# A Poor Choice of Enemies

by

Lucy Dunmore

**Library and Archives Canada Cataloguing in Publication**

**Dunmore, Lucy, 1944-**

**A poor choice of enemies / Lucy Dunmore.**

**ISBN 978-1-896238-15-9**

**1. Title.**

**PR6104.U56P66 2013     823'.92     C2013-901137-4**


Twin Eagles Publishing
Box 2031
Sechelt BC
V0N 3A0
pblakey@telus.net
604 885 7503


www.twineaglespublishing.com

# 1

At the bottom of the slope was a fence that ended up on a back lane and divided the woods from more woods, but not ours, Mr. Balfour's Woods, a place we were always skipping into as children. Guy kept to our side of the fence and headed towards the lane.

"Spider came down here," Guy said. "Nigel and I followed him. He started yapping, worrying at something…"

I followed my brother into a clearing just off the main path. Someone had been digging and it wasn't Spider. Nigel's little Jack Russell might have joined in but these holes had been done with a spade. Two of them were empty, but Guy stood in front of the third...

He looked at me gravely. "Take a look, then, Alice, if you must, but it's not nice."

Deep in the undergrowth and the leaf-mold I peered where Guy pointed.

It was a boot.

A very well-made boot, fit for a country gentleman as it happened, but it had been abused.

So had the foot within it, hand-knitted Argyle stockings peering above the mouldering leather gaiters and the stained tweed breeches above: beyond that the oiled canvas jacket, wide open – well the less said of that, the better, but thankfully the upper torso and head had not been disturbed, and the whole had been lightly dusted over with some of the soil and detritus, probably that which had been dug up to reveal it.

I really didn't want to look any closer.

Although I hated to admit it, my brother was right.

"Spider wasn't to know he mustn't dig here," Guy said, avoiding looking at the cadaver.

"What about those other holes?" I asked. "Spider didn't do them."

"Could be locals after rabbits?"

Yes, I thought, and I'm the Queen of Sheba! Those were

definitely the marks of a spade. Someone knew there was a body hidden here. But I kept that to myself.

"Nicely made boots, though, not necessarily of British origin," Guy said. "This chap wasn't short of a bob or two. Decent piece of fabric, those trousers, once upon a time. Gaiters a bit old-fashioned, though."

I'd never had my brother down as a student of fashion.

"Any of the local great and good gone missing?" I wondered.

Guy shrugged, "Not heard of anyone, but this must have been here some time. I mean it's got to have been here before the winter set in, hasn't it?"

Last winter, the winter of 1946/7 had been dire. The cold had brought the country to its knees for a good four months: it had nearly done for me with pneumonia. The soil would have been under snow for much of it, and like iron afterwards. It had only really warmed up since the start of May, and this looked to have been here longer than that.

"It's on our land, sis," he said softly, exhaling smoke. "Bit of a bugger that, eh? For the old family reputation."

I frowned. "Why would anyone bury a body down here, right out of the way, and then dig it up again?"

It didn't make sense.

Then the rain, which had been threatening since yesterday began to fall in earnest; soft at first, but very soon, drenching.

We stayed, huddled in our light summer clothes, sheltering under the trees until we heard a car draw to a halt down on the lane, then made our way back to the main path to meet it.

Nigel was first out, scampering over the stile, Spider at his heels, yapping. Nigel scooped him up and tucked him under his arm.

I thought: this body had to be brought over the stile!

Unless he was killed here, in situ, after he'd climbed the stile himself.

What sort of person carries a corpse over a stile?

Jeremy, tall and fit, to whom I was engaged, was next out of the Citroen and vaulted the stile.

Well, a very fit person could, I supposed, but he'd need help. I was glad to see him, and ran to him for a hug.

Pa and Sergeant Bloxham followed. They took the stile at

their own pace and made a fairly brisk progress up to where the holes and the dead man were revealed.

Nigel and Guy retold their story. They were walking the dog in the woods, throwing pieces of wood for him, and then he wouldn't come back. They discovered him digging in the earth and saw the boot and the rest...

Nigel had been dispatched to raise the alarm and keep Spider out of the way.

Guy had stayed, to warn off other people. "I didn't want anyone who might have been along to have disturbed it," he explained. "Or be disturbed by it!"

"Quite so, sir," said Sergeant Bloxham, sucking on a drooping pipe.

He had a lugubrious face and I wondered whether he took Sherlock Holmes as a role model. "You didn't actually touch anything, did you, sirs?"

Both young men shook their heads. "Thought it was a job for the professionals, Sergeant," said Guy, brightly.

"Very laudable, sir," said the sergeant. He looked around at us all from under his damp bushy eyebrows. "I suppose none of you recognize ...?" He took a long draw on the pipe. "Well, just a little hope. Not a lot to go on yet."

He let the smoke out slowly. "Well, thank you all for your help. I think that's all we can do here at the moment, and we all need to get out of this weather. If you could give me a lift back to Wethersley, I'll arrange for a couple of men to take over. Until the Inspector comes tomorrow."

Pa drove us home in the Citroen, crushed and steaming.

Sergeant Bloxham took informal statements from us all, which we signed and dated, then made a couple of phone calls and got on his bike, refusing all offers of a lift back to his home.

"I'll not be the most popular man around when I tell the lads they're on duty on their day off, in the rain; the least I can do is be soaked through myself."

# 2

"I see this morning's little discovery hasn't blunted your appetite, Guy," Pa remarked as my brother tucked into Mrs. Mac's rabbit stew with dumplings. It was the first Sunday in June and we were still eating winter food. Fresh vegetables were so late this year. We dined together, as a household, Maman, Pa, Angelique, the Macs, Guy, Nigel, Jeremy and I, around the kitchen table. Spider was in his favourite place by the stove, gnawing his pet bone, having been given a saucer of gravy and a few titbits.

"Nothing like finding a stiff to sharpen one's appetite!" Guy grinned, through a savory mouthful.

"I hope you've washed your hands thoroughly," Angelique sniffed. "I 'ate the smell of death."

Another happy meal at Wethersley I thought, watching Nigel surreptitiously inspecting his nails. As a gardener he was permitted a little ingrained dirt, but Guy, who worked in a city bank, and was heir to the estate, was not.

"No talk of death while we're eating," Maman said. "Where have you all been brought up?"

As if she didn't know!

But of course we couldn't not talk of it. It was hot gossip.

"Why would anyone bury someone here, on our land?" Maman asked, once the subject had been resumed.

"Who doesn't like this family?" asked Jeremy. Not exactly tactful. I had some reservations as to his suitability as a diplomat.

"We have no enemies," Pa said grandly. "We are sweetness and light – surely you know that, Jem, my boy? Why else would you wish to become part of us?"

Maman tapped Pa's hand. "Stop being silly, Roger. It's a valid point."

"Have you upset anyone, Guy?" Pa asked.

"Only my sister," snorted Nigel, answering for his friend. "But she wouldn't have had time to plan a murder, even if she had the brains to. Besides, if she was going to kill anyone, it would be you, Guy, or me."

I chuckled. He'd really opened up since he'd been staying with us.

Angelique sniffed again. "How long do you think the thing has been there?" she asked.

"Recent, but not immediately recent," I said. "The boots and gaiters looked like they had been buried for a few months, but not for years. The police will be able to find out more or less."

"Well that's Sylvia out. She has only really hated me for about a month," said Guy.

"That's not nice, dear," said Maman. "I really don't think you should joke about your ex-fiancée committing a murder." She turned to me. "You haven't made any awful enemies, have you, Alice, dear?" she asked with a raise of her elegant eyebrows.

"Only very recently, Maman," I said, remembering Madame Honoria and Cyril, and a certain bursar. "Or in France, and most of them are dead or too busy rebuilding their lives. No, Maman, I regret to say I've not knowingly brought this shame upon the family."

"Then let us hope it was a random killing, and the perpetrators chose the site of the burial by chance," said Pa.

"And that the poor man didn't have a family missing him," said Angelique. "He certainly must have made a few enemies, whoever he was."

"Justement," agreed Maman. "Now what we need is a swift resolution to this problem with the least possible disturbance to our lives, n'est-c pas?"

Pa lifted his glass. "I'll certainly drink to that!"

We all did.

But it was a vain toast, in water, and none of us believed in it.


The telephone rang shortly after we finished lunch while I was washing up with Jeremy.

Pa took it.

I heard whooping from Maman, and screams of delight.

Jeremy looked at me puzzled. "What's got into them?"

Now Angelique joined in, and Guy's voice boomed,

"Excellent!" from the sitting room.

"In the midst of death there is life, I should think," I replied.

Maman was squealing for champagne.

Pa came through to the kitchen. "You are an auntie for the second time, Alice," he beamed. "And you, Jem, are an honorary uncle. A healthy boy, six pounds eleven by the name of Robin Montague."

"What!" I exclaimed. I knew Maddy and Basil didn't go in for family names, but...

"Robin Montague. It's far better than the alternative," my father said.

"And that was?" Jeremy asked.

"Rupert Peregrine. What a start to give a little chap. He'd be Roo in no time. From a little white bear to a baby kangaroo. At least with Robin he can be an English folk hero."

"Or a very argumentative little bird," I said, rinsing the sink out. "How's Maddy?"

"Very glad to have the little lad in the cradle was what Basil said. They are both absolutely delighted. She will be up to visitors by Tuesday."

"Oh, even Maman?"

"Especially Maman, but that won't stop her. I'll have to drive her and Angelique down tonight. We'll stay at the Stanhope – she likes that. I'll take Guy with me and drop him off. Will you stay here, in case the police come early tomorrow, Alice? I'll go and let the Macs know, now, and find the bubbly."

I watched them go, the car loaded up with baby clothes, gifts for the mother and father, and of course for little Enid who would have to share adulation for the first time, and I pitied Maddy; she'd asked for forty-eight hours grace but they'd not listened, not at all; it was always Maman's needs first.

As soon as they'd disappeared down the drive I ran to the phone and put a call through to Maddy and Bas. They'd need warning.

Mrs. Mac came in. "Quite a day," she said drily. "Will you be wanting tea, because it's on in the kitchen."

Nigel and Jeremy were already there with Mr. Mac. Spider sat under Nigel's chair, chewing his bone.

8

"So," said Mr. MacMurdo, "details please, gentlemen and miss. So we can dispel any dubious rumors."

"You mean disseminate them, surely" I said, lightly, joking.

Mr. Mac shook his head. "No, Miss Alice. If it happened anywhere else I'd gossip like a fishwife, but this is personal. And it's not going to go away easily. Thank goodness Madame will have the new baby to occupy her. You don't think you can persuade Miss Maddy to keep her down in town?"

Jeremy left for London and work after an early breakfast the following morning.

After our night together in my schoolgirl bed, supported and strengthened by a travel trunk, I was looking forward to being back to my Chelsea flat, at least for the few days/nights until Jeremy headed off to his mission. I should have liked to have gone with him, but that would only have been permissible for a wife, and only if the length of time involved were long, so I was here to stay. With the latest developments it was probably the right thing. Of course I'd miss him, but I was used to lonely. That isn't to say I liked it, but I could cope. I'd coped for 27 years before I met him.

## 3

The black Humber bearing Inspector Woods and Sergeant Bloxham turned up at nine. I led them across to the gardener's cottage, but Nigel wasn't there. I checked in the walled garden, but that too was empty. So I led them to the site, where a digging team was already at work. Nigel was there with Spider, distributing tea from flasks into enamel mugs.

"That's very kind," said the Inspector, "but don't stop my lads working. The sooner they can get this chap out, the sooner we can leave you in peace. Now, Mr. Nesmith-Brown, will you tell me exactly what happened?"

I waited for a while, by the stile on the little back road that joins Wethersley to Marsham, musing.

Who was this well-off gent who had been laid low in a clearing that was actually used by locals as a courting ground?

What was he doing there?

Why was he there?

And why did someone want him exposed?

None of it made any sense at the moment; hopefully it would one day soon.

I went back to the clearing where the boys in blue had finished their tea, and gathered up mugs and flasks to take back to Mrs. Mac. Nigel was still talking to Inspector Woods and Sergeant Bloxham, offering them his gardening tools.

So he felt confident enough that they would find nothing to link him with either the holes or the body. I was glad about that. I didn't want him to be a suspect.

As I exited the woods a gray Ford Popular was coming down our drive. I didn't recognize it, but it recognized me. Or its owner did.

He sounded his horn three times loudly and waved. The car slowed and the door swung open. "Jump in, Alice. I was just coming to see you."

It was Sam, Sam Simmons, ace local reporter, grinning like a

Cheshire Cat, with a scrap of bloody tissue stuck to his jaw just below the left ear.

"Didn't know you had a car, Sam," I said, squeezing the baskets onto my lap and slamming the door shut.

"Good, eh? Dad came up trumps when he was over. Said I'd need one for my job, so he and my mother bought me this. I was amazed, I can tell you. Didn't think the aged Ps had that much spare cash after coming all the way across from Auckland. What have you got there?"

"Oh, just some things for Mrs. Mac. Why?"

He drew up round the back of the house and helped me out.

"So there is substance in the rumor?"

"What?"

"There is a body in your woods. Look, you were coming from the woods, there are mucky marks on these mugs... Made by gentlemen of the Force with mucky hands from digging something out. And at a guess, it could be a body. Elementary. It all stands to reason!" He took the baskets from me and headed down to our back entrance. "Come on, Alice. I need a story."

"Ever the journalist! And where might you have got this dubious titbit of information from?"

"I listen to the police frequencies, of course. But there've been rumors for a long time."

"What? Police frequencies I understand. But rumors? Why haven't I heard them? Where did you hear them?"

He blushed a little. "Er... around... yes, that's it. I heard them around."

He stepped through into the kitchen. "Hello Mrs. Mac, how are you?"

"When did you hear them?" I demanded. "How long ago? Who from? And what exactly?"

"Oh, Alice, you know I can't disclose my sources," he said, primly, putting the baskets on the table.

I had helped him previously, given him good copy; of course he could. He owed me.

I smiled at him. "I know," I said, "a man in a pub? But which pub and when? It could be important, you know, and you know I'm good for getting you stories."

"Ah," he said. "Yes, thanks Mrs. Mac, I'd love a mug of tea.

The pub was probably the Angel, and the date was … er, before I knew you, I'd say. Yes, definitely before we became acquainted, so I couldn't have told you, could I? And as nothing came of it, I thought there was nothing in it. None of us did. Just an old toper sounding off." He sat down on a kitchen chair. "Until this morning, when I heard the messages while I was shaving."

Mrs. Mac poured us all tea. "Is that why you cut yourself? Hmm?" she asked. Without letting him answer, she continued. "So whatever it is, you knew about it before this past Easter, give or take a week? Why did you not mention it to us, then, Mr. Simmons? When you had made our acquaintance?"

She was a sharp one.

"Because it was rumor, Mrs. Mac and I don't spread gossip. No, I am the son and grandson of clergymen, as you know."

We both looked at him meaningfully. "Is that so?" said Mrs. Mac. "Is that the whole truth?"

Sam sipped his tea and looked sheepish. "No, actually, I didn't believe it. Besides, it was well before Easter and still snowing, I remember. I waited until the thaw, but there was nothing doing so I discounted it."

"You mean you filed it away for later," I corrected.

I wasn't cross. I would have done the same. But I wanted to know the source.

I went to the dresser and got out the biscuit barrel, opened it and handed it around. There were chocolate biscuits in it, hard to get hold of these days, especially as good as these.

When Sam put his hand in to take one, I stopped him, withdrawing the barrel from his reach.

"A deal – everything you can tell me about your source, every detail, mind, and you can have the biscuit."

He guffawed. "Sell my soul for a chocolate biscuit! You make me sound like Esau in the Bible!"

"Why not?" I asked brightly. "These are infinitely better than a mess of pottage." I waved the barrel under his nose so that the rich dark scent of chocolate rose up to tempt him.

Sam breathed in, closed his eyes and a smile stole over his face. "Yes, alright, then. But I want the story first, before anyone else."

"I don't see why not. But I don't know that there will be much of a story in it."

Sam chuckled. "Of course there will be. You're involved, Alice. Tell you what; I'll take you to see the chap. I think he'd like that."

"When?"

"Around lunchtime. Then you can make up your own mind"

I handed him the barrel.

## 4

The cottage was small, and had seen better days. The thatch was mossy and slipping, any paint that might have been applied to the wood was trying to escape. However, in the poultry yard, the birds looked well enough, kicking up a din as we approached, and the overgrown gardens had been cared for. They were well stocked, and the scent of elder with its cream lace was everywhere. A very organic place.

The door opened before we made it to the garden gate, and a small stocky man, brown from outdoor work came out to greet us with a dog of indeterminate breed. He peered at us myopically, then nodded. "So, Sam, I've been found out," he said. "Which of the bug– perishers ratted on me and for how much?"

"Not Doddy. How's your mother?"

"Not bad considering. Just a bit poorly. Come on in. Who's the young lady?"

"A friend."

He eyed me up and down. "Looks a bit too good for you, Sam. She'll cost a fair bit to keep up, I can tell."

I stuck my hand out to him, "Alice Chamberlain. Pleased to meet you, Mr. Fletcher."

He took my hand, gave it a firm squeeze. "Aye, you'll do, lass. Come on in. I've been expecting you. How can I help you?"

He led us into the parlor at the front of the house, kept for best, and only used for visitors, which, from the dust in the air and on the furniture was not often; the furniture and decorations were hand-downs from the late Victorian period, good, but well-worn and close-packed. In the window on a table a dusty dome of exotic butterflies took pride of place behind the net curtains. On the walls, covering every unoccupied space, were glass and wood cases of stuffed animals and birds, native species, all set in and against habitat backgrounds; their eyes peered out at me, and although I knew they were special fake glass eyes, their dead glares still gave me the creeps. They were too lifelike, articulated, these creatures, on their branches or tussocks, and fitted ill into the ambience of a sitting room.

"My grandfather was the taxidermist," Mr. Fletcher said. "He taught my Dad and my Dad taught me. Unfortunately there ain't much call for the stuff now. Gone out of favor. Like lots of the old ways. Now what did you want from me, Miss Chamberlain. You ain't come all this way to shudder at them unseeing eyes."

My feelings must have shown on my face. "I'm sorry Mr. Fletcher, I didn't mean to offend you or your family. It's just that… they're so lifelike…" I pulled myself together, took a deep breath, and looked at the man squarely. "Mr. Simmons told me that you mentioned to him that a body would be found on Wethersley land, sometime in the winter. I wondered if you would tell me about it." I put on my winning smile. It didn't hurt to flirt.

"Ah, so it's been found then? And you're trying to put it on me, eh?"

"Yes, and no, in that order. A body was found yesterday. And no, I'm not trying to pin it on anyone. I just wondered how you knew."

"What's it to do with you, Miss?"

"It's my father's land. My brother and his friend found it. I am an interested party. Did you tell the police at the same time as you told Mr. Simmons? Did you tell any others?"

He looked at me queerly. "You don't know about me, do you, Miss? No, I can see you don't."

He flung back his head inhaling loudly and then snorting it all out. "Mr. Simmons, Sam, he had ought to have told you," he said accusingly to Sam. "But I suppose I'd better tell you, that way you'll get it straight from the horse's mouth, so to speak."

"That's what I thought," Sam said swiftly. "I didn't want to prejudice anything."

Mr. Fletcher looked at Sam witheringly, and raised his eyebrows. "Indeed, Sam? I don't think so, but no matter."

He looked at me with a twisted grin, his head cocked to one side. "I've got the Sight, see. My family all have it, one way or another. We're seen as different and we don't have it all the time, and we can get things mixed up. Specially when we've been drinking, what is quite a nice thing to do. I enjoy a drink, me."

I nodded. And waited.

15

"My Ma, now, she's far better at all this stuff than me; and she can make sick things better, simply by touching them sometimes; and she knows her herbs and simples, but if someone or some animal she's been looking after dies, they call her a witch and would have her killed, whereas if you go to a doctor or a vet and pays your one and six far too late and the person or creature dies, well, he's done his best. So she lives out here, away from people generally."

"I understand," I said. "But she's not well at present?"

"No, she's fine. Just a bit stiff in her joints with the thundery weather. She don't like the damp, or the damp don't like her. Not her body anyway. Her mind's as clear as a bell. Always has been. She was the one who told me there would be a body found. In the woods, weren't it? In a clearing, on the way to Marsham, where it meets Balfour's land? Got a bit of reputation, that clearing has!"

"Possibly," I hedged, thinking of the reputation.

"Don't possibly me, my girl. If you want me to be straight with you, you gotta be straight with me. I don't like games."

"Fair enough. Yes, it was down there. What else do you know about it? When did it go in? Have you told the police?"

"Lots of questions, eh? No, of course I haven't told the police. They don't like me, and they don't trust me. I'm what's known as an undesirable – like my Ma. We live off the land and the land don't always belong to us, if you get my meaning."

I nodded. A poacher, then, and petty thief. I'd been pretty much the same when the war was on and I was living in the Vercors with the Maquisards. Dammit, it was a survival strategy then, and not a problem then and there. But it would be a problem for Mr. Fletcher here and now, in that the police would have files upon him; he'd be an easy scapegoat for any unsolved crime.

"My brother and a friend and his dog found the body yesterday," I said quietly. "Of course we told the police – but I will not mention any conversation you and I might have to them, although the relevant contents of it might be disclosed without your name being brought in. Will that be acceptable?"

"I think I can work along with that idea. I don't think Sam can, though, but he owes you, don't he? I get the feeling he owes you. Am I right?"

Sam started to splutter denials.

I smiled. "It's just Mr. Fletcher's way of proving he's got the Sight, Sam," I told him. "But he's right. We must be very circumspect at present. When and as the thing unrolls, you'll have your story." I looked at Mr. Fletcher questioningly. "That's right, isn't it?"

He nodded. "Course it is. Now, Sam, what did I tell you, and when?"

Sam looked sulky. "That there would be a body found on Wethersley land. You told me around Christmas, just before, I believe. And you swore you never put it there, on your mother's life, if I remember rightly."

"Ah, well I was a little bit worse for wear that night," he said, shamefaced. "I'd never do that normally. Anyway, she told me she heard a single shot on the wind and felt a pain in the back of her head. It fair knocked her over. When she come to herself, she went to check and saw it in the water-bowl. She said it were like an execution. There were four men there, she couldn't make them out clearly, but one was giving orders and the others were doing the burying; they weren't happy. But the one who was giving orders gave them something – looked like a packet of some sort. And there were someone else there too, with a horse. She could only make out a figure, but the horse was a grey, kept nice, she said. That were it, really."

"Could I speak to your mother?" I asked. "In case she can remember anything else."

"Not at the moment. She ain't well enough to see people. But I'll ask her. I'll let you know. Now you'd better go. It's been nice meeting you, Miss, and I'm sure we'll meet again."

He was already ushering us out. "I'll speak to her soon as she's up to visitors, and I will get in touch, but no police, remember."

"Thank you for your time, Mr. Fletcher," I said. I handed him a card. "I'm not always at Wethersley. If you want to ring me here, please reverse the charges. I'll look forward to your call, and I hope your mother's health restores soon."

We were out of the house and down the path in double-quick time.

"What happened there?" I asked Sam as we reclaimed the car. "One minute all the time in the world, the next clam up and out we go."

"I think you called his bluff," said Sam, backing up the track.

"What do you mean?"

"His mother died last winter. He comes up here when he wants to sober up, and lives quietly for a while. He doesn't believe she's gone. Well, to him, she hasn't. She's still there in her own house, seeing things and telling him things."

My jaw dropped.

Suddenly I was angry.

Sam had been so dismissive of the 'wizards' I had worked with to bring him his last big story, yet here he was dragging me out here on the hearsay of someone whose mother was, for want of a better word, a witch, and communicating to her son from beyond the grave!

"This was your informer?" I spat. "A message from beyond the grave? You really are a journalist, Sam!"

He opened the car door. "No. Nuance, here, Alice. When I heard, she was still alive."

"But I bet she was housebound! Anyone like that could say anything about anyone and start a rumor, that's why witches were put to death," I snapped. "That's why they lived out on the edges of villages, because no-one wanted to be near them. Mr. Fletcher himself said as much."

I climbed into the passenger seat. "Take me home, Sam, please. I'm sorry if I've offended you or your contact; I suppose I was hoping for something more. And you should have told me the situation with his mother being dead, you really should have!"

By the time I'd got back for lunch the body had been removed and all traces around the burial site had been gone over and cleared. Nigel, with Spider at his feet was giving the Macs and the daily girls a gruesome report, but most of it was imaginary.

"You was in the walled garden most of the morning, Mr. Nigel, I saw you there," said Beryl, looking up at him under her eyelashes. "You're a storyteller and no mistake!" Even so, she was saving it all up to spread round Wethersley later; soon no whisper of truth would remain. I wasn't amused, nor, from the look of them, were Mr. and Mrs. Mac.

"What's the Inspector like?" I asked to the company in general.

"Inspector Woods? Seems a bit stiff, but then he's got a job to do," Nigel said. "He asked a lot of questions. I let him have my digging tools – to eliminate me, see? He wanted to know where you were, and Guy and the rest of the family."

"I put him right on that, Miss Alice," said Mr. Mac. "I gave him particulars of everyone's actions yesterday, and all the relevant addresses and phone numbers, including your young man's – I hope you didn't mind, but it seemed the right thing to do. He wants us all to sign the typed up statements, you see."

"Of course. I'm sure that's alright. Thank you for dealing with it. I'm sorry I had to go out."

"And did you learn anything?" asked Mrs. Mac.

"I'm not sure. Not sure at all. Have you heard from Pa or Maman?"

"Your father will be bringing the ladies home, Miss Alice, this afternoon. The baby is well and has all its fingers and toes, and Miss Maddy, sorry, I always think of her as Miss Maddy, her new name's such a mouthful, well she's fit too, but needs a rest. I've made a little cake for her. Would you be so kind as to take it with you, when you go back to town?"

"I'd be delighted to," I assured her.

# 5

I was glad to be back at the front door of the tall terrace house off the Fulham Road in Chelsea once more. My great aunt had left me the freehold complete with sitting tenants on the bottom two floors when she died about a year ago, and, apart from three months in France recuperating from a near fatal bout of pneumonia and sorting my life out, earlier this year, her flat, the top two stories, had been my bolt-hole ever since.

George popped out from the basement to greet me and take my bag up for me. He was eleven years old, going on twenty-five, the oldest son and mainstay of my char, Lily, who occupied in the basement with her three children.

I told him about my new nephew.

"A boy! That's good. There are too many girls about. We boys need to even up the balance," he said brightly.

Obviously his sisters had been getting to him in my absence.

"Is Mr. Jem coming round tonight? Will you be going for fish and chips?"

I smiled. He wanted to ride in the back of the little red Morgan.

I had to let him down. "Yes and no. It's Monday, not a good day for fish. The boats didn't go out yesterday."

I tossed him threepence for the case-carrying, and watched him catch and pocket it in one swift continuous movement.

"Thanks, Miss. I'll tell Mum you're back." He clattered off down the stairs whistling happily. A threepenny piece rarely offended where George was concerned and softened most blows.

I rang my sister.

Basil, her husband, told me she was having a long overdue nap.

I apologized for my parents, and he laughed. "We knew you couldn't stop them, but they've gone now. Would you mind not coming over until tomorrow at the earliest? Neither of us are getting much sleep, even with an extra nanny. Enid thinks he's lovely at the moment, but she hasn't yet understood that he's here to stay."

"Ah, so a little fuss in that quarter will not go amiss," I said. "By the way, Mrs. Mac has sent a fruit cake for you all. I'll hang on to it for you until I see you, but you might ring and thank her."

"I will. How kind!"

There was a scraping of a key in the lock.

"Must go, Basil. There's someone at the door. Love and cheerio to you all."

"Found out who he was yet, and what he was doing?" Jeremy asked, after our kiss of greeting.

I smiled. "What do you think?"

"I think someone's got it in for the family," he said. Then held up his hand to hush me. "No, let me finish, Alice. I really do. I mean, you aren't the average members of the upper classes, are you? You're almost bound to have upset some member of the establishment somewhere along the line, purely by existing."

"Eh? Explain yourself, sirrah!"

Jeremy grinned, and hung his jacket on a peg on the door. "Come on, Alice. I love you all, because of your ... how can I make it sound nice?... Delightful eccentricities, yes?"

I wasn't sure I'd like this, but I'd called his bluff. "Ye-es... Go on...! Although have a care. An upper class eccentric would be something quite different if he or she were middle-class, and mad as a hatter in the lower orders!"

"Oops. Forget I said anything, OK?"

"What! You're backing off? I'm not having that!"

We were sparring, but laughing. I wasn't going to let him off the hook and he knew it.

He chuckled. "OK, you asked for it. Starting at the top, then. None of you are conventional people, are you? Your father's a painter and a free-thinker, your mother's a highly-strung Frenchwoman who keeps her childhood friend as companion, and would spend fortunes on clothes if she could. Your sister is probably brighter than her husband – please don't repeat that, since he is my boss and I do not wish to get fired just yet – your brother is a reactionary, possibly homosexual, and you, my dearest Alice, are ..."

"What did you say about my brother?" I demanded, letting the kettle overflow. "Reactionary I agree with. The other bit?"

His jaw dropped. "Ah…Oops, sorry." He had flushed scarlet. "Er, Alice, the kettle's swamped…"

I turned the tap off, emptied some of the water, put the lid back on the kettle.

"What did you say about Guy just then?" I asked again.

"I'm sorry. I thought you suspected."

"How the hell would I? My brother never talks to me. Not talk like feelings and things that matter." I snapped. "I suppose he told you? Or have you just divined it, or got it from the grapevine."

"Hey, steady on, Alice. I don't mean to upset you."

"Well you are! How can you say my brother is 'possibly'" I emphasized the word, "one of those? He doesn't dress like one, smell like one, or behave like one. He's the straightest, most boring person I know," I spat. "But he is my brother. I don't have to believe this, Jem. Tell me your reasons for saying this. Has he tried anything on you? Has he?"

Jeremy laughed. "Of course not. He'd be far too scared to. Too scared to try it on with anyone, I'd guess, male or female, but I bet it's been tried on with him, at those precious schools your class sends their kids to…" He peered at me, raising an eyebrow.

"It has," I agreed, after some reflection. "Gilles told me, years ago." Gilles, my brother the pilot, who was no more. We two were really close and I missed him. Nothing even vaguely homosexual about him.

"Gilles thought it was just a passing thing. It seems lots of boys go through it, like girls get pashes on the older girls or the younger teachers… it's a way of life in boys' schools."

"Doesn't have to be, and as you say, most of them get over it or at least find the opposite sex more interesting." He felt in his pocket for a cigarette, but stopped himself. "No cigarettes, eh?"

"No," I said. "So what were you saying about boys' schools being breeding grounds of unnatural pursuits?" I asked.

"Some boys actually like it, knowing it's 'wrong' but getting pleasure from it, and being the centre of attention of a very influential boy or master. There's power involved, and that's always exciting."

I thought about my brother.

He was two years older than me. We'd fought or disagreed

virtually all our lives. Gilles should have lived, but Guy was the heir and safe in the bunker under Whitehall during the war, while Gilles had been shot down and I had been in France on government work and Maddy, the youngest had been helping Maman with the evacuees in our home, and working part time in the local hospital.

Guy had never had a girlfriend, as far as I knew. That didn't mean he hadn't, because he kept his feelings very close. He'd had female acquaintances, of course, but no actual romantic attachment known to the family until he'd become engaged to Sylvia Nesmith-Brown, Nigel's sister, earlier this year. In retrospect we all knew it had been a match made in pursuit of money, but we'd all been so happy that he'd found someone at last. Or perhaps a little relieved, even. Yet, when it all went wrong, I felt his broken heart was mostly hurt pride.

I thought about that match, and Sylvia, who had broken it off. She had her reasons, not all of them fit to be aired in polite society, but one of them was that he 'didn't even kiss properly'. She was a big bouncing girl, quite unlike her slender brother, very physical, and had had plenty of sexual experience; no, I'm not repeating hearsay, I had it from her own mouth, saw it with my own eyes. It would appear that although they were engaged, Guy had never tried anything on, which struck me as crazy. You don't get engaged to someone you don't fancy like mad, not in our family.

"Who told you, Jem?" I murmured.

"No-one, Alice." he said softly. "I've been watching, that's all. He doesn't feel comfortable with his life, never has since I've known him. Something's not quite right..."

"You've been checking up on him?" I demanded. "Snooping on us?"

He shook his head. "Of course not! Don't be crazy, Alice. I love you all. It's your very individuality that makes you all so special." He sighed. "And I only said 'possibly'. I may be wrong. Guy will probably find a girl and marry pretty soon – *noblesse oblige* and all that – and provide an heir and spare; forget I mentioned it."

"Oh yes, that's easy for you to say. You make a statement like that and then you say forget it. Sorry, Jem, no can do." I turned my back on him, measured tea leaves into the pot. "It comes as a shock, don't you see?"

He came over to me and put his hands on my shoulders, breathed in my ear. "I didn't mean to hurt you, to distress you. It just popped out."

"Oh yes? So much for your diplomatic training!" I wanted more than that as an apology.

A dry chuckle. "Touché! And you're right. I'm sorry. Forgive me. I have two nights before I go. I don't want my stupid tongue to drive us apart."

I felt him kissing my hair, then continuing, working down to my neck, an attention that normally made me go to jelly, but not today.

Keep going, I thought. He must be able to feel my anger; my muscles were rigid.

The trouble was, the more I thought about it, the more I thought he could be right. And although I had no problems with homosexuality, society did.

It was anathema, a perversion. It just wasn't done, not in the circles Guy chose to move in.

Guy was a great one for doing the right thing. He was Mr. Boring, he was so correct. Or that was the image he wanted to project to people? It was the image he had to project if he was going to get anywhere in his banking career. Mr. Respectable, Mr. Responsible, Mr. Dependable.

If a whiff of anything even faintly untoward got out, he'd be utterly ruined.

Jeremy was wheedling now, whispering. "Alice, I love you. Please, talk to me? I'm sorry. I'm really sorry. Can't we be friends?"

Yes, we could. Of course we could.

I turned. "Yes," I sighed. "We are an odd bunch, and what you say makes sense. But please, not a word of this to anyone. Not a word."

"Of course not. I only mentioned it because…"

"Because you couldn't help it. If you really want to be a diplomat you're going to have to change that and learn to lie! No matter how bad a day you've had."

He looked shame-faced. "Yes, actually, that's quite true. I accept that criticism."

I put my finger across his lips. "Not another word. No-one needs to know your suspicions about my brother. I doubt if Guy even thinks it to be so. If one mentioned it to him – and one wouldn't – he'd deny it completely then knock one down for besmirching the family name. That's the way he is."

I felt his arms snake around me and sighed. We were still friends, still lovers.

Some time later the bell rang. It was our builder friend, Joe, to look at what needed to be done to the house and sort out our building needs. We spent the evening discussing plans, accepting that he would start on Thursday, then adjourned to the Anglesey together. It had been a long day.

I lay awake long into the night. I was alone.

Jeremy was very particular as to when and how he stayed.

If he stayed – which was rare – he would come minus car and leave by the back door before the streets were aired. The little red Morgan was too distinctive and a young woman's reputation could be ruined by a gentleman, even her fiancé, taking obvious liberties, although some liberties were allowed with betrothed people, so long as they were extremely discreet and very careful. Compared to my life in wartime France, my sexual freedom was severely limited. Perhaps that was just how we Brits were, at least on the surface.

Of course the returning heroes were making up for lost time with their wives and girlfriends, there were prams and pushchairs everywhere. But unmarried women … they weren't expected to have needs. Nice girls just didn't.

My brother's ex-fiancée, Sylvia, was the exception to the rule. I wondered how she was getting on. I didn't care for her, but the last time I saw her she was confused, angry and hurting; Jeremy had sweet-talked her out of attacking Guy physically, encouraging her to forget us all and go forward creating her own life as she wanted it. A young woman of twenty, she'd get over Guy. Whether she'd get over the murder of her 'uncles' Archie and Percy Meredith was another matter. She had planned in her own mind to throw over Guy for Archie at Beltane and was used to getting her own way, but Fate was against her this time. The Meredith twins were murdered by a woman they had wronged many times, which just proved that if you sow the wind, you reap the whirlwind.

I wondered vaguely whether to go and see Sylvia, but... no, she wouldn't appreciate it and I had more important things to do.

There were a few things I could do about our defunct friend from our woods: I could cajole Leggy to ask around for me, but it might be even too far for him to find out anything; I could pester Sam, because he'd be pestering Inspector Woods; and I could ring Pa tomorrow, because surely the Inspector would tell him.

And then there was Guy to consider.

Bloody Jeremy!

He'd sowed a seed and it had taken.

He'd done that once before and I'd bawled him out, and the devil had been right all along.

I hoped against hope he was wrong but I had that awful feeling in the pit of my stomach that he could be right. And if he were right, then how many others could see what he saw?

Did men really have a sixth sense about homosexuality? I mean, not the blatant queens, but chaps who aspired to normal family lives, who wanted nothing other than a quiet existence?

What exactly had Guy done during the war? Who had he mixed with? Who were his friends?

I realized I knew nothing about my brother. Was it my business?

Actually, no, it wasn't.

Unless he chose to tell me.

All I was doing was building up speculations and scenarios with absolutely no basis in any sort of fact. Chimeras, taking life from the merest hint of a suggestion.

Better think about the new baby. Robin Montague. I'd look forward to making his acquaintance tomorrow, and making a fuss of Enid and my sister.

I turned my mind from prurient speculations upon my brother's sexuality to presents and treats for my sister and her children, and thence upon the designs and ideas we had come up with for our flat. Finally, about half past three, I must have fallen asleep.

# 6

I was washing up after my meager breakfast when the phone shrilled at me.

My father.

"What is it Pa?" I asked. Although he was an early riser and expected everyone else to be, he didn't normally ring this early.

"Just had Inspector Woods here. Off the record of course. Told me who the dead man was. Have you ever heard of an Edgar Winthrop?"

I shook my head. "No, Pa. Have you?"

He didn't answer.

"Who was he, Pa?"

"Not sure, Alice. Could you let Leggy know, though. And young Jeremy? I'd be very grateful. And not a word to anyone else. Particularly your mother, understand?"

"No, but of course I'll do as you ask."

"It'll be in the papers soon enough. Oh, and yes, the inquest will be held on Wednesday afternoon at Amersham. You will be there, won't you? For a bit of moral support?"

"Of course, Pa. But there's not a problem, surely? Even if the man was killed on our land, there is nothing to link his death to us, is there?" But as I said it, I felt a shudder run down from the back of my head down my spine.

Something definitely wasn't right. And murder was a hanging offense.

"I really hope not, Alice. I'd better go, Chérie is calling me... Don't forget to do as I asked, will you? There's a good girl," and before I could speak he'd rung off.

Which was not like Pa.

I cradled the receiver and hung up my apron.

Two minutes later I was cycling down the King's Road towards the World's End and beyond, to a Mansion block that had escaped Hitler's bombs where Leggy, alias Colonel Legge, had made his home. He had been Pa's commanding officer during the first set of hostilities, and my boss during the more recent one;

he was a valued old friend for whom I worked from time to time. Ostensibly he was retired from Government Service, but he still had connections, and his Antiques and House Clearing Business was definitely an 'on the side' issue.

I chained my sit-up-and-beg trusty steed to a lamp post then headed for the flats.

The lift was ancient and rattled badly, all angular metalwork set into a tiled stairwell, and took me jerkily up to the third floor.

Bobby Gallagher, Leggy's batman, was waiting for me with the door open. "Lovely to see you again, Milady," he greeted, and to my surprise didn't slap on extra blarney. "Leggy's in his usual place. You'll excuse me while I finish my chores?"

He ushered me into the sitting room. Leggy was in his fireside chair when I entered, his big neutered ginger cat, Nuts, purring contentedly on his lap.

He put down the pipe he had been filling with Latakia tobacco. "Alice, how lovely!" he accepted the kiss I dropped on his forehead and grasped my hand in greeting. "How can I help? Is it that body? Do sit down, my dear." He pointed to the chair opposite him.

"Thank you. Yes. Pa said to let you have his name. Edgar Winthrop. I don't know how they found out."

"They wouldn't tell you, anyway. Not unless they wanted to. Told Roger that? Who?"

"Inspector Woods. And Pa said I should tell you and tell Jeremy – although he won't even be here after tomorrow."

"He's going off tomorrow? Well, that'll leave you at a loose end. You could do some work for me, Alice? How would that suit?"

I thought, I've been set up here. Pa and Leggy are trying to stop me from moping – not that I would allow myself to do so, and certainly not let them see me doing so, should I lapse.

"Well, Alice? I've got some work on that may need doing, and you'd be my first choice."

"I'd be honored, Leggy. You know that."

"Good girl, then I'll get some cards printed up for you. Your alias was Sally Carson, wasn't it? You could be a war widow making her way in a difficult post-war world?"

"I could," I agreed.

"Good. Usual rates. Come and see me when your young man has disappeared, and thank you for the information as to the corpse. Isn't it time you went to see your new nephew? Tell Bobby I want him on your way out, there's a dear!"

Perfunctory dismissal and a request to send Bobby in: Leggy had never treated me like that before.

I raised my eyebrows. Then let them drop. His eyes had closed and apart from the gentle stroking of the ginger cat, an occasional puff of smoke coming from the pipe, there was nothing to let you know that he was awake.

"Will do, Leggy. Goodbye for now," I said, as I left the room.

Bobby was waiting outside. "Wait for me in the entrance hall," he whispered as he opened the front door for me. "I'll be there toot sweet."

He met me there five minutes later, eschewing the lift and slipping down the flights of stairs on silent feet. Nobody could move as silently as Bobby Gallagher. "I've got to get your cards printed, Milady. Come with me to the printers. It'll take a day or three, they never do anything fast, but I hardly think that will matter."

"What's it all about, Bobby? Leggy dismissed me like a downstairs maid!"

"Ah, don't take it personally, Milady. He's under a bit of strain at the moment. It's those bloo– damned Merediths. They cast long shadows... And this body, it's not helping. You know Leggy thinks the world of your Pa, all of you, to be honest. He's sure there's more to this than meets the eye."

"So do I, Bobby, but I just don't know where to start," I said, as I unlocked my bicycle.

"Softly, softly, catchee monkey," said Bobby, tapping his nose. "I'm very glad you're working with us, Milady. It'll all turn out fine, you'll see."

## 7

"Well," said my sister, lying back prettily in bed, in a room festooned with flowers and congratulation cards, "I'm so glad someone has seen fit to tell me all about it. People have been whispering – Bas, the staff, Nannie's been biting her lips, and that's a sure sign something's not to be mentioned in front of little me in case I burst my stitches."

She helped herself to a chocolate, then pushed the box towards me. "Thanks for not treating me like a piece of fine porcelain. I knew I could rely on you."

"Oh, I know you're tougher than you look, Maddy. And you've given birth now, so you can catch up on the real world. These sweets are uncommonly good, by the way."

"Start producing grandchildren for Maman and you'll find an unlimited supply, rationing notwithstanding."

"I'll stick to eating yours, thanks. Oh, and we've postponed the wedding."

"Because of my husband, eh? He really does get some strange notions. Still, I'll have a bit more time to get my figure back and I could do with a decent winter outfit."

"Anyone would think you gave Basil the idea..."

She smiled. "Little me? As if..."

She opened the second layer of chocolates. "So now we have another problem on our hands. With Jeremy out of the way for a bit, you'll have to cope alone," she said. "Do you know who that chap was who was murdered, by the way? Do you have a name yet?"

"Not yet," I said, crossing my fingers behind my back. "Why should I? More important, how should I know? I've no links to the police."

Maddy frowned. "Tell me it all again, Alice. I need to get my brain working. Then you can meet young Bobbin."

We went over the discovery once more, but neither of us could get any further. I had not heard of Edgar Winthrop, and I kept his name secret from Maddy, although I didn't like it. Maddy and I had never had secrets. It felt odd, not right, but then nothing about Mr. Winthrop was right. We both knew that this wasn't going to go away easily, no matter what we might hope.

Suddenly there was a rumpus outside. Little Enid, my niece charged into the room, "Auntie Alice, can I have a ride on your bike? I'm a big girl now, really!" she demanded throwing herself upon me.

"Of course you can," I said, catching Maddy nodding vigorously.

Nanny came in bearing the new arrival.

"Auntie Alice, Mum made me a new brother, look! Nanny's got him. He's so little!"

"And I'm very grateful for that," muttered Maddy.

Nanny held out the little white-wrapped bundle to Maddy. I watched her face light up as she took her son, and heard her voice change to a lighter softer tone as she talked to the baby. "Come and see your Auntie Alice, Robin, my boy. She is a very special person and you will disobey her at your peril!"

He had a round pink face, and was already mouthing a smile, his eyes still half-closed in sleep. His head was covered in fine dark hair, and as Maddy put him to her breast his body sighed and relaxed, concentrating on suckling.

"That's a rotten way to introduce me," I said, stroking his soft head.

"You'll get over it. Bring Enid back safely, eh?"

The third dismissal. I wondered what I was doing wrong... or right.

I picked up Enid and took her downstairs. Nanny followed me out. As she shut the door she looked at me questioningly. "It is going to be alright, isn't it? I'd hate Madam to be worried, not with the new baby and all."

"It'll all be fine," I assured her, with more conviction than I felt, repeating Bobby's words. "You'll see."

# 8

After I'd dropped Enid back home (we'd taken a turn round the gardens, she sitting on my bike, me pushing it) I cycled to St James's Park where I caught up with Jeremy, leaning on the bridge inspecting the waterfowl in a desultory manner. His face lit up when he saw me approach, as, no doubt, did mine.

"Last lunch in Britain," I said brightly, dropping a kiss on his cheek. "Cheer up. Tomorrow you'll be taking it in some wonderful exotic spot." I had no idea where – it was too hush-hush.

His face brightened and I got a return peck. "I'll miss you, Alice. I don't know how long this will last, I'll write every day."

I shook my head. "Once a week – and a big newsy one will be quite ample. I'm a lousy letter-writer. You'd just make me feel guilty."

He threw the last of his sandwich at a pelican who had swum over for free largesse, put the empty bag in a bin and offered me his arm. "You're on. I think you've got enough to sort out here. I feel bad about not being around to lend support…"

"We'll cope. Well, I will, and Maddy will. But whether Maman will, or Angelique, or even Guy… We'll just have to see. Anyway, I've got our home to sort out. They might just have to get on and deal with things as best they can."

"You didn't mention Roger," he said after a short pause.

"No," I agreed. "And Pa said to tell you something. The man's identity…"

He shook his head. "I already know. You don't have to tell me…"

"What do you know?" I demanded.

"Let us take a walk off the paths, Alice. And behave like lovers. For the look of the thing." His arm sneaked round my waist and guided me off into the shade of the huge plane trees. I rested my bike against one, then kissed his cheek once more. He smelled nice.

"Tell me," I hissed. "Tell me everything you know. If you aren't going to be here, I need as much information as possible.

And that doesn't mean my going to Basil."

"Basil doesn't have access. You might try your friend Leggy. He rang me this morning."

I kissed him again. On the lips this time, but not too lingering. "More, please, and as you give so shall you receive..."

He chuckled, and disentangled himself then spread his jacket on the grass against the bole of the tree, lining side down. "Milady?" he offered.

I sat, and he sat beside me.

"Give!"

"Alright. The body. We know who it was. There was a British passport in the pocket of its waistcoat. Name and address: Edgar Winthrop. The address existed but no-one lives there now. It was wiped out in an air-raid. We checked the electoral role prior to the bombing. Mr. Winthrop wasn't on it, but a Mr. John Anderson was. So I looked them both up in the records, off the record, so to speak, and discovered John Anderson of that address is the alter ego of a Mr. John Anselm-Jones. Mean anything to you?"

I frowned. The name was familiar, but for the moment I couldn't place it. "You tell me."

"Roger painted his portrait as it happens."

I nodded. "Yes. That's it. I'd forgotten. Of course he did. About twelve, fifteen years ago. It's supposed to be a very good one. There are some really nice artworks in the picture; he's some sort of collector, isn't he?"

He took a deep breath. "Alice, you won't like this. Your father is known to have had some animosity to Mr. Anselm-Jones. It goes back a fairly long way."

"You've got files on Pa?"

"Well, yes. He had to be vetted before he did the royal portraits. We've got files on everyone, Alice, but basically there's also a fairly big one on Mr. John Anselm-Jones."

"But he's just a scholar, a connoisseur, surely?" I said. I'd ask Pa what the animosity was about. Pa normally never held grudges.

He nodded. "You know him then?"

I shook my head. "Not personally. I came across him when working at Lowthers; he authenticated artworks from time to time." I smiled at him. "Sorry, I didn't mean to interrupt. Please continue."

"Right. Now this is strictly off the record, Alice. It will become common knowledge, I've no doubt, but we have to keep it under wraps at the present. This really mustn't go any further. Within the Anselm-Jones file there is mention of something more than simple dislike between him and your father despite his having done the portrait of him, back in 1936; at that point they seemed to be rubbing along together pretty well."

"Pa's a pragmatist, money is money," I said cynically. "Maman can dispose of large tracts of cash, I can tell you. Tell me more about the animosity."

"Well, sometime after that, they just didn't seem to hit it off any more. There were arguments, documented in the gossip columns and it is known that during the war Roger threw him out of Wethersley, although what he was doing there we have no idea."

"Ah," I said. "I'll ask him for you."

"I should imagine our chaps will be seeing to that."

"Your chaps? I thought this was just a simple local issue."

He shook his head. "Alice, darling, how can you be so naïve? Anselm-Jones was a spy. He was also, very likely, a double agent, a traitor."

I let that sink in. It wasn't good news.

"So nice Inspector Woods will be off the case? How soon?"

Jeremy shrugged. "I don't know. Probably after the inquest. It will have come out anyway. It has to. This has got to be sorted. It's all a fetid sore underneath. It's got to be lanced, cleaned, healed. We have to be seen whiter than white, and strong enough to punish traitors when we find them, otherwise what's the point?"

"Will you leak it to the press?" I asked, hoping like mad that he wouldn't.

"Alice, of course not. Trust me. I want to keep it as quiet as possible for as long as possible. I wouldn't have had this happen for the world, you must know that. But like I say, it has come out so that justice can be seen to be done." He felt in his pocket, but his hand came out empty. "Christ, I could murder a fag." He looked at me hopefully. "You don't...?"

I shook my head miserably. "I was hoping you did."

"Bugger! Sorry, Alice." He sighed and then grinned at me.

"It really is lousy timing, isn't it?"

"Yes. I wish you weren't going away, Jem." I sighed.

"Me, too. But we can go and paint the town red tonight. It's all booked. Put your glad-rags on and I shall meet you at eight. Or before, if you like, and we can visit the new-born."

## 9

Leggy's note awaited me. "Come over ASAP, Alice, please."

I backed the bike out of the hallway and headed for the World's End once more.

Leggy let me in himself. "Good girl!" he said, ushering me into his sitting room, which bore the scent of pipe tobacco and boiled fish. He brushed Nuts off a chair and pointed me to it.

"Something's come up, Alice. I need your help."

"I'll help," I said. "What can I do?"

He puffed at his pipe while I waited in silence.

"This job requires someone available this instant, and it will be a bit of fun, Alice, but we may already be too late for the element of surprise."

"Of course. How long will it take?" I asked.

"Oh, a couple of hours or so. We'll be back in time for you to get ready for the evening, rest assured. And this does link with what happened at Wethersley this weekend, my dear."

I checked in the mirrors and backed the Humber into a space a few feet from the main entrance of the International Galleries in Mayfair. Leggy made the transfer to the wheelchair like a professional invalid. I tucked the Hunting Stewart rug over his knees, locked the car and handed him the keys. Then I turned to the task in hand.

I pushed the wheelchair, with Leggy folded in it, looking far less chipper than he ordinarily did, up to the double glass doors. We looked a sight: him as the parody of the irascible old invalid colonel, me a sour-faced nurse, in ugly horn-rim spectacles and a totally unflattering uniform, my hair grayed with talc. I'd modeled myself on the redoubtable Muriel, who looked after a delightful scholar friend. She wouldn't have been impressed.

By now a gallery manager had glided over and together we maneuvered Leggy through the entrance into the deserted cavern of a museum.

"Colonel Alan Stewart, young man. I rang earlier," Leggy barked, extending a hand, "And you are?"

The assistant took the hand and shook it gently, "Delighted, sir. Leonard Parsons at your service. How may I help you?"

Leggy barked over his question. "Knew your boss in the East, young man. Told me to call in if ever I were in London, said there was always something worth looking at here, don't you know! Shame about what's happened to him, but here I am."

The assistant frowned, puzzled.

He had no idea at what Leggy was on about, I'd swear it.

If Leggy hadn't told me that the boss in question was the very same body that Spider had discovered, nor would I.

Leggy looked up at him, tapping his nose conspiratorially. "Business as usual, eh? Well, probably best. In the long run. In the circumstances."

The assistant's face was a blank mask. He retreated to his tried and tested script. "Good afternoon, sir. Welcome to the International Galleries. We have examples of the finest artworks and objects from around the world, here, sir. If you give me some idea as to where your interests lie, perhaps I might assist you, sir?"

"Oh, I'm interested in everything, young man, absolutely everything."

I pushed him carefully into the emporium, where exquisite artifacts were displayed elegantly, some free-standing, others in cabinets. I'd never seen such an eclectic mix outside a state-run museum: it must cost a fortune to run, and money was scarce these days. Only the very wealthy were buying on any scale, the rest of us, scrap metal merchants apart, were just about breaking even. Many weren't even doing that. And here was this Treasure Cave in the middle of London's Mayfair, bursting at the seams with beautiful objects from all over the world... How come?

Leggy was still talking to the assistant. "You might have some pieces I want. I may even have some pieces you want, what's more. I'll just take myself round, don't you know? To the back of the shop, Muriel, where those carpets are, if you please."

I pushed him where the 'young man', Mr. Parsons, forty if he was a day, led us, protecting his stock from the wheelchair, tutting.

I was enjoying myself.

So was Leggy.

"Don't mind her, young man, she's very careful. If she wanders off, she won't break anything, I assure you."

"I'll stay close to you, Colonel," I said.

"No, Muriel, you go and have a look around. Educate yourself." He peered around, surveying the room generally. "Looks like some nice classical nudes over there, my dear. Go and give yourself a treat!"

"Ooh, sir!"

"Won't be anything you haven't seen before, dear, and it'll be in far better shape, despite its age. Go on, chop chop! Leave me here to look at the carpets. If you're good, I might buy you a present. But you'll have to promise to be good, mind." He winked at me, and patted my bottom. "Shoo, off you go!"

"Ooh, sir!" I did my aggrieved bit and humphed over to where he had indicated, struggling to keep in character. Muriel would never have permitted such liberties, any more than the charming scholar would have attempted them.

I'd wanted to be 'invisible', but he'd virtually blown any chance of that; the best hope for me was to be seen just as a menial, that was fine. Menials weren't supposed to have any artistic knowledge or interests, whereas I was a painter's daughter, brought up on fine arts.

The Classical section was small but exquisite, a few pieces of statuary, Roman rather than Greek, possibly later even recent copies, I thought, cynically, as the faces were all intact; among the smaller items, I found a collection of glorious black figure and red figure ware and a jeweler's display case containing some tiny carved jewels and hair ornaments. I gazed at the pots – turning my nose up, because there was some damage, and they were big on naked satyrs with enormous erections, which Muriel wouldn't have countenanced.

I didn't have Greek, so I couldn't read the tiny letters, but I could see the jewels, and lying among them was Abraxas, carved into a carnelian identical to the one that I had round my neck at this very moment, a present from a dead magus. Like mine, this one was set in a silver shank on a ring. I felt a shiver of recognition.

Abraxas, the strange amalgam of a rooster's head, a man's

torso, a pair of snakes or eels for legs, holding a lightning bolt and a sword, the powers of life itself, Earth, Air Fire and Water, dominated by Will, or some would say Spirit, all within one being. The symbol of a truly balanced personality, or so my magical friend Elisabeth Thorburn said, one that had contacted the true life force within and worked with it. I wasn't so sure about that, but mine had opened doors for me.

The jewel around my neck seemed to pulsate in the nearness of its own likeness. The seal of Abraxas, calling out to itself.

I knew I had to have it.

I peered myopically at the rest of the display. It was museum quality, the best, although an eclectic collector had gathered the items. I wondered where it came from. It wasn't the sort of thing you'd come across every day. Even on a very good day! Unless you got up very early and had people looking after your interests and their own at the risk of selling their own countrymen and their heritage down the river.

"Check it all out," Leggy had said.

I dragged myself away from the Classical section, and wandered around the medieval, leaving him the East, Far, Middle and Near.

I had no idea that the Hon. John Anselm-Jones was the *eminence grise* behind the items on sale any more than I had suspected he was a spy. I had understood that he was simply a collector in a private way, and a connoisseur, one of those wealthy English travelers who just did whatever he fancied as he had always had the wherewithal to indulge himself. I hadn't even thought of him as a dealer.

Naïve, of course.

But when he told me, Leggy had smiled. "That's exactly what he wants you to think, my dear. He poses as a wealthy scholar, but there's a lot more going on beneath the surface."

I told myself to focus.

It was difficult to do so and stay with 'Muriel'. She would have been fussing about her charge and looking for dust, of which there was very little. It was a beautifully kept gallery.

Medieval, I told myself. Look at the medieval.

It was, once again, stunning.

High quality items with only minimal damage. Amazing locks

and keys, church statuary and tiny devotional images, lengths of tapestry in faded colours, armour. European, certainly, English, almost certainly not.    This had virtually all come from abroad, and, I would hazard a guess, not necessarily by the most legitimate of channels    There were glass-fronted cabinets, elegant pieces in their own right, filled with smaller treasures, missals, drinking vessels, ranging from silver mounted horn to gold chalices, reliquaries of bone and ivory, what looked like ancient hand-written books in fantastic tooled leather and cloth wrappings, studded with gems, bound in wood, covered by cabochon rubies and sapphires, baroque pearls, and then too, exquisite jewels created by the most skilful goldsmiths for only the most prestigious clients: priceless small-scale items to die for.

And beside the cabinets sat the Lady, who had been carved from a single piece of wood.  Three feet or so high, the black virgin sat on her throne, the blessing Christ Child on her lap, staring impassively out at the viewer; she could only have come from a church, unless, of course, someone had taken her into 'safe-keeping' for the duration of the hostilities.

She was typically French.

I recognized her type, from the one I knew reasonably well, a miracle-working statuette in a village church near where my grandparents lived.  My grandfather was a free-thinker, but his wife, my tiny grandmother was a *croyante*.  If, as her husband said, the Lady had not saved the area from the war, then it was because he hadn't prayed hard enough; the rest of them had been doing their bit, and She had kept the Boche several hundred meters from the door.

This statue was possibly a little larger than the one I had known, but very much the same style.  She was austere, gaunt even, as was the child on her lap, looking out at the spectator, the pair of them, with their hard shell and stone eyes set in the dark polished carved wood.  I could still see the traces of gilding on the carved patterning on her hem and on her crown, on the crescent moon upon which her feet (in very sensible shoes) rested, traces of deep crimson on her dress, green on her cloak.

I wondered why green?

But, of course, lapis lazuli which became the wonderful ultramarine, was the most expensive of pigments, not only because it was a hard gemstone that needed to be brought to Europe from Asia at great cost, but also because of the difficult and lengthy process needed to extricate the color from the powder once the stone had been ground down; no village could have afforded an ultramarine cloak, but they could have managed a green one, and green was the color of Venus, Goddess of Love, and also the color of Nature.

Mr. Parsons came over to me. "She's rather striking, isn't she? From the Marquis de Lanteuil's collection. His widow sent it to us. Twelfth Century. Best possible provenance."

I put on my Muriel face. "Does she work? Does she heal people? I was given to understand that they were for that, black madonnas."

The manager looked confused. "I... I don't know. We only sell works of art here. She is a work of art. That is her purpose, Madam, to be admired. And venerated, of course, by the simple peasantry."

"Oh," I said, putting a finger to my mouth. "I'm probably I'm expecting too much, brought up on William Morris, you see. I thought she would be useful as well as decorative, like those useful dishes with the men with .. well let's say nothing on, chasing young ladies in the altogether... You couldn't get away with those in Woolworths, but because they're a few thousand years old, they're art," I mused.

"Muriel! Come here at once and stop annoying people."

"Yes sir." I'd seen enough, got enough, and from the sound of Leggy, so had he.

I moved across to him and took the handles of the wheelchair.

"Have you seen anything you fancy, Muriel?"

"Yes, sir. In that case, sir."

He took one look at the Graeco-Roman jewelery. "Not a golden hair ornament, surely, Muriel."

"No sir. I want that!" I pointed to Abraxas.

"Then you shall have it, although it's a damned queer thing to ask for." He looked up at Mr. Parsons. "Get her that one. It's Greek isn't it?"

"Er, yes sir. Came from an Arch-Ducal collection in Austria, the Czenins, I believe. Very good provenance." He opened the lid of the cabinet and held out the little gem to me. It was warm in my fingers, on my hand. Once more I felt it link with my own Abraxas.

Leggy looked at me questioningly.

I nodded. This was more than payment.

"Well then, what's your best price – to me, as an old friend and some-time helper of your boss?"

"Why don't we adjourn to the office to discuss it?"

I pushed Leggy to an office of genial proportions set with elegant mahogany furniture, good quality Regency, probably all original, too: a large desk with a tooled green leather top, three library cabinets, glazed above, drawers below, and several armchairs with saber legs and pretty inlay on the backs. There were splendid standard lamps of fluted gold and elegant regency striped curtains at the window, that matched the seats of the armchairs and an Aubusson carpet on the floor. On a silver tray on a table by the window was a tantalus with three cut-glass bottles, each filled with a slightly different colored liquid and sporting a silver label round its neck. An anachronistic state-of-the-art Remington typewriter, perched on an elegant Pembroke table, and a modern typist's chair completed the room.

Mr. Parsons went to one of the glazed cupboards and withdrew from behind the pleated cloth, a ledger, which he brought to the desk.

I had the Abraxas jewel on the leather desk top. There was a tiny string attached to the silver shank, a minuscule label on it. While the manager fluttered through the pages to discover the price, I checked the number attached to the piece and translated.

The code was pretty common. Ask fifty but drop to 30. I handed it to Leggy.

"Tell you what," he told the man, "I'll give you ten pounds, cash, on the nail."

The manager looked up from his search and looked at us.

A sale was a sale, and the gallery wasn't exactly brimming with connoisseurs with bulging wallets.

"Guineas," said Mr. Parsons promptly, "I couldn't do it for less."

## 10

"Now, Alice, what did you make of that?" asked Leggy, as I returned from his bathroom drying my hair. Bobby was pouring tea for us all.

"I'd swear Mr. Parsons didn't know that John Anselm-Jones was dead. He looked quite nonplussed at your comments."

Leggy nodded. "I felt that too. And he looked like a reasonably permanent fixture." He took a cup from Bobby. "Thank you, Bobby. Anything else, Alice?"

I took my tea and sat in an armchair by the fireplace opposite Leggy.

"Yes. There was nothing British in the place as far as I could make out – or precious little. But it was called the International Galleries."

"Quite. He specializes in 'abroad' – it gives him a reason to travel."

"The things I saw could have been genuine market pieces, but I'll check the provenances. I didn't know there was a Marquis de Lanteuil, although I have heard of the Czenins, but whether they collected engraved gems, I'm not sure. The Black Virgin almost certainly came from a church, despite the de Lanteuil connection, and I would say that it came as a result of the war. In fact, I'd say that probably quite a lot came that way. I should imagine that much of his inventory has dubious provenance – why else would the manager impress upon us that it wasn't?"

Bobby chuckled. "They can't pull the wool over your eyes, Milady, now, can they? By the way, you make a great nurse. You could give me a bed-bath any day and I'd be meek as a lamb!"

"Like some of those Priapic satyrs I saw, more like!" I said.

Leggy guffawed into his tea. "Was that what you were giving the chap gyp about?"

"What's one of them?" asked Bobby.

"Never you mind, Bobby. What did you make of the Eastern antiquities?"

Leggy blotted his mustache on a napkin and looked at me

straight. "They're stolen from archaeological digs, or dug up and sold illegally. Can't blame the people, they're poor as church mice. A disreputable dealer will give them what they think is a reasonable price and they can feed their families. But the items get separated, sold on, and the real knowledge, the real price, if you like, is lost, both to the culture that came from it, and to the world in general.

"Carpets are a different kettle of fish. Once-wealthy families in the east are selling their treasures off. I would think most of those do have good provenance and are legitimate – unless they have been stolen. And that is another matter. The thing is, they're still making stuff in the old style, because that's what sells."

"Leggy, are you trying to tell me that Anselm-Jones was a high-class fence?"

"If he was a fence, I think he was a fence with supreme provenance. Why, Edward the Abdicator bought from him, frequently, and he was not alone."

No, I thought, Edward Windsor, our erstwhile king who had married for love, was the leader of fashion and spent like a Maecenas. I'd met him briefly when I came out, and once more a few years later, and wasn't particularly impressed with what I'd seen of him. Oh, he had a certain charm – he was the Golden Boy, and people loved him, but he was indiscreet and totally selfish – which was probably why he had to go. If you liked your men slight, fair and arrogant, with a hint of a lisp, he was for you! I found him vain, self-obsessed. I had far more respect for his unassuming brother, Bertie, who lived a far more 'normal' life before he had to become King George, picking up the pieces and doing a job that he hadn't been groomed for during the war that followed. That took far more courage than 'following your heart' and expecting people to accede to your every whim.

Edward Windsor was in Paris now. I wondered briefly whether he was missing the warmth of the Bahamas, but for a socialite and elitist such as he, not to mention his elegant expensive wife, it must have been four years of purgatory. I also wondered how he felt about being refused his place as bona fide King of Britain and the Commonwealth with the woman of his heart as full Queen beside him; that must surely rankle! I had a feeling he might feel waspish about it: he looked the type.

"You'll maybe have some problems proving it," Bobby said, interrupting my chain of thought.

"That's never stood in our way before, Bobby. We have Alice on our side, haven't we, my dear?"

"Eh?" I said, my mind still on the Windsors.

"Penny for your thoughts, my dear. I was saying to Bobby that I don't want to see Roger set up for this murder any more than you do. We all know he's innocent, but … well, it is on his land and as you know, he bore the victim ill will…"

"You think Pa did it?" I asked, shocked. "That's crazy!"

"Exactly so. But someone knows something, and at present very few people know the true nature and multiple identity of the victim. And one of them is the murderer. That's what and who we should be focusing on. Don't you think?"

I nodded. That made sense.

"Good. Alice, I'm afraid I was a bit rude this morning, my dear. It won't happen again."

He deftly held the flame over the bowl of his pipe and sucked in the smoke, looking pointedly at Bobby, who refilled my cup, giving me a wide grin and a wink. "Have another biscuit. And some more tea., Milady. It will set you up for this evening's frolic."

Basil received us joyfully. He was intensely proud of his family, and enjoyed showing them all off. A genuinely nice man, my sister had found for herself. We cracked a bottle of the Widow then, having left our blessings on the little red-faced bundle, set off to paint the town a similar hue.

We started at the Café de Paris, where we dined expensively and very well, considering the rationing, danced a bit, then went on into deepest Soho which we both preferred for the music and the lack of chi-chi. We did indulge in some cigarettes, but what the hell, we'd not be seeing each other for a while, and everyone else was smoking. We came out into the street at throwing out time – two in the morning - and managed to get a cab back to my place. The little red car was outside.

"What's that doing there?" I asked as Jeremy slipped the cabbie a ten bob note. "I thought you had a care for my reputation."

"It's a present," he said, handing me the keys. "Yours for the duration. You'll need transport while I'm away if things head the way they appear to be going. Just give me a lift back home tomorrow morning, so I can get my traps into a taxi."

I was amazed. And delighted. "I've got something for you, too." I said, dipping into my handbag and handing him a tiny wrapped package.

He opened it as we climbed the stairs. By the time we were in the flat with the light on, he had the Abraxas ring out of it's box.

"Alice, I can't take this, it's yours."

I shook my head. Mine was still round my neck. I pulled it from where it had slipped down below the collar of my dress. "It's yours. Put it on. Can you feel the link between them?"

He slid the ring onto his third finger, where it sat comfortably. I watched his face light up, and felt the tingle response from my own Abraxas. "Wherever did you get it? How?"

"I earned it this afternoon. Keep it and use it. He opens doors, as you know."

"He does more than that, Alice, can't you feel it? It's like a calling device. We could use these, Alice. We really could. I only wish we had more time to practice with them."

It was strange coming back from the airport without him.

He'd taken the envelope that Leggy had given me, with a nod, and placed it inside a the dust cover of a book he would read on the journey and, since we'd said our proper goodbyes earlier, we'd shaken hands like good friends, touching the two Abraxas rings together to link them. Then he'd simply walked through the gate with a smile and a wave and was gone. I found it quietly disturbing. I didn't like the idea of being on my own again.

Back in the BOAC terminal in Victoria it was a fine day and not yet noon. I needed company, so instead of ringing Pa or Sam I rang Thelma and arranged to meet her for lunch at the Prince of Wales Gate of Hyde Park. I took a couple of buses, enjoying the views from up front on the top deck, being driven round my own capital city. The journey filled the intervening time very pleasantly.

Thelma shed her office jacket, waving as soon as she saw me.

She was in her mid thirties, unmarried, and if you took her at face value, a motherly body. She was an exceptional secretary, and never appeared ruffled, oozing calmness and order. Out of work she was a bruising sidecar rider, a very good swimmer, and could handle a heavy motorbike with the best of them. She wasn't thin – but then she was from stocky stock, she said, and she had a failing – a very sweet tooth, a misfortune indeed for anyone during the current restrictions – which Bobby Gallagher, another motorcyclist, to whom I had recently introduced her, was now indulging, probably illicitly.

We found a bench beneath the trees, away from the nannies and the small children playing ball and shared sardine sandwiches and a bottle of pop.

The chat turned to her work – she had taken over my old job at Lowther's Auction Rooms – as I knew it would, and I got my chance to ask the question.

"A name popped up recently, Thelma. I wondered if you'd heard of him. Mr. Arnold used to use him sometimes."

Thelma did a cleaning up job with her handkerchief. "Yes? Who was that?"

"John Anselm-Jones, " I said. "He used to be around all the time. Have you heard of him lately?"

She put her handkerchief safely in her handbag as she reflected. "No. In fact I think Mr. Arnold wanted to contact him over a putative Poussin. Nothing came of it as I remember, but Mr. Arnold said he was often abroad so we got someone else to authenticate the painting. I'm sure it was a Poussin, by the way. Came with good provenance, but was a bit red, if you get my meaning."

"Red bole ground," I said automatically, "Poussin used that technique. Sometimes the glazes he used on top fade over time."

I grinned at her, "Sorry, the artist's daughter's coming out. So you think Mr. Anselm-Jones is abroad? I wonder where."

Thelma shrugged. "Could be anywhere. Mr. Arnold said he had the money to indulge his itinerant connoisseur life-style, I remember. It sounded like sour grapes to me. Was it important, Alice?"

"Probably not," I said. "Forget I mentioned him. Have you seen Bobby recently?"

Her face lit up. "Oh yes. And he let me drive his Matchless. He's not what my Mam would have wanted for me, but I can close my eyes to a lot for that."

I laughed. "You are incorrigible, Thelma!"

Her face lit up. "Thank you, Alice! I have always tried to avoid mediocrity. I doubt if I will ever be famous, but infamous? Oh, I'd settle for that!" She glanced at her wristwatch, sighed and stood up. "Work calls. You won't tell Mr. Arnold, will you? He thinks I'm sweet."

I chuckled. "No, I promise. I won't tell Mr. Arnold. He thought I was sweet, too."

"That's sweet," she said, and we dissolved into giggles. Mr. Arnold was good to work for, and he was lucky to have Thelma, but he had no idea what he had hold of, any more than he had with me. His ideas of what women were... what women weren't.

48

I collected the car from outside Jeremy's rooms in Maida Vale and spent the first part of the afternoon at the library, looking up our body in whatever reference books I could find.

Edgar Winthrop – not a lot. A middle-aged entrepreneur who kept well below the radar.

John Anderson, even less.

But Mr. John Anselm-Jones showed up bright and clear; born comfortably off in 1894, educated at Harrow, then on to Oxford, into the Guards, for a short while, then after the First World War he disappeared overseas for a while, learning his *métier* of antiquary and connoisseur.

I discovered he was a friend of the Royal Academy, so Pa could well have met him there. Indeed he would have been Pa's contemporary, give or take a year, and as Pa said, he knew lots of people. A clubbable man, Mr. Anselm-Jones – he listed at least seven in Britain, and others overseas – with a background in scholarship – the arts, the classics, and the Near East, he had written several books – and seemed to be a well-respected visitor to foreign universities, having a collection of honorary degrees to his name in the Old World and the New.

No mention of a wife, nor of any serious attachment, despite his fifty three years. Not inclined to wed? Or just too artistic? He lived in Bloomsbury, not far from the British Museum, in a house packed with his collections.

I made a note of the address, then checked out Lanteuil, which proved to be the name of several small villages in France. The French gazetteer and 'stock books' told me, as I surmised, that none of them supported a Marquis de.

Out of interest I checked the villages out in Michelin, and found one had a supreme example of a 12th century church, where the carving and architecture was well worth a visit. I wondered whether the Black Mother and Child might have come from there. I penned a letter then and there to M. le Curé of La Madeleine, Lanteuil to post later.

Czenin was a different matter. Polish stock, living in Vienna, the current holder of the title and the collection was before the war a playboy with expensive tastes. The collections mentioned were fine paintings, Baroque musical instruments and 18th century furniture. The classical period was not mentioned, but that didn't mean the Arch-Ducal family had not collected these highly prized carved gemstones. Inconclusive, there.

I left the Reference Section and went into the Lending Library, where I got out one and ordered three more of Mr. Anselm-Jones' books. Leggy had impressed on me 'know your enemy'. I didn't know that he was my enemy, but someone had thought he was theirs.

I drove home and spent the rest of the afternoon clearing the flat as much as possible. Thanks to my recent break-in there was a lot less to do, but I still had some of my Great Aunt Caro's things, family pieces. I needed Pa to look at them, and see if he wanted them; if not, I'd put the best into Lowthers and give Leggy the rest to get rid of for me. Leggy's 'retirement job' running his own house clearance, storage and removal company had its uses.

I rang Pa after six, and asked him whether he wanted any of his Aunt's stuff.

"Have you spoken to Leggy yet? Have you seen Maddy? Did Jeremy understand? Did he get the message?"

"Yes on all counts," I said. "What's been happening at Wethersley?"

"I can't even begin to tell you. Come down and stay. There's nothing for you in town now. Come home for a while."

"Maman playing up?" I asked.

"Don't be cheeky, Alice."

That was unlike him. It was obviously bad at home.

"I can't come tonight. I've got things to do and I've got to be in for the builder tomorrow. I'll come as soon as I can. I've seen the new baby, and he's a darling, just like his mother and his sister. And his maternal Grandpa."

The expected chuckle again didn't come.

Pa must be tense. Not good.

"Look," I said, "if Maman is coming down sometime, she could collect some of your Aunt Caro's things and some of my stuff. I need to free the flat of virtually everything except real basics as soon as possible for several weeks."

"Will it fit in the Citroen?" he asked eagerly. "I'll drop Maman off tomorrow, and collect you and the things. Then you can be with us at the inquest in the afternoon. Will 9 o'clock be too soon?"

"Pa! It'll be far too soon for Maddy if you drop Maman on her at half past eight!"

"Half past nine then. I'll drive you back. We can store the stuff at Wethersley."

"What about Maman?"

"Oh, she'd be delighted to be asked to stay the night."

"Pa!"

"No," he said sadly. "I didn't think you'd like that idea. But she doesn't want to be at the Inquest, says it has nothing to do with her, quite rightly. Perhaps one of us can fetch her, or she could come back on the train. I suppose Maddy does need a rest. Your mother always did for a few weeks after one of you popped out. I'd forgotten. Getting old, you see." He sounded old, sorry for himself, very unlike my father, who was generally positive and brimful of life and fun.

"Pa, what's the matter?" I asked.

"Not over the phone, Alice. I'll talk to you tomorrow. Without Maman listening in. I'll tell everyone you're coming for the duration,eh? They'll all be so happy."

"Er, no, Pa. Just for a day or so, but I will come on and off. I've got to keep my eye on the flat."

"Don't be so silly, Alice. Your place is with your family at a time like this. I'll be there at half past nine. Have the coffee on."

He hung up.

No goodbye, just an order.

Not at all like Pa.

And Maddy would have Maman dumped on her again.

It wasn't fair.

I rang her number and left a message to that effect, and apologized for my parents.

Hell. Things were bad.

I'd been bludgeoned into staying at Wethersley.

Which I didn't mind when things were normal, but now was not normal.

A day or so, fine.

Long term? Definitely not.

I needed to be here, especially since I was working for Leggy, although how, I wasn't quite sure, yet.

I wanted to be here to oversee the building work, and to have a bit of time for myself, not at Wethersley being the oldest daughter of a family all over again.

I put in a call to Sam. He might be able to clarify things on the home front for me.

The phone rang. "Hello Sam! How are you?"

"It's Bar, darling. I've been trying to ring you all day."

"Been frightfully busy, darling," I said, my voice, of its own accord, trilling up the poshness register to match hers. "How can I help you?"

"You tell me. What's all this going on at your country seat? I've just read it in the Evening Standard. Why wasn't I informed? I thought we were friends." She sounded miffed and more than slightly squiffy, but then she was a journalist, society style. She'd have been drinking since mid-afternoon if not earlier.

"Would you believe I know nothing about it? I've been down in London. Jeremy's just been sent abroad. I've been keeping him company until his flight, this morning. I haven't even bought a newspaper. What does it say?"

"Not a lot. I hoped you would tell me, Al." I heard the rustling of paper at the end of the line, "'A body of an unnamed person was recently found in a shallow grave near Wethersley. Foul play is suspected.' Al what do you know?"

"Not much more than that," I said. "My brother and his friend were led to it by said friend's dog, I believe, on Sunday, but we – that is the police and locals are trying to keep it quiet. If the Evening Standard has it, there'll be no chance of that, but I'm going down to Wethersley tomorrow – it's the inquest and Pa wants me there. I can find out then and let you know. My father knew nothing about it, apart from my brother and his friend and his friend's dog discovering something on Sunday afternoon."

"That's all you can tell me? Really?"

"At present, Bar. What you read in the papers is all that I know. Look, if you want, come round for a drink later. I'm up to my eyes in getting the flat redeveloped and there'll be stuff all over the place, but I've got a bottle of my grandfather's wine stowed away. We could share it with cheese on toast? I need an excuse to stop packing things up."

"Sorry darling, I'm off to the theatre tonight. Work. It's such a chore."

"I bet. How's your lovely little photographer?"

"Dating a ballerina, would you believe! Makes you sick. Look darling, if you have anything for me, anything at all, don't be shy. Not after all I've done for you and your beau."

"We are in your debt. You'll be the first to know. Love you. Enjoy your play."

"I'll enjoy the leading man with any luck. Bye for now, darling, must fly."

I cradled the phone.

I had meant what I said, I did want an excuse to stop packing stuff, but I was quite relieved she hadn't taken up my offer.

Sam rang almost immediately.

He, too, was after more information, but I assured him I knew nothing further and that I'd see him at the inquest the following day. "However, I can tell you this. Inspector Woods will not be in total charge," I said. "I had that from someone in town. No names, and only a few moments ago."

He sounded somewhat mollified. "I heard that this morning," he said softly. "He was spitting feathers. So was your mother when I went and saw her. She was brilliant, Alice, said the man had no right to bury himself there on family land. She said there were other people all asking stupid questions and then she went into French. It's a very expressive language, isn't it?"

"It is the way Maman uses it. So you know as much as me. Now how much does your friend the psychic drunkard know?"

"I'm sure he'll get in touch if he remembers something," Sam said, flatly. "Your father seemed very worried. You don't think...?"

"Pa said he knows nothing about it and Pa never tells lies. At least, not that sort of lie. His lies are mostly not to upset people. Like he'll tell a woman she's beautiful when that's what she really needs to hear. Perhaps it isn't a lie to him. He's probably the most honorable man I know."

"Praise indeed. Fair enough. But my editor says I'll have to keep digging. Will you explain that to them, Alice? It's not personal, or intended to intrude, it's just what I do."

"Yes, Sam. I understand. I'm sorry I've nothing more for

you."

"Well, thank you, Alice. I appreciate that. The Rev says to say next time you're down, come to tea. He misses you."

"I'd be delighted."

There was a knock on the door. "Must go, Sam. There's someone at the door. Nice talking to you."

It was George. "The car's still there, Miss. I thought Mister Jeremy was orf."

"He is, George. Went this morning. He'll be there now."

"He's left it for you, Miss?" George's eyes widened. "Cor! What a toff!"

I nodded. "I could murder some fish and chips, couldn't you?"

He beamed. "Cor, yeah, Miss. And Mum says do you need some help with packing stuff away? She's got some old crates and boxes like you said, and the girls are with Aunty Jenny."

Lily, like her son, was wonderful.

After a fish supper, she, George and I cleared and packed away all the remnants of Great Aunt Caro that could be stowed, and lugged them to my landing. "Get Joe and Harry to shift them, Miss, they've got more muscle than us," she said. "Makes them feel big and strong, and they like that."

I smiled. "Good idea. Fancy a drink? We've earned it."

"Me too?" George asked.

"My grandfather's wine? Really? You can have a sip, but I'll make you home-made lemonade if you like." I still had a lemon I'd acquired the previous week, and I barely used my sugar ration.

"I think I'd prefer that, too," said Lily with a grin. "I'm not great on wine. And I don't want to breathe fumes over Aunty Jenny; she's Sally Ann."

## 12

Joe and Harry were shifting boxes down to the entrance hall when Pa arrived and offered to help him pack them in the car when we left. I poured him a black coffee with a hefty slug of rum in it, and passed the biscuit barrel. He got out his pipe. He seemed years older than when I last saw him last weekend, and very very tired. He looked his age, in fact, nudging sixty, instead of being able, as he said, exaggerating slightly, to pass for someone in their mid-forties.

"OK, Pa," I said. "What's happening? You can talk here."

He shook his head. "No, Alice. In the car. No-one can hear us there."

I let him be, drank my own coffee (without rum) and packed a few clothes into a weekend case.

"I need to be in town, too," I said. "I can't stay. I've got commitments here. But I would greatly appreciate an open invitation to come and go."

He stretched his hand across to mine. "Alice, you know you have it. You've always treated Wethersley as your private hôtel," he said with a gentle smile. He looked around at the empty room. "Well, it will be good to know you'll be settled soon. Only Guy left."

"Good Heavens, Pa, you're talking like Maman. There's more to life than getting your children 'settled'!"

He smiled again, wanly. "Yes, I suppose there is. Sorry, Alice. This latest development has really knocked me."

"Reminded you we're all only here on loan?" I asked.

"Yes, but more than that… I don't like the implications…"

"But you've nothing to do with it," I said. "You told me so. And everyone who knows you would take your word."

"I hope so," he said, softly. "I really hope so."

The journey out to the chalk was smooth although the car was heavily laden.

"Right, Pa," I said as Northolt airport fell back on our right. "Give. What's making you so nervous?"

"Didn't fool you, then?"

"Stop stalling, Pa!" I said. "If you're in trouble, I want to know. Remember, I'm family too. It works both ways!"

He chuckled. "Yes. That's good. Right. Leggy came down last night. We went for a walk and had a chat, just him and me. I think I was one of the last people to see Mr. Anselm-Jones alive. Apart from the murderer, of course."

"Ah!" I kept my eyes on the road. "And when was this, Pa?"

"Last November. He left England in October, and that was the last that was heard of him. Went to Verona, according to the papers, and never returned. But he turned up at Wethersley in November."

Ah. That explained a few things.

"You've told the police this?"

"They didn't ask about Mr. Anselm-Jones. Only about Edgar Winthrop whom I didn't know at all. I painted Anselm-Jones once, as you probably know. It was a very good portrait, and at that time we rubbed along very nicely, but later... well, one noticed things, attitudes, behavior, ideals, that sort of thing, and I found him somewhat wanting. When he came in November, we had a flaming row. I told him I didn't want his damned commissions. But we both understood that his visit to me was *sub rosa*; no-one was to know about it and I had given my word that I would not mention it. So I haven't – until now. I'm trusting you to keep mum, Alice!"

I took this on board.

Pa was a man of his word, but he wasn't one to throw away commissions.

He was a very fine portraitist, but Maman could spend for both France and England, given half the chance, rationing or no.

There had to be a very good reason for turning down the opportunity to make his beloved wife happy.

"Was this the first time you did that?" I asked. "Turn down Mr. Anselm-Jones?"

"What?" he asked, negotiating a horse and cart. "What makes you say that, Alice?"

I shrugged. I didn't know. It just popped out. But I must have hit a nerve. "Is it true?"

"Yes, but I thought no-one knew about that. No-one apart from us at Wethersley."

"Tell me, Pa, I need to know everything. Really, I do."

He sighed. "He did come before. I threw him out. He was insulting to a couple of our evacuees. Bloody insulting, damn rude, the bastard! I don't allow that behavior in my house."

"But that wasn't the reason he came, was it? What did he want?"

"He had a commission for me. Which I wasn't inclined to accept, but the real reason I threw him out was for my lads, Marcus and Raymond. No-one treats my guests as he did. Those two lads were suffering enough losing their father and missing their home and friends in London. He behaved atrociously to them, the arrogant racialist pig!"

"And you turned down his commission then?"

"Damn right. It would have meant I'd have to leave you all. I wasn't willing to do that. Not then, and not now. I hope I have some principles left."

I waited for him to tell me what the commission was.

He didn't.

He simply stared forward, clenching his pipe between his teeth and concentrating on the road.

"Are you going to tell me what you turned down?" I asked at last.

"You don't need to know, Alice. Your mother doesn't know. Only I know."

I sighed. He could be very stubborn.

"Would Maman have approved?" I asked. "Had she known?"

"She would have approved of my not leaving you all at that time. It was war time and I didn't want to travel, not the distance that would have been required of me; travel was dangerous in those days, in case you don't remember. She wanted me safe at home, helping with all our evacuees and the land girls, besides, I was head of the local Home Guard. I couldn't have gone, even if I'd wanted to. As to whether she would have approved of my turning down the commission, no. I think she would have wanted me to accept; whether she would have understood why I couldn't do it, I don't know.  Perhaps she would have done, but I thought it best to keep her in the dark, so I didn't tell her."

He glanced across at me.  "This is strictly between you and me, Alice.  I've never actively lied to your mother, but this time… well, I didn't actually lie, just didn't tell the whole story.  And in last November, the same request came in.  I still couldn't accept it.  Even though there would have been far less travel involved."

I waited for the details, but he wasn't going to tell.  "I have principles, Alice, and I stick by them.  I've known Mr. Anselm-Jones for years, and I've read his books.  He's been very influential in his own areas, a scholar who advises on art and *objets d'art*, a clever man, very erudite, and beloved of the great and the good.  If Mr. Anselm-Jones says it's right, then it's right.  Do you understand what I'm saying, Alice?"

"You mean he authenticates things for people and gets a financial thank-you from both buyer and seller?" I asked.

"Just so.  He's a scholar with a very large reputation, and a collector of the first water. He travels widely, building up contacts and putting people in touch with each other and works of art.  Sees himself as a bit of a Lorenzo the Magnificent."

"Indeed?" I said, bearing in mind what Jeremy had said.  Lorenzo de Medici was also a politician!  I wondered just how far politics and art were intertwined in the dubious world of Mr. John Anselm-Jones.

"I wouldn't mind traveling and dealing with fine art," I mused.

"Of course you wouldn't, Alice. And you'd be very successful, you've got a good eye and you get on with people, mostly.  But I'd hope you'd keep your principles.  Integrity.  Without that, Alice, one's nothing."

So Pa was confirming Leggy's and Jeremy's suspicions.  Mr. Anselm-Jones was less than pure white.

I said as much.

"He has no problem with compromising principles," said Pa primly.

He turned off towards the chalk.  "I can't level with you, Alice.  It wouldn't be fair.  But if there comes a time when I can, be assured I will, my dear.  I value your integrity, but I do not want you to become embroiled any more in this than I can help.  The bloody man was found on my land. It's my problem, not yours. Mine alone. I shall carry it."

"Alright, Pa. But I heard it's no longer solely in Inspector Woods' hands. Who's on it now?"

"Some chappie from Scotland Yard, and he's not exactly flavor of the month locally. Putting all the local constabulary's backs up with his high-handed attitude. He was damn rude to Mac as well. Dammit, Alice, a please and a thank-you cost nothing and open a lot of doors that would otherwise be slammed shut."

"Sounds nice. Where's he staying?"

"Would you believe at Larry's? With his stooge," Pa chuckled; our family and that of Larry, the landlord of the local pub, the Wethersley Arms, went back a long way.

"We could call in for a drink on the way home, perhaps?" I suggested, not expecting Pa to refuse.

"Another time, perhaps. I'd like to get the car emptied, and then there's the Inquest. They'll certainly be there, and that will be soon enough for me, Alice."

# 13

I gazed around the courtroom. It was full, and mostly of people who would not be called to give evidence, locals, some of whom had dressed up for the occasion, as well as a sprinkling of journalists. I sat between Pa and my brother Guy. Nigel sat next to him. Sam had nodded to me as he came in, and Rev Simmons came over and shook Pa's hand, then mine, and Guy's and Nigel's. "I'm sure it'll all be fine," he whispered, his dandelion clock hair fluffing out against the brightness of the tall windows.

We were called to order by the Registrar and then the Coroner, and Nigel was asked to speak. He was obviously nervous in his formal dark suit, and spoke softly, haltingly at times. The room was silent, every ear stretching to full hearing, so no juicy morsel was lost. It was probably a disappointment, as what he said was what I had heard before; Spider had led him and Guy to the discovery of the body; he had touched nothing at the scene, and had left Guy there to stay with the deceased while he went to call the police.

"What exactly were you doing in that area?" the Coroner asked.

"Walking my dog, sir. I'd let him off the lead. I thought the woods were safe enough, sir."

For a dog, I thought, but not for the poor chap you discovered.

"Did you see anything that may have led you to guess how he had died?"

"No, sir. I touched nothing. I only looked, and that only for a very short time. I was shocked and repulsed, sir. I offered at once to raise the alarm. I didn't want to be in the clearing with a dead man, and was very glad when Guy, Mr. Chamberlain, that is, said he'd stay with the body."

Guy was called, and stood tall, answered the questions and backed up Nigel's story with times and told how I had joined him shortly after Nigel had gone for help. He had no idea how the man had died or what he was doing on or in our land.

I was called and reiterated how Jeremy and I were driving along the back road from Marsham to Wethersley when we saw Nigel, hugging Spider under his arm, climbing over a stile, and waving us down. He had told us briefly what he had found and I ceded my place in the two-seater car, so that Nigel could put through his emergency call from my family home. I found my own way along the path to where Guy was waiting (not in the clearing) and was taken there. I described what I saw as closely as I could and how Guy and I waited in the woods until Sergeant Bloxham and the others came. During this time I touched nothing.

Sergeant Bloxham reported on his part, and Inspector Woods on his and the revealing and subsequent removal of the body from the site.

The post mortem report was requested, and the room shifted expectantly.

The Pathologist took the stand and reported that the body had been in the earth for some six months, and although there was some evidence of post-mortem trauma, had been killed by a bullet shot at close range into the back of his head.

Everyone jumped!

That was not a murder, it was an execution!

Beside me, Pa groaned.

Both Guy and Nigel gasped "No!".

They were not alone. The room was in uproar.

This just didn't happen in sleepy Buckinghamshire.

Once order had been re-established, the Coroner asked "Do we have an identity for the deceased?"

"Yes, sir," said Inspector Woods. "In fact we have more than one. Edgar Winthrop, alias John Anderson, alias John Anselm-Jones, sir. No doubt you will have heard of the latter?"

The Coroner nodded, "Yes. And do we have any next of kin?"

"Not at the moment, sir. We are still pursuing our inquiries."

"Then I suggest an adjournment? Perhaps two weeks?"

And so it was decided.

Pa and I took our time leaving the courtroom and were catching up with Nigel and Guy who were frantically puffing Senior Services. Pa accepted one, as we made our way to the

Citroen, and drew on it so hard that he started to cough.

I put my arm round him.

"Do you want me to drive?" I asked.

"No, thank you, Alice. I'll drop Guy off at the station and wait for Chérie and Angelique."

Now Sam was touching my elbow, keeping a hoard of other people at bay. "Alice, can I have a word?"

I thought swiftly. "Pa, you go ahead, I'll make my own way home." I dropped a kiss on his cheek. "Ask Mrs. Mac to save me some supper."

Sam and I watched Pa, Guy and Nigel set off in the Citroen.

"Mr. Nesmith-Brown seems very agitated," Sam commented softly, before taking my elbow and leading me away from the Coroner's Court at a rate of knots, to a local tea rooms, where he ordered a pot of tea and whatever cake was available, settling us into a cosy table in an alcove where we could be relatively private.

"He's a quiet person," I said. "You've met him. You can see that."

"Hmm. Possibly. Do you think he knows more than he's letting on?"

I looked up into Sam's war-scarred face. "You ask him. He doesn't say much to me. Not that I've encouraged him. Why are you saying that?"

"I have to. He was very white. And when the names were given out, he went even more ashen. I thought he was going to pass out. And there were people there who were watching him, locals: they noticed too. Did you see them?"

"Sam, I was watching the proceedings," I acknowledged. "I noticed a few people, but there were none that I knew. I'm not local now. I live and work in London mostly. But yes, there was a tall fair chap with a Ronald Coleman mustache; he was eying us all up. He disappeared sharpish once the identity was disclosed. Is he a reporter?"

The tea arrived, and we let the elderly female poured us a cup each, then bring a cake-stand laden with rock cakes, and a plate each for us. "Thank you," I said, with a smile, which was returned. Sam, too, thanked her, paid, then returned to my question.

"He's not a reporter as far as I know, and I know a lot more of them, local and national since you gave me that last story. No, he's local. Calls himself an entrepreneur, but it's a bit grandiose. A bit of a wide boy, I think. He runs a haulage business and has a share in a shop by the church, Broom's Stores, second hand, junk, calls it Antiques, you know the sort of thing."

I nodded. So possibly not quite snow-white. "I wonder what he was looking at us for," I said. "It couldn't just be our good looks."

"It could," Sam said, with a grin. "But I watched him too. It was Nigel he was eyeballing, not you, Alice, and out of the two of you, I know which the average male would prefer to view."

"Thank you, Sam."

"You're welcome. Would you have a word with Nigel Nesmith-Brown? I don't want to scare the chap any further than he is already, and I think he is very scared indeed. I'm sure he noticed the local interest in him, and it didn't please him at all."

"You think they think he purposely discovered the body? He gave his spades and stuff to the police to prove his innocence," I said.

"You could find if they've given them back," Sam suggested.

"And you can find out for me how Ronald Coleman, or whatever his name is, is connected with Nigel, or indeed any of the Nesmith-Brown contingent. The rest of the family were noticeably absent today, don't you think?"

Sam looked up appreciatively from the rock cake he was busy demolishing. "Thank you, Alice. I'd not thought of that."

"The other thing that stands out to me," I said, between mouthfuls of cake, "is that when I found Mr. Jones or whatever he calls himself, he was lying on his back in the ground. If he was shot in the back of the head, he would have fallen forward onto his front. So someone at sometime must have moved him, probably post-mortem, and put him into the grave. He may not have been killed in situ so to speak."

## 14

While we had been talking the tea rooms were filling up. Two men in Trilby hats and long mackintoshes worn open over their dark suits now came through the door. "It's Chief Inspector Murray and his sergeant," Sam hissed. "He's coming this way. I'll introduce you. You'll have to speak to him sooner or later."

"Rather here than in the pub or at home," I said softly. "Stay with me, Sam. Like them, I'd like a witness."

They breasted across to us, swishing their coat skirts against the other tea-takers. I looked up at the pair. One, stocky, pugnacious, whom I took to be the Chief Inspector as he was leading. The other slighter in build but taller, with a similar swagger. I didn't warm to them.

Chief Inspector Murray made a beeline for our alcove, pulled a chair up for himself, and sat down uninvited. He removed his hat and set it on the table beside my plate. Nature had not been gentle with him; short and stocky to start with, he carried extra poundage, despite years of rationing, that his suit couldn't disguise. His thin hair slicked back across his head in black streaks, tipped with gray at the temples, an insignificant framing for the squared off circle of a face whose features were semi-hidden by a thick layer of subcutaneous fat; the nose already showing signs of red veining.

A drinker then, and a trencherman, quantity being more important than quality. He held his face as he held his body, belligerently, but that may have been to compensate for his lack of vertical inches. He must have scraped through the Police height regulation on a wing and a prayer.

Sam introduced us. I realized with a shock they they must have been about the same age, mid-to-late thirties.

Chief Inspector Murray came to attention in front of me and proffered his soft manicured hand.

I gave it a brief shake. "How do you do?"

"I'd like a little chat with you, Miss Chamberlain, and there's no time like the present. I was interested in what you said in court, and I've read your statement, but I'd like to go over things once more. You never know what you might remember if different questions are asked."

I shrugged.

"I can find a few minutes now," I said. "Why don't you sit down and take some tea?" The nippy was hovering and it was only fair that if they were using the tea rooms as an interview room, they paid for the privilege.

"Get some tea, Stonehouse," Chief Inspector Murray told his minion, who pulled up a chair and told the nippy "We'll have what they're having."

The Chief Inspector pulled out a pack of Players Navy Cut, opened it and selected a cigarette, replacing the pack in his pocket. Without taking his eyes off me, he tamped it on the table, flicked the little shreds of tobacco off the end, then put it to his mouth. He used a Swan Vesta to light it, tossing the match, still lit, into the ashtray where it died.

Brash and bossy, I thought. For what effect? Sergeant Stonehouse offered his own case of cigarettes around and discreetly lit Sam's and his, with his Ronson.

"Well, Miss Chamberlain, what exactly happened?"the Chief Inspector demanded.

I went through the whole rigmarole again. Coming back from church, car waved down by Nigel, hearing there was a body in our woods, me deciding to run down and be with Guy rather than waiting at home with the rest of them. I was getting bored with it.

"Why did you go down to the site?" he asked.

Yes, why did I?

Blatant curiosity, but I wasn't going to admit to that. "My brother was down there," I said. "And Nigel took my place in the car, to call the police."

He drew in a long stream of smoke and let it out slowly, eying me suspiciously.

"So?" he asked. "Convenience and …?"

"Moral support; my brother's war was largely official and 'at a distance'; mine was more down-to-earth, I am hardened to the sight of death. He, I think, is less so," I said. "I don't know whether you have brothers and sisters, Inspector…"

He cut me short. "Oh aye. And if it were raining I'd have

stayed inside, particularly if I were a smart young woman in my Sunday best. No matter, please continue."

"It wasn't actually raining when I set out," I said. "It didn't start until I had seen the body and was waiting with Guy for the police to arrive."

"Describe the body again. How much of it was visible?"

"At first I could only see holes where someone had been digging, there were a couple of smaller ones not far away. But then when whoever it was had found the body, well, they had dug up or around it from the feet to the chest. It wasn't nice. I was glad the face was covered. It was lying on its back, Chief Inspector, which, having heard the cause of death, rather surprises me. And some of the spoil had been tossed back over the body, but I think the person who had uncovered it decided to call it a day before completion. Guy said he sent Nigel and Spider – that was the dog; they'd been led to it by him – off to tell the police They didn't think it was their job to dig it up," I said.

I took a sip of tea. Chief Inspector Murray said nothing.

"I was quite impressed by the quality of the clothing," I said. "Class will out."

His face darkened. Obviously I had hit a nerve.

"What exactly do you mean by that?" It was a sneer, but only a hint of one.

"Chief Inspector, I know quality when I see it. The boots were hand-made, the stockings were patterned, fine wool, the gaiters were of good quality, the tweed breeches came from an expert tailor. This was obviously not a member of the laboring classes!"

He snorted. "And if it had been, would that have made any difference?"

"Absolutely not, Chief Inspector. Why should it? But I would still have waited with my brother until the police arrived. If there is foul play it is important that the perpetrator be found. No-one has a right to take life in peacetime."

"So what did you talk about? While you were waiting?"

I frowned. I couldn't remember. "I'm not sure. Nothing significant. I think I told him we'd put back the wedding until the end of October. He wasn't terribly interested, but I didn't expect him to be. He's had a bit of a hard time recently."

The Chief Inspector smiled. "Ah, yes. Now we come to it. Why does Mr. Nesmith-Brown live with your family?"

I shrugged. "He needed a place to live and fetched up with us. I'm sure you've checked us all out one way or another."

He gave a hard sharp smile that disappeared immediately. "Wasn't your brother engaged to his sister? Wasn't there some nasty work going on there? I need the background, Miss Chamberlain. What were those two young men doing in the woods that day? Why there especially? It's got a certain reputation locally, I heard. Who led who down the daisy path?"

His eyes bored into me, cold, hard, insinuating, as he stubbed out his cigarette viciously in the ashtray.

I blinked, breaking the contact and felt anger flowing through me.

No-one has the right to make me feel like that.

I examined my fingernails, systematically, one by one, counting as I did so, calming myself, then stood up.

"I don't think I like your tone, Chief Inspector, and I certainly can't answer any of your questions. If you need this sort of background, you'd better ask my brother and Mr. Nesmith-Brown. As far as I know, they were simply taking a dog for its exercise, nothing more, nothing less."

"Oh, I think there was a lot more to it than that, Miss Chamberlain, and I think you do too," said Murray, slipping another cigarette into his mouth. "I think you all know a lot more about this than meets the eye." He took another cigarette out and a pink-tipped match from his box.

I stood up angrily. "Speak to my brother and to Mr. Nesmith-Brown. You'll excuse me, Chief Inspector..."

It wasn't a request.

I was out of the tea rooms, into the fresh air of Amersham, with Sam on my heels before he or Sergeant Stonehouse could catch me.

Sam started his car. "I'll take you home, Alice?"

I shook my head. "Thanks, Sam, but what I'd like is a decoy. Drive off for me, Sam, as though you were taking me home, would you? I'll talk with you later. Promise!"

He grinned. "Of course. He's a boor."

He opened his passenger door, waited for a moment or two,

slammed it shut then got into the driving seat of his car.

I headed round the corner and back behind the coroner's court, listening as Sam drove off, with Chief Inspector Murray calling out, sounding more Scottish in his anger, and chuckled, and watched the two detectives get into their own car and follow him.

Sam would catch up with me soon enough and I'd have to face Murray again, but dammit, it was round one to me.

During my walk through the backstreets of Amersham to the taxi rank on High Street I thought about what I'd learned today, starting with this morning.

Pa had some secrets to be winkled out, and I didn't doubt I could do that given a bit of time. Whether I'd like what I would learn was something else.

For the first time ever I had seen my father as an old man. Not old to the point of doddery and sick, but the cloak of verve and joie-de-vivre he normally wrapped around himself and all those within his orbit had been slashed to a tissue of rags.

I didn't like that one bit.

And I knew that there were far more nasty creepy things to come out before we could get Pa a new cloak, if indeed we could. This afternoon's disclosures – the identities, the style of death that had been issued to Mr. Anselm-Jones would only make things worse.

I wished, not for the first time, that I had Jeremy here to discuss all this with.

I couldn't talk to Maman, who was, I knew distraught with worry for Pa, and  monopolizing Angelique and worrying the Macs, too.

My sister was too busy with young Robin Montague and the rest of her family, indeed it would be unfair to drop any more in her.

 My brother – well he was my brother and at times a waste of space; although I liked him a lot more now than I did, we saw the world very differently; besides, I had to consider the homosexual angle. That was what the Chief Inspector had insinuated, it was what Jeremy had expressed, and … oh, to hell with it all.

We had a dead body found on our land.

What was it to do with us?

Anyone could have put it there.

Just because it was a well-known corpse… and Pa was known to feel enmity to him when alive...

Why hadn't Guy and Nigel just covered the thing up and lost it?

We were just too law-abiding.

My dear, now dead, lover, Raoul, would be laughing his socks off at the whole sorry mess.

"You never tell the police anything. Never, ever, Alice. They're always bad news, they're always trouble."

That was fair enough during the war in the French Resistance, but here I was in peace-time and in England.

I sat in the back of the taxi, twisting my Abraxas ring, and composed a letter to Jeremy in my head, wondering what he was doing now. I really did wish he was here, or perhaps, even better, that I could be there.

# 15

Before we had supper I managed to get Pa alone and told him I owed my friend, Bar.

"Another journalist?" he said, with a sad smile. "Well, you may as well tell her what happened at the Inquest. It will be common knowledge tomorrow anyway and at least you will have paid your dues. What did Sam want?"

I told him what had taken place, then made my call, and another to Sam, who wasn't in. Reverend Simmons promised to pass on my thanks and extended his own solicitude for our family. "Come and see me when you are next down with your family," he invited. "The angel building fund is coming on very nicely."

The Macs were the guardians of the Day Books, the diaries of the house. The current one lived in the kitchen, but earlier ones were locked in Mr. Mac's cupboard.

After supper I abandoned Pa, Maman and Angelique who were, with Mrs. Mac, listening to the radio, and searched out Mr. Mac. "Can I have a look at the Day Books, Mr. Mac?" I asked, as I hung the tea-towel up over the range.

"Of course, Miss Alice. Any particular year?"

"The last months of 1946. Autumn becoming winter, please."

I searched through November and December, the pre-Christmas activity, which had to go on despite rationing.

Mrs. Mac, Maman and Angelique all busy making things, food and gifts, out of next to nothing, which was all that was available, for the evacuees and their families and all our other friends, and more than pulling their weight in providing food, decorations and presents for the village Christmas party. Looking at the amount of work that went into all this, I was glad to be working at Lowther's Auction Rooms in London. The outgoings and efforts were at first sight constant and pitiless.

Well, almost.

Maman and Angelique seemed to have taken one day a week

off, visiting London, according to the book. On such occasions Pa gave them a lift to the station then returned to Wethersley.

And it was on one of these days that there was a note that a certain gentleman called to see Lord Wethersley; a Mr. John Anselm-Jones. Eleven thirty till twelve on Tuesday 26th November.

And Pa had scribbled a note beside the entry: Strictly No Further Contact With This Person.

In block capitals and red ink.

I heaved a sigh.

The Police would see this and draw all the wrong conclusions.

I closed the book, went back further, starting when we took in our evacuees, which included Marcus and Raymond, and working forward.

It took some time, in 1942, there he was again.

And Pa's writing beside it. 'Refused commission and threw the racialist blighter out. His behaviour to our boys not to be countenanced.'

I groaned, closed the books and locked them back in Mr. Mac's cupboard.

"Find what you were looking for, Miss Alice?" he asked, when I returned the key to him in his sitting room. Mrs. Mac was sitting beside him, her feet on a cushioned footstool, reading a library book beneath the standard lamp. She looked quietly relaxed, for which I was glad. Both Macs worked hard for us.

"Yes, Mr. Mac. And then again, no. But thank you, and keep those books under lock and key, please."

Pa was sitting with Maman and Angelique, both knitting, with a radio play on in the family sitting room. I indicated I was going for a walk.

Dusk was always a magical time.

More magical was the laughter and yapping coming from Nigel, back in his gardener's clothes now, and Spider as they played together along the drive outside his cottage. I remembered how tight and isolated Nigel had been such a short time ago, but here with his little dog, he was carefree again.

Spider, a rough-haired Jack Russell, was delightful, bounding and jumping as though articulated with elastic, racing for a soggy much-chewed tennis ball, retrieving it and daring Nigel to take it off him, but at an instruction laying it carefully at the young man's feet, ready for the next throw.

As I approached, Nigel calmed the little creature, felt in his pocket and brought out a dog biscuit, waiting for Spider to sit up and beg before he handed it over, and rubbed his pet's head, gently. He turned to me. "Hello, Alice. Back for long?"

"I don't know. I hope not. My real home's in Chelsea, but with things as they are..."

Nigel nodded. "Fancy a ginger beer? I've got some indoors. I usually have a glass this time of night on my lawn, such as it is."

I smiled. "Why not?"

We sat on local bodged chairs outside the backdoor of his cottage, with a foaming glass of cloudy drink each, while Spider lapped water from a bowl noisily at our feet.

"It's so nice to have a visitor." He lifted his glass then chinked mine. "Chin chin. I made it myself."

I smiled. "Well done! Cheers, Nigel. And thanks."

We sat down and drank. It was good heady home-made stuff. Mrs. Mac always made it, and must have passed him a plant across.

Finally he said, "Alice, I feel really bad about all this body business. I wouldn't have had it happen for the world."

I gave him a wry smile. "Yes, it is rather a can of worms..."

"I really can't blame Spider; he was just doing what dogs do."

"Nigel, I heard you offering your garden tools to Inspector Woods last week... What happened?"

Nigel grinned. "He took them, kept them for a day or two, and then brought them back, thank goodness. Of course they were not the ones that made all the holes!"

"Good. I didn't think you were the culprit. If you had known something was buried somewhere, you'd have found it first time," I said. He was quiet, but he was fairly astute.

Nigel chuckled, "Oh, Alice, that's priceless! You surely couldn't think I would have done such a thing. After I've been working hard in the garden, I'm not inclined to traipse round Wethersley looking for more digging!"

"Fair enough. Nigel, do you know the man? John Anselm-Jones?"

It was worth a try.

It certainly changed the atmosphere. It was shutters down! He held the glass in both hands, level with his knees and looked at the ground.

I followed his gaze and was reminded of Albrecht Durer's picture of a clod of earth. It wasn't a lawn, it was a microcosm of the universe down there.

I said nothing.

Finally he looked up at me. "I have met Mr. John Anselm-Jones," he said at last.

I inclined my head. "Care to tell me where and when and with whom?" I asked, hopefully.

He sat up, took a drink, put the glass on the grass beside his chair. "I suppose so. But it's not terribly enlightening. No great shakes. I met him in Baden Baden when I was about fourteen. In the Kursaal."

I worked years back on my fingers. It would be 1936.

"What were you doing there?" I asked. I'd whizzed through Germany on my way to Switzerland where I had been sent to be finished, but I'd not actually visited it, either before, during or after the war.

Nigel grinned. "The Cure, of course. Pa must have made some cash so we went. Suddenly, we just upped sticks and went to Germany. Ma was not well, Pa – he was even bigger before the War – he needed to take the waters, too. For some reason they thought Sylvia and I would enjoy the experience, so we were taken out of school and dragged along. Mr. Anselm-Jones was finishing his Cure. We spent a week or so with him, but that was all."

"And you met him again when you came back to England?" I asked.

He ignored the question. "He was an amazing teacher, Alice. He told me about German lime-wood sculptors of the fifteenth and sixteenth centuries, and about the great woodcut printers, Schongauer and Durer, of course. He really opened my eyes for me, you know? Told me how the German people were skilled artists, probably more so than the Italians. We went to a rather dull church, I remember; he made the votive figures come alive. I'd thought them pretty pedestrian and boring before, but then I saw them with fresh eyes. He was pretty special, I can tell you."

I nodded and emptied my glass. So he was a good communicator. That made sense. And he chose to spend time with a rather shy adolescent. Interesting. "Do you like art, Nigel?" I asked.

"I like beauty," he said softly. "Those angels you found, they're fantastic. And what your father did with them, cleaning them up, and then giving them away, that was amazing."

He peered over his glass at me. "Your family is very special, Alice. I've never come across people like you before. Everyone I've ever met was looking for profit, looking for the main chance. My family runs solely on self-interest. They are never happy, never satisfied, they always look for more, something bigger and better. "

He sighed. "No principles whatsoever. Unfortunately they'd sent me away to school  and I had ethics, principles drummed into me there; well it wasn't drumming as such. They sowed the seeds within me and they flourished, so I wasn't particularly popular at home. To survive with my family I learned to turn a blind eye and keep my mouth shut. But it was hard. And it was cruel. What they did to Sylvia and me… It was horrible. Sylvia had her own way of dealing with it. She's a different character from me, far more robust. That's putting it nicely."

I sat in silence. He had never spoken so openly to me before. I wasn't going to  interrupt.

He sighed again. "Well, that's enough about me. What about you? Are you missing your fiancé?"

I smiled. "Yes, of course. But it should only be for a few weeks, and there are far too many other things to keep me from brooding." I stood up. "I'd best be getting back. They tend to keep country hours here."

"I'll walk you back. Spider needs his last walk. You don't mind?"

"Not at all, Nigel. Thank you."


I sat at my dressing table penning a letter to Jeremy.

I was right when I said there were things to keep me busy, but

I missed his presence. I was worried about Pa, and Jem would have been good for him.

Maman needed controlling. I hoped Angelique could manage her, because in the state he was in, Pa certainly couldn't.

I had to keep their visits to Maddy to a reasonable minimum.

And I needed to find out as much as I could about Mr. Anselm-Jones. He must have enemies, but who were they and where were they?

I signed the letter all love and kisses, put it in an envelope and called it a day. I wondered what he was doing and where he was. I still didn't know. I might find out when a letter arrived. He'd probably be sitting in a bar somewhere with a glass of whatever the locals drank, listening to music if there were any available, or he would if he had any sense. I twisted the Abraxas ring on my finger, and ran the picture through my mind. I could swear I caught a wink as he raised his glass to me.

# 16

I took the train back to town on Friday morning, and used the time reading the press coverage. My first stop was with Bar, in her office opposite St. Clement Dane's broken church. She greeted me with a hug and pointed me to her work table where she had laid out information and photographs from the archives.

"You're an angel," I said.

"Fallen, sometimes, but true, generally," she admitted. "Work your way through and I'll see if I can rustle up a cup of tea for us."

I sat down, pulled out a pencil and my notebook and worked my way through, earliest first. This being a society paper, there wasn't a lot of 'news', rather who was doing what and where and when and with whom, which was exactly what I wanted. I began making notes as I turned the pages. Pictures of John Anselm-Jones began with him in the Guards and then continued in the late twenties when he was shown at various receptions and parties, including those hosted by the Merediths. Not that that was necessarily important because everyone who was anyone had attended at least one at some time in their lives.

Book launches and reviews came out regularly, and there were photographs with the great and good of Europe and Asia. Africa and the New World were notably absent.

I came upon one of Pa and him, clasping hands before his portrait. I homed in on it. Both looked relaxed and happy, so it was obviously before the great-falling-out. Royal Academy Summer Exhibition, 1936, it said. So Pa would have painted it earlier that year or possibly late the previous one. Whatever had caused the dissension must have happened later.

I turned the pages, and found Mr. Anselm-Jones in Germany with members of the universities of Heidelberg, Cologne, Potsdam and Leipzig. He had honorary degrees bestowed upon him for his work on the lime-wood sculptors, on Schongauer and Durer. He appeared very content in the company of the German academics, who, I knew, at this time, had to toe the official line. Decadent art, that is to say modern art, was reviled and destroyed, if not then, then very shortly afterward.

So Mr. Anselm-Jones appeared to be at ease with the Nazis. That could well explain Pa's antipathy. But not wholly, because a large proportion of the 'better off' in England thought perhaps Hitler might have something. Communism was far more feared than Nazism.

There were pictures of David, Prince of Wales, heir to the British monarchy, with various women and John Anselm-Jones close up now. And Wallis, there she was, smiling her hard, know-it-all smile at him, shortly after she married the never-to-be crowned Edward VIII. Another shot of the three of them, in what looked like an Alpine hideaway – Bavaria? Switzerland? Austria? John Anselm-Jones welcoming the happy couple to his home in the Oberland. Who sent in these photographs?

Now we were back in UK, an all male group shot. I recognised Leggy, younger admittedly, but it was him, in the background. I knew he belonged to a Masonic Lodge and it all suddenly became clear; the dark suits, the sober grouping, but in the middle stood Edward, all smiles, handing a watch and chain to his grateful friend. The text read 'The King, Edward VIII presents a gold watch to Mr. John Anselm-Jones, in gratitude for services rendered'. It didn't say what the services were, but it did show a close up of the half-hunter watch in its little carrying case and the inscription. It was a beauty and impressed me. The rest of the group, thirteen in all, were named. I copied the names into my notebook, and the date, and on a whim, added the inscription, all in a lovely copperplate script, 'To JAJ from EW, in gratitude and friendship, 1938'.

I turned more pages – and found Pa in the news again; a shouting match which degenerated into pushing and barging, outside the Chelsea Arts Club. Very undignified, and not at all like Pa. No wonder he didn't want to talk about it. It was Leggy who had separated them and calmed things down. Something else I hadn't known.

Bar came in with two earthenware cups filled with brown liquid. "How's it going?" she asked.

"I owe you," I said. The tea was warming; that was the best that could be said of it. I drank it gratefully.

"I'll remember that. But seriously, any time, Al. I was looking through those files and he definitely looks a bit dodgy to me. Not that I should be biased, being a reporter," she added piously.

"You, unbiased? That'll be the day!"

I caught the bus back to my home, and saw that scaffolding had been erected to do the roof. That was quick and I was pleased. I went upstairs to inspect the work, and was even more pleased. Downstairs again I called on Lily, to drop off a few fresh eggs that Angelique's poultry had produced and collect my mail.

"This one came by hand, this morning," Lily said, holding out an elegant white bond envelope. "Nice woman, asking for you, about ten o'clock. Had very short hair, darkish with little blonde tips, unusual."

Elisabeth Thorburn. My magical friend. Daughter of two magicians of some provenance, and ex- and late-fiancée of one Percy Meredith. She lived within walking distance.

"She said it was urgent, Miss," said Lily. "She was a bit put out that you weren't here."

I slit the envelope.

"Dearest Alice," I read, "I've just seen the newspapers. First I'm sending you and your family my very best wishes. I know that you must all be under some stress and that the whole sorry business has nothing whatsoever to do with any of you. I hope that the reasons for this awful event will soon come to light and those guilty brought to justice so that you may all continue your lives in peace. "

Yes, I thought, that would be nice.

I continued reading.

"Alice, I have had you on my mind frequently the past few days. There are three messages that I need to pass on. They are these. Make of them what you will. I'm only the messenger. I don't know what they mean in relation to you and all this.

"Dead people can still cast long shadows. Sometimes they must be exorcised.

"The murderer and the victim are mirrors of each other. Cleanse both.

"Wear the Abraxas ring. He is a protector and an opener of the ways.

"If this is a big vague, sorry. Often what I get from Beyond means nothing to me but something to my sitter or for whom the message is intended.

"If I can do anything at all, for you or your family, please don't hesitate to get in touch. Be assured of my very best wishes to you all,

"Light in extension, Elisabeth"

Curious.

I slipped it in my handbag, with the rest of the mail, including at least two airmails from Jeremy. I would savor those alone; the smile on my face must have told it all.

"Mr. Jem? Good. They came yesterday and this morning."

"I told him not to bother, just one a week..." I said.

"Of course you did, and of course he didn't listen. Be grateful, Alice. He's making up for all those blokes who never write to their girlfriends."

I took the little red car to Leggy's, pondering on what Elisabeth had imparted.

I knew that as a ritual magician she believed that all things came from the One cause, and through the spiritual, mental/creative, astral/emotional realms until they made it down here to the physical and material world, and then, on death, returned back up the levels.

She believed that everything that has ever been or is now on the physical plane will have a counterpart on the higher or upper levels, and though something may be out of commission on the physical, it is not necessarily so on the spiritual levels. Apart from the legacies, not solely physical, that a person leaves in the world after death, there are also emotional and ideological attitudes that will continue, and may be reactivated or even choose to reactivate themselves if the conditions were right.

We were talking about the War Trials at the time. The Nazis had been eradicated on the physical plane, she opined, but they really need to be rooted out on the inner levels. We hadn't done that. We were storing up problems for the future. I hoped she was wrong, but I felt, simply knowing human nature, that she wasn't.

I wondered how one would go about rooting out stuff on the inner levels. She was hinting that I should do this for both the victim and its murderer. I didn't even know the identity of the latter. I'd need her help, and almost certainly that of the Rev Simmons.

But then, I thought, as I caught sight of the Abraxas ring that now sat strangely comfortably on my right forefinger, I have access to a whole circle of ritual magicians. Surely they would know what to do.

Bobby Gallagher opened the door for me with a twinkle. "At a loose end, Milady?"

I shook my head. "Did my cards arrive?" I asked.

He nodded. "Of course. Come in, Leggy's longing to see you."

He was sitting in his usual chair, but the room had been aired. Indeed, it had been cleaned within an inch of its life, and the usual fug was nowhere to be appreciated. The windows sparkled, the curtains and hangings were all clean and fresh, and Nuts sprawled on a new cushion. Every surface had been dusted, and whatever could be polished had been. It was a definite improvement.

"Leggy," I greeted him with a kiss to the cheek, "What has been going on here? It's positively gleaming!"

He looked somewhat sheepish. "I hadn't realised it was that bad, Alice. Neither of us did, and then your friend Thelma came over..."

"You didn't let her set to with mop and bucket!"

"Oh no. It was just something she said as she left. About us being very rich."

I could hear her soft voice right now. "Where there's muck there's brass, and I've found the muck!"

"And how do you like the new look?" I asked.

He shrugged. "I'll get used to it and then it'll go back to how it was... Nothing lasts for long, thank heavens. Now, Alice, I've got your things."

He pulled a folder out of a drawer nearby. "Business cards in the name of Sally Carson. Since John Anselm-Jones has been named in the papers this morning, you might care to have a look at the International Galleries again. But as Sally. The manager won't recognise you if you leave your hair dark and wear your own clothes – I don't think Leonard Parsons would take much notice of women anyway. You're a dealer. You may find out what he can do for you, and how the business is run. I'll be here waiting for a phone call. As much as you can get on the place without looking too nosy. Let me know any leads, and if you can't follow them up, then Bobby or one of his friends will."

He handed the cards over, and a roll of money. "You can't be a dealer without some readies, and I trust you will make us a profit."

# 17

To my surprise, the International Galleries were shut. The Holland blinds were down over the plate glass window, and the metal link shutters drawn to keep out the hoi polloi.

I was not hoi polloi. I was Sally Carson, dealer in antiques and objets d'art, best prices given, discretion assured. I knew that; it said so on my card. I sauntered over and listened, trying to peer through the gaps between the blinds and the window. I couldn't make out very much visually, but from the expletives and scraping sounds I could guess what was happening.

I walked swiftly to the corner and dodged into the mews; the roadway was blocked by a locked gate, but there was no watchman in his hut, so I slipped in through the pedestrian gate, and counted my way along. A large dull green Luton box lorry was being filled from the rear of the galleries. I wandered past slowly, picking my way over the cobbles, glad of my flimsy heels which gave me an excuse to linger.

The lorry was full, packed by people who knew what they were doing, using every cubic inch.

I glanced at my watch; as I did so the salesman, Leonard Parsons, came out, signed a paper and handed it back to the larger of the two men in brown overalls who had been doing the loading. Then he locked the doors to the back of the gallery and I heard him tell the driver that he'd get the gate opened.

I made my way onward more swiftly now, and came out the far end of the mews, then ran to discover what direction the green Luton would take.

Just opposite the mews stood an empty phone box. I slipped in and dialed.

"Armitage Antiques and Removals," said a familiar voice.

"Bobby, it's Alice. Tell Leggy International Galleries appear to be closing down. They've cleared it all into a big van. And the chap who runs it is with it."

"Doing a moonlight in broad daylight, eh? Something must

have spooked them."

I heard the message and the telephone receiver being relayed to Leggy.

"Well done, Alice," he said gruffly, "where are you?"

I told him, and what I'd seen.

"Get the number of the van and any details, there's a good girl."

I'd got the number already, and gave it to him. "It's a Luton box, dark green, no lettering or firm's name."

"Thank you. Are you mobile? You might like to follow it. Discreetly, of course."

"Yes," I said. I would hardly be very discreet in the little red Morgan.

I cradled the phone and made for the car; I pulled a three point turn and made for the corner where, with any luck I would be in time to catch the lorry's exit from the mews.

Serendipity was with me. Mr. Parsons, the manager, had let the lorry out, but it was waiting for him to lock the gate again. I let a taxi pass in front of me while I ripped a headscarf from my handbag and tied it firmly around my head and neck, then slipped on a pair of sunglasses. The manager climbed into the cab, and the lorry pulled out southwards. I turned, and a couple of cars further down, I followed.

It headed south onto Piccadilly and continued down Knightsbridge, passing Harrods and veering left and left again by South Kensington station. At this rate we'd be passing the end of my road, I thought. And we did. I had allowed buses, a couple of drays pulled by matched carthorses, and various other vehicles to get in between us from time to time, but down the Fulham Road I realized my mistakes there.

At Stamford Bridge I got stuck between a parked bus and a cart. I hooted and swerved through. At Walham Green the lorry had disappeared and the lights were against me. I stopped behind a taxi and decided to turn left and return home. It was a fool's game anyway.

Then, as I turned into Harwood Road, I caught the tail end of the lorry turning right at the T-junction traffic lights ahead of me, caught behind a trolleybus.

I followed, all the way up New King's Road, past Eel Brook

Common, Parson's Green, Fulham pottery, and over Putney Bridge.

Traffic was desultory now. An occasional bus or tram, horses and carts, delivery bikes and small vans, but very few private vehicles. I felt so conspicuous. There were, as always, plenty of shoppers along the High Street.

The lorry went straight up, across the lights at Upper Richmond Road, where I was once more trapped, and breathed in the delightful smell of roasting coffee from the tiny importers and suppliers between Putney Main Line Station, the specialist greengrocer and elegant Zeeta's on the corner.

The lorry was getting away, but the lights didn't change. I tapped the wheel impatiently.

I could use a cigarette.

No, I couldn't, I told myself. Because the wind would blow it in my face. Besides, Sally Carson doesn't smoke.

At last the lights turned to green and I was off up Putney Hill like a greyhound.

The lorry was turning left once more. I slowed, let it go into a wide street, bordered by mature trees, which advertised a girl's school in one or more of the grand Victorian houses that had grown up along its sides. I recognized the school at once: one of my contacts in my past life now worked there. She taught elegant Loire Valley French and manners to young ladies. She had been a wizard with the garroting cord, but we all have to make adjustments.

I followed the lorry but pulled into the school's driveway for a moment. Then I got out and watched the green vehicle's progress down the road. It wasn't fast; the road surface was pretty bad, but I got the impression that the driver was looking for something. An address. I watched.

"I say, excuse me, can I help you?" The voice was strident, plummy and the figure from which it emanated was to suit. "You can't just park anywhere, you know, this is a school."

The secretary, I thought. She was in her fifties, going on sixty, in a plum tweed suit with a lace jabot at her neck. Her gray hair was plaited into earphones, which style had been out of favor when I was a schoolgirl, and had, as far as I knew, never made a come back. She wore sensible brogues, with a heel and thick stockings.

She reeked of dyspeptic resentful spinsterhood, and wielded her petty authority like a banner.

"Ah, yes," I said. "I'm a friend of one of your mistresses. I was passing so I thought I'd wait for her, if you don't mind. But I'll park outside if it's a problem." I slipped back into the driver's seat and drove off.

The road was annoyingly empty now. I felt my anger rising at the woman who had broken my concentration.

I dawdled the car gently down the grove, beneath the trees, peering into each driveway, and third from the end on the left, I was rewarded. The lorry was parking up beside a garage.

I passed on, checking the house number and the name "Nutfield Lodge" then went to find a phone-box.

When I'd passed the details on to Leggy I made another call. My brother was at his digs, the bank having closed, and would be delighted to have a lift back to Wethersley for the weekend. I drove back to town, filling up on the way.

Guy was waiting for me on the pavement outside his lodgings. It was an all male establishment, 'done for' by Mrs. Eames, who was a more organized, childless version of Lily. He liked to think of it as Lower Belgravia, but it was really Pimlico.

"I thought you'd be in the Citroen," he said, getting in. "If I'd known it was to be in this car I would have dressed accordingly." He took his trilby off and held it on his lap. "You look very dashing behind the wheel, Alice. Are you going to give it back?"

I chuckled. "I'll probably have to. Why did you get rid of your car?"

"Oh, you know how it is. I bought it because Sylvia wanted it but ate money. I didn't lose out on it, though. Made a small profit, actually," he grinned. "Which was nice!"

He was being very good-natured.

I wondered why. It wasn't his normal manner with me, although Maman said he could be charming.

We drove back through Victoria, Hyde Park and headed out of town via Notting Hill, going west. There were hold-ups along the way, but it was a good afternoon, and we were early enough to miss the five o'clock rush. Indeed by five o'clock I was passing Northolt Aerodrome once more, and neither of us had spoken for some time.

"So," I said at last, breaking the silence. "How's life with you, Guy?"

He shrugged. "As good as can be expected, I suppose, under the circumstances," he said.

"Which are?"

"Oh, come on Alice. It's been a dreadful year. All my plans, I've been made to look a complete idiot, and I've lost my fiancée. And now there's a stiff found on the old homestead. It's not doing my career any good at all."

"It's done a great deal more damage to the stiff," I said drily.

He snorted. "I suppose so. Why did the man have to go and show up on our land? Who put him there? And why?"

"Did you know him?" I asked. I didn't expect any sort of answer.

"Of course I damn well did. I met him quite often. In town, when he was in town, that sort of thing."

My jaw dropped. "You knew Mr. Anselm-Jones? I am hearing you right, Guy?"

"Yes, Alice, you are. I knew Mr. Anselm-Jones. So bloody what? Everybody knew him. He was someone to know. If there were any bargains in the art world to be picked up, he was your man."

"Yeah? What about Pa?"

Guy snorted again. "Pa? He's a painter, Alice. He's not a dealer. He'd be the last to hear of anything good coming up. And although I'd trust his eye, I wouldn't trust his knowledge of prices. I reckon you'd be better at that than Pa is. He's years behind the times."

"Thank you for your compliment," I said. "I suppose you think that because I worked at Lowther's."

"Of course. And because you're interested in artifacts – all sorts of things, not just paintings. Pa's only interested in Fine Art." I could hear the capital F and A. "And of course trying to get me to become a country squire."

"Eh?" I asked. I'd been so tied up with my own life, I'd not given my brother's a thought, once he'd got out of his awful engagement. "What?"

"You mean you didn't know, Alice? He's been putting the pressure on me to take over the estate. He was doing it when I was engaged. Well, I suppose I could accept that – particularly when we were going to get rid of lots of it – but since I've become single again and we aren't going to become developers and wealthy, he's been really putting the screws on. Hadn't you noticed?"

He looked at me and sighed, "No, of course not, you've been too wrapped up in Jem."

And he was right. I hadn't noticed. He sounded very aggrieved.

"Sorry. It doesn't happen to me every day," I heard myself saying. "Do you want to do the squire thing?" I asked.

"What do you think? Wethersley's close to London but not close enough. If I were married I'd have a house in town to escape to, but now Pa's on at me to resign from the Bank and come and manage Wethersley for him."

I stopped at a roundabout. "It was always on the cards, Guy. *Noblesse oblige* and all that. You don't think any of us are free agents, do you? In wartime, perhaps, but in peacetime?" I turned off down a B road towards the chalk.

Guy pulled out a cigarette case and selected a Senior Service.

"Do you want one, Alice? I won't tell, and I've a plentiful supply."

I shook my head.

"Suit yourself," he said, taking a pink-headed Swan vesta from its box and let his hand drop casually over the door of the car towards the tarmac. He brought the light back upward, cupped within his curled fingers and lit the cigarette, tossed the match, now extinguished by the wind, overboard and took a long draw on the tobacco.

"That's a flash trick if you can pull it off," I said admiringly.

He chuckled. "It takes practice. I had lots of mishaps – raw knuckles and burnt fingers."

"Where did you learn it?"

"A flying officer called Desmond." He took another pull of the cigarette. "He was a friend of Gilles. He's dead too."

"You miss him?" I said softly. "I miss Gilles."

"I miss them both. I think of all the chaps who were killed, all the people, just ordinary people, who bought it thanks to Mr. Hitler and I can't make sense of it any more. I mean, I ought to be with those people, yet here I am, and I had the chance to build a new Britain, with Sylvia, and all the time I was praying, don't let this marriage go ahead. Please God, if you exist, don't let this marriage go ahead."

I was silent.

My brother had never been so open with me before. I wasn't going to break the moment.

"I never loved her, you know. It was a chap at the Bank who introduced us. A friend of Algy Nesmith-Brown. And it was suggested that I'd get further up the ladder and more quickly if I had a wife."

"The Bank suggested this to you?"

"My immediate superior told me so, and the manager had let it be known that he preferred married men working for him. Yes. There's nothing odd in that. Most businesses like reliable family men. Isn't that why you are marrying Jem? He needs a wife for his career."

"No," I said at once. "Not at all! I'm marrying Jem because I want to live with him. He makes me laugh. He makes me feel good. If he lost his job tomorrow, it wouldn't be a problem. I'd still stay with him, as would he with me. We work well together. We have fun, and that's been in very short supply for a long time. And I love him."

That shut him up. For a while.

"Then you are very lucky, Alice. I've never felt that about anyone."

"How did you feel about Sylvia, then? How do you feel about her now?'

"Then, it seemed a good idea. I actually quite like the idea of being married and all that, I think she did, too, at the beginning, but now..." he took a long slow draw on his cigarette before continuing. "Now, like I said, I've had an amazing reprieve. And I've made a new friend from the break up. Nigel's such a good lad. I've got a few acquaintances – you know, at work and that, but I've not had a friend for such a very long time. The war took them all, one way or another." He took a final draw on the cigarette then tossed it over the side. "But Nigel can't just stay living as our gardener. It's not on."

I shrugged. "Why not? He's happy enough, and so are the family with the arrangement."

"But I'm not. It's demeaning to Nigel. I don't like it."

I smiled but said nothing.

"Can't you see how it is, Alice? We're treating him like a servant. He's not servant stock, Alice and he shouldn't be doing that sort of work."

"What sort of work should he be doing?" I wondered.

"I don't know, but not laboring. It's not right."

"If you want to start making judgments like that, you'd better take over the running of the estate," I said softly. "But it seems to me that Nigel is happier than he's been for most of his life just tending the walled garden and Spider. Would you take that peace away from him?"

"No, of course not, but dammit, he's a gentleman. He deserves better. And Pa isn't paying him. He told me."

"Who? Pa or Nigel?"

"Nigel, of course. He said he couldn't, wouldn't take any money, so it's virtually slavery."

"Or convalescence."

I turned off past the Wethersley Arms. "Nigel chose to not take payment in cash but in bed and board – he doesn't work all day every day, after all. He's got other irons in the fire, I imagine?"

Guy nodded. "He's got business interests, I believe," he agreed.

"Then if he's happy enough with the arrangement, I can't see any problem."

"But how long can it last?" Guy demanded.

"As long as it needs to. You can always renegotiate with him when you're in charge."

"I suppose so."

I returned to my interests. "So, Guy, you did meet Mr. Anselm-Jones? When was the last time you saw him?"

He snorted again. "My God, Alice, whose side are you on? The police have been asking me that and a whole pile more all week."

"And what did you answer?"

"Sometime last autumn. At a restaurant in town. I was with my boss. He was in the market for some quick investments. Anselm-Jones said he knew of something that might be of interest, but in the end my boss didn't buy."

"You told this to the police?" I asked.

I braked at the big iron gates, and waited for Guy to open them for me. And for his reply.

He struggled with the latches and huffed as he lifted the gates free of the roadway and pushed them aside. I drove through and waited for him to close them after us. He was puffing when he clambered over the side of the Morgan and took his seat again.

"Well," I said. "Did you tell the police what you just told me?"

"You don't let go, do you Alice? You're like a bloody terrier."

"So you didn't?" I pushed the car into gear. I had to get an answer out of him before we got home or the opportunity would be gone.

"I didn't say that."

"Stop prevaricating. What did you do?"

"I had a word with my boss as soon as the papers let it out. He thought it would be wisest to keep the Bank out of it."

So.

"You approached your boss?" I asked.

"No. No, of course not. In fact it was he who alerted me to who the body was. He read it in the papers and was concerned. But at that time the press only knew him as Edgar Winthrop. He told me it was just an alias, thought I knew, and wondered why I hadn't told him about it, but when I said the police had asked me not to, he quite understood. He was very understanding."

"I see. So what's in it for you?"

"What do you mean, Alice? I don't like the implication."

"Does your career start to soar? Or will he drop you in it if anything comes out?"

"Why should anything, as you say, come out?" he demanded pettishly.

I had him rattled.

"Because there are people somewhere who require it to do so. And they are much more powerful than either you or me."

"Rubbish," he said. "I accept that Mr. Anselm-Jones died in a less than natural manner, but why would anyone choose to bury him where they did on purpose? There's no sense to it, it's got to be the work of a passing maniac who later came back and dug him up for his own strange and confused reasons. God knows the war's created enough  mental cases – therefore find the maniac and the problem's solved.  Stop looking for disasters when they aren't there."

I groaned.  True, I didn't know who precisely had caused the gentleman's death, but mere happen-chance – a 'passing maniac', who just happened to be in possession of a  loaded pistol and a spade, simply being in the same place at the same time as a well-known connoisseur at least a couple of hundred yards from the road over a stile in  a sheltered clearing in our woods – well that didn't work, couldn't work.

"You believe it was as you say?" I asked Guy drily as we pulled up round the side of the house.

He looked sullen.  "I want to, I really want to, but it's not going to work, is it, Alice?"

# 18

I was still in the dog-house with Maman and Angelique for running out early this morning, but when they saw who I had brought with me, the sentence was slightly commuted; he may have been over thirty but he was still their little boy, and as far as they were concerned, he was still suffering from a broken heart.

I went in search of Pa and found him in the kitchen with the Macs, polishing the brass and copper that he loved to see gleaming.

"Hi, Pa," I said, greeting him with a kiss. "Elisabeth sends us all her best wishes and is definitely on our side."

He brightened visibly, and started to pack away the cleaning materials.

Mr. Mac took a tray of gleaming gold and copper items to the door. "I'll return these, shall I, sir?"

'No, Mac, leave them here for a while. If they think I've finished, they'll be after me again."

"Possibly not," I said.

"You brought your brother, Miss Alice?" said Mrs. Mac. "That was a kind thought. It'll keep their minds off going to see Miss Maddy. I'll stretch the soup and scramble the eggs."

"Sorry, Mrs. Mac. I thought you were expecting him. I didn't think to phone, and I don't suppose Guy did."

She chuckled. "I was expecting him, Miss Alice."

"You didn't tell me," Pa said, from over his shoulder as he washed his hands at the kitchen sink.

"Must have slipped my mind, sir."

"Nonsense, nothing slips your mind, Mrs. Mac."

He came across and gave me a big hug. "How's my senior daughter, then? Heard from your young man yet?"

I grinned at him, "Yes. And I'm going to go to my room and read what he has to say. I'll leave you Elisabeth's letter," I said, and fished in my handbag. "It's only short. When you've read it you can pass it on to Maman and Angelique. They'll be missing you, hiding away in the kitchen like a naughty schoolboy."

"Don't be cheeky, Alice! As if I would hide from Chérie." The teasing was back in his voice again and a smile on his lips, the first I'd seen for days, so I bit my tongue and refrained from asking whom Mr. Anselm-Jones represented, or for any more information on the aforesaid gentleman and the reason for Pa's antipathy towards him. Pa, and Maman and everyone else, it seemed, wanted to turn their back on the body in the woods, as if ignoring it would make it go away.

I dropped a kiss on Pa's head and ran up to my room where I threw myself down on my bed and opened the two important letters; the rest of the stuff, bills mostly, I would attend to as and when.


I'd never received a letter from Jeremy before so I had no idea what to expect. I sincerely didn't expect him to be writing from a hôtel on the Rive Gauche, Paris.

Damn, I thought, how come he gets sent there without me?

I loved Paris, even this new Paris that had been battered by the Hun.

He wrote as he spoke interspersing little pencil sketches from time to time, showing me a side of him I didn't know existed; he had a mean eye for observation and could report in words and pictures.

'I'd forgotten the smells, Alice. They're what is known in polite society as foreign – that means lots of sewage included! But I recognize your cigarettes, Alice, they're everywhere and I think of you very often! And good coffee. Oh, what a joy to smell real coffee! That reminds me of you, too. Tu me manques beaucoup.'

So the French was coming along

It ought to if he was in Paris!

Of all the places in all the world to be without me!

He gave me the address of his hôtel, and said although he couldn't tell me what his actual mission was, he could tell me lots of things that were not to do with it – like how much he loved the place. He'd never come across a pissoir before but had taken a turn in one at need, and for the experience. He described the city, the food, the jazz.

Oh you lucky lad, I thought, you get to go to hear the best black American players and I am stuck here!

I should be over there with you, sipping apéritifs on Boul' Mich'.

And he agreed.

What he actually said at the end was, "When I've finished this job, why don't you pop over for the weekend? It would be great!"

Get behind me, Satan!

No, actually, don't. Of course I would go. No-one need to know, and we could lose ourselves among all the other lovers. I resolved to do so if at all possible, then enjoyed the sweet nothings at the end.

The second letter was shorter.

"Darling Alice," it read "I had to send you this at once. I was in the Place Vendôme when who do I see coming out of a very fine jewelers but Sylvia Nesmith-Brown, looking very sophisticated – which I must admit is not a word I would normally associate with her, but so it was. On the arm of a middle-aged gentleman of swarthy complexion.

"I was going to be discreet and just nod, when she ran up to me, gave me a hug and introduced me to her companion. He is a diamond dealer, from South Africa, so she says, and she told him, "Felix, darling, this is the man responsible for you and me getting back together. I told you about him, didn't I? It's Jeremy Arkwright. He told me to follow my dream, and I did, didn't I?" Then she kissed him very tenderly on the cheek, and said to me, "May I introduce my fiancé, Mr. Felix Van Buren?"

"Well, I knew she was a fast worker and always got what she wanted, but I didn't expect that. She was sporting a very large solitaire diamond, so I guessed it was true. Mr. Van Buren shook my hand delightedly. He spoke English with a slight Afrikaans accent, and thanked me for sending her to him, and invited me to join them for supper in a couple of days time. I've got to go, Alice! Apart from anything else he might give me a good price on some stones.

"Sylvia said to give you her love, but not to tell anyone where she was. It seems they will be married when their business in Paris and Amsterdam is done, and will set up permanent home in

South Africa. She said she was starting afresh, and wanted to put all the old life behind her, understandably. I hope she can manage it, but I'm not putting any money on it.

"Darling Alice, I will let you know more when it happens. Give my love to everyone, but keep a large chunk for yourself, I love you so much, Jem xxx

p.s. Meet you through Abraxas at 10pm your time nightly? See if we get anything? It's worth a try! "

That gave me something to think about. Abraxas, certainly. I would do my very best to be available at 10 pm, of course I would, but the rest, too...

Sylvia sophisticated!

And on the arm of a person of wealth and power.

He must have been someone the Merediths had introduced her to.

But why would a man like that want to become engaged to, let alone marry, a girl like her?

Perhaps because she would be very very obliging and make him feel younger? Perhaps she had changed, grown up after the May fiasco.

Perhaps what Jeremy said to her had borne fruit.

I hoped so.

And I was glad she'd not be in my immediate vicinity.

Paris was fine, Amsterdam was fine, but South Africa was definitely far better.

I wondered whether she asked for anonymity because she wanted it, or because she wanted me to tell people where she was and who she was with, but I doubted that she was that devious.

Anyway, it was none of my business, and to bring her up in conversation here would be pointless.

She would have her anonymity at Wethersley at any rate, for the moment.

## 19

After supper Guy suggested a game of bridge, which Pa and Maman enjoyed. Angelique cast me a questioning glance. Neither of us liked the game, and usually one of us had to play to make up the foursome, but Nigel was with us.

"I'd like to play, if you don't mind," he volunteered.

"What an asset you are, dear," Maman said gratefully. "You'll be most welcome. Now you two can go and do whatever it is you both need to do," she said eying Angelique and me.

I was about to say I hadn't got any plans, but Angelique nodded. "Oh, we have much to discuss," she said. "Come, Alice, a walk would do us good."

We ended up outside her part of the estate.

Officially she was Maman's lady's maid and companion, but she was family, my best auntie, and we had all called her Tantange as children. She had married our chauffeur who had happened to be Pa's batman during the First set of hostilities – when I was very young. We drove ourselves now, the last war had seen to that, and, sadly, to lovely Uncle Matthew. He and Angelique had lived in a cottage the other side of the house from the old stable block (Pa's studio and the garages), where she still lived most of the time, although she also had a room up at the House.

Beyond was her secret kingdom. She might be a fine dressmaker – this was how she literally made some pin-money – but she was a better still poultry raiser and during the war had also turned to pig rearing with the help of our evacuees. The patch behind her and Matthew's home was where her non-human 'family' lived.

We put on aprons and rubber boots and fed and watered the fowls. I didn't like them close up, particularly not the gander who was vicious.

"You didn't bring me out here to tell me about poultry," I said, as we closed the gate to the yard behind us, mission accomplished.

"No, I didn't. The body. What have you found out, Alice? Have you worked out who killed the man, when, why, how and why he should be dumped on our land? I take it that's what you're doing."

I smiled. 'Our land'; she was more Wethersley than we were in her head. "I am trying to do that. And no, I've found out nothing."

"You know he was here last November? Marie-Thérèse doesn't know, but I do. Roger talks to me. Sometimes he needs someone to talk to who is a little less volatile than Chérie."

I'd always suspected as much, but it was good to hear it from the horse's mouth.

"Did he tell you what it was about?" I asked.

Angelique shook her head. "Not totally. He said it was private, very private. But it seemed that someone, someone very high up, wanted a portrait, and he didn't feel inclined to paint it. He said pressure was put on him, there were threats and accusations which shocked and annoyed him so much that in the end Roger threw him out. He was wild as fire!"

She looked me full in the eyes. "Alice, he wouldn't tell me who the sitter would have been, and I've never ever seen him cast away an opportunity to make money. Heaven knows we need it."

"It's that bad?" I asked.

Pa never spoke about money to me; I took it there was enough. We always seemed comfortably off, but Maman spent it freely, being of the opinion that there was always plenty so why should she stint herself or anyone else; it was there to be spent, that was its purpose.

"I think the Wethersley-Marsham project actually had some merit," said Angelique thoughtfully. "Oh, not the way it would have been if those awful men had had their way, but financially we could do with some extra input. Roger needs to paint to generate some more cash, but no-one's wanting portraits these days, now that cash is so short. We can survive, I believe, but the estate needs some new ideas and young energy taking care of it, which is why he's been pressing Guy to consider taking over the running of the estate..." she drifted to a halt.

I saw the flaw.

I voiced it.

"But Guy's always full of get-rich-quick schemes that fall

over before they've been built!" I said.

"Justement. But who else? Gilles is no longer with us... You are going to marry that lovely young man and probably end up the other side of the world, like your sister. It has to be Guy. It's not as though he hadn't known he would have to take over, and he certainly wants all the goodies that come with being the heir. It has to be him," she said emphatically.

I shook my head. "No, it doesn't. But he'd have to earn enough to pay someone to do it for him. What about Nigel?"

We had tidied the feed buckets away and were getting back into normal clothes and shoes.

"Well?" I said.

"Yes, I've been giving that a bit of thought."

"Well?"

"I'm not sure about him. He was with Guy when the body was found. He knew the man, too."

"So did Guy, so did Pa and Maman, so did lots of people."

"But their sister was not engaged to Guy, and their families are not necessarily bad lots."

"You think Nigel had something to do with this, Angelique?" I asked.

She shrugged, "Could be. Why not? Why did he take the dog down that route?"

"I thought the dog was taking them for a walk, that's what I understood. They were letting him lead."

Angelique frowned at me. "Alice, who told you that?"

"Why, Guy, I think. That was what I was led to believe. Guy and Nigel both told the coroner they had let him off the lead and he was taking them for a walk."

Angelique sucked in air between her almost closed lips. "Now think again," she said. "Come, we'll go for a walk while it's still light. First we'll go to Nigel's house and from there we'll go through the woods."

I didn't like the sound of that, but I went along.

It was a very fair step. Oh, nothing beyond the stretch of the two young men and Spider would have been up to it, no problem.

But it was an odd place to come.

We all knew it as children, had played there, delighting in the smooth springy turf and its seclusion. But we never stayed later than about five, even in summer. It didn't have a sinister reputation, quite the opposite, it was a place sought out by lovers in search of a bit of privacy, and we had been chased off more than once, even though it was our land. Of course, we didn't tell, because the threats we received were too awful to disclose.   We kept it to ourselves, and shared the place with the lovers, leaving them the evening and the night, and often the daytime too. I'd forgotten that, but as I dropped down into the woods with Angelique, my pre-war summer memories returned.

Gilles and I had once sneaked out after bedtime and waited and watched, but although there were sounds of a sultry and suggestive nature it was too dark to see what was going on, so we went home, somewhat let down by the whole experience. I hoped, now, that the lovers, whoever they were, had enjoyed their time there more than we had.

Angelique stopped and put her finger to her lips. "Just observe," she whispered, gliding behind a tree.

I followed her lead and gazed down the path through the trees and ferns to the clearing. The police had removed all their tapes now, the holes newly infilled stuck out like  wounds in the turf even in the late evening light. It dawned on me that that was probably what it looked like when the body had been put in, possibly a bit more camouflaged, but certainly not grown over. It had been placed so that it could be discovered. Only the extreme winter had intervened.

I started to move.

Angelique grabbed me back behind the oak. "Look, Alice, see who is coming..."

I frowned. I could see no-one.

"Listen then. I can hear people on the road."

She must have ears like radar. I could hear nothing but the breeze in the leaves, the occasional call of a bird and the thudding of my own heart. But I waited.

And waited.

And then I heard it.

Giggling, then laughing, then voices. A male and a female. Young, younger than me, but in their twenties. And I watched. He climbed the stile at the bottom of the path, then handed her over, but as she stood above him his hands shot up her skirt. I heard a squeal, and she jumped down. She said something and he laughed. He was carrying a car rug. They walked up the path, cuddling and fondling as they did so.

Now they reached the patch of new infill. He flung the rug across it, and she casually stepped out of her knickers and lay down upon it. He joined her.

I heard him say, "I hope you aren't going to play as dead as that old codger they took out of here," and heard her giggle and pull his head down to her face, guiding his hand inside her blouse.

Angelique chuckled. "It must make a pleasant change from that cold flat gravestone in the churchyard," she whispered. "Shall we leave them to it?"

I nodded. "They seem to know what they're doing. Did you recognize them, by the way?"

"Oh yes, but it wouldn't be wise to mention any names."

We turned back. In the distance as we came out of the woods, we could see the lights on downstairs at Wethersley.

"Good church-going folk?" I asked.

Angelique smiled. "Well church-going, at least. Everyone does around here."

"Ah," I said. "Not quite everyone."

My brother and Nigel hadn't gone last Sunday.

"Justement."

"Thank you, Angelique," I said. "You realize it doesn't make the matter any easier."

"Of course. But that's a minor problem. What I want to know is whether Nigel knew the body was there. And if he did, why is he saying nothing. Also, he has access to a spade – not that virtually every house in the neighborhood doesn't, but … You'll have to have a word with him, Alice. With them both."

I sighed.

I'd just got on reasonable terms with my brother; I really didn't want to go back to how things were. And I liked Nigel. I didn't like Angelique's implications, but they did need looking into.

"Why me?" I asked.

Angelique sniffed and shrugged gallicly. "Because, Alice, you're the only one with your head screwed on round here."

When we got back to the house the card playing was over.

Maman's face was a tight hard mask, so she'd obviously lost.

Guy and Nigel were puffing cigarettes and drinking beer looking very pleased with themselves.

Pa was filling his pipe thoughtfully. "Beginner's luck? I don't think so. You two have played before."

"Not as a team," Guy admitted. "I used to partner Sylvia, and we always lost." He grinned at Nigel. "It's good to be on the winning side for a change!"

Maman sniffed. She normally won.

Pa lit his pipe slowly, then through the curls of smoke said, "Yes, Guy, it is. Enjoy it while it lasts. How much did you owe, by the bye?"

Before he could answer Maman had stamped over to him and put her finger imperiously across his lips. "Not a word, Guy! Your father has no right bringing it up here. It's between him and you only." She glared at Pa.

For a moment I thought he would stand firm and demand an answer, but after a long second he subsided. "I bow to your greater delicacy, my dear," he acknowledged. "Angelique, Alice, did you enjoy your walk? You were a very long time. It's almost dark."

Nigel started. "Good Heavens, so it is. I'd better take Spider home. Thank you all for a splendid evening."

I watched him as he moved round to say his good-nights. When my turn came his hands, although hardened by use of the spade and hoe, were cool and light and he smelled of rosemary. He was comfortable with us, and that was good. Guy and I saw him to the front door.

"Cheerio, old man. Thanks for the game," Guy said, slapping him on the back.

"My pleasure. Sleep well." Nigel skipped down the steps barely touching them, high on happiness, his pockets jingling.

Spider scampered after Nigel and cocked his leg against the hedge, then distracted, found a hole beneath the yew and started digging. Nigel grabbed him by the scruff and tucked him under his arm before waving goodbye.

I remembered Angelique's words.

Did Nigel know the body was there?

Had he set out that way on purpose, with the aim of discovering it?

Had he dug it up, and blamed the 'discovery' on his dog? It wouldn't be an impossibility.

Or would it?


"Why do you keep picking on me?" Guy asked testily, draining the last of Pa's whisky into his tumbler. "I've had it up to here. You and the police, you all ask the same questions and you never bloody let go!"

I raised my eyebrows.

We were alone, which was just as well, and he'd done a quarter of the decanter since I'd returned. I'd stuck to soda to keep my head clear. Besides, whisky was neither cheap nor commonplace - although Pa always managed to have access to it, despite what Angelique had intimated.

"Well, did you choose the route?" I asked. "What were you and Nigel doing there that morning?"

Guy sucked on the cigarette and let the smoke out slowly. He was sitting in Pa's chair by the fireplace. I wasn't sure he looked right there but it would be his place when Pa either handed over the estate or was no more.

I pushed the thought aside as Guy sighed.

"Murray's men have asked me that," he said softly. "They insinuated all sorts of things."

"So how about you tell me? I'm discretion personified, Guy. I can keep secrets. You can trust me on that. And you'll feel better. A trouble shared is a trouble halved."

I didn't believe that, but it might work.

"I'm not sure I have the right to tell you," he said at last. "It's not that I don't trust you, Alice, believe me. I … I have loyalty, too."

"And the police are pressuring you?"

"Damn right! It's not on."

"A man has been killed, Guy, executed even. Surely you can see that's serious. It's not accidental death. Someone will swing for it. Literally. I don't want it to be any of us! So anything you know about anything could be useful. Do you understand?"

He looked up through a haze of smoke, sulkily. "It's not to do with us. Not our family."

"Then whose?" I asked.

He gave me a belligerent stare, took another pull on his cigarette, let the smoke out slowly, then shrugged.

"Nigel's?" I pressed. "Was it he who led you to the body?"

Guy sighed. "We went for a walk. That was all."

I bit back the temptation to say 'down Lovers' Lane' and said softly, "Tell me, Guy. I won't tell the Aged P's."

He nodded, and smiled. "They don't need to know anyway. We went for a walk, that was all. We went there because Nigel wanted to go there. Not because of it being Lover's Lane or anything like that – he just wanted to walk the boundaries."

I wondered: why did he mention Lover's Lane, and more to the point, why did Nigel want to walk our boundaries? I said nothing.

The drink made Guy reminisce. "I went down there with Sylvia once – well, we stopped the car by the stile; it was blowing up a gale and there were snowflakes all around us but there we were safe and warm. She was a bit forward, a bit frightening actually. Then we had a row and I drove her home. It was always like that..."

I crossed over to my brother and put my arm round his shoulders. "God, Guy, why the hell didn't you tell someone. It must have been horrible."

He took my fingers and stroked them. "Who could I tell? I'd got myself into it. I was as keen as she was at the start. I liked the idea of being engaged, being married, being respectable. I don't think ..." he sighed, sniffed and took a long slug of Pa's whisky, then let my hand go. "But that's not what you are asking. Nigel wanted to walk the boundaries. That was it. So we started off at the gate and turned right, walked along the road then came over the stile and up the path. Nigel was shuddering. I asked him what was the matter. He wouldn't talk."

I waited.

And waited.

"Then what?" I asked.

"He began shivering. It wasn't a cold day, not at that point. I was quite worried about him. He was white as a sheet. Then he moved off the path into the undergrowth with Spider and came out into the clearing. Someone had been digging... Spider started at the body. We had to stop him..."

103

"Why didn't you tell all this earlier?" I asked softly.

"I couldn't. He... we... well, we both sort of made a pact. He didn't want to get into trouble. He's had enough, Alice, his life's been full of the most horrendous things. I couldn't let him suffer any more."

"So you cooked up a story about Spider. Nigel knew that someone, something was buried here? How could he keep silent?" I demanded.

"He didn't know. Or not the full extent. He knew something nasty had happened here. He didn't know what or who or all the whys and wherefores, I swear it."

"I'm sure you do. I'm not sure that I do, though. He took you there. He knew something had gone awry there, and he brought it to light and cast a blight over all of us. That family..."

I peered at my brother and shook my head in puzzlement. "How the hell did you manage to get mixed up with them? Who was it who introduced you? A colleague at work? Your immediate boss?"

I didn't expect an answer but he dropped his gaze and nodded enough for me to see I'd hit the spot.

I groaned. "Then, Guy, you've got to ask yourself why, and what's in it for them, and more importantly where you stand?"

I could see by his face that he had been doing just that.

I couldn't help him any more, as he said, he'd have to deal with it.

But I did need to know more and he wasn't the person to ask.

I went over and kissed him lightly on the head. "I'm going to bed now. I'll keep my promise, but things are looking bad, believe me."

I sat before my window looking out at the summer night sky and the countryside. I was angry.

I could see Nigel's cottage – our cottage that he was using – and was furious that he'd not been completely honest with me.

It hurt.

I'd been totally taken in by him when I'd shared his ginger beer.

All this week he'd been hiding the truth.

He'd known something was there, something nasty, something that would affect our family, the family he professed to be very fond of, and he'd said nothing.

I was disgusted.

I could have used a cigarette. No, I really could, but I had none and I wasn't going to beg or steal, neither was my way.

I took the hairbrush and started to brush my hair, and as I did so thought about Nigel and his family, the Nesmith-Browns.

He had had an awful life, that was true.

I knew without Guy telling me of the various sorts of abuse, physical, of a sexual nature and psychological, that had been perpetrated upon him, so I could see mitigating circumstances for what could have been taken for cowardice and certainly being less than honest. I wondered how much he really did know and whether I could wheedle it out of him.

It was just past ten now.

I looked up at the moon and thought of Jeremy in Paris.

Why wasn't he here when I needed him?

I twisted the Abraxas ring, and called into the ether, but got only a feeling of warmth, nothing more.

I tried for several minutes, but was still consumed with irritation and jealousy, the annoyances of just about everything going on around me, and the fact that I couldn't get through to him made it worse.

I could have screamed.

So much for magic!

I took refuge in the letters, and fell asleep rereading them, then suddenly, at midnight sat bolt upright, wide awake, feeling the ring tingling on my forefinger.

I heard in my head his apologetic tones. "I'm so sorry, Alice, I've been working. Had to be at a reception and couldn't get away. I bet you're asleep now. Sleep well. Know you're loved. I'll try to make it tomorrow night at ten your time. Love you."

"Love you, too," I mumbled back, then slid back down onto the pillow, wondering whether indeed we had connected or whether it was just wishful thinking.

Either way, it was fine by me.

# 20

Nigel was earthing up potatoes when I entered the garden next morning. I hailed him and wandered over. "Got any for Mrs. Mac?" I asked.

He stuck his fork in the earth at the end of the row and came across wiping his hands on the back of his trousers, a wide smile on his face. "Not yet, I'm afraid. Alice, how nice to see you. More ginger beer?"

"Maybe," I said.

We went into the cottage, Spider following. I bent down and scratched his cheek, letting him lick my hands. We were friends.

Nigel poured us all drinks and we went out to his lawn. "So to what do I owe this visit?"

I took a sip of the ginger beer. "I need some information, Nigel. I won't promise that it won't go any further than these garden walls but your name will not be mentioned. I don't tell lies, but I can be very discreet, especially to my friends, and I count you as a friend, Nigel. You've been a great friend to my brother, and we, all of us appreciate that."

I watched him as I spoke.

There was fear, puzzlement, uncertainty, and then a gushing sigh, and a soft moan.

I seized the moment.

His eyes were down and his shoulders hunched. He looked like a stricken schoolboy rather than a man of some twenty-five years.

"You say you love our family," I whispered. "Then you must answer my questions, because if not, Pa is going to get in serious trouble."

His head jerked up. "Lord Wethersley? Roger? How? It's nothing to do with him!"

"What do you mean, Nigel?" I asked.

He sucked in a breath between his teeth then groaned. "Oh God, Alice! How can I tell you without causing all sorts of problems for everyone. It's wretched. I'm wretched. I suppose

Guy told you…?"

I shook my head. "My brother told me nothing at all, honestly. So what do you know?"

I do believe he was almost ready to tell me, but there was a shout of greeting and the garden gate swung open.

My bloody brother!

I watched the eye contact.

Nigel leaped to his feet, and they clasped hands, clapping each other on the back.

Bugger!

As he turned to bring another glass for Guy, he caught my eye and mouthed "Later. I promise," and that was that.

I certainly didn't want to embarrass him in front of Guy.

I downed the last of my ginger beer and stood up. "I'll take some herbs up to the house, shall I, Nigel? Thanks for the drink."

I beat a hasty retreat into the walled garden, picked a bunch of mint and some fresh parsley, then headed back to Mrs. Mac.

"Thank you, Miss Alice. That Murray creature is in with your father."

I raised my eyebrows. I hadn't heard a car.

"It would be a kindness to interrupt, I'm thinking," she said tartly. "He's a fellow Scot, but he leaves a lot to be desired."

Indeed!

"In Pa's study?" I asked.

She nodded. "There's a coffee tray. It'll give you an excuse," she said. "Mac's occupied."

I tapped at the door and entered.

There was an atmosphere. Pa was leaning into his chair-back while Mr. Murray had a haunch on the Pa's desk and was lowering over him threateningly.

I strode grandly into the room, bearing the tray like a weapon.

"Morning Coffee, gentlemen! We mustn't let the niceties be abandoned, now, must we!" I trilled; I'd learned that at finishing school, but my sister was far better at it than I was. She wielded a trilling voice like a machete through jungle.

All I got for my pains was a glare from Chief Inspector Murray and a grateful sigh from Pa.

I set the tray on the low table in front of the fire place and began to busy myself with the jugs and crockery, interrupting whatever had been going on by requests for milk or sugar so that Pa could regain his composure.

"Miss Chamberlain, we meet once more. We never finished our last conversation," Murray growled, heaving his ham off Pa's desk to greet me.

He held out a hand, which I grasped and shook almost imperceptibly, then helped himself from the plate. Two ginger nuts and two short-breads, which was both greedy and cheeky since there were only six biscuits. I handed him a milky sweet coffee, then took Pa's over to him, and the remains of the biscuit plate.

"Thank you, Alice." His voice was calm but I could hear the gratitude. "You've met the Chief Inspector, then?"

I nodded. I'd not gone into details of our meeting. Pa hadn't asked.

"Miss Chamberlain," Chief Inspector Murray said, from the leaded glass window, where he was standing four-square against the light, "A few minutes of your time, if you would be so kind. Yes, your father may be present, of course. I'm sure he'd like to hear what you have to say."

I frowned, wondering what he'd be asking. "As you wish, Chief Inspector. I'd be happy to answer any sensible and relevant questions."

Pa's lips twitched, a good sign, and he reached for the last biscuit.

"What do you know about the deceased?" Murray asked, turning to face me.

Against the light I couldn't read his expression. I moved across to the window so that I could, putting myself close to the Victorian leaded carrels, holding my head high.

"Personally, I never met him. I only know of him by repute – I've read a couple of his books in connection with my work – I used to work for Lowther's, the Auctioneers. He was considered an authority."

"So you've never met him? You are quite sure of that? Your father painted his portrait before the war."

"Indeed, but I would have been away at school at the time,

surely. Besides, Pa did most of his painting in his London studio. It's generally more convenient for the sitters."

"Not this one. We know this one was done here. In 1936. Early in the year, isn't that right, my Lord?"

Pa looked miserable, but nodded. "Yes. The portrait was shown in the Academy Summer Show."

"What do you remember of that year, Miss Chamberlain? You must have seen the man around here."

Eleven years ago. A time of innocence.

I cast my mind back. Before the tentative unpleasant peace, before the horror of war, back when my family was whole, before Gilles had been shot down, before Angelique's husband had been shot, before the wild flower meadows had been grubbed up, when, despite the depression, the days seemed to be long and sunlit. A different world completely.

"I was being finished, Chief Inspector, and then I came out. I was in Switzerland, Paris and London and my head was full of fashion, balls, having a good time and meeting all sorts of people, particularly young gentlemen. What Pa did while I was making my entry into society was not of importance to me. I didn't meet his sitters, although I did meet his friends. Ergo, Mr. Anselm -Jones was not one of Pa's chosen friends."

Murray's lips curled as I spoke. He obviously didn't approve of my way of life, but that was his problem, not mine.

He sneered when I stopped talking. "You are quite sure of that? I understand they got on very well together."

Pa frowned now. "I didn't exactly say that. I said we had a working understanding. We were business, not leisure."

"And he came here again, didn't he, during the war, my Lord? We have that from his diaries. What was that about?"

Pa sighed. "I don't remember."

Oh, heavens!

The Chief Inspector now turned to Pa. "What, my Lord?"

"I don't remember," Pa said.

And here I was with Murray. We both knew Pa remembered very well.

He rolled forward towards the desk, his heavy head shaking from side to side. "My Lord, I don't think I can believe that. I think you could recall what it was about if you gave it a bit of attention. I think you are trying very hard to recollect right now, and I think you are going to tell me very soon indeed, now in fact."

From behind the pushy Scot I nodded at Pa, and mouthed "Best you do tell him,"

Pa sighed. He looked thoroughly deflated.

"Come on, my Lord, I know your memory of the meeting is returning. Won't you share it with us?"

I wondered whether we should have a lawyer present, but it was too late now.

"He came during the war as you said. I can't remember the exact date, but he came with a commission. He was acting as an agent for a third party. He offered me a portrait commission and I turned it down and him out. He was extremely unpleasant, behaved despicably to a couple of my evacuees, a high-handed racialist bully. I don't tolerate that sort of person, Chief Inspector."

Pa's blue eyes were blazing with righteous anger.

Murray let out a long slow breath. "Thank you, my Lord. And the commission was?"

"That, I am not at liberty to say. And since I didn't take it, I fail to see how it can be significant."

"Ah, Lord Wethersley, who is to say what is or what isn't important? A man has died, brutally on your land, and you had a certain animosity to him, that we know. You tell me he was acting as a go-between, between you and a secret other. Now it could be that that secret other is very important."

"No, Chief Inspector, I give you my word on that." Pa pulled out his tobacco pouch and began to rub a little knot of dark aromatic tobacco between his hands, prior to filling his pipe.

"The word of a gentleman?" snapped Murray.

"Just so, Chief Inspector, and I could be equally offensive and say the word of an English gentleman. I have given you as much on this visit as I can. If you need confirmation, I imagine the two young lads would remember. He treated them disgustingly. My wife will have their details."

"Your wife met him?"

"She has met him, but only socially. He is, was, a very urbane man, which was why he was so successful."

"You mean your wife liked him?"

Pa shrugged. "My wife appreciates good manners, Chief Inspector Murray, as do we all at Wethersley."

Murray snorted slightly then tried another tack. "Now why were your son and his friend down in those woods?"

Pa's eyes widened and raised to the ceiling. "I suggest you ask them, Chief Inspector. We've never been a family for locking the grounds away. That's a public area. Why should they not be there?"

"I've heard it was a place where courting couples would go…"

"Courting couples go anywhere they can find a bit of quiet as I remember," Pa said chuckling. "Do you suppose that Mr. Anselm -Jones was finished off by a jealous husband?" He grinned up at the Chief Inspector. "Well, it makes as much sense as any other theory, doesn't it?"

"Why didn't you tell me about Mr. Anselm-Jones' visit before, Lord Wethersley?"

"I didn't remember it."

"Indeed. And are there any other visits you couldn't remember, that have just sprung back into your mind?"

I felt sick. I knew Pa should come clean, and I knew that Murray was offering him an olive branch, but Pa was obviously not thinking straight.

He frowned, "I'm not sure that I can tell you anything else, Chief Inspector," he said softly, stuffing tobacco into his pipe and busying himself with setting fire to it - his sign that the interview was over.

I felt the waves of annoyance coming off Murray and exasperation of my own, if I were to be truthful.

I collected the cups and plates onto the tray.

As I left the study Pa called "Alice, get that address for the Chief Inspector from your mother, would you? She knows the lads in question."

I saw the Chief Inspector out about ten minutes later, handing him the address. The two young men would not be available, being aboard ship, but it looked like we were co-operating.

"My brother and Nigel were at his cottage about half an hour ago," I told him. "If you want any more information you might find it there."

"You know something?"

I shook my head. "You seem to have an interest in the two young men. I was just being helpful. Goodbye, Chief Inspector Murray, I have things to do."

I told Mrs. Mac I'd be out for lunch and went to the garage to find a bicycle. I needed some fresh air and exercise, but mostly time to think.

# 21

Reverend Simmons greeted me with joy. His halo of flyaway silver hair almost quivered with it and his blue eyes shone. "Come inside, my dear Alice. I was just thinking how nice it would be to see you again."

We passed through to the garden at the rear of his Georgian vicarage. "It's good to see you again, Reverend Simmons," I told him as our handshake grew into a warm hug.

"Is this a social call or can I help in any way?" he asked at last. "I was sorry to hear of the discovery, but of course it has nothing to do with your family."

"Not as far as I know," I said. "I hope it hasn't, but no, this is a social call. How are you? How are the angels?"

"We're all extremely well, thank you, Alice. Did you know that Miss Thorburn has made a very generous donation so that they may have a home attached to the church? She's a very remarkable woman, Miss Thorburn. Sees beyond the immediate, if you get my meaning. And very generous. Sold off some jewelery that she said was no longer necessary; she said it was time to redress the balance."

He peered over his glasses at me. "You wouldn't know anything about this, I suppose?"

I said nothing. Hoped the puzzled look did the trick. I suspected it was the gold and diamonds that Percy Meredith had lavished on her. Left to her own choices I knew she preferred silver, nor would she have deemed it appropriate to keep his gifts.

"Of course you wouldn't," he said answering himself. "No, don't worry about it. I can see you don't. Anyway Sam's done very well by them; he'll be on the radio next week, did you know? And someone's interested in publishing their story. Yes, they've been working very nicely for him. And for the church, too. There are lots of visitors, the interest is quite phenomenal. I sometimes wonder where it will all lead, but I'm not complaining."

We wandered around the garden, chatting away like two old friends, although we had only met three months ago. The sense of tranquility that Reverend Simmons emanated was what I needed at that moment.

I said "Has Sam any theories on how that man came to be in our woods?"

The lined face frowned a little. "Oh Sam always has theories," he said at last. "I don't hold much with them. But I would suggest you go and see Mr. Fletcher again. Do you know where he lives?"

"The ... er ... taxidermist?"

"That's the chap. Sam saw him yesterday. He said he had something that might interest you. He, Sam, that is, told him to get in touch with you, but the chap didn't seem too keen. Sam felt he wanted him to be a go-between."

"Did Sam try to ring me?" I asked.

"Yes, of course. But he didn't know you were here. He thought you were in London. He tried last night, and then tried Wethersley, but I understand your mother ..." He twinkled.

"Ah!" I smiled. "She must have forgotten to tell me. She's got a lot on her mind at present."

He nodded. "It's all been a bit of a strain for Lady Wethersley, hasn't it? Please give her and your father my very best wishes when you get back, and again, if there is anything I can do, you, they, only have to let me know, Alice."

It was half past one when I finally leaned the bicycle against the fence and walked up the path.

Mr. Fletcher came round from the back to greet me. "Miss Chamberlain, nice to see you. You got my message. Fancy a drink?"

We settled on old local bodged chairs, me with a jug of water and a tumbler, he with a tankard of brown ale, just short of being engulfed by the burgeoning greenery that this week's sunshine had brought forth.

"So what have you to tell me, Mr. Fletcher?" I asked.

"You got a young man at Wethersley, ain't you? Not your family. Pale lad. Dark hair, not a lot of it. Bit of a misfit?"

I frowned. "Possibly. Why?"

"No, not possibly. I'm being straight with you. You got him there or not?"

"Yes, we have someone of that description, although I don't like 'bit of a misfit'."

"But it's right, ain't it? You know who I mean? Good." He lifted the tankard and took a long draw of beer then licked the foam from his upper lip. "He found the body, didn't he?"

"Well, yes," I said. It had been in the press, local and national. "So?"

"How did he know it was there?" His eyes were bright and bird-like. "Did you ask him that?"

I shook my head. "He said the dog found it."

"Dog had been led there and pointed to it, I'd say. That lad knew all about it, knew where to look."

"You mean he was there when it happened?" I asked. I didn't like this. "He was part of it?"

"Well how do I answer that? I don't rightly know, if you want the truth. I don't think he was there when it happened, but he was around, if you get my meaning. He wasn't party to what happened at all, and he didn't understand what was happening at the time. But someone thought he did, and put the frighteners on him something cruel."

"You are quite sure?" I asked.

"Mother never lies," he said. "She sees clearly and she's been around your place lately and seen the boy."

"Only he's not a boy," I said. "He's twenty-five, a grown man."

"Physically perhaps, but inside he's a little hurt kiddie, ain't that right?" Once more the bright questioning bird-like stare.

He could have got that from gossip. There would be plenty of that around both our family and Nigel living with us.

I wondered, once again, what the Nesmith-Browns were doing, how they were. I didn't care for them, apart from Nigel, and I was beginning to go off him at this particular moment.

Mr. Fletcher took another long haul on the tankard. "Now here's a funny thing, Miss Chamberlain. A very funny thing. You'd think the young lad's family would care for him enough to let him know that they were quitting the country, wouldn't you?"

Local gossip?

"Do you know that for a fact?" I asked, suddenly on edge.

"I know that their house is closed up, emptied out, just this week. The living-out women were laid off without so much as a by-your-leave yesterday. Well, I say laid off. When they turned up for work yesterday they found the place all locked up, deserted. Not a soul around, not a horse in the stables and everything that could have been taken gone. You might ask why the family is doing a moonlight flit. And why they haven't informed their lad."

I nodded.

I finished the first glass of water and poured myself a second. "Indeed," I said at last. I knew there was not much love lost between the family and Nigel but I wasn't going to say so.

"He knows more than he's letting on, Miss Chamberlain." Mr. Fletcher emptied the frothy ale into his tankard. "He knows a great deal more than that, Miss Chamberlain. You tell him I said that. And if you don't believe me, you just get yourself back on your bike and take a peek at his family home as it is now. There were people depending on the money they earned there and they ain't been paid. There'll be a lot of ill feeling about that!"

Below the chalk hills and spring line villages down in the clay valley, set beyond the village in a loop of the stream that would eventually join the Thames sat Marsham Court.

I'd never been inside the house although I'd passed it all my life and glimpsed it through the trees. I'd not known it as a child – the incumbents were an aged couple who didn't socialize – and by the time the Nesmith Browns settled in we were under wartime restrictions and I was mostly elsewhere. Guy knew it, of course, and said that the interior owed at least some of its style to Modernism, unlike Wethersley, where the only parts that had been modernised in my lifetime, apart from the installation of electricity, were the plumbing and the kitchen. Pa insisted on the former, Maman, Angelique and Mrs. Mac, the latter. Décor and furniture were pretty much as Granddad and Grandma left them, good quality late Victorian and Edwardian stuff that would last another hundred years at least if treated right. It worked for us.

I cycled up to the driveway and was disappointed; unprepossessing, an oblong box with a mock classical portico, attendant stabling and other outbuildings along one side, rendered and, some time ago, whitewashed. Every window was shuttered fast, giving it a blind appearance. It felt empty, uninhabited, closed down.

I parked my bike against a portico column and looked around. I tried the front door, but of course it was locked. I went round the side of the house to the rear door. That was locked too, but the scent from the rose beds coming from the weed-free parterres in the garden was a delight and the lawns were well trimmed and rolled flat as a bowling green. The gardener was a good one who had worked hard. I doubted he would have been paid, from what I knew of the Nesmith-Brown's habits.

I turned back to the outbuildings, but they were empty and padlocked.

The family definitely wasn't coming back.

Despite Mr. Fletcher's words, I wondered whether Nigel had known.

## 22

"What!" I demanded. "Sorry, I didn't mean to shout, Mrs. Mac."

"No offense taken. I said the Inspector's got the day books. Mac said to tell you."

I groaned. The cup of tea was welcome but the news wasn't.

"Has Pa contacted his lawyer?"

"Mac says yes. But it won't be long before there's ructions."

"Where's Pa? And more important, where's Maman?"

"She and Angelique went down to Wethersley – there's a bring and buy sale - with Mister Guy and Young Nigel who were going for the cricket. It's a local match, Wethersley v Marsham so not to be missed. Your Pa's in his study waiting for Mr. Myddleton. Mac's with him."

I nodded. "Thank you."

"He's hiding something, isn't he, Miss Alice, and it's choking him." It wasn't a question, it was a statement, and all the worse because it was true.

I nodded.

"Who or what is he hiding?" she asked. "Mac can't get it out of him. He's tried, God knows, he's tried. I've never seen Mr. Roger so eaten up before."

"Me neither. And I've tried, too. I don't think Maman knows. I'm pretty sure he wouldn't have mentioned anything to Guy. Perhaps Angelique…?"

"Angelique would have told me if it were important, and it looks like this is. She's worried, too."

"I'll go up and see him. Do Guy and Nigel know what's happened?"

"No. They all went out before the Chief Inspector came along. I doubt they'll be back before nightfall. Larry and May will be doing good business, you know how cricketers like to celebrate their victories."

"And their defeats," I said drily. But Maman and Angelique would be home before five.

I nipped upstairs to freshen up then went to Pa's study and knocked on the door.

This time I waited.

"Who is it?"

"Alice. Can I come in?"

He opened the door himself. "Of course you can. Mrs. Mac told you?"

I nodded. "Want to tell me anything?" Mr. Mac was standing by the window and I caught the flicker of a smile on his normally well-schooled face.

"No, thank you, dear. I'll tell what I need to – and if I need to – to Mr. Myddleton. The fewer people who know, the better." He still looked as though he had the weight of the world on his shoulders. "Well, Alice, where have you been all day?"

Mr. Mac coughed gently. "I'll go and see if I can be of use elsewhere, sir," he said, looking at me, then at Pa.

Pa smiled. "Thank you, Mac. I'm sorry to have taken so much of your time. I do really appreciate it. Of course you must go. Alice will keep me company until Mr. Myddleton arrives."

And afterward, too, I thought, but didn't voice it. I smiled at Mr. Mac as he closed the door. "Thank you for looking after him, Mr. Mac."

"My pleasure, Miss Alice, and sir."

The door closed almost silently. I listened for his footsteps, but they didn't sound. Pa caught me, and chuckled softly, which was nice.

"You can leave us alone, Mac. I know you're listening," he called.

Through the door came a muffled voice. "Very good, sir and miss. I was just ascertaining that I wasn't needed after all." And soft footsteps followed, disappearing towards the stairs.

"I am really incredibly lucky," Pa said at last. "So, Alice. Where have you been?"

I told him.

Everything.

A few months ago he wouldn't have given a toss for what he called 'woo-woo', but now he didn't dismiss it out of hand.

"We'd better have a word with young Nigel then. Who do you think would best deal with this? Guy perhaps? They seem to be thick these days."

I thought about that. "Perhaps a word with both of them," I said at last. "Separately, and then together. I've tried, but it's never quite the right moment. But the Nesmith-Browns doing a flit – do you think Nigel knows?"

"Well no-one here knew, which is surprising with bush telegraph, but I should think he'd find out soon enough if he's down at the cricket. There'll be people laid off without a by-your-leave from his parents. I'm sure he'll be able to tell us when they flew the coop when he gets back."

I nodded. I hoped he was alright. People get angry when they're let down by their so-called betters.

A quiet knock on the door, then Mr. Mac ushered a short portly person of Pa's age into the room. "Mr. Myddleton, sir," he enunciated suavely then waited.

I shook hands with Mr. Myddleton after Pa.

Pa looked at me and nodded his head towards the door. Mr. Mac watched poker-faced but I knew he was grinning inside.

"I'll leave you two together then, shall I? Or might you need me here as a witness?"

"If we do, we'll call you, Alice," Pa said. "But I think you have other things to do, dear, a young woman like you."

"Her Ladyship will be back soon, Miss Alice," Mr. Mac said formally as we left. He closed the door behind us.

"Thanks, Mr. Mac," I chuckled. "This family seems to be lurching from disaster to crisis and back again."

"I hope to God it will soon all be resolved once and for all," Mr. Mac said softly as we went back to the kitchen.

"Do you think God will help us out of this mess?" I asked.

"Just a figure of speech, Miss Alice. I think we must help ourselves out. God got us into it. Or possibly the Devil, in whom, I must tell you, Miss Alice, I do not believe for one moment."

Maman and Angelique burst in some ten minutes later, laden with 'bring and buy' loot.

"Nowhere near as good as it used to be," Maman said, dumping three string bags on the table in the living room, beside Angelique's three. "But it was fun and we won a cake! A treat for all of us. Where's Roger?"

I told her.

"What's he doing there? I thought he'd be painting on a nice day like this. He could do with some fresh air."

Angelique said, "Shall I go and fetch him?"

I shook my head. "There's someone with him?"

"Who?" asked Maman, perking up at the thought of guests. "Anyone nice?"

I shrugged. "Yes, if you call Mr. Myddleton nice."

"Mr. Myddleton? You mean the solicitor? I've been telling Roger to get hold of him all week, but would he listen? Well, good. I wonder if Mrs. Mac could stretch supper. I'd better check before I go up."

"It's not a social visit, Maman," I said quietly. "I'm sure Mr. Myddleton has made arrangements for his evening. It is Saturday, after all."

She nodded. "Yes, dear, I'm sure you're right, but I did want to tell him about our new grandchild. We're catching him up, now. Only one more to go."

"Don't look at me," I said.

"Well, not yet, I should hope. Not until next August at the earliest, all things being equal. But I do expect you to do your duty."

Angelique, unpacking her bags behind Maman, rolled her eyes.

I laughed. "My duty isn't to produce offspring so that you can flaunt their number to Mr. Myddleton, or any of your other friends!" I told her.

I liked the idea of children, but not yet. Neither of us did. There were things to be done before we gave in to breeding. Sorting out this current problem for a start. I suddenly felt very alone. I couldn't see a way out unless the truth came out – from everyone – but they all seemed to be hiding things.

I sifted through the booty. "Haven't I seen this blouse before?" I asked.

Maman chuckled. "You don't miss much, do you?"

Angelique's round face creased with amusement. "She couldn't bear to part with it, even after she'd thrown it out!"

"Well it all goes to a good cause. But look at this cake!"

Wrapped in greaseproof, in a brown paper bag, was a Dundee cake, a rare and exotic delight to us in these days of rationing.

"How many tickets did you buy for a chance at that?" I asked.

"Quite a few," Angelique said drily. "But we know the baker, and she's very very good."

"Not Mrs. Mac?"

Their faces told it all.

I didn't believe them!

"Why?" I asked. "You could have asked her to make one for us."

Maman shook her head. "She made two. This way the village gets our support and we get a cake. *Noblesse oblige.* Isn't that the British way?"

"And what if you hadn't won?" I asked. "Despite all those tickets?"

"Oh, but that would never have happened. Not with Angelique drawing the raffle."

I shook my head. "And no-one said anything? No-one noticed that?"

"Good heavens, an insignificant thing like that? Of course not," Maman said. "Oh, and did you know that Nigel's family appear to have done a moonlight flit, and not paid their staff off properly. The village is in uproar. There are some very angry people down there."

"Nigel and Guy?" I asked. "Hello, Maman, your heir and his friend are down there. Is there likely to be trouble?"

Angelique's lips pursed. From behind Maman she nodded, then waved her hands – possible, but …

I took the message.

Maman shrugged. "Why should there be? It's not they who've abandoned people."

I didn't wait to hear any more.

The little red car swooped down off the chalk into the village.

Colored bunting fluttered gaily over the village green and the pub which was doing a roaring trade. It looked wonderful, most bucolic, deck chairs and summer clothes, the sound of leather and willow and all that sort of thing, a typical country village summer afternoon.

Only it wasn't.

I skidded to a halt and leaped from the car, slamming the door behind me.

At the back of the pavilion there was nasty business going on. A knot of bodies tangled, not large, not obvious if you weren't looking for it; a huddle of large lads were in a noisy and threatening ring and someone was in the middle.

I ran towards it.

I grabbed at the arms of two men and pulled them forcibly apart, charged between them into the circle, spitting fire, breaking the closed circle, thrusting its components outwards and backwards.

"Gentlemen! What is happening here?" I demanded of the crowd in general.

I got away with it.

I was a woman.

They didn't dare touch me!

Nigel was on the floor, blood and snot all over his face.

Guy, bless him, was doubled up and breathing heavily with some very bloodied knuckles.

The ringleader, a strong fair-haired lad who had certainly seen active service and knew how to give as good as he got, held the other men back, a couple with bloody noses, and looked me up and down.

I didn't know his name, but he knew who I was.

He dropped me a foppish mocking bow.

"Well, well, well, rescued by a lady, eh?" he drawled, looking disdainfully at Guy and Nigel.

He eyed me. "You don't want to be getting mixed up with this, Milady, this is between us and him!" he pointed down at Nigel, and spat. "No cause for either of the Wethersley clan getting involved in Marsham business," he said soothingly and spun a glance round the rest of the Marsham men.

"Let the lady and her brother go. We'll hang on to the other one."

I stood up tall and looked him in the eye. "I don't think so. We all go together, that includes all of you, but I need to know what your grievances are with our friend. Then perhaps something can be done."

Nigel was wiping his face, struggling to his feet, "I don't know what they're talking about, truly I don't!" he said.

"Yeah, and I'm the Queen of Sheba," said a rough voice from the crowd.

"And a very beautiful lady you are, too," came another. Which eased the tension somewhat, and I was glad of it.

But now a newcomer arrived, running, pushing his way into the center of the group.

I recognized him at once; despite the fact that he was wearing cricket whites and was padded up in Marsham colors; the tall chap with the Ronald Coleman mustache who had been at the Inquest simply took over. Like the senior lion in the pride, he stamped his not inconsiderable presence over us all.

"What are you lot playing at?" he rasped. "Don't you know that bloody haggis-basher has his Incident Room in the Village Hall? Do you want to draw attention to yourselves?"

"But Les, his bloody family have skipped the coop and welshed on payment and he's saying he doesn't know anything about it," replied the ringleader. From their looks I guessed they were related. "We gotta do something! They've been getting away with it for too long, the bastards."

"He's been living with us since the start of May, how should he know?" I retorted. "I didn't know the Nesmith-Browns had left the area – if that's what you are saying."

"Well they bloody have. And they've left owing wages. They're a bunch of parasites, and no mistake, and what you lot are doing getting mixed up with them, I don't know! We got no problems with Wethersley, just leave him to us."

The cricketer shook his head. "Not here, Joey, don't you ever think?"

Now Guy chipped in. "Look, none of us, and that includes Nigel, knew anything about this. I'm sure if there are wages to be paid, if you let us have the amounts, Nigel will settle it, won't you Nigel?"

Nigel stood up gingerly and looked around the group, "Of course I will." He dug in his pocket, and continued, "I'm grateful for you gentlemen for bringing this state of affairs to my notice, although I must admit the way you caught my attention leaves a lot to be desired."

He blew his nose noisily into a less than spotless handkerchief. "Now gentlemen, can I buy you a pint? And if you let me know who is owed what, I will see that the books are balanced as soon as possible. I am not to blame for my family's lack of honor. You will be paid what is due. You have my word on it."

It was the longest speech I had ever heard Nigel make, but it went down well.

"Good lad," said the cricketer, "And least said, soonest mended, eh? We'll forget this ever happened. There's a tap over there, you can clean yourselves up, and then we'll take up your offer like good fellows, eh. Come on, look lively, chop chop!"

And as he spoke the little knot of men glided away in ones or twos, either to the tap, with both Nigel and Guy, or to the pub.

The cricketer turned to me. "Les Broom, Milady. I know who you are." He held a hand out for me to shake, which I found myself doing automatically, while he continued "That was a brave thing you did, just then. I wish I had a sister or a friend like you to watch my back."

He must have been about five years my senior, and held himself well. Definitely a lot of presence there, and I could feel electric charges beginning and knew he could feel it too; he had tawny eyes, and knew how to use them, but two could play at that game. I stared back, smiling, daring him to pull back first.

Then from the field there was a shout of 'Out!' and some cheering and cries of 'Shame' and 'Well played'.

The contact broke.

He flashed me a smile and let go of my hand, turned to look at the state of the game. "Excuse me, Milady, but it's my turn to give Wethersley a thrashing, no offense!"


I sat at the bar with a lemonade while Nigel and Guy and a couple of the Marsham men finished cleaning up in the Gents.

"Bloody family," one of the knot of attackers muttered, sipping at his free pint beside me. He was older than the others, in his late forties, weather-beaten, a countryman who worked outdoors.

I raised an eyebrow to encourage him.

"Nothing but bad luck round here, that family."

He turned to me, looked me in the eyes. "Watch yourself with that one. A leopard doesn't change its spots. Them and their fancy friends – they've never been anything but trouble."

He took a stub of a cigarette from behind his ear and lit it carefully. "You heard about little Cissie Laycock, did you? It was one of their fancy friends as killed her. They never caught him. She never did tell anyone his name as I heard. Told everyone she had someone who promised to look after her, and just before she died she was all smiles and bright-eyed, pretty as a picture, blooming, she was.

"Poor little scrap. She wasn't bright, She didn't understand what looking after meant. She thought she would be married, but instead … Well, you know how it goes. One of their friends – he told her everything would be alright, only it wasn't. She died. The family weren't too pleased about that, as you can imagine."

He eyed me purposefully. "I, for one, wouldn't blame them if they took the law into their own hands, know what I mean?"

I did; they had a legitimate grievance if that were true, though nothing official would be done – the shame, the lack of evidence, people's attitudes to 'unlawful' pregnancy and terminations.

We lived in barbaric times and thought ourselves so bloody civilized.

I nodded sympathetically. "Poor little kid," I said, softly.

"And that daughter of theirs, that Sylvia, what a nasty piece of stuff she turned out to be, eh?"

My ears pricked up.

I said quietly "My brother had a lucky escape there."

The man looked at me. "Yes. Yes, indeed." He took a long pull of his pint, wiped the foamy mustache on the back of his hand.

"She disappeared from here about three four weeks ago. For her health, I heard it said. Now that can mean anything, can't it!"

I smiled. "I disappeared at the beginning of this year for my health," I said. "I had pneumonia rather badly. Somehow I don't think..."

"No, milady. I wouldn't dream of thinking anything other than that for you. She just ain't in the same league. We all thought that it would be just her as went, sort of after she broke it off with your brother. None of us expected the others to up sticks. I take it that lad will make sure the wages are paid?"

"As long as they are honest accounts, yes. We will make sure of it," I said quietly.

I didn't know how much cash Nigel had to hand, but it would have to be done and done fast.

While Guy and Nigel downed the last of their pints, I fired up the car and drove over to them.

They clambered in gratefully, Guy, who was heavier and wider, beside me, Nigel sitting on the folded down roof, legs between the seats, grasping the windscreen top with his hands.

"Marsham Court?" suggested Guy.

"If it's no trouble," Nigel added through puffy lips, one with a fresh scab forming. "I need to check something."

I said nothing, but turned the car, giving a final look at the cricket field, where Les Broom was knocking up runs with style. He had just hit a four, but stood easy at his crease and turned his head as we set off, and waved, then executed a stunning exaggerated bow.

I grinned, waved back and blew a kiss.

Guy looked at me strangely, which made me grin even more widely.

Marsham Court was no distance in a car. Nigel had his house keys with him and used them. We went in.

He gazed around the empty house aghast.

"Everything, they've taken everything," he kept repeating as we moved through the empty white-painted rooms.

"You really didn't know this, did you, Nigel?" Guy said quietly.

"I told you. I told them," he turned his eyes to us both. "I've not had any contact with my family since... since the end of April... No, that's not right, because Sylvia came to Wethersley, didn't she? And I did go back to get a few things before then, clothes and a few books and stuff when I knew they'd all be in London. I've not seen any of them, I swear it. I had no idea they were going to leave, or how shabbily they were going to treat their staff. Like I told them in the village, I've been at Wethersley since the beginning of May."

No stick of furniture remained anywhere. The place was cold and dead.

Nigel went to a wall safe in the study and dialed the code in. The door clicked open at his touch.

Inside was bare.

"Bastards!" he hissed. "The rotten lot."

"What's up old man?" Guy asked.

"They've taken my passport."

"No they haven't, I've seen your passport, it's on the shelf in your kitchen along with your ration-book and your cheque-book."

"No, not that passport."

Nigel looked at us both. "Look, I know it's a bit dodgy, but we all had two passports. We've always had two. Since I could remember."

"You mean like Maman and Angelique? You didn't tell me you had dual nationality," Guy, the law-abiding friend, asked.

Nigel looked embarrassed. "Er... not exactly. We didn't always travel as Nesmith-Browns, you see."

I saw only too well. "And now they've taken your one, sort of disowned you?"

"Something like that. Look, they're so shabby. They had no right to treat other people like they did. Those people need their money, they've earned it. And my bloody family have just let them down, dropped them all in it, and me too."

"You've no idea where they've gone?" I asked.

"Leave him alone, Alice, can't you see he's having a hard time?" Guy said.

Nigel shook his head. "No, Alice is right. I need to talk to someone. Someone official. My mind's made up."

He relocked the safe. "Go ahead. I'll catch you up."

Guy and I walked out of the echoing house back into the sunlight towards the car.

"They bashed him up, Alice," Guy told me. "Four of them. We were watching the cricket. I went into the pub to get a pint, and they took him round the back of the pavilion and belted him. Because of his bloody family. They wouldn't listen to him. I heard him and weighed in, then you turned up. Let me say, sis, you were amazing. But... what's all this about?"

"Search me. Are you both alright? I mean nothing broken? Nothing too hurt?"

"Only our pride," he said with a wry smile. "We'll survive. I think Nigel will be sore for a few days but I'm fine. Just a few grazed knuckles that I can pass off as the results of cricket. I don't like violence, Alice, particularly when it's four or more on to one, but I really enjoyed laying those punches. I would have punched the rest of them, the ones who were hiding the action, too. I was bloody angry. It was worth a few grazed knuckles."

## 23

We drove back swiftly in silence and crept in through the back door.

Mrs. Mac blew an angry sigh at the sight of us. "Where the deuce have you been? Your father's gone off with Inspector Murray and your mother's going haywire. Go and give Angelique a bit of a hand, please Miss Alice."

"Any possibility of tea, Mrs. Mac, for a pair of battle-scarred soldiers?" Guy asked, giving her a hug. "Nigel has had a little contretemps with the locals."

Mrs. Mac lost her firmness. "Heavens, you've been fighting! Why on earth did you do that?" She took a close look at them both and melted. "Well, sit yourselves down and I'll get you something..."

I stomped off.

Maman would be in her own room, I could hear the shrieking in French, and Angelique trying in vain to pacify her. It was pretty bad if Angelique couldn't work her magic. I went to the cupboard that housed the more interesting bottles that remained. I found the guignolet – a cherry drink with warmth and Provençal provenance, which she loved, and which usually had a calming effect on her volatile nature. There wasn't a lot left, I hoped it would be enough.

Maman opened the door when I tapped on it.

"Where were you, Alice? It's just like you to *fuir comme un anglais* when we need you. That idiot écossais has taken your father into custody. And Roger let him. How can I be expected to be calm in such circumstances!"

She cast a baleful eye at her friend Angelique who was rolling her eyes to heaven.

"I've found some guignolet, Maman," I said softly in French. "Why don't we sit down and remember the cherry trees at Grand-père's?"

She snorted. "I don't know who or what you were mixing

with, but you've got a very strange accent, ma fille," she sniffed loudly, but was distracted from her tirade.

"Some very strange people, Maman. I was serving my country, both my countries," I reminded her. "It wasn't always easy, and it wasn't always with gens comme il faut, but we did our best. I'll drink to their memory. Will you join me? A toast to my rugged maquisards with their drôle d'accent, living and dead?"

I filled the three small glasses with the deep red liquid and handed them out.

We raised our glasses to the French Resistance and to S.O.E., and sipped the warmth of summer cherries which had continued their delightful existence all the way through the recent hostilities. I found myself wanting to cry. Too many memories, good and bad, and I'd invoked them to take Maman's mind off the present. Raoul. I had Jem now, but his death still hurt, and the fact that nobody bothered to let me know, although as they said, they didn't know where I was any more. But they could have tried to find out. They knew my real name, some of them. They just didn't think of it. After all we'd been through together. I sipped again and swallowed back the tears.

Maman was silent. The memory of the war brought her back to reality.

Angelique nodded appreciatively. "C'est tres bien fait, Alice," she mouthed.

Praise indeed.

"And to Grand-Père's cherry trees, la Belle France," I said, raising my glass once more and sitting on the sofa next to Maman. I put my arm round her. She was tiny, such small narrow bones; I had forgotten how slight she was.

"Now very calmly, what's been going on while I was out just now?"

I listened, I calmed, I listened some more.

Both Maman and Angelique were outraged.

Inspector Murray had come in and taken Pa, with Mr. Myddleton, luckily, to his head quarters.

"They've arrested Pa?" I blurted out, before I could trap my tongue with my teeth.

Maman drew away from me, shuddering. "Alice, you have an awful way of putting things. I don't know where you get your manners from. I have struggled to bring you up to be diplomatic, but..." she sighed, sipping the cherries.

Angelique sniffed. "Your father is helping with inquiries," she said quietly. "Although why he couldn't do that here, I don't know."

Yes, I thought. They're going to put the screws on him because he has been less than truthful because of his damned scruples.

To be honest, I'd expected it, but not so fast. Not good news.

"Mr. Myddleton will make sure he will get back for supper," Maman said, "I told him expressly to do so."

I nodded. "Of course," I said.

I wasn't sanguine although Pa's position still packed a lot of clout locally.

"Do you know what Pa's not saying?" I asked.

Maman frowned. "I don't know what you mean, Alice! Your father is the most honest, upright and ethical man on earth. Why would he try to hide anything? It's that awful Scotsman, he's obsessed."

She sniffed loudly. "And if I hear anything else disloyal from you about your father, I shall be severely disappointed in you, ma fille."

I shrugged and left her with Angelique and the last of the bottle, and went down to the kitchen.

Mrs. Mac had completed the cleaning job on Guy and Nigel, applying sticking plaster wherever she could, and had provided mugs of tea and thin slivers of cake as shock treatment. The boys were regaling the Macs with their adventures, and the disappearance of the Nesmith-Browns.

"Without paying the staff off?" Mrs. Mac said. "I'm sorry Nigel, it's your family, but that's despicable."

"I know," he nodded, speaking thickly through bruised lips. "I don't think it's the first time that's happened, though."

Suddenly, he had all our attention.

"It's happened before?" I asked. "When?"

He shrank back into the chair. "We..ell... When I was at school we moved every few years. I wasn't involved with the moving because I was away, but Sylvia said it was always a swift decision to go, almost overnight, and they'd got it down to a fine art.

"Pa always said God helped those who helped themselves, and you should never look back. To both my parents, people were to be used, not cared for. They needed staff to keep them in the style they wanted to live but didn't have the wherewithal or the inclination to pay for it. Not unusual, really."

"So a trail of disgruntled people left in their wake," Mac said, his voice icy calm.

Nigel hung his head. "I would say so, Mr. Mac. I'm not proud of it. In a way I deserved the drubbing I got. Those people had a legitimate grievance."

"But not against you, Nigel," said Mrs. Mac. "And violence doesn't serve any purpose at all. Certainly not here. It doesn't bring the jobs or the money back, does it? Or affect the perpetrators of the crime."

Nigel shook his head, sadly. "But it might make a few people feel better, even if I feel awful."

"Nigel," I said quietly, "You said you wanted to speak to someone official…"

Nigel got up, took his plate and cup and saucer to the sink. "Yes. I think that would be a good idea. Thank you, Mrs. Mac. Might I take you up on that aspirin you offered?" He rinsed the crockery and put it on the draining board.

"Right, then let's go."

"Mr. Guy, you had better go along too."

"Of course, Mr. Mac, but where are we going?"

"To rescue your father from the clutches of the Constabulary."

"What! Why didn't anyone tell me?" Guy demanded.

I smiled sadly at him.

"OK, OK, we have been a bit full of ourselves. Where is Pa?"

"Amersham police station," Mr. Mac said. "The Citroen has a full tank. Go and save the family honor."

Sometimes I wondered who was in charge here.

Mr. Myddelton met us outside the police station. "They cannot keep him, they cannot charge him," he said, puffing at his pipe. A good blend, fragrant and rich. "He will be out in a few minutes. I wish he will speak, but he refuses to."

He gave us both a look. "You don't think you might be able to give him a little nudge, either or both of you? For Marie-Thérèse's sake if not for his own?"

"He hasn't spoken to you?" I said.

The lawyer shrugged, fiddled with the pipe. "Not fully. He's admitted that Mr. Anselm-Jones has visited – well, it was in the book, wasn't it? And that their meeting was less than cordial, but not the reasons for the dissatisfaction between them. He refuses to budge on that. But where does that get us? Mr. Anselm-Jones was here in Buckinghamshire last November. That's all. He could have gone anywhere afterwards."

I saw the flaw, of course, and so did Guy.

"But Anselm-Jones went missing in October, surely?" he said.

Nigel coughed politely. "I think I may be able to help here," he said. "To whom should I speak, Mr. Myddleton, sir?"

## 24

By half past eight Pa was back at Wethersley, under what Mr. Myddleton referred to as 'a mild variant of house arrest'.

Maman screeched and threw herself at him as he tottered, shell-shocked by his ordeal, out of the Citroen, and would have laid him out had not the car door supported him.

Mr. Myddleton, the advance guard, put his arm gently round her shoulders and drew her away with the utmost delicacy.

Pa caught his breath, leaned forward and kissed her gently on the forehead. "Tout va bien, Chérie," he breathed.

Mr. Myddleton took Maman in one arm, Pa in the other, and pointed them towards the door. Guy and I followed. Angelique and the Macs came through the front door and cheered Pa in.

"The conquering hero returns," Guy sneered.

"Better than 'Home they brought her warrior dead.'"

He looked at me, shocked. "You don't ...?"

"Not while Mr. Myddleton is on our side, but I think a great many favors have already been called in."

"But Pa is a Lord," Guy said. "Surely that counts for something!"

"With the feeling in the country as it is at present and a Labour government? You're joking. We're seen as decadent, oppressors of the noble working class, or hadn't you noticed?"

Guy pulled a face. "Yes, but anyone who knows Pa..."

"Quite. But the masses, if they cared to look at him would only see him as a painter of posh people. What use is that to anyone? How does that help rebuild a country fit for working men to stand tall in? Anyone who does know Pa will agree he is the most generous of men, he looks after his tenants, helps people whenever he can, he actually believes in a sort of socialism, but that won't count with the communists when he opens his mouth, when any of us do. And there are far more of them than there are of us."

"Hmm!" Guy bit his lower lip. "Do you think they'll take

over the country, then, Alice?"

I shrugged. "No idea. But I do know that we can't count on favors any more."

"We never did, surely," Guy objected.

I looked at him witheringly. "What about when you brought your fiancée, sorry, ex-fiancée, and her family and the Merediths over for a dinner earlier this year? When we killed the fatted calf – and for whom! People round here helped us to do that. We're incredibly lucky that we still have a bit of money, good friends and roots in the country. Ordinary people in towns really suffer, without access to the sort of food and favors people like us take for granted."

Guy sniffed. "That radical boyfriend of yours been turning your head?"

I laughed. "Jem, radical?"

He let out a sigh. "Well, that's good. I owe the chap and I like him, but I couldn't let you get involved with a red. I mean, I know it's fashionable in certain quarters, but it's a bit off, isn't it?"

I bit my tongue. It had been going so well, but I suppose it was my fault for bringing up the disastrous engagement.

I chose my words carefully. "You don't think Jem would hold the job he has if he hadn't been checked out as sound, do you?"

I knew that, although we had been thrown together in an attempt to get him into Society and he worked in Whitehall for the government, his background and sympathies were not totally with we privileged few, and I was with him, as in fact was his boss, my sister's husband, Basil, who was public school through and through, and, I believed, Pa and Maman, in fact everyone with any sort of common sense.

I gave him a wan smile, "Now tell me exactly what happened this afternoon, then we'll call the police station to see if they've finished with Nigel; he could probably do with a lift back."

Guy didn't hold back. He knew several of the assailants by name, local boys who had gone to war and come back from the fighting as men, expecting things to be different, 'infected' as Guy put it, 'with socialism and their rights'.

They had young families now, were the coming generation, and were looking out for themselves and their friends the way they'd been trained to in the army.

"I was never one to gossip," he said primly, "but it seems the Nesmith-Browns were not popular. Larry told me that, on the QT, while he was patching me up. Said no-one would say a word against Pa and us lot – well, not to our faces, I suppose – and people were happy to work for us because we were decent, and we belonged.

"Nigel's family were incomers, and even before this happened, considered 'takers', chancers, not exactly straight. He actually said the locals were glad to see the back of them, but wanted their due – understandably."

"How's Nigel going to pay those wages?" I wondered.

"Ah, that's all sorted out. Larry will collect and check over the invoices and pass them across tomorrow. We can get the cash here by Monday evening, I should think, and do a pay out in the pub. Don't worry about it."

"Good, the people need the cash as soon as possible. It would put Nigel in a good light too. Especially if he dropped in an extra quid each. It'd be a small price to pay."

But there was a lot more stuff to know, I thought.

Perhaps I'd go and see Larry some time? No, I'd see May, his wife, and ask about Cissie Laycock; I'd get a lot more out of her.

We went indoors.

Mr. Mac said, "We are all in the Library, if you'd care to join us for a celebratory sherry, before supper, Miss Alice, Mr. Guy? And might I say, very well done, both of you?"

Guy followed him. "Excellent, a chap could use a drink!"


I used the Citroen to pick Nigel up. It was dark now, the pubs were closing; folk were pouring onto the streets. Some poured into the police station, rowdy with Saturday night spirit.

Nigel clambered, wincing, into the back of the car.

"Thank you so much for this, both of you. After paying for all that booze earlier I don't have cash for a taxi and I really didn't fancy the walk."

I watched him settle through the mirror. He shrank into the dark cushions, and into himself as he had done when I'd driven him and Guy back from that awful Beltane meeting, the same haunted look in his eyes.

Guy noticed too. "What's the matter, old chap?" he asked.

"Look, nothing can get you now. You've done the decent thing, haven't you?"

Nigel sighed deeply, and nodded. I put the car into gear, pulled out into the main highway, and headed for home, driving on autopilot, listening avidly.

In the back, Guy was lighting cigarettes. I heard Nigel cough as he took his first draw. He wasn't a smoker normally. "I should have come clean at once. I've just been cowardly. Hoping it would all blow over."

"What do you mean?" I asked, as kindly as I could.

Guy snorted. "Leave him alone, Alice, he's done in."

"No, I need to talk, Guy," Nigel said. "It will help me sort things out in my head, too. I've told each of you bits of it already, but there's more. Quite a bit more."

We sat in Nigel's tiny living room topping up gin, from a half bottle Guy had managed to buy from Larry as we passed through Wethersley, with ginger beer.

Nigel swallowed two more aspirins, and accepted another Capstan full strength.

He had told us that he had known Mr. Anselm-Jones rather better than he had admitted earlier.

Like Guy, he had passed the war in a desk job – his uncles had seen to that. The Meredith fingers were found in many pies then, and Mr. Anselm-Jones had links with them – though you'd not find them easy to document – hearsay only, and that unlikely. He stayed with both the Merediths and with the Nesmith-Browns, but under a different name.

"I only ever knew him as Uncle Edgar in England. In my family you got used to extraneous uncles and aunts turning up and you learned very quickly never to ask questions. You were usually asked to be nice to them in one way or another." He gave us a knowing look and shuddered. "Uncle Edgar had certain preferences and luckily for me they were for young women."

I glanced across at Guy. Had he..?

Nigel caught my look. "Oh no! Not Sylvia, she was far too obvious for him to be even vaguely interested. He liked them young, slender and dark. And when I say young, I mean very young."

"Children?" I asked.

"Possibly. Certainly under the age of consent. And not the ones who were ... er ... developing. Little skinny girls with fronts like ironing boards and big eyes, 'wondrous waifs', he called them. He said he loved their innocence. Of course, in the East, they were freely available, for a small price."

Guy looked at me, sickened.

Nigel looked at us both, "I never said he was a nice person. Then again, he also liked young men, but well-built, muscly ones, so again, I didn't feature there, for which much thanks."

He frowned. "A couple of the chaps who thumped us today, they knew him. Two of them. I recognized them."

"Ye-es," I encouraged.

"I don't know their names. Or where they live. But Uncle Edgar knew them. Last year he knew them. I saw him with them, out in the woods a couple of times. He liked going for long walks whenever he stayed with the parents. He'd been doing that for some time, since before we left Cambridge and everywhere between. Always off for walks mostly alone or with some young man or wondrous waif for company. He'd often bring back something for the pot, so no-one questioned what he was up to."

I began to feel the hairs on the back of my neck quiver. "Who did you recognize today, Nigel?"

"The good-looking ones, of course. The one who started it and the one who came in and finished it."

"Did you tell the Police this?" I asked.

"No, I said there'd been a slight misunderstanding but wasn't pressing charges. This isn't about me. It's about... well lots of other things. Let me get my thoughts in order. They're a bit woolly at the moment."

He gave a shy grin. "I don't suppose we could have a cup of tea? This gin isn't helping."

I made the British panacea. It was no use expecting my brother to do it.

As I opened the door to bring in the tray I heard my brother hiss something. They looked as guilty as any pair of amateur conspirators could.

I dispensed the liquid. The boys stirred sterilized milk into theirs, I took mine neat.

"Uncle Edgar used our place when he needed to be inconspicuous."

"Ye-es…" I could wait.

Nigel sipped the tea. It was too hot and burned his bruised lips. He put the cup and saucer on the dresser by his side.

"He used it as a place to meet people."

"Ye-es.."

Guy began to speak but I flashed a warning look and shook my head.

"These were people who didn't need to be seen to be here. Foreigners. Wherever we moved to, we made sure there was reasonable access to airfields or tracts of flat pasture. It was part of the deal."

"You told all this to the Police?"

He nodded. "Oh yes."

"What about Leggy after the May Day fiasco?" I asked.

"I think so. He knows we entertained a lot. And there was always enough food, even in the hardest days. We ate a lot of rabbit, mind, and pigeons."

"Don't we all!" muttered Guy.

"When was the last time you saw Uncle Edgar?" I asked.

Nigel was silent.

Guy said very quietly, "You might as well tell her. You've told me, and you'll feel a lot better when it's out in the open."

"Yeah, and now the family's no longer here… Last November, the far end of it. I'd heard he was missing, but I'm sure I saw him walking down the back road that runs from Marsham towards Balfour's and Wethersley Woods. I was coming home for the weekend and had taken a taxi from Amersham. I said nothing to the cabbie, because it was none of his business, but I mentioned it to Ma when I got home.

"She said 'Rubbish, Nigel, you must have imagined it. We've not seen Uncle Edgar since summer.' She said it too quickly, which is what she did when she was lying. It was like she had to get the words out before the truth rushed over them. But I know it was him, in his usual country clothes. He was a very particular man, keen on good quality – well, it went with the job, didn't it?"

"Then what?" I asked.

A smile fluttered across his face. "I'd forgotten," he said. "I went upstairs to my room and passed the room he normally used. The door was open and one of the staff was doing the place out, but I could smell his tobacco. He had his own personal blend, part Turkish, made up for him. You'd recognize it immediately, once you'd become accustomed to it; it was like a signature..."

Yes, I thought. Mine used to be Gauloise, and Jem's Pasha. But although the scent of tobacco lingers, it doesn't linger three months, even in a closed up room.

"Anyway, it was an odd time of day for doing a room, late afternoon, but I didn't say anything. Then later that night when we were at dinner, Ma brought it up.

"She said 'Nigel thinks he saw Edgar this afternoon!' and there was an awful silence. Everyone was waiting for someone else to speak; Pa was red-faced, Sylvia looked daggers at me, and Ma actually looked scared.

"Then Uncle Archie, who was staying with us, said very definitely, 'Nigel must be very much mistaken. And if he knows what's good for him, he'll not mention this again to anyone. Anyone ... or else!' And he drew his finger across his throat, you know.

"Then Pa spluttered, 'Haven't seen the man since summer. I hear he's gone AWOL, not that it's any of our business, do you hear, Nigel?'.

"So I muttered something about being confused, not completely sure, in fact now I came to think of it, it couldn't have been him, and the tension subsided. But Sylvia looked at me through narrowed eyes and sneered, then looked up at Uncle Archie who patted her on the hand, and the look changed to smug.

"But it was him, I'd swear it; and as I looked back out of the cab window there was a chap coming towards him with a shotgun and a dog, like they were going off to bag a few pigeon or something. Which was odd, as it was very damp and becoming misty. I thought what a strange day to go shooting. It didn't make sense."

We sat in silence for a while. I felt shivers creeping up my spine.

"Did you recognize the other chap?"

He shook his head. "Just a figure in the mist. Loose dark jacket, cheese-cutter cap, I think. Nothing I could actively recognize. He was waiting by the gate at the other end of that track. You know, the other end, close to Marsham. There's a farm nearby."

I noted the place. I knew it. Why hadn't I thought of it before? There are always at least two ends to track, even if one peters out.

"And that was the last time you saw him?"

"Yes. Like I said, it came up at dinner that evening, and I was told in no uncertain terms that I'd best forget I'd seen anything, not that anyone would believe me if I did mention it, which would not be a very good idea at all, if I hoped to see Christmas."

"You've kept quiet all this time?" I said sadly. "You've known Pa was in trouble, yet you've kept quiet?"

"I'm not proud of myself, Alice. It's been really hard, but my family have ways of dealing with things that you would not imagine. It's better now the Merediths are dead, but I wouldn't trust them not to do something drastic."

"Well they're not here now. Have you any idea where they are?"

"I don't suppose they'll be in the country by now. They've lots of contacts abroad. And I doubt they'll be using their usual names or a British identity."

He stretched out his hand for the teacup. "I didn't mean to cause all these problems, I really didn't."


I lay on my bed writing to Jeremy on onion-skin airmail paper.

It had been my turn to apologize for missing our ten pm Abraxas meeting. But I twirled the ring now.

It was one thirty in Paris, and was half past twelve here and Wethersley was silent. I could sense him in a tall narrow room with overlarge furniture and heavily ornate wallpaper, sleeping soundly. I leant over him, heard his soft regular breathing, and dropped a kiss on his cheek. He stirred slightly, and mumbled my name. "Love you," I said. "I'll try to keep our date tomorrow, Jem. You'll understand why I couldn't be there when you get my letter."

I went over Nigel's story in my head.

The date he furnished the Police with was that of the weekend after Mr. Anselm-Jones's abortive visit to Wethersley. And the fact that Archie Meredith was a house guest of his parents. Now Archie Meredith was dead and the other Nesmith-Browns had disappeared.

Pa wasn't off the hook, but life looked a lot less bleak for him now.

Of course, there would be a search for the Nesmith-Browns under that and their other name. Being cynical I didn't hold much hope for that. If you've got one false identity, why not others?

I told Jem everything, the whole sorry mess and just about everything that had happened this very busy day. It took ages, and by the time I was signing off with love and kisses, I'd had enough of it all.

I was still annoyed with Nigel, who could have at least shown some backbone and some loyalty to us as a family; more to the point, I was back again out of charity with my stupid brother who had supported him in keeping quiet when he should have been encouraging him to come clean. Maman was just being French and dramatic about everything, Pa was feeling sorry for himself and hard-done-by, and Angelique and the Macs expected me to make everything better.

I missed Jem dreadfully. I was still young, I wanted to feel young again. I needed someone – specifically him – to talk to, and, please, it wasn't a lot to ask, to laugh with.

I listened to the night sounds of the country; perfectly nice but not what I wanted. I felt so lonely.

What I really craved was a Soho dive with some loud brash band, and a dance floor with Jem, a packet of Pashas, a few drinks. I would have danced my blues away and felt loved.

That would have set me right, but there was no band, no cigarettes, and no Jem.

I sealed the letter in its thin blue envelope  then pulled the curtains and got into bed. Alone and dissatisfied.

## 25

Angelique and I skipped church so that she could kit me out as Sally Carson.

When I was a child she used to dress us up, and we all loved it. Her eye and skills were immaculate.

I went from me to someone very unlike me in a few easy steps.

Firstly a pair of old horn-rims that Grandpa had disowned when I was a child, that had been converted to clear glass for 'dressing up' – Giles and Guy used to fight for them. Then a rather lumpy cardigan that had come in yesterday from the Bring and Buy to be unpicked and re-knitted. There was nothing wrong with the color, a soft heathery pink, but everything wrong with the style as far as Maman and Angelique, both petite women, were concerned – a combination of lacy and lumpy, and far too long for either of them. It actually didn't look too bad on me, but then I had Pa's 'English' height.

She found me a sensible gray skirt and a cream blouse to go with it, and a blue-pink lipstick and rouge, not my usual colors at all.

"Gloves – ecru crochet for summer, grey leather for winter, shoes, beige or black according to season, and a grey jacket if we can find one. And a hat."

We dived into the dressing up box and spent a happy morning sorting through the ancient clothes. Some went back to my grandmother's time, all folded away and smelling of mothballs.

I found what I was looking for, and another skirt and blouse that would pass muster.

"Wear your hair pushed back," Angelique suggested. "With combs or Kirby-grips."

"It looks terrible that way," I objected.

"Then no-one will recognize you. You look suitably English now." She made it sound really bad. "Flat shoes would be a good idea. Sensible ones. You want to look trustworthy."

I chuckled. Looked at myself in the mirror. "You'll be suggesting lisle stockings next."

"For winter, yes. And a Burberry. That hides a multitude of sins and says money. Jewelery? Are you married?"

"Soldier's widow, making my own way in the world," I said. "Perhaps a ring or two, some nice beads, nothing too flashy. And a watch. I've got those things."

I stowed my new wardrobe in a cloth hold-all ready to take home.

Being with Angelique had lightened my mood. I'd forgotten how long it had been since I had laughed, really laughed.

We were both still laughing when we went back down to the kitchen to help with the lunch.

Mrs. Mac turned to us gratefully. "You have no idea how good it is to hear that sound. The place has been like a graveyard this past week. It's only a week ago, isn't it? And it feels like a lifetime."

It did indeed, and as I took my place at the big table with the knife and the basket of vegetables, in the company of these two women who had nurtured me from birth, the final bit of last night's loneliness fled.

"I'll find out who those lads were, they shouldn't get away with such things," Mrs. Mac said quietly as we peeled and chopped. "One of the girls will let me know, you may be sure of it."

I said nothing. In a way I agreed with Les Broom.

"Did you know about the Nesmith-Browns disappearing?" I asked.

Mrs. Mac frowned. "Not enough for me to be able to say anything. I'd heard that there was a horsebox at Marsham Court but the story was that Sylvia had taken her steed with her to a friends for a holiday, a few weeks ago, but nothing more than that. I wasn't surprised that they weren't at the inquest. Now it's obvious, but not at the time. Leaving must have been quite a sudden decision, though. No-one seems to have any idea where they've gone – or they're not telling." She nodded towards the gardener's hut.

"I don't think he knew anything about it," I said.

Angelique sniffed. "He squealed well enough last night, Guy told me. I wouldn't put anything past that boy. Bad blood. He'd have let Roger go to the gallows rather than have said anything. Who was he protecting?"

"I don't think he thought anything through," I said, surprising myself at supporting Nigel.

Mrs. Mac sniffed. "He needs to learn loyalty. Who took him in in his hour of need? A bit of loyalty wouldn't go amiss. He may have been brought up very badly, but he's old enough to make his own decisions now, and old enough to know right from wrong. I'm sorry he was hurt, but he should have spoken up sooner. And Mr. Guy supporting him! I don't know what the place is coming to."

"Where is Guy?" I asked.

Angelique sniffed again. "Where do you think? He's not with your father or your mother, he's not here, or as far as I know with Mac. And he's not gone to church."

"Nigel will be pretty uncomfortable today. He could probably do with some company."

"He's got that dog," muttered Angelique, chopping parsley fiercely. "Nasty little creature. That was the cause of all this bother. Pity it wasn't put down!"

Mrs. Mac raised her eyebrows over her glasses. "Gallic," she mouthed at me, and nodded.

Angelique caught us. "I 'ave not gone Gallic!" she spat, then began to chuckle. "Oh, no, it's just that I am so glad that Roger and Chérie are off the 'ook. But if it hadn't been for that dog and that young man, we would never have had to go through this."

"What's done's done," said Mrs. Mac. "I hope they can find whoever did it. But if they can't, nothing's going to bring him back. It's just a pity he was dumped on our land."

We worked on in companionable silence, occasionally chatting, but mostly not, each of us in our own thoughts.

I had seen Pa and Maman at breakfast; they were late, in fact, which was unusual, but a weight appeared to have left Pa's shoulders.

"If the dratted man was seen round here after he left me, then I've nothing more to add. But I'm surprised at young Nigel. If only he'd come to me and talked. I thought he was my friend," he told me as I poured his coffee.

I nodded.

"But perhaps we must forgive him for being loyal to his own family. After all, blood is thicker than water."

"Even if it's pig's blood," muttered Maman. "But he did look very battered last night, and he will feel and look even worse today, so I suppose that was God moving in mysterious ways."

She ignored the questioning looks that Pa and I gave her. "And I for one am very pleased with God at the moment. He has my vote for the present time."

I finished the vegetables and cleared away. "I'll go and see the invalid," I said. "See if he's up to Sunday lunch."

Angelique sniffed, but Mrs. Mac nodded. "It's thanks to him that we're having one," she said. "He can coax fruit and veg out of the ground as well as any professional gardener I've ever known. If he's too poorly to come over or feels wrong eating in public looking like a piece of raw meat, I'll send it over. Tell him that, would you, Miss Alice?"

"You're too nice, Mrs. Mac," I told her.

Angelique nodded in agreement.


They were sitting outside with bottles of brown ale playing ball with Spider and chatting.

I joined them and sat on the grass having ascertained Nigel was 'pretty fair, considering' and definitely keen to join us for lunch.

"The chaps who did us over," Guy informed me, "are from the far side of Marsham. Larry told me who they were when I bought the beer."

"You've been down to the village? That's quite a hike." I was impressed.

He grinned at me. "Took the bike. It was going begging. Fancy a jar?"

He went in and got a glass for me and twisted the stopper free. The ale foamed upwards. I wasn't a brown ale girl normally, but it hit the spot today. The weather was warm with a slight breeze, a perfect early summer day. I wiped the foamy mustache on the back of my hand. "Who are they?"

"A couple of ne'er-do-wells. Joe and Les Broom, cousins, not brothers. I'm quoting, by the way. A bit flash, you know? Weren't backwards coming forward before the war, but after they come back from North Africa, thought they were really something. Set themselves up as hauliers with a lorry and took work wherever they could find it, and they'll buy anything, shift anything, no questions asked, Oh, and they've a little business in Amersham, second hand shop with allied services, for the look of things – to appease the tax-man, know what I mean?" Guy did a very fair imitation of Larry.

Well, yes, I did. But I thought that there was probably a lot more to Les Broom than that. Apart from flirting with me, he had a quiet authority about him, and enough nous to want to keep things quiet, away from Chief Inspector Murray. Now why would that be?

I turned to Nigel. "Did you know them at all, Nigel?"

"No. I knew some of the cricket team, but not that well. I didn't spend much time down here, as you know."

"You're quite sure?" I asked.

"I'm not holding back, Alice. I saw Uncle Edgar with them a couple of times, perhaps more. They're big chaps, well built, confident, and they looked like they knew how to take care of themselves. I kept out of their way."

"So where would they meet Uncle Edgar? Did they come to the house?"

Nigel shrugged; looked across at Guy under his lashes. "My sister, she knew them. I'm sorry, Guy, but ..."

Guy shook his head. "It's okay, old man, I'm not in love with her any more, say what you like."

"She knew them. I saw her with one of them once, in Amersham, coming out of the cinema."

"She could have been a go-between?" I suggested.

"Between them and Uncle Edgar? Why? I don't think she was particularly fond of him. He wasn't particularly fond of her, either. At least, not in the way she expected. No compliments, no treats. I think he hardly noticed her."

That, I thought, would have been tantamount to an insult.

I finished my beer and stood up. "See you both back at the house for lunch, then. Usual place, usual time."

Sam's voice crackled down the phone. "I can meet you this afternoon, Alice. I'll pick you up at two thirty? We could go for a drive."

It wasn't what I had in mind but there'd be no eavesdropping by local telephone operators.

I was at our gates with five minutes to spare, and he showed up on the dot. I climbed into the little Ford.

"So what's up?" he asked, revving up. "Any new developments for me?"

"Possibly. What do you know about Joe and Les Broom?"

He frowned as he drove down the hill towards Wethersley. "Broom and Broom? Apart from junk shop just behind the church? They have a lorry and will shift anything relatively cheaply, I've heard. Used by local firms. House moves, deliveries of all sorts, that sort of thing. And of course the junk shop."

"Is it just junk?" I asked. "I mean real junk?"

"Mostly. But I wouldn't put it past them to have dodgy stuff, too. In the back, no questions asked, no answers given, take it or leave it, that sort of thing. Why, Alice?"

"They picked a fight with Nigel and Guy yesterday, at the local cricket match."

"OK. Why?"

"Not sure. You know that Marsham has been vacated by the Nesmith-Browns?"

"Without coughing up the wages, I heard last night." He turned right at the Wethersley Arms. "That's not a nice thing to do."

"I know, but beating up the only remaining family member in the area is equally nasty, particularly since the family has disowned him."

"Is Nigel seriously hurt?" he asked.

I shook my head. "Nothing broken, but he looks a mess and will look worse. He recognized the Brooms, although he didn't know their names. Larry told Guy who they were."

"So is he going to put in a complaint?"

"No, he thinks it would be counter-productive, and he's probably right."

Sam nodded. "Want to take a look at their shop?"

I gave him my very best smile.

Broom Stores was in a row of small rather run-down shops

off to the left of the churchyard. A grubby shop with peeling paint and overstuffed with items that had once been desired. It wasn't open, of course, today being Sunday.

Peering through the chain-link metal grilles that protected the dusty windows I was hit by sense of glorious disorder; everything that could possibly be put on show was on show. Which didn't tally with my impression of Les Broom any more than the items for sale did.

This was junk, I could almost smell it just from looking, from the battered chairs and cupboards, through boxes of much-played gramophone records, the odd wind-up gramophone, paintings, crockery and chipped glasses full of used cutlery. Roughly-folded sheets, bed covers and curtains were piled up on a sideboard, sheet music on a table, and in the center of the window in pride of place was a jeweler's display case full of brooches, rings, hat-pins, tie-pins and seals, all jumbled together. Beside it was a chaotic arrangement of boxes and tools to the left, balanced by scruffy rows of books and magazines to the right. Pre-War clothes hung from a rail along the door or draped over a wooden towel rail close by.

"I can't imagine they sell much. How long have they been here?" I asked.

Sam shook his head. "I don't think they were here before the War, but the Rev will know."

I looked up at Sam and smiled. "Thank you, Sam. I appreciate your help."

At half past five he dropped me outside Nigel's cottage.

Since they knew each other, I walked back to the house alone.

This morning I had intended to skip back to London before nightfall, but now I wanted to stay on and visit Broom Stores tomorrow morning. I checked with my parents who were happy about that, and Guy, who wasn't, until I promised him a lift to the station early that would get him to Pimlico by eight o'clock so that he could be changed and at his desk by 9.30.

"It's lovely to have you both here," Maman said, sipping tea. "And getting on so well together."

"Oh, we can do it sometimes," Guy admitted. "Isn't that right,

Al?"

I nodded. "On occasion," I agreed.

We were in the lounge, just the three of us and Pa.

The Macs were in their house, Angelique had gone off on her bicycle, having been called out to help someone with a wedding dress, Nigel had gone back to his cottage for an early night.

Pa said, "I suppose this is the wrong time to bring this up…"

We all eyed him suspiciously.

Guy began, "If it's about what I think…"

But was stopped by Maman. "It doesn't matter, Roger. It needs to be dealt with and we are so rarely just the four of us."

Guy took a deep breath, set his jaw and leaned back in the armchair. "Okay. I can take it."

Pa said, "You mean you will take on the running of this place, Guy? That's wonderful news!"

My brother frowned. "No. I most certainly don't. Well not immediately. Look, I've got a career to carve out. Anyway, you aren't ready to give up yet, surely?"

"Oh, no, dear boy, but you do need some training. You need to decide whether you want to do this, keep the family line on, after we've gone, in this house, or I could make alternative arrangements."

Maman put her dainty hand over Pa's long bony one. "That's what we need to talk out, you see, Alice, Guy. Neither of us are looking to fade away yet, but we need to consider what we will have in place when we finally do. You know, Guy, that traditionally it is the oldest son who takes over the family home and all that goes with it. We would love you to carry on this tradition, but if you feel you can't… well, naturally we shall be disappointed, but …"

"But you would do what?" Guy asked, suspiciously.

"Well, Alice's young man might like to take it on," suggested Pa. "I must say I'd prefer you to do it, but if you really don't want to…"

"You'd give my birthright to a complete stranger!" Guy gasped.

"Oh, no, Pa, you can't do this," I said. "You're using Jem as a lever and he's not even here to defend himself. And he's got a career to build too."

"Well, you could take it on, Alice," said Maman. "I'm sure

you'd make a very good job of it."

"I'm not stealing Guy's birthright," I said drily.

"Thank you, Alice. I appreciate that, even if it does drop me back in it."

"You're welcome, Guy."

I looked at Pa. "Why do you want Guy out of the Bank, Pa?"

That got their attention. All of them, Maman included.

She was the first to speak. She trilled, just like her youngest daughter did when she had something unpleasant or untrue to say.

"Whatever makes you say that, Alice?"

I smiled and tapped my nose.

"Well, now I come to think of it," Guy blustered, "I think Alice is right. You don't want me working at the bank, do you, Pa? You were hinting at it before I got engaged, but you really started putting the pressure on me to settle down here when there was a possibility of a marriage. And now you are still doing it. Why?

"We all know that eventually I will be duty bound and all that to take over the estate, but you've still got plenty of life in you, Pa, and you, too, Maman. Neither of you look anything near your ages. Surely you can enjoy it now. I mean the war's over, and although it's hard at the moment, still, we should all be getting back to normality pretty soon. You'll both be in clover."

Pa raised his eyebrows. "That's how you see it, is it, Guy? A short while ago you were all in favor of selling off most of the land in order to make money. Tell me, my boy, what would the bank advise?"

Guy looked puzzled. "How can I tell you? I'm not privy to the situation here or to all the ideas they might have, I'm not senior enough. I mean, you weren't for the development at all, I know that, and it happens that in that particular instance you were right. But that was because of who and what was involved."

"Exactly," said Pa. "But the bank – your bank, if I remember rightly – was all for putting up as many houses as we could cram in, and selling mortgages at quite incredible rates to just about anyone."

"It would have been very advantageous to us, Pa, and to the

Nesmith-Browns; we would have all stood to gain a great deal."

"And so would the bank, never forget that! And for precious little work, too."

"Banks are in the business of making money – mostly for themselves. Surely you know that?"

"But it was the people from the bank who introduced you to Sylvia's people, to the Merediths, and now I discover that it is they who have put you into contact with John Anselm-Jones. Do you understand what I'm saying?"

"Where there's muck there's brass, Pa. Money is a filthy business. Money stinks but we can't live without it. I've probably met a lot of nice people through the bank, too."

"Yes, dear, of course you have, but we haven't had that privilege," said Maman. "And I was really looking forward to seeing you settled."

I eyed Guy and he eyed me.

"I'm off the hook for the moment," I waved my left hand in the air, flashing my engagement ring.

Guy laughed. "Is this what it's all about. Me getting a wife? Why didn't you say?"

Pa said, "We think you'd do far better if you found some nice local girl, you know, well-brought up, but a country girl. There must be a few knocking about round here. You've just got to go out and hunt them down. And with Nigel, it will be easier, the prey always hunt in pairs," he twinkled. "N'est-ce pas, Chérie?"

Maman smiled at Pa. "Oh yes. And Guy, you must go where the girls go. You'll never find them in a bank, any more than Nigel will find them stuck in a walled garden!" She looked kindly at Guy. "A nice respectable local girl, that's what you need, dear. Think about it, Guy. You know it makes sense."

Guy snorted. "That's what I thought I did have!"

He pulled out his cigarette case and handed it round. Maman and Pa both took one, he lit them both and his own.

"OK, I made a mistake. But I'm really not ready to get married. Not yet. I like living in London. I quite enjoy working at the bank. Give me a couple more years at it, then I'll come back and learn all there is to learn and settle down to being a boring old country squire – if I haven't made my, our fortune." He held out his hand to shake on the agreement.

Maman took it and shook. Pa was reluctant.

"What's up, Pa?" Guy asked.

"I would like to say this to you. Be very very aware of everything you do or say, of everything that is said to you while you are at work. But yes, my boy, I'll allow you two more years as of tonight. Make your fortune, and make ours too. If that's what you want. I'm sure your mother will be delighted. Now how much was it you wanted?"

# 26

Monday.

I parked by the church of St. Michael's and All Angels and walked up the lane alongside. The church clock tolled nine.

At Broom Stores a frail gray-haired woman was struggling with the mesh grilles.

She had the padlocks in her hands, but the grilles stayed put; she could shake them on their hooks but couldn't lift them free.

I stepped in. "May I help?" I asked, taking over.

I had youth, strength and reach on my side. The grilles slipped off the hooks and down to the ground.

She looked at me gratefully but embarrassed. "You shouldn't, Miss, you'll get your nice clothes dirty."

"It's no problem. I want to visit the shop anyway," I said. "If you just unlock that other padlock?"

Between us we got the shop open, the grilles hidden in the back room.

She turned to me, puffing slightly, "Thank you, Miss, thank you so much. I don't usually have to open up. I usually just cover while they have an afternoon off."

She looped her bag, a soft cloth affair with ring handles which I was sure contained knitting, over the back of the chair behind a table that served as a desk. "How can I help you, Miss?"

"I'm looking for a present for my young man," I said. "And a bit of jewelry, perhaps? I saw some in the window. Could I have a closer look?"

"Of course, of course. Is it a birthday present?"

She tottered, tiny, with bird bones, hair the colour of a sparrow's chest, papery yellowish skin, a sweetheart of lipstick daubed across her thin lips, her knitted skirt and cardigan hanging off her, between the dusty chaos to the front of the shop. With effort she retrieved the display case and brought it back to the desk, unlocking it with a key from her cardigan pocket.

"It's a bit of a jumble. I've been meaning to sort it out," she said, apologetically. "You know how things are, though, when you're all alone. Have a look through, Miss."

"Thank you." I opened the glass lid and dipped in my hand.

"I ain't seen you before," she said, watching as I examined the jumble of merchandise. "You ain't from round here, are you?"

I shook my head. "Just visiting. I'm always on the lookout for anything a bit different in the jewelry line." I took a card out of my bag. "Just a bit of an interest of mine," I told her, untangling a silver chain of dubious provenance.

"You might be lucky there, but I wouldn't have none of that stuff if you paid me. I just mind the shop while Les and Joe are busy. I'm their auntie."

I delved into the case once more. Gilt chains with no gold content, blackened bits of silver, a couple of nice hat pins and a porcelain brooch of flowers, pretty but chipped on some of the petals. Not to my taste at all.

And then I saw them. The seals.

They were not any old seal.

Apart from anything else they were hallmarked silver, but the carved stones inset were the giveaway.

They were antique cornelians, like those in the British Museum, and, more to the point, like the Abraxas that I had round my neck, like the Abraxas Leggy had bought for me from the International Galleries.

I looked at the little ticket and read the code.

Cheap. Even though this was not a prime London outlet, they were too cheap.

I continued looking. And found a scarab bracelet.

Now I know that there was a vogue for all things Egyptian in the Twenties but this was not imitation.

At least, the scarab was not.

The mount was new. Well, a lot newer than the stone.

I put that and one of the seals aside and let the woman fiddle amongst the tangle of stones and metal.

She looked up at me. "Does your young man have a watch?" she asked.

"He likes watches," I said.

"Only, I just remembered." She tugged at a drawer in the desk, and brought out an envelope. "I think this is just lovely. I like a man with a watch and chain across his waistcoat. It may be a bit old-fashioned, but I think it's so smart."

She tipped the contents of the envelope onto the desktop.

I had to stifle a gasp.

It was amazing.

"It's rather heavy and a bit old-fashioned but your young man might like it. I can't think why the lads don't have it out on show. I suppose it's because of the inscription."

I was hanging onto reality by a thread. "Er, inscription?"

She took the watch and opened the back. "To JAJ from EW in gratitude and friendship, 1938," she read. "A good jeweler would be able to get rid of that, the metal's quite thick, then you could put your own in, personal, like."

She smiled up at me, longing for me to buy it.

"I'm sure Jem would love it," I said. "Now, a price?"

She frowned a little. "Well, it's got to be worth a tenner, hasn't it? And you wanted those other little trinkets? Twelve quid the lot?"

I searched in my shoulderbag. I had to have it. It was a lot of money, but thanks to Leggy's float my purse provided it; I carefully counted the last two pounds in small change, for the look of the thing, and asked. "Will you be here all day?"

"Oh yes, I should think so, just me and my knitting, but I've earned my wages, thanks to you, Miss." She put the money in the envelope that had held the watch. "I expect I'll be here most of the week. The lads've got work in London somewhere in the daytime. You'll be wanting a receipt?"

"Thank you."

In my hand was the very watch that Edward VIII had given to his friend, John Anselm-Jones. No wonder 'the lads' had kept it hidden in the desk. I wondered where and how they got hold of it!

I had to work very hard to look calm and nonchalant. This little woman had possibly, unwittingly, positioned a rope around her nephews' necks.

She scribbled the details of the sale on a sheet of note-paper, stamped the shop's name and address at the top, and the date at the bottom and handed it to me. "Do you need a bag, only I've not got many."

"Save them, I've got a bag here," I said, stowing my purchases in my handkerchief and then in my hold-all. "Goodbye, and thank you so much."

"You're welcome, Miss. Please call again."

I went straight to a phone box and rang Sam, to ask him to keep an eye on the place. "There's something going on there, but I'm not sure what, yet. I'll let you know as soon as I do have something concrete. And thank you for your help."

I was putting the phone down when I saw Chief Inspector Murray making his way up the passage towards Broom Stores.

I let him enter the shop then fled back to the car.

All the way back to London I wondered whether I had acted correctly.

I had acted on instinct, and was in any case unwilling to give up a ten quid gold half hunter to the man who had harassed my father.

More to the point, how did it get into that grubby little junk shop?

Broom Stores.

I'd only come across Les Broom this past week a couple of times, once only to talk to, and that cut short by the cricket.

I didn't see him as a junk dealer. He was far too sharp for that, had too much presence. And yet he was aware of the Chief Inspector's presence and didn't want to attract his attention...

Now why might that be?

I deposited a newspaper parcel on Lily's kitchen table.

"Spring onions!" she cried in joy, unwrapping it. "Oh, how wonderful! And radish and lettuce. Oh, Miss Alice, that's a joy. And parsley. And mint. Oh, my!"

I grinned. "Sorry I couldn't get the meat or the fish to go with it," I said. "Look, I'll be away for a bit, but I'll drop in from time to time, but I may look different, so warn George. I'll be Sally Carson. Mrs. A long lost acquaintance of Yours truly. I don't need to be recognized."

Lily grinned. "Oh, you going underground or something? George will love that. He'd probably apply for the job of your son if it were the school holidays."

She stopped from putting the vegetables safely in the larder and said "But be careful, Miss. There are some nasty people out there."

"And I'm one of them, Lily. Any chance of a cuppa before I go and see what a state my flat's in?"

"Course there is, and there's a couple more letters for you, too. One's an airmail."

I slit it open immediately, but it wasn't from Jeremy.

In a way, it was better. It was from Père Raymond Laval, of the church of La Madeleine, Lanteuil, telling me that during the recent hostilities, two of the church's most treasured possessions, a jewel-encrusted Book of Hours by a follower of the Rohan Master and the Lady and her Son, along with a quantity of liturgical plate, had been looted by German Forces. They had overrun the village, burnt houses and generally caused mayhem.

Monsieur Le Curé then added something that made the hair stand up on the back of my neck.

"With these troops, Mademoiselle, was an English man. I had seen him in the church before. He came with the Sieur de Lanteuil, and had seen our treasures in years gone by. I was led to believe he was a connoisseur of beautiful sacred objects, and showed him all we had. He was most erudite and very interested. Our Sieur was proud of his knowledgeable friend. Then Our Sieur was killed by the Germans, and this man came with the troops who ransacked our church. Forgive me if I am wrong, but I feel betrayed by this elegant erudite devil of a man."

He sent a full description of the Book of hours and the missing statue, which I read avidly, adding, sadly, that he was not sanguine of seeing them again, but prayed that the Lady and her Son might find a way to return to their home village. He was even less hopeful for the Book of Hours; paintings and jewels could be recycled for a great deal of money, he opined, and in these days, it seemed to him, greed was greater than honor.

Poor Père Raymond Laval.

Leggy was waiting for me in the still fairly pristine flat in the World's End. "Roger rang this morning to tell us what's happening, but I'm sure you have some more," he said.

I showed him the watch and told him how I had come by it.

He took it carefully and said nothing for some time, probably sorting out what he was going to tell me, but eventually I got confirmation that it was the same one I had seen in the photo archives in Bar's office.

"My dear Alice, I do believe I saw this presented. Sometime before the start of the last war. It will be photographed, in the society papers. And yes, it is important. Edward Windsor. Well, we knew he was friends with John Anselm-Jones, and he quite liked giving presents, so long as they didn't cost him too much, Mrs. Simpson apart. This was probably given to him previously, but he disliked the pocket watch, much preferred the wristwatch, more modern, don't you see, more up to date. John Anselm-Jones was delighted with it, you know. He always wore it, always..."

He looked up at me with approval. "So it was in a drawer in the Broom Stores? We'll have to take a look to those lads. I'll get Bobby onto it. You are too close."

"Then look into what happened to Cissie Laycock and when. And I meant to tell you ages ago, the other end of the path leads across to a lane leading to Marsham – and there is a gate on it, not a stile. The body could have been brought that way."

"Yes, I heard that. And also that the body had been shot in the back of the head by a German pistol from the First World War. Your Pa didn't bring one back with him, did he?"

I shook my head. "Not as far as I know."

"Good. Lots of soldiers did, you know. Anything else to tell me?"

I told him about Jeremy seeing Sylvia in Paris.

His eyebrows rose. "A jewel dealer? That was fast. I wonder who introduced her to him. I could hazard a guess, but ..." His voice had a trace of admiration in it.

Then I handed him the letter from the Curé de Lanteuil which he read nodding to himself. "Pity he doesn't give us a name. Did you see anything like the Book of Hours at the galleries?"

"I saw some ancient books with jeweled bindings," I said. "I couldn't say the one the Curé mentions is one of them, although the Rohan Master's style is quite distinctive."

"Then we'll have to find out. Now, Alice, I want you to go to Putney. I've had the house under surveillance most of the weekend and as far as we know there is no-one there at the moment. You might care to go on the knocker?"

## 27

The day was close, and I parked at the far end of the street, well away from the girls' school.

I took my cards out and meticulously went to the first house, knocked, waited, then as there was no reply, scribbled a dated pencil message to say I would be calling again the following evening after six; it would give the occupiers time to discuss the possibility of selling to me and a time when they'd be back from work.

The second house was equally silent, and I went through the same drill. The gray air seemed turgid, I felt the first drops of rain.

Damn.

I'd not thought of an umbrella nor of putting the hood up on the car. I decided to do the latter – there's no joy driving sitting in a puddle, and it wasn't my car after all. I found a headscarf in my shoulder bag and knotted that under my chin as I trotted back up the semicircular drive of Nutfield Lodge.

It looked just as dead as the other two houses, late Victorian, set in its own grounds and supporting fine growths of both ivy and Virginia creeper. Picturesque in a late nineteenth century way.

I tripped up the five steps to the front door. I may have been 'trade' but I wasn't going round the back. I rang the bell, and heard the chiming inside, a pleasant sound.

And then I heard voices.

Or at least one very querulous female voice.

I couldn't actually make out the words, but it felt like an inopportune time to be calling, so I scribbled on the card and slipped it through the letter box then started down the steps.

I was halfway to the entrance to the avenue when the door opened and a woman, her hair tied up in a headscarf, wearing a floral wraparound overall, called out to me.

"Coo-ee! 'Scuse me, Madam. Are you Mrs. Sally Carson?"

I turned, "Yes, can I help you?"

The pink face creased into a wide smile. "Oh I think you may well be able to help us very much indeed."

She ushered me through the front door, past two sets of fine luggage to a small side room that was used as an office.

Inside, shouting down the telephone stood a woman of some sixty years or more, dressed in a severely tailored suit that echoed the style of her youth.

Beside her, in a simpler utility suit and blouse, a younger woman was trying to calm her.

The char held my card out to the younger woman, and introduced me. "Mrs. Sally Carson," she said. "Might be just the job, Ma'am, begging your pardon. I'll make some tea."

The younger woman took the card and read it, nodding. "Thank you, Mrs. Green, you'd better bring it in here. There's no space anywhere else."

She turned to the older woman and flashed the card in front of her. "Mother, we may be saved. Put that phone down, there's a dear, and come and meet Mrs. Carson."

All this time I was trying not to look at the older lady.

Staring was rude, and besides that, I wanted to see what sort of place this was.

It was obviously a gentleman's study, and from the looks of it, a military gentleman who served abroad.

I smiled at the younger woman; "I'll come back later if it's more convenient," I offered.

The older lady pulled a set of spectacles from her reticule and stuck them on her nose, "Mrs. Sally Carson, buyer of antiques and objets d'art, well, well, well. How very fortuitous. Who sent you here?"

I shook my head. "No-one, Madam. I'm visiting the area. It's what I do, a little discreet buying and selling, ever since my husband was shot down. One doesn't want to go under."

The old lady peered over the top of her glasses. "Another war widow? Well, that's the three then, I'm Mrs. Dugdale, widow of Brigadier Dugdale, Royal Fuseliers and this is my daughter Fanny Dugdale Hurst, widow of Captain Freddie Hurst, the same regiment. Only Mrs. Green retains her husband here. He was Home Guard. So, no-one sent you?"

"No, Mrs. Dugdale. But if you have any little items you would like me to evaluate, I should be very happy to do so."

"Oh, I have a few things. You'll need deep pockets!"

"I'm sure we can sort something out," I said.

"I'm sure we can," said Mrs. Dugdale. She looked at her daughter mischievously. "I can't see any problem with that, can you?"

"None whatsoever," said Fanny Dugdale Hurst. "Mrs. Carson, would you care to come with us?"

The place was packed.

They had unloaded the lorry not into the garage as I had thought, but into the downstairs reception rooms, piling it high and deep, one room full of furniture and rolled-up carpets, the second with tea chests and other cases.

"This," enunciated Mrs. Dugdale, imperiously, "is where one would normally dine with one's guests, and that room there is our sitting room where tea and other comforts are normally taken. As you can see, we are unable to use either. My son, Ferdy, God rot him, who also lives here, has allowed his so-called friends to use our home, my home, as a repository for God knows what trash. We are just about to get ready for Wimbledon; guests will be arriving tomorrow, staying until the first week in July. We do this every year, have done ever since the children were small, and the fool could hardly have forgotten."

She took a deep breath. "I know you mentioned small antiques and objets d'art – there are some here among this, but really, Mrs. Carson, I would be so grateful if you could simply take the lot. What do you say?"

I needed to think.

Firstly there was the legality of it all.

And then, all I had was a little red car.

But I looked at the boxes and furniture piled up, and knew that everything that had been at the International Galleries, including the office furniture, was there.

I turned to Mrs. Dugdale. "Mrs. Dugdale, I'm sure we can come to some arrangement, but, and I must ask this, do you have permission to sell this property?"

"Of course she does," said Fanny Dugdale Hurst, "I heard my brother tell her he wasn't going to do anything with the stuff in any haste, but if she wanted it out that badly, then she should call someone in and get it shifted," she looked me in the eye daring me to gainsay her, which of course I wouldn't, then added "for a price, of course."

"That's exactly right, Mrs. Carson," corroborated Mrs. Dugdale. "So can you help us?"

"Ladies, I think I can. I don't usually deal with such large loads, but I have a friend, a military man who does. I could ring him."

"Be my guest," said Mrs. Dugdale, grandly, and led me back to the study.

She sighed. "I'll leave you alone to make your call. It will be such a weight off my mind to have my home back. I was staying with my sister and only returned this morning to prepare for the Wimbledon influx. You can imagine..." she left, closing the door behind her.

I dialed Leggy's number.

"Armitage Antiques, Good morning, how may I help you?"

I told him.

"I'll be over within the hour," he said. "Mrs. Dugdale? Brigadier Dugdale's widow? She was quite a looker when I was a young lad. I'll bring Bobby, the boys and the van. Well done, Alice."

I opened the door, and the two women stepped forward. "My friend Colonel Legge will be pleased to call within the hour," I said.

"Excellent." Mrs. Dugdale drew us into the study once more then called, "Mrs. Green, dear, bring the tea in, will you?"

While the two ladies took tea I inspected the items for sale. Or some of them. Most of the smaller pieces were wrapped in newspaper; I opened a few of the little parcels and saw, amongst other things, the Lanteuil Black Virgin.

As I held her up against the gray light coming in through the rain-spattered window, I felt a zing of recognition. I pulled M. le Curé's letter out of my bag, and reread the description, checking off the details, one by one.

It was identical. I stuffed the letter back in my bag and put the Lady and her infant son gently by the door.

As I was doing so Mrs. Dugdale came out of the study and

saw the statue.

"Who on earth would want that?" she shuddered. "It's so primitive and beastly, a thing for idolaters. What my son was doing with people who collect stuff like that, I don't know! He was brought up C of E. There's never been a taint of Catholicism in our family. Why, his father leaned towards non-conformism!"

"What does your son do, Mrs. Dugdale?" I asked, re-wrapping the Madonna.

Mrs. Dugdale sniffed. Obviously her son had lost star billing in her esteem.

"He tells me he is in investments. In a city bank. I must admit I didn't expect this sort of treatment, and he's been so cavalier about things this past month. That was why Fanny and I went to stay with my sister in Bournemouth; he actually drove us out of our home by his strange behavior. I suppose it could be problems at work, but he never speaks to me about that, after all, I'm only his mother, what would I know?"

I moved over to the desk and slid the drawers out, examining them, then inspected the undersides of the chairs, the drawers and doors of the bureau bookcases. They were all in very good condition, all empty.

Mrs. Dugdale frowned. "These are very nice pieces, Mrs. Carson," she said. "I'd like you to make me an offer."

I sucked my teeth.

I knew worth when I saw it, and did not want to appear tight-fisted, but there was no way I was going to blow all Leggy's readies.

I started low. "A hundred pounds!"

I watched her face, "I could do with a bit more than that." I nodded. I'd go up to a hundred and fifty if necessary, and that was generous. The working wage of a fully-qualified tradesman was less than a tenner a week, and that was on a very good week. I was offering ten weeks' wages already, but the goods were worth it and more.

"A hundred and ten. I can do that cash..."

Her daughter came in at that point. "How about a deal for everything?" she suggested, as the bell rang.

I breathed a sigh of relief.

Mrs. Green let Leggy in, and introduced him.

"Colonel Legge, Madame. Colonel Legge, Mrs. Dugdale and Mrs. Dugdale Hurst."

He charmed the socks off them, he really did, standing smartly to attention, mentioning mutual acquaintances, smoothly bringing them back to business and flirting in the nicest possible way.

He winked at me as I watched in amazement.

Watch and learn!

He made them feel valued, beautiful and let them make decisions, although he gently guided them towards what he wanted that decision to be, as he spread banknotes before them on the desk in two tempting one hundred pound rows. I watched the ladies eye the cash and then each other, wanting to take it but unsure.

Leggy turned to me. "We can sort this out later Mrs. Carson, but would you like to add anything?" I peeled four white fivers from my stock, "I have seen some of the stock, Colonel. I think it's worth a bit more, and the ladies have been so reasonable, I'd like to be generous."

And they bit it.

Some time later I while Bobby and one of his friends were clearing the International Galleries into the back of Arkwright's lorry and Leggy was taking tea with the ladies, Mrs. Green touched my elbow. "Thank you Mrs. Carson. You've done us all a great favor. I hope you'll do well out of it."

"I'm sure I will, Mrs. Green," I said, slipping a white fiver into her apron pocket. "If you hadn't called me in... I always show appreciation."

"Thank you, Mrs. Carson, thank you very much indeed," she said, stroking the note.

"Tell me, Mrs. Green, were you around when this all turned up?" I asked.

She shook her head. "I only do when there are people here. Mr. Ferdy Dugdale left on Friday morning, so I did a clean and tidy up because I knew Madam was coming back this morning, and when I let myself in I found this. I was right put out. Then Madam and Mrs. Fanny arrived and everything blew up. Madam must know where Mr. Ferdy is, because she got him on the phone. That was her shouting – only you never heard that from me. I'm here now daily until the Wimbledon guests are off. We take in payers, you know. There's a tennis court out the back, grass, nicely kept, and a quiet garden, with a croquet lawn, too, so it's a nice little earner. What Mr. Ferdy was thinking of, I don't know, but he hasn't been himself lately."

That was twice I'd heard that. I wondered about that.

Mrs. Green walked back into the house and down the stairs into her domain.

Leggy was making his farewells to the ladies, and I joined him and did likewise.

"Give you a lift, Colonel?" I offered.

"Delighted, Mrs. Carson, delighted. Those two know their way home."

## 28

As I sped back down Putney High Street Leggy turned to me. "Slow down, Alice. Now, Mr. Ferdy Dugdale. What do you know about him?"

I decelerated, and thought. "Not a lot. He's not been himself lately according to both his mother and Mrs. Green, the Char. And he works for an investment bank in the city."

"Good. He works for Bathurst's Bank. Mean anything?"

I whistled softly. That was the same bank that Guy worked for.

"What do you know?" I asked.

"It's all to do with the Merediths. Roger hinted there were things that needed looking into when they first broached the Wethersley Marsham project, so I looked."

I waited. He was busily stuffing his pipe, when I crossed over Putney Bridge.

"Which way now, Leggy?" I asked. The lorry had vanished, having hit the lights right.

"Bear left, then right on Fulham Road and keep going. Our repository is on Finborough Road."

He held a match over his pipe and sucked hard, urging the tobacco to light. Then as I turned right, he continued.

"What I saw was disturbing. Mr. Ferdy is Guy's immediate boss by dint of dead men's shoes. I don't think he is an ethical person. And he's running scared at the moment, so dangerous."

"Why do you think that is?"

"Noticeable since the Merediths met their demise, and accentuated since Mr. Anselm-Jones turned up dead," Leggy said. "And also, he is also attempting to blackmail Guy."

I clenched my teeth, determined not to say anything, but I suspect the way I clutched the wheel gave the game away.

He gazed across at me. "Ah, you didn't know. I'm sorry, Alice..."

"It explains a few things, lately," I said icily. "What's Guy gone and done that needs hiding from the world?"

It took me some time to bring the words out; I was dreading the reply would be 'unnatural practices', or something along those lines. I really didn't want my brother to be blackmailed because of his sexuality.

"Oh, nothing much. He's only a mark because he's so straight and proper," Leggy said, stashing his tobacco pouch back in his pocket. "And because he wants to make a perfect impression on everyone."

"But if it's what I think, it could ruin him," I said.

That stopped him. "What were you thinking, Alice?"

I didn't say. "Tell me, Leggy. Tell me what my stupid brother has got himself mixed up with, for pity sake!"

Leggy frowned at me, shrugged, puffed on his pipe and blew out the aromatic smoke. "What lots of young men do, that's all, but he went in a bit deeper than most."

"Ye-es. So why is he being pressured?" I was really worried.

Leggy chuckled. "The bloody little fool spent time in gaming houses and had to borrow money to pay his debts, Alice. That's why he sold his car. I admit it's not a trait you would want in a banker, but it was a banker who introduced him to the casino, and who is putting the squeeze on him now."

I let out the long held in breath slowly, and said a silent thank you to Them Upstairs (Elisabeth's usage).

What a twerp! What an utter twerp!

Leggy chuckled. "I don't know what you were imagining, Alice, but I seem to have relieved you. I don't want to know, by the way, and I am glad that you think blackmail is preferable."

"Guy and his bloody get rich quick schemes!" I muttered. But I felt as though a huge cloud had lifted off me. I hadn't realised how much I'd been carrying for my stupid brother.

"Exactly. We must get him out of the clutches of Mr. Dugdale and, if necessary, out of Bathursts."

I passed the Red Lion pub and the Granville Theatre at Walham Green and carried on past the Chelsea Football Ground at Stamford Bridge before I spoke.

"Is Pa paying his debts?" I asked. That would explain why we needed money!

"He has done, some at least. And Guy has foresworn the casino, as far as I know. It was all Meredith and Nesmith-Brown induced, via Mr. Dugdale."

"And it would seem that Mr. Dugdale was also involved with John Anselm-Jones," I said. "Or at least with Mr. Leonard Shepherd."

"Whom the police are investigating as we speak. I don't think there will be much problem with him squealing."

"Show him the thumbscrews?" I suggested.

"Alice, really, that's barbaric... I think not, but not a bad idea."

Beside a tall lock-up Bobby and his friend, Jack, were unloading furniture and boxes onto the pavement. Leggy slipped a key in the padlock, twisted it, and the chain fell free. The repository – a grand word for an unprepossessing storage facility already half full – smelled of old clothes, dust and damp. It wouldn't be a good place for some of the fine pieces we had just bought. I said as much.

"It's just a holding pen," Leggy told me as the first boxes were shifted in. "I'll arrange better for the stuff that needs it but I had to act fast."

I waved the letter from the Curé de Lanteuil. "Any chance of me getting the Lady photographed and sending him a copy? And I'll try to get more details out of him regarding the Englishman."

He nodded. "Off you go, then," he said, "I'll see if there are any Books of Hours. The boys can do the hard work, that's what I pay them for."

I went to the corner of the road where there were a pair of public phone boxes, and rang Bar.

"Alice, darling. Do you have a story for me?"

"Not exactly. I've come across a black virgin and I need her photographed as soon as possible. Is Tom free?"

"A black virgin? How exotic. I'm sure Tom would be free to photograph her, what's her name? Where did you meet her?"

Ah! Not what I'd meant to portray!

I chuckled. "No, sorry, Bar, I said it wrong. Think medieval Black Madonna and child statue... possibly obtained illegally from a church in France..."

"Oh, Alice. You'd got us both all fired up on the wrong track.

Tom is nodding. Can you bring her to the studio here? ASAP. And I need to know all about it. By the way, what is it about you and religious icons? I never had you down as a believer."

By three thirty I had the Lady rewrapped and tied in her blanket on the passenger seat of the car, and three copies of four views of her in black and white in my handbag. I was out of my Sally Carson look. Bar had looked so askance at my grayed and slicked back hair and the horn-rims that while Tom took the photographs, I restored Alice Chamberlain to her more usual look.

I drove back via Bathurst's Bank, as I had promised to meet my brother and take him and the money (Nigel's) down to Wethersley that evening.

I drew up outside the Bank as he and another, somewhat older man, wearing a very smart trilby above an elegant dark suit, stepped out through the door onto the pavement. I hailed Guy and got a wave back.

"Alice, excellent timing. Let me introduce you to my immediate superior, Mr. Dugdale. Mr. Dugdale, my sister, Alice."

It was the most natural thing in the world, but I felt the shiver that shot through Mr. Dugdale's body, and the anger that crept through the thin slit of his dark eyes, before he realized he was leaking information. He schooled his face and stance, doffed his hat and shook my had graciously.

"Miss Chamberlain, delighted to meet you at last. I've heard so much about you, all of it good." He smiled; there was a hint of gold inset into his upper left canine that went with the wolf's eyes and the Windsor knotted silk tie.

"So you are Guy's boss, Mr. Dugdale. I've heard very little about you. My brother can be the soul of discretion where his work is concerned. Lovely to meet you, sir."

I turned to my brother, "Guy, can you move that parcel into the back of the car for me? It's something I got for Pa. I think he'll like it. No, don't unwrap it, there's a love, I'll never get it so tidy again."

I watched as my brother struggled fitting the statue into the boot/rumble seat, then smiled up at Mr. Dugdale. "So nice to have met you, Mr. Dugdale. You will forgive us rushing off, but we've a long way to go. Goodbye." We shook hands, as did he and Guy, before he hailed a taxi and climbed in. Wherever he was going, he'd be in for a shock.

"Got Nigel's cash, then, Guy?" I asked, as he settled in the passenger seat, clutching his briefcase to his chest.

"Oh yes, Alice. Do you know, I'm quite looking forward to tonight."

"Good. Can I come along?"

"I'm surprised you asked," he replied. "You normally suit yourself."

"True. Your boss," I said. "I'd never even known his name before..."

"Did I not tell you? I must have forgotten." But it came out awkwardly, and I knew he had been told to keep quiet.

"So what's he like? As a boss, as a person, as an asset to the bank?" I wondered.

"Hey, Al, you ask a lot. I heard you tell him I was the soul of discretion." He pulled out a packet of Senior Service and helped himself to one. "You don't mind?"

"No. Go ahead."

"Still off them?"

I nodded, and waited while he lit up and inhaled.

Then he turned and said, "Let's put it this way, he's not my favorite person by a long chalk. But here's something odd, Alice. I was going past his office this morning. Normally the place is as silent as a tomb – there's talk, obviously, but it's quiet, respectable, discreet, you know, a sort of hushed reverence for being in a temple to money. But as I passed, I heard him shouting down the telephone at someone. Well, I couldn't let that go by without eavesdropping, could I? It's amazing how long it takes to retie a shoelace sometimes."

"Good for you, Guy," I chuckled. "What was he saying?"

"Well, I don't know who he was talking to, but he was pretty irate, voice raised in anger and annoyance, I'd say, and what I actually heard was this: 'If you've got a problem with it, then sell it. Sell it all. Get rid of it and we'll say no more about it. It's brought nothing but trouble and you're just adding to it. Get rid of it.' I don't think he was talking about stocks and shares or a working company. You just wouldn't do that to a client, would you? You'd be out on your ear without a reference!"

I smiled. "Would you be prepared to sign an affidavit to that effect? Swear to that in a legal situation?" I asked.

Guy choked on his cigarette, then beamed at me. "Oh, Alice, would I! Oh yes, yes, yes!"

# 29

I dropped Nigel and Guy at the Wethersley Arms around half past seven; they set up in the public bar, which was already busy and full of tobacco smoke. I left them to it, then went round the back to the kitchen where May was busy on sandwich duty.

"Can I come in, May?" I asked, tapping on the open door. It was a warm evening.

She looked up and smiled. "Of course you can. Your brother and Nigel here, then?"

I stepped over the threshold into the low room and joined her at the table. "Yes, just setting up. Do you want a hand? I don't suppose you want me in the Public."

"I think the rules are relaxed this evening. There are women owed money, too. In fact there are more women owed than men. I hope they'll all be hungry after they've been paid."

I sat beside her and scraped butter on then off slices of bread while she filled them with ham paste and pickles. She was a warm person, rosy-cheeked, wrapped in a floral crossover overall and headscarf, like Mrs. Green's, but her grey curls were not so easily constrained.

"So what's new up at Wethersley?" she asked.

"You tell me. You have the great detective here."

She sniffed. "Your Pa and Ma looked a bit more jaunty than they have been when they popped in here for a drink today, so I guess things are looking up for them."

"Yes. But they still don't have the murderer. Or should I say executioner?"

She shuddered. "Oh, don't say that, Miss Alice. It fair gives me the creeps. Things like that don't happen around here, shouldn't happen anywhere."

"No, perhaps they shouldn't. On another subject, what do you know about Cissie Laycock?"

"Cissie? Oh, poor little scrap. Buried her last winter, yes, just before Christmas, I think. Such a waste of a life, for all she was pregnant. Oops, shouldn't have said that!"

She stopped her spreading and looked me in the face. "You didn't hear that from me, by the bye, but that's the gossip, and very much off the record, if you know what's good for you. The way she was beaten up! Horrible! She didn't stand a chance, a gust of wind would have blown her away. They never caught the chap who did it, either. Surprised me, that. Why'd you ask?"

"Someone said her name somewhere, and I couldn't place the family," I said vaguely. "They from Marsham?"

"Of course; you'll find them all in the graveyard there. She was the last of them, apart from Billy, her Dad. They looked after each other; her Mum died when she was about six, and they only had each other. And of course the Brooms kept an eye on them; you'll be knowing them?"

"I've come across them."

May looked up from her work. "Billy Laycock married Elsie Broom, that's the sister of Les Broom's dad and Joe Broom's dad. It's quite a large family, and they're very close, if you get my meaning. Cross one, cross all, great to have on your side, but the very devil if they've taken against you. Be warned, Miss Alice."

"I'll remember that, May. Thank you."

"Now, Billy Laycock was gardener up at Marsham Court since the year dot. He got Cissie a job there before she even finished school, she must have started when she was about twelve. I heard she was very good, could be relied upon to do whatever was required and do it well. She often came home with extra cash or presents from the visitors, and the Nesmith-Browns were always having visitors."

Oh dear, I thought.

May caught my face. "Yes. That crossed my mind, too. Particularly afterwards. I mean, it's not something that would enter your mind if you'd seen her. You'd never believe she was pushing sixteen when she died. She had the body of a ten year old, but I suppose it was developing, because she couldn't have got pregnant if it weren't ready. She was such a skinny little slip of a thing, great big eyes, pale pale skin and bones like a bird's."

"'A wondrous waif'" I quoted.

"Yes, Miss Alice, that's exactly what she was. Poor little girl," she wiped her hands on a tea towel and began piling sandwiches

175

on two large platters. "You staying for a drink?"

"I'll have one when I come back for Guy and Nigel," I said. "I'll go and say goodbye to Cissie. Thanks, May. I didn't realize it would make me feel so sad."

"Then cut a few roses off for her from me, too. Let her know she's remembered – and forgiven. Though there's nothing to forgive, is there? She just got unlucky."


I drove through the golden summer evening in the Citroen with a deep melancholy upon me. I knew what the Nesmith-Browns were capable of, and the thought of another child being lured into their sordid circle sickened me.

Marsham church was on a slight rise at the north end of the village, which had grown up beside the little river, a tributary of the Thames. The tower, square and gray was the only visible part as it was hedged all round by dark yews.

A beautifully-maintained Pre-War Humber Super Snipe was parked hard beside the lychgate, not a car I'd have expected to see around here, and, as I drew up beside it, Les Broom came out from the churchyard, followed by an older slighter man, in working clothes, and opened the driver's door.

I stepped out of the Citroen.

"Well met, Milady!" Les greeted, ever flash. "Just who I wanted to see. Is that lad of yours down at the Arms, because Uncle Billy needs his wages."

"He is. I'd get there fast, if I were you, there's a fair crowd up there."

He smiled. "Then what are you doing round here?"

"Keeping away from the tobacco smoke, it makes my eyes water. But I'll be going back to pick the boys up later."

"Then I will be delighted to buy you a drink, Milady. Come on, Uncle Billy, let's get what's owed you. I'm dying for a pint."

The little man climbed into the passenger seat and I waved them off. Then I went round to my passenger seat and picked up the little bunch of deep red scented rambling roses, and ducked beneath the lychgate.

The cold hit me.

The churchyard was in shadow, the yews keeping all the low golden warmth out.

I wandered around, peering at gravestones, I had no idea where the Laycocks were buried, and I wished I had a cardigan. The grass was longer than it should be, and running to seed, interspersed with purple knapweed and creamy yarrow, tall daisies and soft blue devil's bit scabious. Bats were already out hunting the late flying insects in this dark place, whereas in the evening sunshine beyond the yews the swifts and swallows still held sway in the aerobatic displays.

Sometime later I found the Laycock graves well hidden in a quiet chilly corner between the north transept and the chancel. On one was a cheap pottery vase filled with a bunch of fragrant white roses and jasmine.

I read the latest inscription. 'Cecilia Mary Laycock, born 20th November 1930, died 1st November 1946, a flower who failed to bloom.'

I wanted to cry.

I stood for a while thinking of what I knew about her – which was precious little – and knew she didn't deserve this, then knelt and interspersed my deep red blooms with the white flowers in the vase.

"This is from me, Cissie, you don't know me, but I'm getting to know you, and from May at the Wethersley Arms. She wants you to know that you are remembered with love, and you are forgiven for whatever sin you think you committed. We both feel you were greatly wronged. The person who did this is dead, too. But I expect you know that. Wherever you are, Cissie Laycock, rest in peace." I kissed the Abraxas ring on my right forefinger and pressed my hand on her name, tears running down my face.

As I rose to my feet, I heard a sigh, I swear it, but it could have been the wind.

Wiping my eyes, I made my way as swiftly as I could to the lychgate and the light. I passed through and the living warmth fell golden on my bare arms. It was good to be back to the real world again.

I thought about Cissie on my way back to the pub. She died on the first of November last.

Would her father have tried to kill John Anselm-Jones?

Would he have had access to a gun, particularly a German pistol?

No reason why he should, but then again, he might have, and of course, he had family.

I had Nigel's word that Archie Meredith was at Marsham Court, and had told him to forget he had ever seen John Anselm-Jones there in November, although he knew he had been.

But Archie and John Anselm-Jones were friends, as were the Nesmith-Browns, even if they were all less than pure white.

Archie had told Jeremy and me that if people got in his way, well, they might have to be removed. He and Percy had threatened us in such a way before Lady Finching killed the pair of them.

I parked beside the pub, still juggling people with means, motives and opportunities, and went in.

Guy and Nigel were putting away their receipts in the now empty cash-box. Sam was with them, and came across to meet me. "Alice, I've been looking for you," he greeted me, "What will you have?"

"Hello Sam! A half of shandy would be lovely."

From his stool by the bar, Les Broom, waved and made drinking signs. I went across. "Sam's getting me this one, but I'm sure I can join you for a while afterwards," I said.

"I'll look forward to it," he said. "And be careful what you say to that one," he nodded at Sam. "It'll be in the local papers in no time."

Sam looked at him with a frown as Larry pulled our drinks.

"Just telling Milady you're good at your job, eh? No offense."

Sam's face softened. "None taken, Mr. Broom."

"Oh, it's Les, my friends call me Les, and any friend of Milady's is a friend of mine."

I was about to say you may regret that, Les, I have some friends that might do you a disservice, but Sam handed me my drink, so I raised it, and said, "Cheers, gents," and took a draw. Sam and Les did likewise.

I turned to Sam. "I made Les's acquaintance at the cricket match," I said. "He was scoring like a demon."

They both relaxed, having something in common to talk about, and I wandered back to Guy and Nigel, who were drinking up free beer.

"Where did you get to, Alice?" asked Guy.

"Couldn't deal with the smoke. Went to help May with the sandwiches. Do you want a lift back?"

"Not yet, we're just starting to enjoy ourselves," Guy said, as Nigel handed him another pint and a plate of sandwiches.

"I need to be back by a quarter to ten," I said.

"OK, Alice. We'll be ready by half nine, I need to be back for work tomorrow."

I went back to Sam and Les Broom, where the last match was being discussed, and sat, listening. It was refreshing to hear men talking about something normal, a shared interest, with enthusiasm.

Behind Les, his uncle, Billy, was slowly counting out his cash, stashing it about his person in various pockets. He smiled, patting it, as he did so, then pulled a stub of a roll-up from behind his ear, and carefully lit it with a Vesta. Les Broom heard the noise, and turned back to him.

"You ready for another, Uncle Billy?" he asked. "And you, Milady? Sam?" then called the order to Larry, waving a ten shilling note.

He was paying for the beer when an angry Scottish whirlwind forced himself between Les and Sam, Sergeant Stonehouse stood behind me. "Mr. Broom, a word in your ear, please."

"Certainly, Chief Inspector. Nothing you can't say here, though. I'm among friends."

"I hope you are, Mr. Broom. Are you the possessor of a large green Luton lorry, registration no... "

My ears almost left my head. I listened to the number and knew it at once. The one I had given to Leggy last Friday.

"If you've done your homework properly, Chief Inspector, you will know that I am. What is it supposed to have done? I assure you it's been in the garage having its engine sorted since last Thursday. I only got it back this morning. The mechanics will bear me out."

"I've no doubt they will, Mr. Broom. I'll be checking with them. Which garage?"

"A1 at Amersham, Chief Inspector. So what's up? What have you got that you'd like to pin on me, eh? Look, why don't you sit down and have a drink. There's no need to stand there fuming and thirsty. Sergeant Stonehouse, can I stand you a pint too?"

Sam and I shifted along so the detectives could get to the bar. Larry poured a couple of pints and handed them across.

"So you weren't in London in your lorry last Friday?"

"Not me, Chief Inspector. I was here, well, not exactly here, but you know, in the area. Out and about. Doing this and that, as you do." His voice was casual, slow, almost mocking.

"Anyone see you?" asked Chief Inspector Murray.

"Lots of people, I should imagine. I'm quite memorable."

"I've no doubt. So you weren't in London on Friday, and your lorry was in the garage? Do you know, Mr. Broom, I'm not sure I can believe that. I have witnesses..."

"Then bring them to me, and let them tell it to my face. I was here. The lorry was in the A1, that's how it was. I'll drop my diary in to you tomorrow morning. OK? Now, let's just have a nice friendly drink, eh? Cheers, gents, bottoms up."

He raised his glass and gave the police a grin before downing his half in one and calling for another.

I finished my drink and stood up. The bar was good and lively, but I'd heard enough. "See you, Larry. Enjoy your evening. Lovely to have met you Mr. Broom, but I've an appointment." I looked at Sam meaningfully.

"You off so soon, Milady? I don't blame you. You deserve better than the Public Bar," Les told me, with a grin. "Off you go, and enjoy yourself. You off too, Sam? Well lucky you! And don't forget to come down to the cricket club, eh? We can use all the help we can get." He gave us both a wink.

Guy and Nigel were playing darts now. I told them I'd be outside in the car when they were ready.

Sam joined me outside shortly after. "What was that about?" he asked. "Was it something Chief Inspector Murray did?"

I shook my head. "No, it wasn't."

"So?"

"Sam, this is strictly under wraps. If I level with you, not a word to anyone, promise?"

"Not till you give me permission," he said, doing a boy scout salute.

"Good. Then let me tell you that I know for a fact that last Friday afternoon Les Broom's lorry was in London. I don't know who was driving it, but I followed it from the rear of a John

Anselm-Jones business, fully laden, to what I imagine was thought a place of safety in Putney."

Sam whistled softly. "So Les Broom knows John Anselm-Jones?"

"Don't know. He could simply know the business front man – John Anselm-Jones kept very much in the background. But that lorry was not in the A1 Garage at Amersham when Les said it was."

"I'll check on the way home," Sam said. "I need to fill up."

"Have you got anything for me?"

"Cissie Broom; I checked with the Registrar at the hospital and the County Coroner. She actually died of wounds inflicted by what looked like a good beating, but she had also, very recently, had an abortion, which was turning nasty. She wouldn't have made it either way," Sam said sadly. "Do you know who the man was who caused this? She was too far gone to say when she was brought in."

"Not got chapter and verse, but I suspect it was Mr. John Anselm-Jones, alias Edgar Winthrop. He was known to fancy, and I quote his name for young girls: "wondrous waifs"."

"Oh Hell!" Sam cursed.

"So he will have made some enemies round here," I said.

"I'll say. But he will have made enemies wherever he went, I should imagine, if he was predatory on young girls. People are very protective of their daughters, and rightly so."

"Not always, sadly," I said, remembering Sylvia Nesmith-Brown. She was encouraged, groomed for sexual stardom by the Merediths and her parents. And in other cultures, where there was hunger and life was cheap... I was so lucky to have such a privileged existence.

I wondered whether Uncle Edgar had ever been seduced by Sylvia's charms, despite what Nigel believed. He was, after all, by his own admission, away at school for a lot of the time.

Sam pulled out a briar and filled it with tobacco, took his time lighting it, then said, "Murray is looking for the Nesmith-Browns, now. Did you know?"

"No, Sam, thank you. I doubt he'll find them. They seem to be pretty good at slipping the traces and disappearing into the wide blue yonder, according to Nigel."

"Yes, so he said." So he'd spoken to Nigel.

"I don't see Algy Nesmith-Brown as a murderer, certainly not an executioner," I said, breathing in the aromatic smoke that was curling, blue in the evening light, from Sam's briar. "He's a coward and probably a bully. Blackmail, yes, I can see that, and confidence tricks, swindles, no problem, but not murder."

"But no-one knows what a person is capable of if the situation requires drastic measures," said Sam. "The war taught us that."

I wished he hadn't said that. I had killed – it was that or be killed and at that point, I was very keen on staying alive and keeping my friends alive, too, so I did what had to be done. I hadn't enjoyed doing it, and I never wanted to go through it again. The memory came back with a jolt, and I forced it back down under layers of rationalism, but I still wake up shuddering and guilty from time to time.

"I don't think Algy was combatant," I said at last.

"Nor in the first war," Sam said. "I checked. And I'm with you. He'd hurt or harm, swindle or blackmail, from what I've heard, but killing in peace-time is a hanging offense, and I don't see him stupid enough to risk that. And he'd keep his nose as clean as possible, let others do the dirty work."

"What could John Anselm-Jones have been doing? And who the hell dug him up, and why?" I mused. My brain was going round in circles again.

Sam puffed at his pipe again, sending out another cloud of fragrant smoke. I sniffed at it. I could have murdered a cigarette. I thought of Jeremy in Paris, then checked my watch. It was twenty past nine, and I'd a date with him at ten.

"Sam, could you go in and remind Guy and Nigel that I'm here. I need to get home for an early night and I can't legitimately see Les Broom again."

"Of course. Although he thinks I'm with you."

I chuckled. "You are a reporter, you can go anywhere at any time with anyone you choose," I said.

# 30

Pa, Maman and Angelique were listening to the radio when I got in. "How did it go?" they asked.

"Very well. But it's raised some further questions," I said.

Guy and Nigel entered with a wooden crate of bottled beer, faces wreathed in smiles. "A drop of Larry's best," Guy said. "So you can share our success."

"Everyone else will join us, yes?" Nigel asked.

There were three assents. I checked my watch. "Just a small one, then, Nigel, then I'm for my nest. It's been a long day."

I managed to reach my bedroom shortly before ten, and did a calming, the way Elisabeth had taught me. When I was centered I lit a candle and held my Abraxas ring in its light.

It was so nice to be alone, or rather, away from the outside world in my own quiet space.

I took a few deep breaths, let my gaze drift over the room, and the treetops, dark against the afterglow of sunset, and felt at peace.

Silently I thought about Jeremy, and called his name. I could see him, in my mind's eye, sitting at a table in the same hôtel room, jacket off, with a pen and pad beside him. He was more organized than me.

I heard my name – in my head, of course, or even in my imagination – and felt a great welling wave of love. So for a while, I did nothing but bask in it and return it. And then, I got thoughts whipping through my consciousness.

"Alice, the rings are special. They really do open doors. I was wearing it yesterday, and a someone in our service approached me. When I mentioned Lord Finching he nodded, and said he knew Thorburn and his daughter, whom he held in high regard. He said the rings don't belong to people, they choose their owners. I know, a bit airy-fairy, but he taught me how to use it. I know you're getting this, but it doesn't matter, I'll put it in the post to you."

I could sense all this, and particularly the overwhelming excitement that he could communicate clearly this way. I must admit, it was pretty amazing. I could hear him, in my head, almost as though he was in the same room. I hoped he was receiving as well as transmitting.

Jeremy, I asked, have you seen Sylvia? Do you know where her parents are?

No. I got your letter today. I'm glad Roger's off the hook. I miss you all so much, but things are very interesting here. Will tell you all when we meet, but … I can't keep this up. I just need to tell you I love you.

And again I was swept up in a huge wave of love for some half minute, and then it was gone.

I set the ring back on the desk, and came down to earth with a thump. Despite the warm night I was suddenly cold and shaking.

Whatever he was doing, he was doing it right. And perhaps I was, too.

I knew from my last foray into magic that I had to get back to the here and now as soon as possible, so slipped my warm dressing gown over my clothes and headed for the kitchen.

Never had warm milk and biscuits tasted so good!

Back in my room, I went through the experience, and made notes. Then I made notes on what I'd learned today. They were necessarily brief. I set the alarm for 6.30, then turned the light out.

But before I went to sleep, I did another call to Jeremy, just for the hell of it. It settled me nicely.

I hope it did the same for him.

## 31

Tuesday morning and I was back in Chelsea. I'd dropped my brother off at his digs at eight, then went for a swim at Chelsea Baths. The rhythmic movement of the strokes as I did the twenty-five lengths gave me time to think.

Guy and Nigel were happy with their work of the previous night. They had paid all the back wages owed and put a few extra pounds in, but what they couldn't do was replace the jobs that were no longer there.

It had been a sharp reminder lesson to them both.

Neither had ever really wanted for money, any more than I had, but we were all from the privileged classes and had no dependents. The villagers who 'did for' the nobs like us were in a very different situation, and any and all work would be considered, for there were young families to feed. Guy had suddenly been brought face to face with the reality of what needed to be done, and he had talked and talked all the way into town. He, we, needed a project that would provide work and stability for those people. He had talked with Pa, Maman and Angelique late into the previous night.

"Does this mean you'll be changing your mind about making your fortune in the bank?" I asked.

"If we can get the right project, I can do both," he said. "The bank will finance the right project, I'm sure."

"Just make sure it is the right project," I told him as I dropped him off. "And watch out for Mr. Ferdy Dugdale."

Leggy had his door open as the black metal lift rattled to a halt. I followed him into the flat. His sitting room was piled high with files, ledgers and boxes.

"There's tea in the pot, Alice, help yourself and find a place to sit, this is all the paperwork from Nutfield Lodge. We're in for a long day."

"Did you empty the secret drawer?" I asked, pouring myself half a cup of very black tea and topping it up from the hot water jug.

"In the bureau or the one behind the bookcase?"

Ah, so I couldn't teach my grandma to suck eggs.

I settled in at the dining table and dipped randomly into the box in front of me.

A card index on a spiral, one of several, with a bakelite semi-circular cover, marked E-K. I opened it and flicked through the cards, expecting to find business contacts and useful firms – tailors, office suppliers, the odd restaurant – such as Mr. Lowther had on his desk.

The first card was just such a one: Eastmann Photographers, of Charing Cross Road, with the contact name Willie. Then came Easy Printers, Victoria, Herman, and Eccleston Wines in a Mews off Eccleston Square, and Bumble. Nothing odd about that lot, and I saw someone (hopefully not me!) having to contact all these people. It could be a job for life!

I flicked over the next card and gasped.

Leggy heard me. "What have you found, Alice?"

"Edward and Wallis, Duke and Duchess of Windsor," I said. "A lot of crossings out on their addresses, but there is a Paris address and phone number." And a funny little sign there, too, in the top right corner, red ink originally crossed through several times with more red. A bit indistinct - probably an over-drawn doodle.

"So what's the surprise? You knew they were friends. The watch, my dear. Keep going."

So I kept going. And by half past ten I had found quite a few more of the great and the good of Britain, some names I knew personally, including my father's old friend, Padraig Flynn, the artist, who had, I believed, a few secrets he didn't want bruited abroad, and all with odd little red inked squiggles at the top right. I flicked through the index again, removing these cards, then started on A-D.

More red squiggles. I extracted them. And when I reached C, there was Pa, Roger Chamberlain, Lord Wethersley, artist, Wethersley, Bucks.

"Leggy, Pa's in here," I said. "But no red squiggle by his name."

"Obviously not important enough," he said, with a grin. "Be grateful."

"But Padraig Flynn is."

Leggy looked up, suddenly interested. "Who else?" he barked.

I read the cards out, starting with the Windsors. Leggy listened attentively now. When I came to a halt he nodded. "Good work, Alice. I guessed as much. Keep going. I want every one of those squiggles out, then we'll be getting somewhere."

He was my boss, war-time and current. I wasn't going to ask why, although I would have liked to have been privy to his thoughts. I fairly whizzed through the rest of that spiral, and the two others, L-R and S-Z.

We spread the cards out across the table, now cleared of extraneous boxes and files.

"What do you notice about these people?" Leggy asked.

"Most of them are well-off?" I hazarded. "Not Padraig, perhaps, and the last I heard Algy Nesmith-Brown was not exactly flush."

Leggy nodded. "What about the others?"

I gazed at the random spread of cards and that was just what it looked like, a random spread. "Some good names there, I suppose. He moved in high circles, nothing we didn't know already."

"Padraig Flynn, young lady!"

"Soldiers of the Dawn," I said.

Padraig headed that secret organisation and had been after the angels as much as the Merediths had. I liked Padraig, and since he had taken up with another of Pa's old artist friends, Emily Shotton-Fell, I liked him more. She had brought out the more caring side of his nature.

As to the Soldiers of the Dawn, the run-ins I'd had with the few I knew of, Padraig apart, had been unpleasant, but I still had little idea of their ideological standpoint, apart from the fact that there was some ceremonial involved. Leggy and Bobby knew far more but were very tight-lipped about them. I knew that the Soldiers of the Dawn wanted the angels that Jeremy and I had recovered from various 'safe' houses to be restored to their rightful place in the church of St Michael and All Angels, which Reverend Simmons served, but what their purpose was for the angels I still didn't know. And I couldn't find out from Padraig, couldn't let on I knew of Padraig's involvement with them, although he did wear their badge on the dashboard of his car. If I ever got a lift from him, I'd ask, out of 'female nosiness'.

"Tell me about them," I asked.

"Right wing. Far right, Alice. I might even go so far as to say Fascist. Look at the rest of the names..."

"You mean Nazi tendencies?" Surely not Padraig? But I'd keep an open mind.

Leggy puffed on his pipe, which had gone out again. "Let's say there feels to be a German connection..."

I looked again at the names. Certainly Edward Windsor had family connections with Germany, several top families had. When Victoria had married Albert, Germany was our friend. And the Nesmith-Browns visited there before the war, according to Nigel. But, although it was unpatriotic, certainly at the start of hostilities lots of people had thought Hitler was right, were, and always would be anti-semitic, racist, and thought that Order was All, Might was Right, and wanted to hang on to their deeply-held nationalistic values, that they saw being undermined not just by the working classes and Jews, but by Communism too.

"What do you make of the squiggles?" I said. "What was he trying to hide?"

Leggy puffed his pipe back to life then delved in his waistcoat pocket for a magnifying glass. He held it over the card with Edward Windsor written on it and focused over the scrubbed out mark.

Enlarged it looked very different.

Under the overscoring you could just make out a tiny crown topped by a swastika.

# 32

A Nazi king?

Or possibly a king controlled by Nazis.

If Hitler had won?

And Mrs. Simpson would have been his Queen, of course she would. He would have insisted, and Hitler would have assented to such a small thing, for a puppet king. I shuddered at the thought.

What about the rest?

Would they have got sinecure jobs? Would there have been rewards for favors rendered?

I took the magnifying glass and picked up cards at random. All of them had the Swastika symbol more or less scribbled over.

Leggy watched me, sitting back in his chair, puffing clouds of aromatic twisting smoke upwards to the nicotine stained ceiling. "Someone else did the scrubbing out," he said. "Not very thoroughly, either. Do you think it was Mr. Parsons? In a panic?"

I thought for a moment. "Do you think he, John Anselm-Jones, was blackmailing these people? Only there are quite a few..."

"And they wouldn't take kindly to it," Leggy mused. "Perhaps blackmail is too strong a word. Let's suggest a calling in of favors for his continued silence."

"Sooner or later, one of them will not be able to pay up," I said. "Or unwilling."

"True. And sooner or later one, or several, or even all of them, if they knew what was going on, would take it into their heads to free themselves from his demands."

"These are powerful families, they would have the motive and the means."

"I'm sure they could find the opportunity, Alice. So who were the nearest to the grave?"

"Oops!"

"Indeed. Which is why I find it odd that Nigel should have

been the one to find it. He must have known it was there, whether he was party to the killing, or indeed the revealing, or not. I'll have another word with the boy. He talks to me." Leggy put his pipe down and pointed to the spiral card index. "Find his bank, Alice, or banks, will you?"

I flicked through the indices. There were several banks listed, but the first that turned up was Bathurst's in the City.

Leggy smirked.

I gave him the contact names: Jellicoe and Dugdale.

He smirked even more. "I will have a little word with Mr. Jellicoe," he said, hauling the telephone towards him. "As a fellow Freemason, don't you know?"

The smell in the bank was one of old ledgers mixed with metal polish and cigar smoke. Beneath the high ceiling motes of dust floated in the sunlight pouring in through the high narrow windows. There was the sound of silence, of, I fancifully thought, money growing.

My heels clacked and echoed on the black and white marble tiled floor as Leggy and I were shepherded by Mr. Jellicoe, in morning suit and starched wing collar, past the silent row of tellers behind brass screens, to the body of the bank, past the offices of minions towards his own inner sanctum.

Up the wide staircase with more bright brass-work, along a dark corridor punctured by tall oak doors, one of which bore my brother's name, another, Mr. F Dugdale, we finally came upon Mr. Jellicoe's office. He seated us and ordered tea, "Or something stronger?" he suggested to Leggy.

Leggy shook his head. "Need to keep a clear head, Henry," he said.

"Exactly so," agreed the portly bank manager.

"So can you help us?" Leggy asked. "I know it's a lot to ask..."

Mr. Jellicoe smiled. "It's more than a lot to ask, Colonel. I would be in breach of the bank regulations..."

I noticed the 'would'; I waited for him to continue.

"... if the man were alive." He looked at us over the top of his gold wire-framed spectacles. "Mr. Dugdale was his contact here. Would you like me to fetch him?"

Leggy shook his head fiercely. "No, no, we'd rather work just with you, Henry," he said.

Mr. Jellicoe nodded and smiled. "Might be just as well, Colonel." He was about to say something else but thought better of it. "So. Strictly within these walls, sub rosa and all that... Mrs. Carson? Colonel?"

I put my finger to my lips and nodded. Leggy did likewise.

Mr. Jellicoe led us to a door at the far end of his office and pressed a button. The door drew back to reveal a small modern lift. We went down three floors.

When we got out we were beside a large door, steel-clad with another lift to our right, beside which was a small sturdy two-tiered trolley.

Mr. Jellicoe opened the door, first with a key from his waistcoat pocket, then with a combination code which he dialed in behind his hand.

Within was a room filled with numbered boxes, floor to ceiling. He had John Anselm-Jones's details and found the box at once. Opening the door with a smaller key he delved within and found a large deeds box, which he withdrew with some difficulty.

"It's suprisingly heavy," he said. "You couldn't get the trolley?"

I brought it in, and with Leggy's help he tipped the box gently onto it, shut the door and hustled us back through the vault door, locking it carefully behind him while we put ourselves and the trolley in the lift, then squeezed in himself.

On reaching his office he dialed his secretary on the internal telephone. "Mrs. Naylor? Thank you for the tea. Now would you cancel all appointments for the next hour or so? I'll get back to you at let's say half past three."

The deed box was on his desk. We all looked at it and then at each other. What we were about to do was breach of trust, but under the circumstances...

Leggy nodded at Mr. Jellicoe who humphed and took another tiny key from his pocket, and muttered something about being the executor anyway, and fitted it into the lock. It scraped slightly, then sprang open.

I crowded forward. Mr. Jellicoe looked in then whistled softly.

"I didn't expect this," he breathed. "Lend a hand, Colonel, if you will."

What came out, between the two pairs of elderly hands, shone gloriously under the desk lamp. They laid it carefully upon the blotter, and we all gawped.

Before us was a brick of purest gold, an ingot so shiny and wondrous that it lifted your spirits. I had never seen gold bullion before. Any gold I had known personally was small scale for personal adornment. This was different. It was somewhat smaller than a house brick and solid through and through. No wonder it was heavy.

Impressed into it was the double-headed eagle.

"There's another one," Leggy said.

"Good heavens! I'd no idea. Where did he get these from?" Mr. Jellicoe wondered.

"Don't ask," I said.

These were almost certainly once personal adornments, stolen from anyone whose face didn't fit the ideology, and melted down. I felt a deep wave of sadness, pain, melancholy and sorrow rise over me and dropped into a chair, overcome.

The two men had the second gold bar out, and now were bringing forth envelopes.

"If they're open, you can read what's inside," Mr. Jellicoe said. "I can't let you open them if they are sealed."

Leggy eyed him appraisingly. "I think we are talking national security here, not the legal rights of a corpse," he said softly.

"Let me clear it with the Directors, Colonel, please?"

"Of course. I don't want to get you in hot water. But the fewer who know, the better."

"Mrs. Carson, would you pour the tea?" Mr. Jellicoe asked, nodding to a table and chairs at the far side of the room where a tea tray stood.

"Of course. Milk and sugar?"

I was glad to have something to do. The gold had disturbed me.

I wanted to know what was in the envelopes, but the gold was enough to link John Anselm-Jones to the Nazis, and I was sure that the papers would confirm it. I carefully poured three cups of tea, two with milk and sugar, and kept my own black.

I was so busy with my own raging thoughts that I didn't register the telephone conversation. It would be the old boys' act, and I knew we'd get permission from the Director when I saw Leggy take the handset and greet the person on the other end jovially as an old friend.

Public schools, eh?

He handed the receiver back to Mr. Jellicoe with a satisfied nod, and came over. "Well done, Sally. I could murder a cup."

We sipped tea together while Mr. Jellicoe finished his call and fished in his drawer whence he brought out a disclaimer sheet. "You'll sign this for me, Colonel? Just in case!"

He took his tea, and looked at each of us with a mischievous twist to his rather dour face. "Nazi gold, eh? Who would have thought it? And at today's prices..."

I watched the calculations go round his face and the smile broaden. "... a pretty penny!" He downed the tea in one, put the cup back in the saucer on the tray and made for the box on his desk. "So what other dark secrets did Mr. Anselm-Jones have hidden away in my vault?"

There were documents, in both German and English, formal and informal. The German was lost on me. I could order a meal and ask for a room, the bathroom and say please and thank you in that language should I ever have occasion to do so, and that was about it. I left that to Leggy and Mr. Jellicoe who both had a far greater knowledge of that language than I did. They were bubbling with excitement.

"This is dynamite!" Mr. Jellicoe breathed, then lapsed back into German.

"Good God," Leggy muttered. "This is far worse than I thought."

I picked up a sheet note-paper that had fallen to the floor in the excitement. It was fine deckel-edged, with an embossed address at the top: Berchtesgadener Hof Hôtel. Below was a list of names, familiar names, with Edward Windsor and Mrs. Simpson at the head, those I'd read earlier in the day.

Not guests, but 'Friends of the Reich', to be rewarded.

It was signed, Adolf Hitler.

I nudged Leggy's arm.

Passed the sheet to him.

Very definitely the stuff of blackmail.

## 33

It had to go higher up. It couldn't go to Chief Inspector Murray. It was, as Mr. Jellicoe said, dynamite.

"Thank you, Al .. Mrs. Carson," Leggy said.

Mr. Jellicoe eyed the list. "I'm leaving this in your hands, Colonel," he said. "I want nothing to do with it. Some of these are my clients."

"Let me consider what action should be taken, if any," Leggy said. "I will confer and get back to you, Henry, if that suits you?"

"That would be perfect, Colonel. I'll see you out, then put things back as they were," Mr. Jellicoe said, shaking our hands and hustling us to the door. "So lovely to have done business with you Colonel Legge, Mrs. Carson."

As he led us down the corridor, my brother Guy came out of his office. I froze. Made a minute shake of my head at him.

Guy's jaw dropped.

"Don't just stand there, Chamberlain, the Colonel and Mrs. Carson are leaving. Perhaps you could see them down for me? I'm rather pressed at the moment."

Guy stood to attention. "Of course, sir, a pleasure. Come this way, sir and madam," he said.

Mr. Jellicoe hustled back into his sanctum while Guy led us swiftly down the stairs and out through the main hall to the front door.

"What's happening?" he asked in an undertone as we crossed the black and white tiles. "Dugdale's all of a twitter, was supposed to see Jellicoe and then it was canceled."

"Nothing that need concern you at present, Guy," said Leggy. "Mrs. Carson here will be interested to learn what happens to him, don't you know!" he tapped his nose.

"Oh... er... Of course. Nice to have met you Colonel, Mrs. Carson," he said, opening the front door for us and shaking our hands formally.

"Nice to have met you, too, Mr.... er ... Chamberlain, wasn't it?" I replied wickedly.

The traffic was thick outside, the afternoon warm and heavy.

"What now?" I asked.

"I need to think, and to see some people," said Leggy. "If you really want you can go and help Bobby and his friends cataloging in the warehouse. But I think we've done enough today. Take the rest of the afternoon off, Alice. You've earned it."

So I went home, back to the flat, where I picked up my mail – an airmail from France - and ripped it open, reading avidly.

Jeremy didn't disappoint.

He had been at various functions, official and otherwise, where he had met the Windsors briefly, 'I hadn't realized they were so short, Alice, or so dismissive – but I was H.M.'s government and I suppose they were a bit miffed with us', and Sylvia and her jewel-dealer Felix at greater length. She was besotted by the Windsors and had taken to wearing 'Wallis blue' although, he added acerbically, it didn't match her eyes any more than it matched Mrs. Simpson's. He drew a little sketch of the three of them dining at Le Crillon. Well, lucky you!, I thought as I read their menu. 'Not bad for a lad from Southport. I owe it all to you, Alice. I got my knives and forks right and used my napkin correctly, didn't bring politics or religion into the conversation, and behaved most decorously, which is more than could be said for Felix who told several dirty jokes with the brandy while massaging Sylvia's thighs. He's quite old, but besotted by her. I think Sylvia's done very well for herself. I hope it works.'

What a romantic! But I hoped it worked too, in a way. It would keep her out of the country, and a jewel dealer must have access to enough of the readies to keep even Sylvia's material needs satisfied.

I read on. 'I've made some good contacts, not just useful, but some really nice people, which is real bonus - I hope you'll like them when you meet them. Meantime, in haste, I love you, keep safe. See you on the inner tonight.' Then an inky thumb print with a capital J scrawled over it and in brackets in fine cursive script 'Jeremy Arkwright, his mark' and a line of kisses.

I looked at the clock. The little car was at Leggy's, so I walked back there to get some fresh air and pick it up. Then I drove to the warehouse, and knocked on the closed door.

Bobby Gallagher opened it, grinned widely and welcomed me in. "Are you looking for anything particular, Milady? We can do you a magnificent deal on Regency furniture."

I chuckled. "You're not selling that yet, are you?"

"For the right price," he said, locking the door behind me. "And I'd do a special price for you, don't you know?"

"I am looking for something, actually, Bobby. A Book of Hours." I sniffed in the musty air. It really wasn't a good place to store quality items.

"And that would be?"

I pulled out the Curé's letter, "An old book, tooled leather, with jewels inset, filled with illuminated prayers, and pictures. Made around five hundred years ago. Have you seen it, Bobby?"

His face creased into a frown. "What is it with you, Milady? First it was the angels, then that old Madonna and Child, and now you're after a prayerbook. Have you actually decided to embrace the true faith after all? There'd be delight in Heaven if you did, sure enough."

"Not as such. But I would like to see any ancient books you may have, as one of them may have come from the same source as Madonna and Child, which I have left, with Leggy's approval, with my Pa, for safe-keeping."

"And you want to give it back? Like the Angels? How will we ever make a living with you giving stuff away as soon as we get it in?" He was teasing, of course.

"If it's the right one. Just let me look round the book department, please Bobby?"

We sidled and threaded our way between furniture – not all the International Galleries items – and tea chests full of stuff, until we reached a desk with an anglepoise lamp on it, and an office chair behind it. "Take a seat, milady," Bobby said, grandly sweeping the papers and the over-filled ashtray to one side. "I will fetch you the box you require."

He disappeared into the gloom and returned a minute or two later, dragging a packed tea chest. "There. I hope you find what you're looking for. If you could hold the fort here for half an hour, I've got a couple of errands to run." He winked at me.

"OK, Bobby, but don't lock me in!"

"Certainly not. You can lock yourself in from the inside when I've gone. Thank you, milady, I'll be back as soon as I can – shouldn't take long," and he shed his brown overall, picked up his jacket and was off between the piles of furniture and bric-a-brac on his swift silent feet.

I followed him, more slowly and noisily, waved him off, locked the door then went back to the desk and the tea chest, filled with books.

I dipped in and picked out the first book. It wasn't what I was looking for, but was pretty good – a printed book bound in marbled card with leather spine and corners, the title and author embossed on the spine in gold: The Age of Fable, by Thomas Bullfinch. An old friend, older than the one my great grandfather had bought, whose stories Pa had read us on cold winter evenings when we were small.

I put it aside, marking down the title, author and date of publication on a foolscap notepad, then dipped in again. The books were in piles, but not as carefully packed as they might have been, particularly given their age. I noted them down on my pad and set them to the side of the desk, in piles of six or eight.

Then I got to the books they had managed to wrap, before packing and sending to their place of dubious safety. Leaves from the London Evening News (morning edition) of a week previous, enfolded the precious volumes. I was no bibliophile, but I knew that a first edition of The Adventures of Tom Jones wasn't something one came across every day. I cataloged it and re-wrapped it, writing the title on the newsprint.

I went through the parcels; not all the books were British. Italian and German, Swiss, Netherlandish and French, they all popped up, but these were printed works, with or without engravings or woodcuts. I cataloged them and set them back in their wrappings with their titles on a table whose top I had cleared onto a chair.

Then, under this layer, I hit the mother lode.

Ancient books, wrapped in pieces of soft faded once-red velvet curtaining.

Below these modern makeshift covers were the original cloth wrappers, fifteenth century textiles of deep dyed silk, velvets or brocades, woven with threads of pure gold, embroidered in silks and precious metals by long dead needle-workers, fitting protection for the jeweled and gilded covers which in turn hid vellum illuminated and limned by artists and copyists whose skills and eyes rendered the words and prayers into miniature scenes, calligraphic meditations that could only be marveled at. Books of Hours, Missals, for private devotions, and others, that looked as though they had come from abbeys or churches, music written in a strange notation, with Latin texts beneath.

I didn't know where they had come from, but I would say continental rather than home-grown, from the style and the richness. Henry VIII and Cromwell had seen to it that precious little remained in England.

I didn't know how to catalog these. They required specialist knowledge, that of a medieval historian or bibliophile. I did a quick resumé of each of the glorious books' exteriors and wrappings, then, having turned a few pages tentatively and drowned in the beauty of the bright colors, the tiny gold bosses, the tender scenes, closed them and moved to the next one, checking each against the Curé's description.

There was a knock on the door, and Bobby called that he was back; I shimmied through the furniture and opened up for him.

"Sorry I'm late, milady, I got caught up. Did you find what you wanted?"

It was early evening now, people were passing, coming home from work, perhaps going for an early pint. I was astonished. I know it had been a busy day but the last few hours had passed in a flash.

"Well?" he asked.

I shook my head.

"Let me find it for you, then," he said, doing a double-take at the piles of books, the catalog sheet and the wrapped parcels. "Jeez, milady, you've been working like a Trojan!" He peered into the box. "One more. Let's hope it's the one you want."

He leaned over the tea chest and brought out a parcel swathed in grey-green faded curtaining and put it on the desk. Tenderly he unwrapped the fabric to reveal a fine deep purple wrapper. "Oh, Milady, what have we got here?"

I got out the Curé's letter again. "Book of Hours, 15th century, 20 cm by 15 cm – that's roughly 8" by 6"," I read.

"Well, it's a book, that size give or take a quarter inch. Leather and wood decorated with gold leaf, gold and jewels – pearls, big odd shaped ones, and ... I think they are garnets and a beautiful big sapphire, cut like big circles..."

"'Three baroque pearls, two garnets and a large sapphire, all cabochon cut, and five small agates'" I read from the letter. "Open it up, Bobby."

"It looks like a calendar of some sort."

"That would be right, a calendar of church feasts. It tells you when and to whom you should pray."

Where did I drag that up from?

But Bobby nodded.

"Show me the pictures."

He handed the book over. It was a delight. We held it under the anglepoise and gasped at the beauty together, going through, page by page.

I tried to remember anything I had ever known about the Rohan master. All I could recall was a representation in the Book of Hours of the Master of Rohan of a naked man making a good death – with God looking on and an angel fighting the devil for his soul. It was emotive, almost expressionist in its handling, with Gothic daiper-work in red and black and agitated forms.

The little paintings in here had the same daiper-work, the same agitation in the drapery, and the same realism – the corpse I remembered was a real suffering individual – in faces and clothing.

I looked at Bobby. "You found it!"

"Where did it come from?"

I translated the Curé's letter for him.

"Then we shift all of these little jeweled books at once to a place of safety, milady, and I buy you a drink. I could murder a Guinness."

We locked them in the safe at Leggy's. He had returned from various meetings while I had been in the warehouse. Amongst other things, he had arranged for a very secure and dry lockup for what he called the Nutfield Hoard.

He looked elated, particularly with the discovery of the Book of Hours, and took my letter. "Write back to the man and tell him we may have some good news but we need to hang onto the Book for the moment – it's a legal necessity. As far as I'm concerned he could have it back tomorrow, but it's not down to me."

## 34

I cried off the drink and climbed into the little red car and headed home, turning right into the Fulham Road after the Watney's brewery. Opposite St Stephen's Hospital a figure waved frantically at me, flagging me down.

I immediately drew up. "Elisabeth! Whatever is it? Can I take you somewhere?"

She climbed in beside me; she was still wearing mourning black for her friend, Lady Finching, rather than her ex-fiancé, Percy Meredith, whom that lady had murdered, but she looked wonderful, with simple amethyst studs in her ears and the amethyst pendant that I had worn for a short while, instead of the full flashy set of gold and diamonds that Percy had insisted on. "No – well, yes, I was coming to see you, but I'm starving, aren't you?"

I hadn't thought about it, but now she mentioned it. "Ravenous!"

"Good. Let's go for dinner. South Kensington, Alice and I'm paying."

"Never let it be said I tried to stop you, but I do need to freshen up a bit first," I said. "I've been in a very musty warehouse."

"Of course. Your hair looks a bit dusty." That was kind. I looked like Sally Carson, who had been pulled through a hedge backwards!

I came out of my bathroom sweet-smelling in fresh clothes, my hair still a little damp, but clean and curly. Alice was back.

"What were you wanting me for?" I asked, as we clattered down the stairs.

"May I not just wish to see a friend?" she asked back.

I smiled. "You may just wish to see a friend, but you'd not waste a social occasion on just social. Oh, and thank you for the letter. I'm sorry I wasn't in and that I didn't get back. I've been somewhat busy."

"I know. And not just with the refurbishments."

"Hey, you're not keeping tabs on me again? I gave you that jewel back!"

"Oh, Alice, of course not." She poured herself into the passenger seat of the car. "But I know you well enough to understand that you will be fighting for justice for your father and your family, and also for the victim. How's it going?"

So that was it.

"Messy and confused. Too many skeletons creeping out of the cupboards."

I went straight on past the underground station, wondering where we were going. From now on it was all Museums, not a restaurant in sight.

Elisabeth sighed. " 'Twas ever thus with such people. Park here, Alice, in front of the Museum, and we'll walk the rest. It's not far. You don't mind Polish food? I love this place, it's like being in central Europe. My mother was German, but her family were from further east, and I have Polish friends who recommended this place to me. It reminds them of home as it was before Hitler, before communism."

When I entered Daquise, I, too, felt at home. Elegant, but simple, I could have been anywhere in Mittel Europ, among émigrés and amateurs of pierogi and bigos. certainly it didn't feel like London.

Elisabeth was greeted as a respected and valued customer and we were shown to a table at the far end of the room, set for four. The waiter lit the candle and held out our chairs for us.

"Are you expecting guests?" I asked.

"We'll see," she said, settling herself comfortably. "Do you have any cigarettes, Alice."

"Unfortunately not," I said.

She called to the waiter who returned with a pack of ten, a continental brand from the script and the number of consonants on the card wrapper. She took one and handed me the packet.

Yes, I did.

I even found my cigarette holder at the bottom of my handbag, brought it out of retirement and fitted the cigarette into it. The waiter held out a Swan vesta and waited as we inhaled. The tobacco was dark, with a touch of Turkish in there. I thought of Jeremy. He would like it.

I enjoyed the moment and let the remains of the day drift from my shoulders.

Elisabeth said something to the waiter and he nodded and went away, leaving the menu, two sides of close typescript, on the table. I looked at it, non-plussed.

"I'll order, if you want," she said. "You can read the translations if you feel like it but they don't do the food justice."

The waiter returned with two stemmed narrow goblets of light yellow beer, transparent as glass with a high foamy head, and set them before us gravely.

Elisabeth ordered then, as the waiter withdrew, lifted her glass. "To us, Alice. And to those we love, and most of all, to Magic!"

I raised my glass and clinked hers. "I'll drink to that, with pleasure."

The beer was ice cold, light, sparkly with a hint of bitterness, and very welcome.

I turned to her, dabbing my lips with the napkin. "Thank you for this, Elisabeth, I had no idea how much I needed good company and to just stop for a moment."

She chuckled. "I think I do. I've been doing pretty much the same sort of thing. The temple is almost ready, but I've been working through all my father's stuff – he sorted lots before he died, but there are always little things that get through the net and I've been dealing with them, and setting up the circle, and reading all those diaries you gave me. I knew he and my mother were good magicians, but I didn't know just how good. They're a hard act to follow."

"You'll manage, Elisabeth," I told her, and I meant it.

"Thank you, Alice. From you I appreciate that."

"Reverend Simmons said you'd made a donation to the Angels' building fund," I said. "He thinks you are a very remarkable woman."

"I am. But I had to do something decent with all that jewelry Percy bought me. It was ill-gotten and the angels need a home."

I took another draw on the cigarette, another sip of beer. "You mentioned something in your letter that I'm not sure about. I understand that dead men can still cast long shadows, but you said the victim and the murderer are mirror images, and I should cleanse them both. What did you mean by that?"

She looked around, peering at the door, possibly searching for eavesdroppers, but the restaurant was by no means full yet, and the clientele, mostly older than me, were concentrating on eating, speaking to each other in Polish or Czech, or reading foreign newspapers. No-one seemed interested in we two unescorted women at the far end of the room, which made a pleasant change.

"Yes, I know I can talk freely here, Alice. No-one bothers a lone woman at Daquise, another reason I like the place. Have you found the murderer?"

"No. But I know quite a bit about the victim, and he wasn't what he wanted people to believe he was. I can think of quite a few people who would wish him dead."

Elisabeth raised her eyebrows. "Indeed? The papers hinted that it might have been an execution?"

"Quite. It takes a certain sort of person to shoot someone in the back of the head."

"Probably easier than shooting them, looking into their eyes, while they plead for mercy," she said slowly. "It could be a hit job. Or not. But certainly two not very nice people – mirror images of each other. Both a bit ruthless and not what they would have people believe they were."

I thought about that and nodded, "OK. But how to cleanse them? Or cleanse the areas they have influenced. Or possibly the site. I don't understand what you mean, Elisabeth, and in any case that's your province. Or Rev Simmons's."

"And you aren't involved in Magic, Alice?"

"Not this sort of stuff, that's advanced work, surely?"

"How will you ever learn if you don't try something?"

"You're doing it again, Elisabeth, answering a question with a question. Why do you do that?"

"Why do you, Alice?" she teased.

I chuckled. "What do you mean? What do you mean to do?"

"I don't honestly know. Try to set everything back in balance, I suppose. It would need people I can trust in the circle. And then cleanse the area and hopefully all those affected by the event." She grinned. "Of course, it's only an idea, but someone's got to do it. Are you up for it?"

I gasped. "You brought me here to ask me this?"

"Not exactly," she replied, and looked towards the door of the restaurant.

It burst open, admitting a tall fair man in a dark suit of American cut. He bounded in, greeted the staff like old friends, and strode up towards us radiating raw energy.

"At last!" Elisabeth breathed. "I was wondering where they'd got to."

She stubbed out her cigarette and stood up to greet the man. "Stefan, how wonderful to see you again! Where is your friend? You've not left him behind?"

He took her hand and pressed it to his lips. "Gnädige frau, would I dare? He's paying off the taxi."

He held onto Elisabeth's hand and gazed into her eyes with his own pale gray ones.

I felt the electricity between them like a jolt.

Why would she bring me along?

She surely would want to be alone with him.

If I were her and someone like him kissed my hand and called me 'gnädige frau', I certainly would!

He was stunning, tall and well-built, about forty, perhaps a little more, but fit, his hair brushed back from his brow in two gold wings, high cheekbones under the pale eyes, and a straight nose, a strong jaw and a soft sensual smiling mouth.

I was definitely surplus to requirements.

But then the door opened again, and my jaw dropped.

Another man entered, as tall, but leaner, with dark hair, and was directed to our table. I let my cigarette holder drop into the ashtray, leaped to my feet. He was the last person I expected to see, but the only one I wanted to see.

It was Jeremy.

# 35

He did try the gnädige frau move but I was having none. I was in his arms and delighted to be there. Not for long, but enough to show I cared, and a quick peck on the lips, then a beaming smile, which was returned, and I led him to the table.

"Now, introductions and explanations, please," I said, looking at the company, who were beaming just as much as I was.

Elisabeth started first, before we took our seats. "Alice, this is Stefan Paretsky, my very dear friend. Stefan, this is Alice Chamberlain, Lord Wethersley's daughter, of whom you will have heard, both from me and from Jeremy, I am sure."

He nodded gravely and bent over my hand. As he lifted it to his lips I saw the ring – on his little finger – he had large masculine hands. So Abraxas ruled here too.

"Enchantée," I said and smiled. And as we sat, Elisabeth too pulled out a ring with the familiar decoration and slipped it on her middle finger.

So four of us, each with Abraxas on our hands, one on each of the fingers.

I looked at each of my companions, head full of questions.

Jeremy said, "The job I was sent to do is done. I was called home. I'm not sorry."

"Nor I. But...?"

"Stefan and I have been with Leggy and Bas and various others all afternoon," he said. "We have permission to tell you what you need to know and Leggy says that you should keep us up to date."

I shook my head. "I need to get that from the horse's mouth," I said. "Is there a telephone in here I could use?"

There was not; so I made my excuses and left the restaurant. I found a phone box a block away, and with Jeremy cramming inside with me, dialed Armitage Antiques.

"So, Milady, I was wondering how long it would be before you rang," Bobby said. "I'll pass you to Leggy."

I heard a scuffling as the receiver was handed across and

Leggy's voice boomed in my ear, "Alice, how are you enjoying the little surprise I sprang on you? No. Don't answer that and don't thank me. You may pass on anything and everything to your companions of this evening. Anything you think relevant, although I have been updating them and they me, this afternoon. And don't think of coming in to work before noon tomorrow. Have a good evening. Goodnight."

I looked up at Jeremy. "OK, I have clearance, but you've got to tell me all you know, too."

"How much time have you got, Alice?"

Back in the restaurant Elisabeth and Stefan were chatting over pierogi and beer. The waiter brought ours.

"So?" asked Elisabeth.

"So I can tell you what I know, but how did you get to become involved with this?"

"I asked Leggy if he wanted a bit of help," she said, matter-of-factly. "And he said why not. He's known Stefan for years. Worked with him during the war."

"Polish Air Force," Stefan said.

"And now?" I asked.

"I adapt. I can prove useful to the Free World."

"And much more, I'd say." I looked at Elisabeth and then at him. "You're working magical partners, aren't you? But what has magic got to do with all this?"

"Nothing, yet. But there will be a need, later," Elisabeth said.

"I won't speak here," I said.

"Then we'll walk for a bit after dinner," Stefan said.

So we ate the pierogi, the slow-cooked cabbage dish whose name I couldn't pronounce, Stefan and Elisabeth regaling us with stories of their past: they had met at her grandmother's house in the early 1930s and had hit it off immediately.

"But you knew all about her and Percy Meredith?" I asked.

"Of course. And I'd worked with the angels with her parents. I wasn't going to let them be defiled. So when Elisabeth said she had an idea we talked it through. You know the rest. And thank you, by the way, for your part. You played it perfectly."

I frowned. It didn't seem to me that I was playing at the time.

"You weren't … I don't know, jealous? Of the attention she was getting from Percy?" I asked.

Stefan shrugged. "Jealousy is such a tawdry emotion. Elisabeth knew what she was doing. I had, and have, complete confidence in her integrity. And in the end," he chuckled, "I am here with Elisabeth and Percy isn't. He who laughs last..."

True, but the ice-pale eyes must reflect an ice-cool head and heart.

Elisabeth patted my hand. "Oh, don't be such a romantic. It had to be done. You know that, and a bit of buttering up a vain old man, who incidentally, I actually came to like a bit in the end – although I couldn't stand Archie or the way he manipulated his younger twin, or anything they stood for, was a small price to pay for settling a lot of scores. Although there is still a lot of clearing up to be done."

So that was it...

The waiter brought the bill. None of us had room for dessert and the tiny glass of orange flavored vodka was enough. We paid and shook hands with the staff, and left, walking together up Thurloe Place to the quiet area beside the Brompton Oratory, where there were benches and low walls around a small green, possibly once a cemetery. There we chose a bench in the shadow of the fine domed Catholic church, and shared our knowledge.

I learned that what I had discovered that morning in the spiral files, although kept from the Great British public was confirmed by files in secret places, and that the two ingots of Nazi gold were probably 'acquired' as a sweetener for use when Hitler would bring Edward and his Queen back to their true station in life. There would probably be other hoards in other places.

As for the other names... both men said the majority were known to those who guarded our national security. These people would be interviewed, quietly, but firmly. "We cannot allow them to have people killed, no matter what pressures may have been put upon them," Stefan said.

No, I thought, but you and Elisabeth allowed Lady Finching to murder the Meredith twins, even planned it. I kept that thought to myself, and said, "You think there may have been a contract on John Anselm-Jones?"

"What else? People don't like being blackmailed and they

couldn't go to the police, now, could they?"

"No. I suppose not. But he didn't just rub the rich and powerful up the wrong way."

"You think it's local?" Jeremy asked, waving a cigarette case full of Gauloises at me.

I nodded and took one, and fitted it into my holder. "I think there's as much a chance as someone coming in from on high. Simply because of where he was found. Why else would he be there?"

"And you still don't know who uncovered it?"

I shook my head, then inhaled as Jeremy lit my Gauloise.

"Not Nigel, then?" he asked, lighting up Elisabeth's and Stefan's cigarettes, and then his own.

"I don't think so. There is some ill-feeling towards him locally. And there are links between him and some local people," I said, and told them about Cissie Laycock.

Elisabeth shuddered. "She worked at Marsham Court? What do Algy and Anthea have to say?"

"They've disappeared," I told her. "The place is empty, locked up."

"Why didn't you say earlier, Alice? Sorry, forget I said that. I hope they can be found. I'd say the answer lies with them."

Jeremy looked at me. "Have you met the Laycocks?"

"I've met Cissie's uncles, one to talk with, and he's telling lies to the cops, and I've seen her father, but not to talk to. He was gardener at Marsham. He puts flowers on her grave regularly."

Jeremy looked at his watch. "If we set out right now we could be at Marsham in three quarters of an hour."

## 36

It was dusk when we drew up beside the The Cricketers, at Marsham, but a warm evening, and people were sitting at tables outside enjoying their drinks. It was just Jeremy and me in the car; Elisabeth and Stefan had elected to go back to her place to catch up. He had murmured something about missing Beltane and she had licked her lips and smiled. Well, good for them! I didn't know where I'd be sleeping tonight, but I, too, had hopes.

I recognized Sam's little Ford and the Pre-War Humber Super Snipe that Les Broom drove the previous evening, parked next to each other at the cricket club fence. Jeremy saw Sam first and hailed him, and we both wove our way between the tables to where he and Les were ensconced with pints.

Sam did the introductions, and Jeremy went to get the drinks. I hadn't expected it to be this easy, but Sam and Les were obviously now fellow sportsmen, and enjoying each other's company. Or possibly using each other to find out more about what was going on.

"When did Jeremy get home?" Sam asked. "He's her young man," he explained to Les.

"Pity, but a lucky lad, eh?"

"This ... er ... morning," I said, with some hesitation.

"And the first thing you think to do is nip down here?" Sam asked. "Not even down at the Wethersley?"

Damn!

"Oh, we've already been there," I lied.

I felt Les's eyes on me. "What are you up to, Milady?" he asked. "Do you know something I don't?"

"What about?" I asked. "I know lots of stuff, I nearly know the lot!"

His face cracked into a grin. "No, you don't. But you do know something, don't you think so, Sam?"

"Never knew a time when Alice didn't know something, Les. Ah, here's the refills, good man, Jeremy."

Three pints and my half of shandy were duly distributed and

sipped at.

I looked at Jeremy. "I need to make a phone call."

I'd spotted a phone box by the bus stop just up the road beside the churchyard. I knew I must get us a bed for the night at Wethersley, because if we had been seen, there would be hell to pay if we didn't stay there.

Maman answered the phone. "Alice, I've been waiting for your call. Are you and Jeremy staying tonight?"

How did she know?

"If it's no trouble. I suppose Leggy told you."

"Oh no, dear. I just had one of my suspicions, you know. Good. We'll expect you in the next hour or so. Don't be too late, dear. Roger and I would like to see you both before we go to bed. I'm so glad Jeremy is back in England with you, Alice."

"So am I," I said softly.

Don't tell me Maman was getting psychic, I thought, as she wittered on about having the blue room aired and made up. "See you soon, then, Maman."

I replaced the receiver and was about to leave the phone box when a short angry whirlwind blew through the lychgate and down the road to the pub, fetching up in front of Les Broom's table. And it started shouting at him.

I hastened down the road too. I recognized the figure. Billy Laycock, Les's Uncle, Cissie's dad. And he was angry. Wild as fire.

"Someone's put red roses on my Cissie's grave! They've no right to, everyone knows she was pure, that's why she only has white flowers. I gotta find who it was, Les, and I'll have 'em. So help me, God, I'll kill 'em. Defiling a young girl's reputation like that!"

Les stood up and grasped his uncle to him, shushing him, like a father might calm an angry child by a forceful cuddle, patting his back.

"Don't take on so, Uncle Billy," he murmured. "It probably wasn't meant as an insult, just a bit of kindness from a passing stranger."

Uncle Billy wouldn't be stopped. "Don't be daft, Les-boy, everyone hereabouts knows she only has white flowers. Everyone. So someone's up to something, and I'll have 'em, so I will. You don't insult me or my poor dead lass like that and get away with it."

There was a crowd round the table now, locals all out for a bit of gossip to pass on.

"Sit down, Uncle Billy," Les said firmly, and forced the man down into what had been my seat. He looked around him, and spied his cousin, Joe and tossed a shilling at him. "Joe, fetch Uncle Billy a pint, will you? And see if anyone knows anything about these bloody flowers."

I watched as Les's head shook infinitesimally from side to side and Joe's head inclined a fraction as he received and understood the message.

"OK, Les. Your usual, Uncle Billy?"

The older man subsided. "Yes, Joe, ta, lad." He dug in his jacket pocket and pulled out a packet of Woodbines. Busied himself with the selecting and lighting of the comforting cigarette. Les patted his knee. "It's alright now, Uncle Billy. I'll go and fish the offending flowers out, OK. I'm sure no-one meant any disrespect. Not from round here, they know how you feel, and if it was someone else... well, how could they know?"

Quite, I thought, being the person responsible for this outburst. But it had shaken me.

Jeremy caught my eye and stood up as I approached, giving me his chair. "It's fine. My sister sends her love, she was sorry to miss us," I lied. "She's back home now."

"Then we'll go as soon as you've drunk up," he said. "If you'll excuse us, Les and Sam?"

"Give them my best wishes at Wethersley," said Sam.

"And I'll see you both later," said Les. "And we'll catch up, eh?" He winked at us both. "See what you gone and done, Uncle Billy, you've scared my nice friends away."

Uncle Billy scowled at us. "You've no call to be having friends like them," he muttered. "They ain't for the likes of you!"

"If it weren't for this young lady and her brother, Uncle Billy, you'd not have been paid yesterday," Les snapped. "So keep a civil tongue in your head."

The older man looked surly, ready to start up again, but Les stopped him.

"And I'll make friends as and where I like. You can stick in

213

the past, but this war we've just fought has killed that world, and that's the best thing it could have done, given the common people a voice and a chance to make something better, so shut up, OK?"

Billy Laycock took a long draw on his Woodbine and looked at his nephew with disdain. "Bloody communist! You ain't got no respect."

"Then don't drink the beer I've just bought you, you don't have to," Les said, as Joe came back with a pint of mild and set it on the table before his uncle. "Any idea who did the flowers, Joe?"

The blond man shook his head. "Nah, I asked around, but no-one knows anything. They wouldn't of course, but they are shocked. It'll be all over the village by closing time. If there's someone as done it, we'll find out. Then we can deal with it."

"Possibly," shrugged Les. "Now, you off, Milady? I hope you sleep very well, very well indeed!"

"Cheeky bugger," said Jeremy with a grin as we got back in the car. He raised his hand in farewell as we passed the group.

"You know who put the red roses on the grave?" I asked

"You? Just a guess. But you didn't know, did you?"

"Of course not," I said. "How could I have known?"

"Then steer clear of Billy Laycock, Alice. He's one angry man, possibly a bit mad."

Although my sister Maddy was not there, we were greeted with open arms by everyone who was – Angelique, the Macs, Pa and Maman were all delighted to have Jeremy back. I was just an afterthought, but that was fine by me.

"You were in Paris!" Maman squealed. "What did you do there? Who did you see?"

"Oh, you know how it is, everyone who was anyone, present company excepted, was there. The noise, my dears, and the people! It was too too much!"

Noel Coward, eat your heart out.

Pa hooted. "So hush-hush, eh?"

" 'Fraid so. But I did see someone you know, and not connected with what I was doing," he teased.

"And?" asked Mr. Mac.

"You're surely going to tell us," purred his wife.

"Yes, I think I am. If you promise to keep it under your hats."

They all nodded, eager for gossip.

"Sylvia Nesmith-Brown was there."

That bombshell hit its mark and shut them all up for a moment.

Then Angelique said softly, "And her parents?"

Jeremy shook his head. "Just Sylvia, looking very smart, I must say, and on the arm of her new fiancé."

"So just Sylvia," mused Maman. "I wonder how she managed to fetch up in Paris. She had no money at all last thing I heard, none of them did, and Paris isn't exactly cheap. She'd need somewhere to stay, of course, and clothes, she couldn't do Paris in the clothes she wore here, she'd be a laughing stock!"

"Oh, she's changed. You wouldn't have thought it was the same person – she's got poise now, and of course a very rich fiancé!"

"What's he like, this fiancé?" asked Pa.

"An older man, closer to your age, Roger, if not older," Jeremy revealed. "A South African businessman who sells all round the world. She's done well for herself. If she can bring him to the altar, she will be looked after very well."

I watched the faces as they considered the information. Sylvia was not yet twenty-one, and her putative husband was nudging sixty. Not that that would worry her; she was ready to cast in her lot with Archie Meredith who was more than twice her age, rather than marry Guy. For her marriage was definitely a business deal, and it needn't be a long deal. Divorce settlements would be forthcoming if necessary, but given twenty years or so she'd be a merry and wealthy widow of forty, set up to enjoy herself in whatever way she chose. It wasn't the way we functioned at Wethersley, but we could all see the merit of it.

"Well," said Pa, breaking the silence. "I need a drink after that."

We all did. There was more chatter, gossip, catching up, but all the while I kept remembering Maman's question: how did Sylvia get the cash to get to Paris? I didn't believe that the fiancé provided it, I really didn't.

I sipped my brandy and let my mind wander.

When I last saw Sylvia she was demanding her engagement ring back from Guy – who had no intention of returning it after it had been thrown in his face. She was that desperate for a some sort of financial support. The Nesmith-Browns had not paid the staff for weeks and were known to have emptied the stables recently. The house? It had been part of the Meredith empire – owned or leased to one of their companies and lived in by their lieutenant, Algy and his family. So nothing tangible there that they could turn into money. There must have been something stashed away somewhere, but I guessed that would be in the parents' hands, and possibly tied up.

So where had Sylvia got the wherewithal to get to Paris and set herself up there well enough to attract a new protector? I had no doubt that she knew the man previously, that he had been one of the people she had been naughty but nice to at some time or other. But how would she know he was there, would be there, or would even want to see her? She would need money to finance her fishing trip. And she had none.

Drinks consumed, people began to go to bed.

I wasn't ready to retire. I needed to unwind.

"Pa, I need a bit of air," I said.

"Of course. I'll lock the front door, so take the back door key. You'll keep an eye on her, Jeremy, won't you?"

"Of course, but I think Alice can take care of herself."

Pa grinned. "I see you've been told. Come on, Chérie, let's go to our nest."

We took the glasses down to the kitchen and rinsed them while the Macs and Angelique went out to their own cottages, then we too went outside into the cool night.

## 37

"Do you think he'll turn up?" I asked, setting off to the woods.

"I think so. He read the message when I slipped it to him, and nodded," Jeremy said. "It was lucky timing. Sam had gone to the Gents and Uncle Billy hadn't yet appeared. Damned lucky!"

The moon was half full, but the stars were bright, or they were until we reached the trees. Our torches weren't much good either. We kept to the paths, somewhat overgrown, until we got to Mr. Balfour's fence, then we turned left along it, until we came to the turning into the little clearing. We made enough noise to warn courting couples to cover up, but it was pushing midnight, and most people, even passionate ones, were in their own beds by now, recruiting their energies for the next day's work.

The clearing was empty. Above the ring of trees the sky, dark indigo with ice diamond points in it, sent a pall of silence down upon us. Already nature was covering up the holes and diggings with fresh new plants, but I still felt the hairs on my neck standing upright. It hurt here. The peace of the place had been violated. I felt its anger. This was a place where people came to express their love to each other – fair enough, it may not always have been legitimate, but it was love all the same – and it had been stained with murder.

Jeremy stood in the center of the clearing and looked around, his face stern as it often was when he was thinking. He twisted the Abraxas on his finger and walked over to where he body was found. I moved across and stood beside him, on his left, then, with my Abraxas tingling on my index finger, I drew with my mind's eye a globe of light around the two of us, before letting my inner senses spiral forth, beyond the sphere. I did all this instinctively, without thinking. I don't know what I was searching for, but it certainly wasn't what I got.

I found myself whizzing widdershins until the spinning slowed and I came to rest exactly where I was standing now. Around me, it was winter, cold with sleet in the air, and early evening, the sun already below the tree tops. There were shapes, people within the clearing but I couldn't make them out clearly, they were just three shapes, male, seriously angry, shouting, menacing each other, hatred and blame cast on all sides. Now another shape pulled them apart, trying to bring order to the chaos – I felt he was saying something, someone's coming, and trying to stop the noise. Then two more figures came into view and joined in the shouting, the blame, the hatred, augmenting it until there was a sudden loud crack and such pain, and then nothing.

Nothing at all. Just blackness and I was kneeling on the soft turf, shuddering.

Beside me, Jeremy was on his knees, leaning forward on his hands, coughing, gasping for breath.

I put my hand out to him, stroked his face. He looked across at me through watery eyes and managed a grin. "Nobody said it would be easy!"

Slowly we stood up. I didn't know what he had experienced, but I'd find out later.

He took a watch from his pocket and checked the time. "Any time now."

I checked the watch. "Leggy gave it to you?"

"Insisted on it. Said it could be important." He replaced the watch. "Are you alright, Alice? That was pretty fierce."

"Never better," I lied. "I could murder a fag."

"Gauloise?" he asked. "They were so cheap it would have been churlish not to buy some."

Les arrived, whistling, as we were lighting up.

He accepted a cigarette and looked at me. "So, Milady, what do you know? Why have you called me here in the middle of the night?"

"When you first met me last Saturday, you said you wished you had a sister or friend like me to watch your back," I said, breathing out the smoke. "I'm offering to grant that wish."

He looked puzzled. "In what way?"

"I heard you lie to Detective Chief Inspector Murray yesterday," I told him.

"Oh, please! That's ridiculous!"

I shook my head. "I followed that lorry from Mayfair – the International Galleries – to Nutfield Lodge in Putney. On Friday afternoon between two and three, I'd say. It was full of furniture and artifacts, some of which I know for a fact to be stolen. I know Detective Chief Inspector Murray would be interested in this."

"So tell him. It's my word against yours. I'm a respected businessman round here. Why would I send my lorry to London when I've got work enough round here – especially when it was in for an overhaul."

"My word against your, too, Les. I'm a Lord's daughter and unfortunately that still counts with most people. Why should I lie? What good would it do me? But I'm not here to shop you to DCI Murray, I'm here to find out who killed John Anselm-Jones. I'm not saying you did it, in fact I'd like to give you a chance to explain and clear your name before we go any further, and I do want to be your friend, but you've got to play straight with me. You see, there's a whole host of people who wanted the man dead, I just want to make sure we find the right one."

"What business is it of yours? Why don't you let the cops do their work?"

"If it had been the local bunch, I would have. I trust them."

He took a long pull on his cigarette, then said "Yes. You know where you stand with them. But Milady, Alice, what makes you think I had anything to do with the death of this man?"

I looked at Jeremy, who had been standing some way back from us. "You tell him," I said. "No, Don't tell, show him."

Jeremy sauntered over and pulled out the pocket watch, "Do you recognize this?" he asked, handing it over, shining his torch on it.

Les took the watch and shrugged. "Nice half-hunter. Should I?"

"Look inside the back," Jeremy said, flicking the watch open and focusing his torch so that Les could see.

"Just some old dedication," Les replied. "Takes the price down."

"Not this dedication," Jeremy said. "This one lifts it up considerably. Look." He dug into his inside pocket and brought out two pieces of paper.

Les examined the first – the photograph of Edward Windsor presenting the watch, and the watch itself, with the inscription. "Yeah, OK, so that takes the price up."

"Do you see who it was presented to?" I asked. "John Anselm-

Jones. Who was buried in this clearing. Now do you see?"

"No. I can't see what you're getting at, not at all. Look, I've got a busy day tomorrow, I need to get some shut-eye."

"So do we, but not just yet. Alice bought this watch this morning from your shop in Amersham, and we have a receipt. So how did you come by it?"

I looked at Les seriously. "You must admit, it looks a little dubious that you should have the dead man's watch in your possession, a watch that by report was given to him by the Duke of Windsor, in friendship, and something Mr. Jones was never without," I said. "Especially when your lorry was seen shifting the dead man's possessions to a place of safety. So tell us what really happened, Les. And then we can all go home to bed."

I didn't think he would.

I thought he'd try to bluff his way out, but he sank onto the soft turf and lit a cigarette from his case, offered them around.

Jeremy took one, but I thanked him and passed.

He looked up at me with a grin. "So Auntie sold that watch to you? She was so chuffed. You got a real bargain, Milady. Even without that inscription."

"How did you come by it?" I asked.

"My bloody family. Jesus, they can't look after themselves. Like Joe at the cricket match. What a twerp, trying to beat Nigel up in broad daylight with that bloody DCI swanning around looking for 'abnormalities'. I told you, we've got no trouble with Wethersley, but Marsham people have had so much trouble with the last bunch at Marsham Court, you wouldn't believe."

"I would. We've had trouble with them," I said drily.

"Your brother's well out of it," Les said. "Although the plan for building and extending the villages would have brought decent paid work in. We could use some of that round here."

"So where did you get the watch? It came off a dead man who would not have willingly given it up." Jeremy said.

"Look, I'll tell you what I can tonight. I need to think. It's not just me to consider, you understand.? I need to talk to people. But I will tell you this, hand on heart and swearing to whichever God you think may be listening, that I didn't kill that man. Why would I? I worked for him from time to time. It would be like biting the hand that feeds you."

So he did know John Anselm-Jones, and he did work for him. "How did you meet Mr. Jones?"

"Ah, I didn't know him as that. I knew him as Edgar, Edgar Winthrop. I still think of him by that name. I met him at the cricket. I make lots of contacts that way. I learned in the Army that people will pay for things to be done, and pay very handsomely if they have a dirty job that needs doing. I don't mean, you know, mucky stuff, women, drugs and that. I mean shifting rubbish or making things look new or better, just clearing up after people who can't or won't do it for themselves. So when I came out I got some wheels and set up. I shift anything now – from manure and hay to finest antiques, and if you need something cleaned or cleared, I'm your man. Well, sometimes I am, because I've got others working for me now, too, family, of course. Someone's got to look after them."

"So you met John Anselm-Jones at the cricket and he wanted something moved?"

"Yes, Sylvia had told him about me, and me about him. She hated him, because he didn't fancy her. And no, I didn't either, far too brassy, but you don't turn a meal away when you're hungry, just because you don't like the plate. I think she liked to think of me as her bit of rough-trade," he chuckled.

I grinned up at Jeremy, who had suggested that he was mine. He looked at Les and said, "Do you know where she is now? Or any of the Nesmith-Browns?"

He shook his head. "Only the lad, Nigel, if he's still at Wethersley. The rest of them have upped and gone. I heard that Sylvia went first, then the two horses, then the rest of them. People knew something was up, because there'd been no visitors since the start of May, and there were always visitors, always parties of some sort or other."

"So what happened to John Anselm-Jones?" Jeremy asked.

"He did something that he shouldn't. To a member of my family."

"Cissie Laycock?" I hazarded.

"I thought it was you must have put the flowers on her grave. How did you come to hear about her?"

"Just something in passing. And I wouldn't have put red roses on if I had known that it would have caused so much distress."

"Yes, well, Uncle Billy's had a lot to put up with, but he ought to have been glad that someone else was thinking of her. Your secret's safe with me, you know that."

"Thank you, Les."

"Cissie was Billy's only remaining child. His wife had died before the war and he had brought up Cissie by himself. He's not an easy man to live with. She must have had it hard, but he did have a regular job and money, and as soon as he could he got her a job in the house, so she could earn her own living. She was was a very obedient girl – he'd knocked that into her – so if she was asked to do something, well, she would..."

Both Jeremy and I groaned. Les looked at us sympathetically. "Yes, I can see you've got the picture. Sylvia hated her, because, as she put it, she'd nothing of a body, yet she could have certain people round her little finger."

"John Anselm-Jones?" Jeremy said. "Uncle Edgar?"

He nodded. "Sylvia had had her eye on him because he traveled a lot, and she liked traveling. In style, I mean. She wouldn't be happy going third class. Edgar, I mean Mr. Jones, was known to travel First Class. Everything about him said that, and she wanted some. It didn't put her off having a roll in the hay with a piece of rough, but she was looking for something smoother, older, and richer for a more permanent set up. And Cissie had queered her pitch with him."

"Don't waste your tears on her," Jeremy told him. "She's engaged to a jewel-dealer of senior years and great wealth, who travels the world."

Les looked up in surprise. "When did you last see her?"

"A couple of days ago in Paris. Why?"

"How'd she get there? They were all broke at the end. On their uppers. That's why they did a moonlight flit."

"Don't worry about that for the moment. What happened to John Anselm-Jones?"

"Cissie died. You know that? Good. Uncle Billy felt he was due some sort of compensation, and as I knew the man, I suggested to Edgar, er Mr. Jones, that he meet up with Cissie's father and discuss her death. It was all very normal, civilized. He was by far the most civilized of the people who visited that house."

I sniffed. "He was a blackmailer," I muttered.

"Was he now? But there, I suppose we were about to do something likewise. Put the screws on – how would it look for a respected cultured gentleman to have had carnal relations with an under-age girl and procure her an illegal abortion? He'd have given a lot to hush that up. And I assure you, that that was all we intended to do. Cross my heart and hope to die. All Uncle Billy wanted was a bit of cash – and probably a bit more, then a bit more, as they do, but there was honestly no call for murder. None of us had that in mind, although Uncle Billy may well have wanted to give him a good kicking – once he had the cash!"

"So what went wrong?"

Les ran his hand through his fair hair and stroked his mustache. "Er, I suppose that was down to me, truth to tell. But I hadn't foreseen where it would lead, honest. I told Sylvia what we were going to do. She was hot to be in on it, but I said no. Then she pouted, stuck out her lip, the way she does when she doesn't get her way and said, she would be there no matter what. I told her not to be so daft. She took the hump and stormed off, cursing me. But I remember chuckling, because I'd not told her a time or date, so I forgot about it." He lit another cigarette. "I guess she must have told her Uncle Archie. Once he got involved...."

"You mean Archie Meredith?" Jeremy asked.

"Just so. He and Sylvia turned up, she on her horse, they must have watched Mr. Jones go out and taken the other route to the clearing. No-one would have seen them. It was dusk in winter, gray and cold." He shivered at the memory. "Anyway,we didn't hear them, either. Not until they were right on us. I was trying to calm them all down! We needed a civilised debate, but Joe and Uncle Billy were shouting and grabbing at Mr. Jones, they've both got hot tempers, when suddenly, Archie Meredith pulls out a pistol and shoots him in the back of the head. Just like that, cool as you like. Then he turns to Sylvia, and says, 'There you are, my dear, that's how you do it. Now, bring the shovels, Sylvia, and you lot – that's us – start digging. We need a shallow grave. So he can be found easily when the time comes.' I always wondered what he meant by that, but he had the pistol trained on us, and although Joe had his shotgun – we were supposed to be after pigeons – it was the other side of the clearing.

"Sylvia brought three shovels from his car. We dug. It was

hard, even for Uncle Billy, who was used to it, because the earth was cold and damp. He got a shallow grave alright. We dragged him over to it and rolled him in, face up. It was messy work, horrible. Uncle Billy started to cross his hands over his chest, but Archie stopped him. 'Leave him,' he said. 'and don't be tempted to take his money. No, whatever he was going to give you, I'll give you twice, to keep your mouths shut. That money needs to stay here, with the body. I don't want this corpse to look like a robbery. I've got my plans,' and he taps his nose.

"Well, me and Joe and Uncle Billy took the money off Archie, of course we did. Two hundred each. Archie Meredith and Sylvia left us filling the grave in. She went back on her horse, she was breathing heavily, I think she'd got a real charge out of watching it all, she liked danger. He tapped her thigh then went to his car, which was parked down by the stile.

"Once the car had gone Uncle Billy kicked hell out of the body, and took the watch. He said the bastard would have no need of that where he was going, so he might as well have it."

"What did you do with the shovels?" Jeremy asked.

"Put them into a local auction with some other stuff as a job lot from my next house clearance. Don't know where they are now."

"And the watch? How did that get into your shop?"

"Uncle Billy got into a muck sweat as soon as the body was found – he used to use it, enjoyed it before then, but after that he was scared and brought it to me. I didn't know the significance of the dedication; I put it aside in an envelope to deal with later but you were too quick for me."

He took a final puff at his cigarette, and then stabbed it out in the grass, sighed heavily. "There, Milady. I'm not proud of it, but that's how it was. Do you still want to be my friend?

# 38

I looked at Les. He was completely in our hands, and he knew it. He had admitted to aiding and abetting a blackmail attempt – which he needn't have done – but denied murder. I was inclined to believe him. And yes, I did want to be his friend. He was between a rock and a hard place.

Jeremy got out his cigarette case. This time I took one. "Alice?" he said, "Your call."

I put the cigarette into my holder and let him light me. Inhaled, and let the smoke out slowly. Then he lit Les's and his own cigarettes. Les looked wretched. But he had something on me, too. And Uncle Billy was not the nicest of people.

"Yes, Les," I said at last. "I do. But you need help. I know someone, we both know people, who can help you if you tell them what you've told me. It goes above DCI Murray. It's political – you know what that means?"

"Shit!" Les breathed. "That's really bad news."

"Not necessarily, Les," said Jeremy, gently. "It could work in your favor. It's a can of worms, I agree, but your part in it is pretty peripheral. I can see it being hushed up. Big names are involved, lots of clout..."

Les smoked for a bit. "What do you want me to do?" he asked at last. He sounded like a man beaten.

"Come with us tomorrow. Meet our friends," I said. "Tell them what you've told us."

"I'll think it over."

"Amersham station, by ten o'clock tomorrow," I said, getting to my feet. I was damp from the dewy ground, stiffening up and I wanted my bed.

We set off back to the lane, all of us, in silence.

"Hope to see you tomorrow, Les," I said, as we turned off at our path through the woods.

"We'll see. Goodnight, both," he said and disappeared into the shadows beside Mr. Balfour's woods.

We parked in the station car park at a quarter to ten. No sign of the Humber Super Snipe, but there was still time for him to show up. We crossed to the ticket office and bought three tickets, then went to the news-stand and browsed at what reading material was available, in between keeping an eye open for Les Broom.

In the event, he found us first. He arrived on foot, dressed in a navy suit with a blue-grey trilby, shoes polished to a brilliant black. He made the normally dapper Jeremy, who was wearing yesterday's clothes, look sartorially imperfect. Formally he greeted us, doffing his hat to me and shaking our hands.

"Thank you for coming," I said, as we went through to the platforms and found seats on the first train for London.

"What choice do I have? I want to prove my own and my family's innocence of murder. I imagine DCI Murray and DS Stonehouse have me down for the lot." He sat opposite me, by the window.

Jeremy sat beside me. "Tell me, Les, do you know someone called Dugdale?"

Les looked blank. "Doesn't ring a bell. Should I?"

"Possibly. And Leonard Shepherd?"

"Him, yes. International Galleries. Pernickety, but paid up front, always. I actually knew him from the army. He was always picking up odd bits and pieces, always had something going on, and I was his driver for a time – he was in troop entertainment, ENSA – Every Night Something Awful, and some of it was dire. I thought he'd go on the stage when he came back or run a theatrical agency, something like that, but it seems that he got an offer he couldn't refuse. He turned that gallery, which was a bit of a grubby barn when I first saw it, into something classy. Did a good job selling, too. I got that from several dealers, and from Edgar – Mr. Jones. Thought the world of him, he said. But then he used to say that about everyone. Probably meant nothing."

He eyed us carefully, "Now, I've put myself in your hands, and you know it. Tell me what your interest in all this is? And why you want to help me. You don't know me. You'd never even heard of me a week ago, I bet. Then suddenly, you, Milady, keep on turning up wherever I am. It ain't for my good looks, now, is it?"

I smiled. He was a good-looking chap and he knew it. A fair-haired Ronald Coleman, right down to the mustache. And he knew how to present himself. I could see why Sylvia would have been drawn to him – for dallying not marrying.

"The good looks are a bonus," I told him with a smile. "I work for an old soldier, a colonel, who was in SOE during the war. He is a friend of my father and my old boss. He brought me in when it was discovered who the corpse was. It was found on our land and there were hints that my father was involved in the murder, possibly the perpetrator of the crime."

"Bloody Hell! Sorry. No. Not Lord Wethersley! He hasn't got a mean bone in his body."

"Thank you, Les. Is that the consensus of opinion locally? I'd be very happy if it were."

"Can't speak for everyone, but I'd say it's not far off. Look, I'm not a great fan of the nobs, but as nobs go, your Pa's one of the best. I told you, our lot have never had a problem with Wethersley."

He turned to Jeremy. "What about you, Jem Arkwright? I know you are engaged to Milady here, but you're grammar school made good, same as me, am I right?"

Jeremy grinned. "Spot on, Mr. Broom, and I also hail from oop North. But I've lost a lot of my accent and Alice has taught me manners, so I can mix more easily with the nobs. I work for her brother-in-law and His Majesty's Government. My interest is in the Meredith twins and their long shadows. I know what evil men they were beneath the veneer of civility."

"Right. I'd not recognized that until that evening. I'd not come across them personally, but I'd heard tales, as you do." He looked around, but there was no-one within earshot. "I heard they were murdered recently. Bloody good job too. Whoever did it did the world a favor. Don't suppose either of you would have anything to do with that?"

"We were there," Jeremy said. "Someone beat us to it. But there's a hell of a lot of sorting out to do. Do you know why Meredith killed Mr. Jones? Or why he brought Sylvia along? It's a bit weird, that, isn't it?"

"Never knew his reasoning, but I knew he had planned it for something. I mean, why would he stop us emptying the bugger's pockets otherwise. He wanted the money found. Edgar, Mr. Jones, he always had a good wad on him, in a leather wallet lined with oiled silk – odd that, I thought, when he showed me, but he laughed and said you should always protect your banknotes then they'd protect you." He grinned. "Didn't work this time, did it?"

"Did Sylvia know about this wallet?" I asked.

"I should think so. I imagine she would have told Mr. Meredith what we planned and that fitted in with what they both wanted. She hated Mr. Jones. What Meredith's problem was with the man, I don't know."

We had reached Harrow on the Hill, and the carriage was filling up. We applied ourselves to our newspapers, Les, distinctly annoyed by the slowness of the journey, muttered, "I could have got us to wherever you're taking me much faster in the car, and got us back faster. I've got a business to run, you know. I'm only doing this as a favor."

"And it's greatly appreciated," I told him.

At Baker Street, we changed to the Circle Line to Gloucester Road, where we picked up a cab.

"World's End," Jeremy told the driver.

Les raised his eyes heavenward, "Blimey, lay it on, why don't you!"

But it dropped us at the pub of that name which Leggy used as a meeting place when needed.

We entered the saloon, and found him sitting at his favorite table in a snug out-of the way corner, where, because of the mirrors behind the bar, he could keep tabs on what was going on in all parts of the room. He stood up and greeted us all, shaking our hands heartily.

"Mr. Broom, so glad you could make it. Alice, Jeremy. Bobby, get the drinks in."

Bobby took orders and went to the bar.

"And you are, sir?" asked Les, sitting down between Leggy and Jeremy.

"An old soldier, Mr. Broom. That's really all you need to know. I'm afraid you'll have to take me on trust, sir. But both of these two will vouch for me."

Les frowned at Leggy, looked questioningly at Jeremy and

me.

"Yes," we both said.

"So it seems they will. Perfect love, perfect trust, eh?"

I started. I'd heard that before.

Elisabeth had said it some time ago, and I'd asked her why. "It's an occultist thing, Alice," she said. "Witches, actually. How you go into ritual, how you treat people you work with, your brothers and sisters in Art? In perfect love and perfect trust."

Leggy smiled at Les. "Oh I'm on the level, I assure you," he said.

Hell, now here was Leggy quoting Freemasonry. What was going on?

"Fair enough, squire," Les said. "But I need some assurances."

"And they are?"

"That my family will not be brought into this mess. Not publicly. As I see it, you want the murder tidied up, and I can help there, but I don't want my or my family's names brought into it, OK? Least said, soonest mended, know what I mean?"

Leggy sucked in his breath, then pulled out his pipe and set about filling it. "I'll do my very best, Mr. Broom. A man can say no fairer than that. We want the killer found and if possible brought to justice. Anything that may be... shall we say, er, periphery?... well that can be passed over, in the grand scheme of things. As you say, least said, soonest mended." He held a Swan vesta over his pipe and sucked to get it started. "Will that do?"

"Before witnesses, here?" Les asked, looking at Jeremy and me. "On the Square?"

Leggy let out a cloud of aromatic smoke. "On the Square, Mr. Broom. On the level."

"What do you want to know?"

"Everything. And then more." He smiled as Bobby brought the refreshments - beer and a plate of ham and mustard sandwiches. "Mr. Broom, the floor is yours."

We sat and listened while Les told his tale, more succinctly this time, but basically the same as he had told us the previous night.

"Why did you tell me about the attempted blackmail?" Leggy

asked when Les had finished.

Les shrugged. "It's true. But it also gives our lot a reason for bringing Edgar Winthrop or Mr. Jones to that place, even if it's not a particularly honorable one. I'm telling you how it was." He applied himself to his beer then ran his tongue over his mustache. "I'd be grateful if you could see a way to keep that out of things. Uncle Billy has suffered enough. I don't need that sort of publicity either."

"But you would be willing to swear, privately, that Archie Meredith was the murderer."

"Very privately. Between ourselves. That's all. How could I go to court and say this without implicating my uncle and my cousin? Find Sylvia Nesmith-Brown. Ask her what happened. She was there. She watched Archie Meredith shoot Edgar – Mr. Jones."

Leggy nodded. "So you tell me. What sort of gun did he use?"

"A pistol. Well, a smallish handgun. It was all very sudden. Out of his pocket, used, and then back in his coat again. I couldn't describe it. And before you ask, I don't have one. I've got a shotgun, and a license for it, so has Joe. We use them strictly for the pot, rabbits and pigeons mostly. We're country folk."

"But not averse to a bit of blackmail?"

"I prefer to call it getting our due. But we don't kill people. Cissie was killed. Taken for a ride by someone who should have known better and treated her better. That bastard deserved to die, but we didn't do it, and we wouldn't."

"So why didn't you blow the whistle on Archie Meredith at the time?"

"And involve ourselves? No, it was better this way. Or that's what we thought. Look, sir, we saw Archie Meredith shoot a man in cold blood. You don't cross a man like that, believe me. We kept our heads down!"

"Mr. Leonard Shepherd? You knew him?"

"Of the International Galleries, yes. I told Mr. Arkwright and Milady I did. I was his driver sometimes in the Army. He used me when he needed me when we got demobbed, we kept in touch."

"And Mr. Ferdy Dugdale?"

"Never heard of him."

"Your lorry moved International Galleries in toto to his house in Putney. And you're telling me you never heard of him?"

"Yes. OK, Joe and I shifted the stuff, but no names, no pack-drill. Len Shepherd came along in the cab and told me where to go; the house was empty, he had the key. He told us to put the stuff into the house. It was a bloody hard job, I can tell you. Took two trips, and was heavy work."

"How much were you paid?" Leggy asked.

Les grinned. "I haven't been paid yet. He's got the bill. It'll come in due course. One of the reasons I work for him, he always coughs up at the end of the month."

He checked his wristwatch. "Look, I've got a business to run. I've told you all I know."

He took a case from his pocket and handed us each a card. "If there's anything else you need to know, ring me. If I'm not there, someone will take a message and I will get back to you as soon as I can."

"Do you believe him, Bobby?" asked Leggy, when Les Broom had left.

"All except the last bit. Sure he got paid up front and cash. You want me to track him?" Bobby was already exchanging his suit jacket for a lightweight summer one from his briefcase and a cloth cap.

Leggy turned to us. "I think it's a case of find the lady, and if possible her parents, as Mr. Broom suggests."

He delved into his own briefcase and brought out a manila envelope. "I want you and Jeremy back in Paris, as fast as you can. If she won't co-operate, use your initiative. And Alice, you will be witness to this statement, but you'll be traveling under the name of Sally Carson and it will be she who will sign the statement, understood? Here's all you will need."

He handed me the envelope. "Your passport in that name. I'm not having Marie-Thérèse bawl me out for sending you and Jeremy on a pre-nuptial honeymoon, but Sally Carson, widow, is a different matter. She would approve of that, and actually said you should buy what you need for the wedding while you are there."

He chuckled at my dropped jaw.

"Maman knows what you're up to? And approves?" I asked.

"She said to get some dress patterns and some fabric," Leggy said, still chuckling. "Something for yourself and for her and Angelique and also for your sister, if you can manage it. She needs some new clothes and trusts your judgment. Angelique will make them up."

Jeremy was laughing into his beer. "She's got you trained, too, Leggy?"

"Marie-Thérèse had me trained from the first time I set eyes on her, Jeremy. By the way, I've settled it with Basil. And there's something else, Alice. You can deliver this to Père Laval, but I want confirmation and receipts and a signed and witnessed statement from him too."

He brought out another small parcel sealed in brown wrapping paper and handed it across. He was trusting me with the jeweled Book of Hours.

"Only he must open it."

"Understood," I said. "But he knows me as Alice."

"Take your real passport as well, then. He's never seen you. Now, off you both go. There's work to be done!"

## 39

I was going to Paris!

I was going back to France, and with Jeremy!

Someone Upstairs must have heard me. I was truly grateful!

We went back to my flat where, after looking at the improvements and explaining to Lily we would be away for a time, I packed a suitcase and took a taxi to the nearest tube. Jeremy went home to unpack and repack sorting the laundry in between. I went to Baker Street where I made a phone call then caught the next train to Amersham to pick the car up.

It was a slow journey but I used it to sort out things in my head. Sam was waiting for me at Amersham Station.

"I'm glad you rang, Alice," he said, doffing his hat. "Tea?"

"I could murder a cup, Sam," I said. "What's new?"

"After last night I checked up on Billy Laycock. He's got a violent temper. You know that Cissie was beaten up before she died? Well, bush telegraph mentions her mother being prone to walking into doors and tripping downstairs. I thought you needed to know."

It was what I suspected. "Do you think Les Broom knows?"

"Come on, Alice, he must suspect. But he's a nice bloke and a damn good cricketer."

And, of course, that meant everything.

We had a cup of tea and a slice of cake at the station café, then I placed my suitcase in the back of the car.

"Where are you off to? Anywhere nice?"

"France," I said. "Work. I'll get back to you with the story as soon as I can, Sam. And thanks for tea. Love to the Rev, too."

We shook hands and I drove off, straight back to The Boltons, where Jeremy was waiting for me with Elisabeth and Stefan, the latter in a gray paint-stained overall, having been helping her finalize her temple.

More tea.

"Alice, you will work with us?" Elisabeth asked. "Jeremy

will if you will, and we need you both."

I thought about it. It wasn't a problem.

I looked at him. He nodded imperceptibly.

Magical partners, eh? Well, we could be a force to be reckoned with, so why not?

"I'd be delighted to," I said. "And I'd consider it a privilege."

Her face creased into a smile. "I'm so glad. I pride myself in being able to spot talent when I see it. Next working Midsummer. I had a word with Lord and Lady Wethersley. It might be nice to work down there. Do a bit of healing of an area?"

"Could we not do it here?" I asked after the shock had worn off. "The locals like to use it in the summer."

"We'll wait until they've gone back to their own beds," Stefan said.

Jeremy chuckled. "You are a city boy, Stefan. If it's a fine night, they won't bother."

"I'm sure we'll sort something out," Elisabeth told him. "When you get back, eh?"

And we were off, in a taxi once more, the little red car now in the tender care of Stefan and Elisabeth, until we returned.

We arrived at our hôtel on the left bank at dusk. The taxi-driver brought our luggage to the door, accepting our fare, our tip and our thanks without a word, the stained stub of a Gauloise hanging from his top lip, then swerved back into the traffic. While Jeremy took the cases in I stood on the pavement, looking around and breathing in the scents around me – dark tobacco, coffee, fresh bread from the baker's next door, horse dung, a faint hint of garlic, and the undertones of bodies and urine, and as a couple of women passed me, the fresh light scent of lily of the valley, *muguet des bois* – and sighed with delight. It felt so good to be back among the faded grandeur of tall apartment blocks, some bullet-pocked, with their fancy ironwork and shutters, amid the language of my other people.

I went in and stood by Jeremy at Reception. "Mrs. Sally Carson," I said in French. "I believe you have a room for me."

We were shown up in a lift not dissimilar to the one in Leggy's block, to a pair of rooms on the top floor. Jeremy tipped the porter well, and we went in. My room was identical to the one I had 'seen' on our late night link-ups. So was his. Tall and narrow with a bed, a wash-stand with a jug and basin, a bidet by the side and a slop bucket, a mirror above it, placed relatively low. The water was cold, but it would do. The towels were scrim and there was the tiniest block of soap I had seen to that moment. I sat on the bed. It was a French double, which meant it was short and relatively narrow, but the French are generally not a tall race. A huge armoire stood between the window and the end of the bed, with a small table and two stick chairs beneath the window. It was no worse than many other rooms I'd stayed in, better than many, apart from the horrendously intrusive wallpaper, but that was local taste. Through the window, against the fading pinks and golds of the evening sky I could see the Eiffel Tower. A very definite plus!

There was a scratching on my door. "Mrs. Carson? Coming for a bite to eat?"

The hôtel kitchen was closing down so we went out, to a local Brasserie filled with students that offered Casse-Croûte à tout heure where we were served with a plate of saucisse de Toulouse and purée and a carafe of red. Not exactly haute cuisine but full of flavor and filling. It definitely hit the spot. We were working out our plan of campaign when a tall man, in flannels and a sports jacket, approached our table.

"Jeremy, dear boy, I thought you'd been recalled," he greeted. "And who is this charming companion?"

"Chucked back, I'm afraid," Jeremy said, standing up and shaking hands with the newcomer. "Laurence, let me introduce Mrs. Sally Carson. She is working with me."

"Enchantée," I said, taking the outstretched hand.

"Ooh, and she speaks the language too!"

He shook my hand limply. "Delighted Mrs. Carson. Are you here to keep an eye on him for his fiancée? No, don't tell me. Your secret's safe with me, young lady. Laurence Fairfax at your service."

He pulled up a chair and sat down, turning to Jeremy. "What are you up to, then, or is it too hush-hush?"

"We're working for Leggy," he told Laurence Fairfax, who tapped his nose, knowingly.

"Anything I can do?" He turned to me. "I work in the Embassy, so if you need anything, simply ask. Although it's a bit up and down at the moment, we've got the builders in."

I thought for a moment. "Any chance of access to an English typewriter?" I asked. French ones had a very different keyboard. I could use both, but for typing up a statement in English, an English one was obviously easiest.

His eyebrows rose. "So you really are working."

"Justement," I said. "I can use a French one at the hôtel should I need to, but an English keyboard would be extremely helpful."

"I'll see what I can do," he promised, and called for a glass and another carafe and proceeded to drink most of it while regaling us with the latest gossip about the Ambassador and his wife, the Windsors and the great and (less than) good of Paris society, then as suddenly as he arrived, he stood up, shook hands and said he must be off.

I thought it was the empty carafe, but Jeremy nodded at the door, where Laurence Fairfax had his arm over the shoulders of a dark-eyed Arab youth.

"It takes all sorts," I said as they drifted out into the night. And I thought for a moment of my brother, Guy. Laurence Fairfax's style would have been anathema to him.

Jeremy must have caught my thought. "In Paris, anything goes," he said. "Particularly at the Embassy."

Back at the hôtel Jeremy telephoned the Crillon, but was informed that neither Sylvia nor her new fiancé were answering the call. "Well at least we know they are still staying there," he said. "Unpacking and bed?

# 40

While I finished my coffee in the lobby, he tried the Crillon again. This time he got an answer from their suite. He waved at me, signaling me to come over and take the spare ear-piece.

Sylvia was on the line. "No, Felix," I heard her say, "It's just that woman I was telling you about. The one I met at the Louvre, remember? She wants me to meet her for coffee this morning. You're busy, aren't you, darling, and it would be such a treat. I could show her where the best shops are... Oh, thank you, darling, I love you to bits. I'll meet you for lunch at the usual place, Felix, yes?"

Now, loud in the ear-piece, "Yes, my dear, I'd love to meet you. Say ten o'clock, you say where."

"Le Café de Paris, on the Champs-Elysées?" Jeremy suggested.

"Wonderful, I'll be there. See you soon. Looking forward to it."

He replaced the receiver. I lay my ear-piece beside it. We paid the receptionist for the call and smiled.

I honestly didn't recognize her at first. I was sitting inside the Café, looking out at people generally, when an elegant young woman dressed in blue approached Jeremy at his table on the terrace. He greeted her with a double bise and held out a chair for her.

The last time I had seen her she was angry, hurt, wearing a monstrous black coat and threatening my brother. She had seemed huge, almost dwarfing him in bulk.

Today, she sported a tightly corseted top with a deep plunging V-neckline, to show off her be-jeweled cleavage, and three-quarter length sleeves, a skirt that hit mid-calf billowed out from below the belt below, supported by many petticoats – very much Dior's New Look, although almost certainly made up by a clever local seamstress – which suited her far more. Her fair hair had been cleverly coiffed beneath a tiny hat, her shoes and bag were elegant and polished. She looked a different person – older, elegant, poised – dammit, she made me feel dowdy in comparison, and precious few people achieve that. But credit where it's due. She'd done an excellent job of re-creating herself.

Jeremy raised his arm to the waiter and ordered. That was my signal to make my way out to them. As I did so, I noticed a dark-haired chap in a blue and gray checked suit wandering across the road from the Crillon, keeping Sylvia in view, staring even. Well, she was looking good, but this was no louche ogler. There was something not quite right about him. He looked purposeful, and yet as soon as he spotted me stare back, became just another person in the street.

I hurried out to join them, and Jeremy stalled her greeting.

"Miss Sylvia Cavendish, may I present Mrs. Carson, Mrs. Sally Carson." It was firm. And actually the first time that I had realized that Sylvia, like me, was traveling under an assumed name. We even shared the same initials.

We shared a brief hug and double bise and I took a seat. "Well, Sylvia, this is nice," I said. "You look very well. I heard you were engaged."

Now the old Sylvia came out. "Yes, and well, too. I heard you were, too."

We admired one another's rings. Hers was a very large solitaire diamond, naturally, set in platinum. Her necklace, bracelet and ear-rings were a set, that sparkled with diamonds and sapphires, to link with the Wallis blue, and she wore them well, a very fine advertisement for a diamond-merchant. My own jewelry didn't match and was far less grand – but each piece was a precious gift from Jeremy and that was all that mattered.

"What are you doing in Paris, Al... - er - Mrs. Carson?" she asked

"Working with Mr. Arkwright, and you can call me Sally. It seems we are both sailing under false colors."

Sylvia frowned. "What do you mean?"

"Cavendish?"

"Oh, that? It's one of the names the family always used. Sounds posh, Duke of Devonshire and Chatsworth and all that. Opens a few doors. As you can see." She took a sip of her café-crème. "I do love Paris, don't you? So you really are working, not just here for a good time?"

Jeremy said quietly, "Sylvia, how did you manage to fetch up here? Last time we saw you in England, you were quite different."

She smiled. "I told you. I took what you said to heart. I've always trusted you, Jeremy. I hope you understand that." She smiled in his face and put her hand on his arm gently.

He smiled back, and just as gently removed her hand, laying it carefully on the table. "Sylvia, I know you and your family had no cash," he told her bluntly. "How did you get here and set yourself up?"

"I thought about what you said and wondered where I would really like to be, if I could be anywhere in the world. Then I discovered Uncle Edgar's address book in Pa's desk. I went through it, and found Felix. I've known him a few years and I've always had a good time with him. He's a very generous man. He may be old, but he's full of fun, and pretty damn good in bed, and he always comes to Europe in the summer. So I decided to hunt him. And, see," she waved her be-ringed finger, "it worked!"

"He paid for you to come over here?" I asked.

"Oh no! Good Heaven's no! That would have been no good at all! It would have been far too obvious and I would have lost the upper hand. Felix thinks I have my own money, so he refuses to let me pay for anything. If I'd been dependent upon him from the start he wouldn't have had any respect and could easily have ditched me as soon as he got bored. No, I came here under my own steam and set myself up. There was an almighty row at home with Ma and Pa. They said we should all go and live in South America somewhere, it was easy to live there well on little money and there were rich people to be nice to down there – Buenos Aires, I think. Wherever that may be."

She helped herself to a cigarette from the case Jeremy had left on the table. "You don't mind, do you? Thanks..." as he lit it.

"Do you know much about South America? I don't, and what I do didn't sound much fun. Apart from anything else, it's a bloody long journey back if you don't like it, and I like Europe. So I said I wasn't going with them. I said I'd make my own way. I wanted to go to Paris. They weren't happy about that. They're probably too well-known in Europe."

"So?"

"Well, I asked for some cash, but they said they didn't have any, but they were already selling things off. I'd had enough of them. I knew where there was some money. So I took it. Three hundred pounds, plenty to set me up here and buy me some lovely new clothes. It was wonderful. And then Felix turned up, and we just had fun."

She inhaled appreciatively, then inspected the lipstick stain on the end of the cigarette. "I must get a holder," she said, then looked up. "It's all turned out rather splendidly, I think."

I fitted a Gauloise into my holder and accepted the light he held for me. "Yes. You've done very well for yourself, Sylvia," I agreed. "Where are your parents, now, may I ask?"

She shrugged. "Don't know and don't care. I've done with them. And with my whining brother. You can tell him that. I don't wish him any permanent ill, but I don't want him getting in touch hoping to borrow money. They took his passport, you know. They don't want to know him either. Not that he'd be of any use to them. He's not much good at earning money, and that's what they'll be needing. I would have been more use, but I'd had enough of them. They depended on the Merediths to support them, we all did. And then that bloody mad woman went and killed them both! It was horrible." Her bright face began to quiver, to crumble as she remembered.

"It's over, Sylvia," Jeremy told her gently. "Put it behind you."

"I do, I have, but it still comes back sometimes. It wasn't nice, seeing someone you had just made love to get killed before your very eyes." She looked at each of us, searchingly. "I don't suppose you know what I mean."

"I watched good friends die during the war," Jeremy told her softly. "Slowly, too. And in terrible pain. It still comes back sometimes. But life goes on."

She nodded. "I tell myself that."

"Me too, Sylvia. I watched a village being gunned down, with friends in it, mostly women and children, and a few old men. I could do nothing. Just sit back, hidden, with those who had managed to get out before the shooting started, hoping they wouldn't find us. It's not nice, it doesn't go away, but other things, nice things, take its place."

"Bloody war!" she spat. "Everywhere you go people are still going on about it. Far worse here in France than in England. I can do nothing about how they suffered but they do all keep going on about it."

"They were occupied," I said. "They got it first hand. I was here. Well, not exactly here, further south, but it was pretty bad wherever you were if you were French. It wasn't nice."

She looked at me in amazement. "Whatever were you doing?"

"My bit. Liaising with the Free French. I'm half French if you remember."

"But why didn't you stay in England? It would have been so much safer!"

"I'm half French. It seemed the right thing to do – and I had some great times, as well. Wouldn't have missed it. I had so much freedom."

I looked across the terrace. The chap in the blue and gray suit was back, and taking a seat opposite so he could keep an eye on her. He ordered a coffee, then got out a newspaper, but didn't read it. I hoped he was out of earshot, and more fervently that he didn't speak English. He didn't look English by the cut of the suit, but he wasn't French, either.

Jeremy stabbed out his cigarette. "Sylvia, you know we want the best for you," he began, lowering his voice to a caress.

She frowned. "Well, of course you do, Jeremy. You're a dear man and Al – Sally is lucky to … er … be working with you. What are you actually doing?"

He said, "We know where you got the money to set yourself up, Sylvia. And it has caused a lot of problems, particularly to Lord Wethersley."

Her face dropped. "What? Oh, God, you won't tell Felix, will you? It would be too, too awful."

"So why not tell us about it?" I asked softly.

She shuddered. "I couldn't. That was worse than having Archie die in my arms, no, really it was. Really, I can't. I've just got myself settled. You can't tell on me. That would be too cruel."

"Yes, it would," Jeremy agreed, his voice a whisper now.

"But we can offer you a deal. You sign a statement as to what happened, and we let Sylvia Cavendish get on with the rest of her life as Mrs. Felix Van Buren? We need to know everything, and you are the key to it all, aren't you? You know exactly what happened to John Anselm-Jones, or Edgar Winthrop, don't you? I don't want to tell Felix what we know, nor do I want to tell the police – but if I had to..."

The color drained from her face. "What do you mean? Who's been spreading rumors? It's their word against mine..." but her heart wasn't in it. It was considering losing face with Felix, the last successful roll of her dice. I don't believe she had ever thought of the illegality of her actions before, either.

I pressed on, "Tell us what happened last autumn. It was before you got engaged to Guy, wasn't it? We know about Cissie Laycock, if that's any help, and we think we know why and how things were set up. And it took some guts to disturb the corpse, I'll give you that. I wouldn't have done it. But then, I wasn't in your situation."

The new fashionable young lady returned, and gave a quick smile at the compliment. For someone who had not yet reached 21, she had lived hard and it showed in her hurt face while she considered for a moment. But she was tough. She'd had to be to survive.

She took a long draw on her cigarette, then put her chin up and exhaled slowly. "So if I give you what you want, you'll leave me alone and promise never to tell Felix?"

"Yes," we both said.

"If you sign a written statement to that effect," I added. "You can sign it as Sylvia Nesmith-Brown, no need for Felix or anyone else in your new life to know."

"No-one will give a toss in South Africa," she said, dismissively. "It's Europe that'll be the problem."

I was about to bring out my shorthand note-pad, but checked the chap in the blue and gray suit with the newspaper. He was leaning forward, watching us attentively.

I looked at Sylvia. "I think we should go, now," I said, then raised my voice somewhat. "We have some shopping to do, don't we? Let's get a taxi, eh?"

She pouted. "I rather fancied another coffee," she said. "Or something else."

"Trust her," Jeremy whispered. "There's a chap who has had his eye on you ever since we've been here. No, don't look, just get up and leave. I'll watch him then join you both." He gave us his special smile and spoke somewhat louder. "So sorry you have to leave, ladies, but if you must, you must. Shall I call you a cab?"

"No, there are plenty available, we'll pick one up," I said, rising. Then I dropped my voice. "Third café along, inside," I said softly as I gave him a goodbye kiss. "See you later, eh?"

Sylvia stood and did the same, and trotted after me. "Which chap?"

"No, don't stare, Sylvia. It's rude and you don't want to scare him. Late thirties, blue and gray check suit in the corner. Look casually back to Jeremy and you'll see him. Subtle is the name of the game. Have you seen him before?"

She turned back and waved at Jeremy, doing the same little girl wave that she'd given him the last time I'd seen her. Not a good idea, if the chap was on her tail, but she scanned the café well as she linked my arm like an old friend, and said, "Yes. He's at the hôtel from time to time. Not a guest. But he's well-known there."

"Does Felix know him?" I asked, stepping out faster, guiding her swiftly onwards.

"I don't know. I could ask him. Why"

"No, don't bother, he's probably no-one important. I'm just a bit suspicious, but you don't want anyone overhearing what you are going to tell us. This is strictly between the three of us. It will go higher up, but I give you my word that it will not be common knowledge."

I turned her briskly between the tables of the Café George V, through the doors and right to the back of the bar, where we sat facing each other, me facing the the entrance, she the exit via the kitchen, on deep red banquettes finished with gold. "I don't want us to be seen or overheard, OK?"

## 41

Jeremy strolled in some five minutes later and sat beside me.

He had watched the chap in the check suit rise, throw a few coins on the table, then saunter out to follow us. Jeremy had casually stuck his leg out as if stretching – I would have loved to have seen it – and managed to hamper his progress to the sidewalk, and then spent some time apologizing profusely in a mixture of French and English. The man was impatient to get on, and said so in no uncertain terms, pushing Jeremy aside. But by then we had disappeared. There were taxis ferrying passengers all along the Champs-Elysees. We could have been in any one of them.

Sylvia listened delightedly. "Gosh, Jeremy, this is so cloak-and-dagger. Is this what you do? And you, Al..., sorry, Sally? How exciting! Where did he go?"

"Down across the Place de la Concorde towards the Rue de Rivoli. That's where the shops are, isn't it?"

I got out my shorthand notepad and pencil, and rested them on the table. The drinks arrived: café-crème for Jeremy, americano for me and a guignolet for Sylvia, who loved cherries, and wasn't averse to alcohol. It was a treat, something she'd never tasted before, and would probably help loosen her tongue.

Jeremy leaned towards her and offered a cigarette from his case.

She smiled, took one and allowed him to light it for her. "Thank you. This drink is lovely, what's it called again?"

I told her and wrote the name down for her. "It's a digestif really, from my mother's part of the world. My grandfather makes his own. I'm glad you like it."

Her eyebrows widened. "Makes his own? What from? How?"

I shrugged, "Cherries, alcohol, sugar, a few special secret additions. Every family has its own recipe."

Jeremy lit his own cigarette, and looked at Sylvia. "Not here to discuss booze, Sylvia. You've got to meet Felix for lunch and we need to have sorted this all before you go off to meet him, without you becoming three sheets to the wind."

She chuckled. "Oh, he doesn't mind if I have a little drink, but you're right. What do you want me to say?"

We looked at each other. The truth would be nice, I thought, but held my tongue.

"What do you know about John Anselm-Jones?" Jeremy asked. "Or do we call him Edgar Winthrop or John Anderson?"

"Call him Edgar. I was told to call him Uncle Edgar." She took a long draw on her cigarette. "He was a friend of my parents, I think Mum had a crush on him years ago, but I only met him when we went to Baden Baden. I was told to be nice to him. Ma flirted with him. I was surprised at that, but Pa just laughed it off, said it was funny. You see, I don't think Uncle Edgar actually liked women – we were too gross for him. He was ... er ... you know, artistic, if you get my meaning. He liked young girls – but not me. I was too knowing, he said. He liked innocence, children, pale skinny girls with nothing under their vests and big melting dark eyes. I was too round, too boisterous, too blond and too pink for him. Well, it was his loss!"

She looked at us, daring us to comment, but we didn't. I let my pencil fly across the pad in my own variant of shorthand – I could read it back but it wasn't pure Pitman and was pretty awkward for others to decode. It often came in useful, as long as I didn't leave it too long, as sometimes even I had difficulty transcribing it.

She sipped the guignolet. "Pa said Uncle Edgar liked well-built young men, too, so Nigel was no use to him either. But we did do him the occasional favor, taking stuff from wherever he was to wherever he wanted it. That first time before the war, we carried quite a lot of his things back to England in our suitcases. Customs didn't bother with us. For some reason they never did when he had given us things to bring back..."

"What sort of things?" I asked.

She wrinkled her nose. "Nothing special as far as I could see. Bits of jewelery, sculpture, small scale, things that you could hide in a suitcase. A picture or two, books, I think, stuff wrapped up in brown paper quite often; I wondered why he couldn't just post the things. I wasn't particularly interested, to be honest. I got nothing out of it."

"This was when?" Jeremy asked.

"Before the war, and then again, after it. And during, although we didn't travel, he managed to. He came down to our place with Uncle Percy and Uncle Archie. They knew each other."

"What were their feelings towards each other?" I asked.

"Archie told me he was dangerous, said he should be done away with. That was later, though. At first they were friendly enough. A bit of you scratch my back, I'll scratch yours. Percy didn't pay him a great deal of attention. Percy always agreed with Archie, anyway. He was weak. And once Lizzie Thorburn got her claws into him, he was useless. Archie was really cross with him – and her – but he said they were playing a long game. He used that phrase a lot," she added thoughtfully.

"Did you know what he meant when he said it?" I asked.

She shook her head. "And he wouldn't have told me if I'd asked, just tap his nose, knowing like."

"So you knew Edgar before, during and after the war?"

She nodded. "He came to us at Marsham as soon as we moved in. And then he caught sight of Cissie Laycock when she was cleaning his room." She shook her head and gave a hoot of laughter. "He was lost! He'd found his ultimate wondrous waif!"

"What was she like?" Jeremy asked.

"Skinny as a rake, but great dark eyes, pale skin, and long dark hair that never stayed put, always wisping out and down. And she adored him. He treated her very gently, I noticed. Paid her attentions, but … how can I put it? He was careful of her... We all knew it would end in tears because there was no future in it. He was old enough to be her grandfather! She'd gaze at him with those big dark eyes, she absolutely adored him. I caught her sitting on his knee once while he read poetry to her. She was stroking his hair, and gazing at him with that silly besotted look, and when they heard me, she skipped off, picked up her feather duster and disappeared pretty damn quick. Uncle Edgar looked daggers at me. 'See what you've gone and done, she was enjoying the poem,' he snapped. He gave her nice things, too. Never gave me any! And money. For a new dress, a new pair of shoes, a treat, that sort of thing. I wondered what she did to earn it, to be honest."

"Did your mother have a word with her?" I asked. I could

imagine Maman putting up with that sort of thing going on under her roof. There would have been words! And probably a new position for the young girl.

She shrugged. "Why should she? Edwin was a generous guest, and she wanted to keep him sweet. Apart from cook-housekeeper all the staff lived out, including Cissie. Although she would stay overnight sometimes, if she were needed. She was a very biddable girl, would do anything you asked. She liked staying at our place. I don't think she got on that well with her father. He was our the gardener, I didn't like him at all. A sullen, angry man. Not like his nephew..."

"Les Broom? Or Joe Broom?"

"Joe? Please! He's going nowhere, and he's insulting to boot. But Les, I like Les." She smiled, then her face went hard. "What did he tell you? He had no right to. He swore he never would, made me and Joe and Billy Laycock all swear to do the same, too."

"I'm sure he did," Jeremy told her. "But we want your story, Sylvia. All of it. It's the only choice you've got. You don't want to go to prison as an accessory to murder, do you?"

Her jaw dropped. "Prison? But I didn't do it!"

"Nor for robbing a corpse – I'm sure there's a law against that, too," he pressed.

The face crumpled. "That's not nice, Jeremy. I thought you liked me..."

"I do. Which is why I'm trying to help you. But you must help yourself. So speak. And don't leave anything out."

So she started, and I wrote. How Cissie Laycock started to bud, and this, to her and her family's surprise, didn't put Edgar Winthrop off. He was truly smitten. Adored her, brought her more presents, and was seen sloping off with her on long summer evenings, returning beaming like a satisfied cat.

"They did it at the same place he was killed," she said. "That's why that place was chosen. Billy wanted money, and wanted lots. I think Les and Joe went along to make sure Uncle Edgar delivered. Les always liked Cissie, like his little sister, she was, he said. Joe was just extra muscle. But Billy, her dad wanted to kill the bloke who ruined his daughter's life."

"Understandably," I said.

"Huh, you didn't know him. He's a vicious piece of work. I saw him kicking the hell out of a dog once, because it had displeased him. I bet he did the same to Cissie if she did something wrong – and that wouldn't be difficult with a man like him."

Her glass was empty, so were the coffee cups. I ordered another round, not coffee, though, we'd both had enough.

"Who actually shot Edgar?" I asked.

"Uncle Archie. I suppose it doesn't matter now he's dead. He was really angry with him, for some reason. So was Pa, around the end of October. Ma wasn't too pleased either. I think he had something over them, but I didn't know what. So when he came down in late November, there was an awful atmosphere. Cissie was dead by then, and Uncle Edgar was really hurt and angry. I told Les about it. We were sort of seeing each other. On and off, you know. He said he was planning something with Billy Laycock. They both thought Uncle Edgar was responsible for Cissie's death although there was no actual investigation. I don't know how it got hushed up," she added, frowning.

"Why was Edgar in the area?" I asked. "Surely now Cissie was dead...?"

"He said he had a commission for someone. Highest sort. Secret sort of thing, but it had something to do with your Pa, Alice. I don't know what it was, but he wasn't best pleased when Roger turned him down. Got really shirty. That cheered Uncle Archie up no end. He was already working on the Wethersley-Marsham project and said he could use a bit of extra leverage, and then he suggested I made a play for your brother. To please him, I did. Uncle Archie is very generous when you please him. And Ma and Pa thought it was a brilliant idea. Of course, I'd have a title, and Ma was thrilled at that."

"So what did Archie decide to do?"

"He said he'd get rid of a thorn in all our sides. And he'd make sure none of us were bothered again. I said 'How?' and he made a gun with his hand and went mimed shooting it, then blew on the fingers. Then he asked if I wanted to come along and watch – I'd have to help, but I wouldn't have to shoot anyone. Of course I did. I couldn't miss such an opportunity!"

Jeremy looked at me, but I dropped my gaze to the note-pad. I'd have run a mile, but, of course, I'd witnessed death. She probably hadn't, and she would have done anything for Archie Meredith.

"So what did you have to do?" Jeremy asked, softly.

"Well, for a start, I had to find out the where and when from Les. And how much they would be asking for from Uncle Edgar. That was easy enough. We went to the pictures and then for a drive in his car afterwards. I was nice to him, he was nice to me...

"So I told Uncle Archie, and he was really pleased with me. That was nice. We had a lovely time and he promised me a present soon afterwards. Then, on the day, we went to the other end of the path, separately by different routes, him in his car, and me on my horse. We waited, and then, when we heard the shouting, we just went up there – Uncle Archie on foot, me on Moonlight."

She inhaled deeply, and then released the smoke as she remembered. "They didn't hear us, they were making far too much noise. We could hear them as soon as we got on the main path, well before we went through the woods. Billy Laycock was really angry, grabbing hold of Uncle Edgar and trying to nut him, screaming about him killing his daughter, and Joe wasn't exactly quiet.. Les was trying to pull them apart and gain some sort of order. I think he wanted to just get the money and run – until the next time, of course, but Billy and Joe weren't having any. They wanted blood!"

"Then?" I asked.

"It was misty, I remember, and Uncle Archie looked awesome, all in black. He just strode into the clearing and barked at them to stop.

"Billy Laycock hopped back, afraid, so did Joe. Uncle Edgar must have recognized the voice as he dusted himself off. He was standing with his back to Uncle Archie and didn't turn round. I suppose he wanted to keep his attackers in view. I heard him say, 'Well, thank you, Archie, you´re just...' and then there was a crack as Uncle Archie shot him in the head. It was so sudden, like a snake. I nearly wet myself!"

"What then?" Jeremy asked.

She shrugged. "Well, he fell down. And the Brooms just gawped, shocked. They hadn't expected that at all. Uncle Archie told me to get the spades and ordered them to start digging. Of course they did. Uncle Archie never took 'no' for an answer and he had a gun.

"We stood and watched. It was getting dark, and pretty grim. But Archie wouldn't go until they'd put Uncle Edgar in the hole. Then he gave them a lot of money. Twice what they were asking Uncle Edgar for. He checked the body, and told them he wanted the money to be found. It was another long game."

"Did you know what he meant?" I asked.

"No. I think it may have been something to do with putting pressure on someone. He liked to do that, have something over people. I didn't ask. I was too shaken up. I'd watched him kill someone, and that was enough for me. I'd never seen that before, except on films and that's all fake anyway."

"Didn't you feel sorry for Edgar?" I asked.

"Not really. He wasn't much use to me. I could have had a good life with him, but he wasn't interested, and he was still thinking of Cissie."

"When did the others leave?"

"Don't know. We left them filling in the grave. Billy Laycock was bending over the body, but I didn't want to stay on. Les came to me the following day and told me it was all sorted and none of us must ever let on, made me swear, said the others had, and it would be best for all of us if I did."

"Did Archie swear? With you?"

"No, just told me to keep quiet if I knew what was good for me. Then he gave me a lovely new watch that I'd set my heart on."

She stubbed out her cigarette. "Of course, Nigel came that evening, saying he was sure he'd seen Uncle Edgar from the taxi. Ma told him he'd not been around for some time but he wouldn't let it go until Uncle Archie put the frighteners on him. Pa and Ma knew to keep their mouths shut. They weren't stupid."

"Then what happened?" Jeremy asked.

"Nothing. Oh, I got engaged to your brother, Guy. It seemed a good idea at the time, but he wasn't very forthcoming in any way. I think he'd been put up to it, too. And when I had that talk with your sister, Alice, sorry, Sally, well, I knew I couldn't go through with it."

She took another cigarette, lit it herself and looked at us both.

"I'm happy enough to stick to one man as long as he's rich and satisfies me, gives me everything I want in the way of travel, the best of everything, a good life. Guy couldn't do that even if he wanted to, he's too 'proper', and the possibility of a title doesn't make up for him being Mr. Boring. Besides, he'd want children, heir and spare, and I don't want any, even if I could have them. And I'm not sure that I could."

"What about Felix?" I asked.

"Felix understands me. And he doesn't want kids. He wants a glamorous young woman on his arm who can show off his jewels to their best advantage and treat him well in bed. He's got sons from a previous marriage. They'll take over the business when he's ready, and we'll just have fun. He says I make him feel young again. And he makes me feel pretty damned good! I hardly ever think of Uncle Archie now."

"So on to this year. You decided to come to Paris. How did you fund it?" I asked.

"You know that, Alice. I dug up the body and took the cash. It was horrible messy work at the dead of night, and I filled in a bit, but it was all too much to finish filling in. The money was in a leather wallet lined with oiled silk. It hadn't rotted, I'm glad to say, but it was awful, touching a dead body. I didn't realize how people change, or disintegrate after they die. Nasty smelly oozy work. But the cash was intact. Three hundred pounds. I threw the spade in the river, had a shower, then packed a few things, all my jewelry, including both my passports, and called a taxi the following morning, and waited by the stables for it. Saying goodbye to Moonlight was hardest of all, but I had to go. I got a flight to Paris, and started changing myself, living my own life. I doubt my parents even noticed I was gone until the afternoon. Did they tell the police?"

"They did not. They let on you'd gone away for the good of your health, then they sent the horses away, I heard, and shortly after disappeared themselves, without paying their staff. Nigel picked up their debts. There's a lot of ill-feeling locally," I told her.

She sniffed. "Not my problem. I won't be going back. And someone will have a nice horse. He'll have sold himself, he's so beautiful. Felix has horses in South Africa, did you know?"

I shook my head. She really was a piece of work!

I didn't want to hear about Felix, didn't want to hear any more to be honest.

I let Jeremy ask more questions, and made a few more notes, then put my pencil and notebook back in my bag.

"What time are you supposed to be meeting Felix, Sylvia?" I asked.

She looked at the clock over the bar. "Good Heavens, is that the time? Have we done? I do hope so, I must fly!"

She stood up, smoothing her skirt over the mass of petticoats, picking up her handbag. "When can I sign this thing? I need to get this sorted out as soon as possible so I can get on with my life."

She gave us both the double bise, lingering slightly longer on Jeremy than she needed to.

"I'll ring you," I said.

She nodded. "Must go, thanks for the drinks. Please stay in touch. Au revoir," and she was gone, out of the café, out on the pavement, hailing a taxi.

Jeremy raised his eyebrows at me and shook his head.

"Don't say a word," I muttered as I finished the last of my citron-pressé. "I guess we'd better see if your friend Laurence has managed to find me a typewriter."

# 42

Back at the hôtel he'd left a message. A typewriter would be made available to me at the Consulate, all I had to do was go there and ask. That was far better than I'd hoped.

We took a prix-fixe menu in a local restaurant, huddled together with local office workers, sharing the carafes of red to wash down the céleri rémoulade, bœuf bourguignonne and crème caramel, then, after a small espresso, went back to the hôtel. I read out my notes, Jeremy wrote them down in a more formal manner then together we checked through and made a decent report. When we got to the British Consulate it was closed for the afternoon. It would open tomorrow at 9:30.

"We could find out how to get to Lanteuil," I suggested.

"Go to the station? Which station?"

I shook my head. "Nuance, not station, stationer's. They all sell railway timetables."

Some three hours later I woke up.

On my bedside table were scrawled notes of train times and changes. On my pillow was Jeremy's head, looking remarkably peaceful and young in slumber. I dropped a kiss on his forehead, then slipped on a bathrobe and went down the corridor for a shower. When I returned he was still sleeping, so I penned a letter to Père Laval saying we would be down to see him on Monday, asking him to contact the hôtel to confirm this would be convenient. I got dressed and went down to reception and asked them to post it for me, and for a pot of coffee for two to be sent up.

He was awake. "You look very fresh!" he commented. "Where have you been?"

"I've ordered some coffee," I said. "You might care to get dressed? For the look of the thing?"

"I might," he agreed. "I'm sure they are used to such situations here, but I could use a shower."

By the time the coffee arrived the bed was made and all was ship-shape. I poured my own and sat by the window enjoying the view over plane trees in full leaf, across roofs to the Eiffel Tower and beyond.

Jeremy returned, as spruce as I was, came over and kissed the back of my neck. "I could get used to working like this," he said.

"Me too. Tomorrow the typing, then we'll get her to sign it. I wrote to Père Laval. We'll go Monday unless he contacts us before then. The trains are rubbish on Sundays and he'll be busy anyway."

"So we have a weekend together in Paris! Yes, I could really get used to working like this." He poured his coffee, added a spoonful of sugar and pulled out the other stick chair and sat down. "I don't think I've ever had a better job, and certainly never a better partner, Alice. Do you fancy going dancing tonight?"

Then he chuckled. "I could never have said that to any other person I worked with!"

Despite, or perhaps because of, a late night on the town listening and dancing to some of the best black musicians I had ever heard, we were waiting on the Consulate steps when it opened the following morning, and asked for Mr. Fairfax.

Shown to his office through signs of remodeling, we found him, slightly jaded, shuffling a pile of papers between his hands. He perked up when he saw us. "Ah, Jeremy and the lovely Mrs. Carson – may I call you Sally? - the typewriter. How are you both enjoying Paris?"

He took us back down the main hallway and into another office, devoid of people, but with a couple of large desks, both with Remingtons, and typist's chairs. "Paper – top copy and flimsy – are in the top drawer, carbons in the second. Envelopes are in the bottom one. There's eraser there too, but I'm sure you won't be needing that. If you want to send reports, I can get them through swiftly through the Bag."

I settled myself at the nearest desk and started organizing myself. One top copy and three flimsies, interspersed with brand new carbons, slipped into the machine. Laurence Fairfax didn't appear to want to leave. He was chatting to Jeremy, who was telling him about bands we had heard.

"Oh, jazz? The place is alive with it. I've been told that

some of the musicians are very good, but it just sounds like a din to me. I went to an Arab restaurant last night with some friends. Amazing. I thought Muslims didn't drink until I came here. But alcohol is an Arabic word, would you believe!"

I got our report out. "Jeremy, would you read it for me? I can type as you speak, it would be quicker. And of course we could change things as we go along if we need to."

Jeremy sat beside me.

Laurence Fairfax headed back to the door. "Well, I can see you've both got work to do. Come and see me when you've finished. We could go for a drink."

"Thank you, that would be nice," Jeremy said.

"Thank you, Laurence, for being so helpful," I called after him.

By noon we had a decent statement and a report to Leggy finished. We took the statement for Sylvia to sign with us, but let Laurence have the report with an unsigned carbon copy enclosed to send through the Bag.

At that moment an older mustached man entered the office. He wore his clothes with supreme confidence, his dark hair slicked back to a patent leather shine. Laurence and Jeremy both stood to attention. I looked up into his face. He smiled at me. "Ah, Mrs. Carson? Colonel Legge said you would be accompanying Mr. Arkwright. Everything OK?"

"Yes, Ambassador, thank you. Mr. Fairfax has been remarkably helpful."

"So he should be, that's his job," he chuckled. "Well, Jeremy, what will your fiancée say about you having such a lovely partner-in-crime? I hope she's not the jealous type."

I pursed my lips – it was a compliment, in a way, – and tried to look unconcerned.

"Alice is a very understanding woman," Jeremy assured him, quick as a flash. Perhaps he was diplomat material after all.

"She'd have to be. But I'll not tell. Your secret's safe with me. In Paris anything goes." He shook hands with us both, lingering a little too long over mine. "And anything you need, just ask. Anything!"

His gaze said it all. He was propositioning me.

But, of course.

I was a widow.

And widows, like divorcées, were fair game.

So that was Alfred Duff Cooper. Married to the beautiful Lady Diana Cooper, and playing away with so many others that the gossip-mongers couldn't keep up. He did have a certain animal magnetism.

"He likes you!" Laurence Fairfax breathed, as though it was the ultimate accolade, when the Ambassador had left the office.

"That drink, Laurence?" Jeremy offered. "If you can get away."

"Oh, you heard what the Ambassador said, 'in Paris anything goes'!"

"Can I make a phone call first?" I asked.

"Be my guest! I'll just freshen up and let my secretary know we'll be out."

I dialed the Crillon. Sylvia was unavailable but they would pass on a message for her to ring me at my hôtel when she got in. Laurence Fairfax returned, and we went out, dropping off Leggy's letter with his secretary in the front office, into the bright sunshine in the rue d'Anjou.

We started with a drink – just the one – but pretty soon it became two, Laurence leading the way, and then it became lunch. By then Jeremy and I were drinking Evian, but Laurence continued emptying carafes of white – it was Friday and we were eating fish – and talking all the way through. We paid the bill and excused ourselves after the riz au lait, leaving him to his own devices. He was already calling for another carafe.

When we got back to the hôtel there was a message waiting. "I can meet you at the Sacré-Coeur this afternoon at three thirty, on the terrace overlooking Paris. I will wait until four. Sylvia".

It was 2:30. "Ever visited Montmartre?" I asked Jeremy.

"Actually, no. Artists stronghold, isn't it?"

So we went sight-seeing, enjoying ourselves among the steep streets and stairways, and having a wonderful time, just being lovers in the most romantic city in the world. At a quarter to four we got up from the café just off the Place du Tertre where we had stopped for a restorative coffee and made our way towards the great white basilica.

Sylvia was waiting on the terrace, leaning over the parapet, looking out across Paris. And nervous. She was smoking fiercely and kept looking at her watch, expecting us to come either by the funicular or the steps, although I doubt she would have deigned to walk up from Pigalle. Again she was in blue, but the skirt was close-cut, and mid calf. She wore a tight little bolero, a stunning little black hat with a froth of a veil, shoes with wedges, low cut at the front, and a tiny clutch purse, but all the same jewels.

When she caught sight of us she relaxed, threw down the end of the cigarette and came across to meet us.

"Thank goodness you came. I couldn't have stood here much longer, there were people constantly harrying me. Now, where can we go to sign this?"

"The church is probably more private than a café," I said.

So we went through the great portals and sat about halfway down the nave, in the middle of a row of pews, and under the wonderful mosaic of Christ in Majesty, I handed her the statement to read.

"Where do I sign?" she whispered.

"Read it first," Jeremy told her. "Never sign anything without reading it."

Her nose wrinkled. "But there are three pages..."

"When you've read it, you can sign – and we will witness that you have read it, understood it, and signed it on this date in this place. That's the way it has to be done, for your sake," he said. "Otherwise it might have something in that was untrue. You wouldn't want that, would you?"

He was flirting again, and she was loving it, and looked into his eyes and said "No, Jeremy, but I do trust you."

"Don't trust anyone in this life," he told her. "Surely your mother told you that?"

"Or Uncle Archie," I added. "Read it for him."

She looked down at the papers and worked her way slowly through them. I understood now why she didn't want to read them. Her lips moved as she followed the words, and often stumbled.

I hadn't realized she found reading difficult. I doubt she had had any regular schooling after the age of eleven, and she wouldn't have necessarily had much quality education before then. I was shocked, but amazed by her confidence, by the way she covered up her relative lack of literacy. In my world no-one left school without being able to read and write properly and do basic arithmetic – adding, subtracting, multiplication and division: it was what you paid for. I didn't enquire into her numeracy, but the school had taken money for false pretenses where reading was concerned.

At the end of page one, she looked up at me, pleading. "I don't have to go on, do I?"

"What if I read it to you? I swear to read exactly what is written here and Jeremy will verify it, won't you?"

"Of course."

"That would be wonderful. You won't tell Felix, will you?"

So I read, slowly and softly, and she listened attentively, nodding.

At the end she looked at me amazed. "God, Alice, you're so clever! It's exactly what happened. Give me the pen."

Quietly, using the briefcase as a rest, she signed, as Sylvia Nesmith-Brown, and we witnessed and dated, all the copies, blotting each one as it was done.

I handed one to her.

She shook her head. "She doesn't exist any more," she said. "This is the start of my new life."

I put the papers and pen back in the briefcase and stood up, ready to leave. Sylvia had already moved down the center of the nave, up towards the high altar, where she knelt and gazed up at the huge mosaic, her lips moving silently. Both Jeremy and I waited, some way back, until she'd finished and lit her candle, before we made our way out together.

Back in the open air she looked different.

Brighter, somehow.

"Let's celebrate in Paris, eh?" she said. "My treat! Let's take the funicular, it's such fun."

So we traveled down the hill in style, and then started walking south through Pigalle, Sylvia chatting away about how much she enjoyed being out in Paris. She seemed in no hurry to return to the hôtel, but was enjoying roaming through the red light district, even in daylight. "It never closes, did you know that?" she asked. "Soho's positively stuffy by comparison. No wonder people come to Paris!"

Eventually we reached the Rue des Martyrs – it was all downhill still – the road that joined the old city of Paris to the hilltop village of Montmartre, and found a bar that did please her, on the corner of Rue Navarin.

It had been a fair walk, and the day was warm, even a bit steamy. I was glad to sit down outside with a Perrier-citron. The quarter was busy, but not bustling.

Rue Navarin was pretty, one particular house drew me. It was only three stories high, but it was a little jewel in the French Renaissance style, the windows adorned by pretty ogee moldings, all regular, slightly flamboyant, but really charming.

I was admiring it when a large shiny limousine came from the far end of the road and parked beside it.

Jeremy followed my gaze. "Nice car!"

"Where?" asked Sylvia.

I nodded the direction.

She turned to look. "Good Heavens!" she said. "Look who's getting out. Well, I never!"

As she was speaking a chauffeur had come round and opened the passenger doors. A stylish woman in a tight turban adorned with exotic feathers, stepped out from the front, and a man in a pale gray lounge suit and matching hat, from the rear of the car.

Before they had crossed the pavement, the door of the house opened and they entered. It closed immediately behind them and the chauffeur put the limousine into gear and purred past us, turning left down the Rue des Martyrs towards the center of Paris.

"You know who that was?" I asked.

"Of course. It was the Duke of Windsor and Wallis."

"So why the surprise?" Jeremy asked. "They live here, in Paris."

Sylvia started to giggle. "They can do as they please, I say, but that house..."

"Yes?"

"It's a *maison close*, a brothel."

"I thought they were all closed down last year," I said. "There was a law passed."

She giggled some more. "Do you think that means anything? A lot of the cheap ones, perhaps, but some people are above the law. And that is a very special sort of brothel. Very exclusive,

Felix told me. He takes the occasional client there. It's not your usual sort, you see, not just women turning traditional tricks, it's for people with very specialist tastes and the money to indulge them. I suppose it opened especially for those two. They're very exclusive."

We all lit up cigarettes, each of us considering what we had just seen and what Sylvia had told us. Then Sylvia said, "I can't wait to get back to tell Felix. I wonder what their tastes are."

"I'm not hanging around until they come out to ask them," Jeremy said with a grin. "They could be hours if they're fit enough!"

We took a taxi back to the Crillon, and saw Sylvia safely back in.

She trotted over to the bar towards a large man with graying curls, dark eyes. On seeing her his face creased into a wide smile that boasted gold, and gave her a hug and a double bise. "Sylvie, chérie, you're back early. How lovely!" and as he did so a man in a check suit, to whom he had been speaking, slid quietly backwards along the bar, taking his drink with him.

Beside me I felt Jeremy stiffen for an instant. He had recognized him, too. Sylvia, however, only had eyes for one person, Felix.

Sylvia introduced me to her fiancé. He was deeply tanned and wore his black suit and tie with panache; his gold cufflinks, tie pin and signet ring all sported discreet diamonds.

He kissed my hand, then both cheeks and said "Truly enchanted, Mrs. Carson!" then he turned to Jeremy. "What are you doing here. I rang the embassy and they told me you'd gone back to cold England."

"I did. And then I came back."

"I can see why. I thought you were faithful to your lovely young Englishwoman," Felix said. "Well, she's not here, so the least I can do is buy you all a drink and you can tell me what you've all been doing this afternoon."

# 43

The waiter brought the cocktails, making a big deal on serving them up. Behind him the check-suited man made his escape. I followed him with my eyes as he strolled out of the bar towards the main reception area.

"Cheers, all, bottoms up!" Felix boomed, raising his glass high. We all did likewise, and clinked to friendship, Sylvia linking her arm through his as she drank.

I took a sip of the White Lady then excused myself to powder my nose and left the bar. Check-suit was in one of the phone booths, speaking in an animated manner. When I returned from the loo he had gone.

I went to reception and asked, in my best Loire Valley French, who the man who had been using the phone in booth six was, as I thought I recognized him – only it had been such a long time...

"Monsieur Brouk? He's not a resident, Madame. He works for some of our guests from time to time, very discreetly. That's all I can tell you."

I frowned. "Brouk? No, I must have been mistaken. Thank you so much."

I gave him my best smile and a small note then returned to the bar. Sylvia and Felix were ogling each other, hands on each other's thighs; Jeremy and I were definitely de trop. We drank up, thanked them and escaped out onto the Place de la Concorde.

Back outside the sun was sinking low. I told him what I'd discovered.

"Brook. I wonder how you spell that. I'll ask Laurence. Do you think Felix had her tailed?"

"Wouldn't you?" I asked. "I know they look all lovey-dovey in public, too much so, to be honest. But what do we know about him?"

"Does it matter?" Jeremy asked. "We'll ask Laurence that, too. Let's find a telephone."

He was in. "Jeremy, dear boy, I'm just going out. Can't it wait?"

"Probably, but I'd prefer it not to."

"OK. I'll do my best, but be quick."

"All you can tell me about Felix Van Buren and a chap called Brook."

"You don't ask much, do you! Felix Van Buren, diamond dealer and merchant, owns mines in South Africa. Rich as Croesus. Currently doing business in Europe. To the best of society and anyone else with cash for his merchandise. On first name terms with them all, including the Princesse de Polignac and the Windsors and our own dear Ambassador and his lady. They love him. He is a very smooth operator."

"Off the record?"

"Darling, you wouldn't want to know! He's rich because he's made himself indispensable and removed all the opposition. I have that from his Excellency. And he's known for catering for all tastes, if you get my meaning."

"Anything to do with the Meredith twins? Or John Anselm-Jones?"

"Of course. Birds of a feather and all that. What was the other name?"

"Brook. Medium to tall, medium build, dark hair swept back. Wears a grey and blue check suit, an odd cut, definitely not English tailoring, may work free-lance, possibly for him."

"Ah, Brouk with a 'U'. Yes. South African passport, like Van Buren, amongst others, I hasten to add. He's a general leg-man for people who want things done, no questions asked, so I've heard. Ex-military, I believe, through the school of hard knocks. If you want my advice, leave both well alone."

"Thanks, Laurence. I owe you one."

"Of course you do. Must dash. I'll be in touch. Got your number."

We crossed the river and headed east along the Boulevard St Germain, looking for somewhere to eat. Café Flore filled the gap; later I discovered we may have been eating in the presence of French intelligentsia, including Jean-Paul Sartre and Simone de Beauvoir, but that night I was with Jeremy and we were discussing the day. The mahogany and mirrors, the comfortable

French furniture, and the noisy clientele were noted, but it was the enjoyment of a bottle of Nuits St Georges, steak-frites-salade and floating islands with each other for company that made the evening special.

Back at the hôtel the receptionist handed us mail and messages: one from the Père Laval who would meet the train that left Paris at 9:27 for Blois on Monday, two others, one for each of us, in very grand envelopes from the British Embassy.

Jeremy ripped his open while I was reading my message.

"Hellfire!" he muttered. "I could do without this!"

"What?"

He held out a deckel-edged card inviting him to a reception on Monday evening. "I should think yours is the same," he said. "Damn, damn, damn!"

"Oh, come on, Jeremy," I said. "It'll be good practice for you, mixing with the great and the good." I smiled.

"It's bloody Leggy, isn't it? He and Bas stitching us up. I bet they know I left my penguin suit in London," he muttered, then, "What's this?"

In with his invitation was a scrawled note from Laurence Fairfax: 'You'll need the correct attire - I've got a spare, should be able to find something to suit you, sir – pardon the pun! Cocktails and dressage at my place, 7 pm, Monday. Bring Mrs. Carson! I can accommodate her too if needs be.'

## 44

I didn't fancy being accommodated by Laurence Fairfax, so the following morning we obeyed Leggy's orders and visited Boulevard Haussman and the Grandes Magasins – Galeries Lafayette, Au Printemps and the like. There was far more to buy here than in London, and best of all, you didn't need coupons. I blew a lot of money that day, on metres of silk, velvet and workaday cotton, dressmaking magazines from which an able seamstress like Angelique could create templates, and all the sundries, interfacings, bindings, lining fabric, buttons and fasteners, and had some fun matching up threads so they would be virtually invisible. Besides some new and beautiful underwear, I also invested in a little black dress, my own, like Jeremy's penguin suit, being at home, and a tiny matching hat, more a velvet headband adorned with a cloud of gossamer veiling. As a widow, Mrs. Carson would naturally wear black at a formal occasion. The dress was very simple and off the peg (a grand peg, it must be said!), and I went into the fitting room so they could make the necessary adjustments to it; I was happy with it, but it did look sombre. I had to think about something to lift it. Even a widow needs a bit of color in her life.

While I was being fitted up, Jeremy took himself round the rest of the galleries. We met up for an early lunch in the Galeries Lafayette restaurant at noon, both of us delighted with our purchases.

"I'll show you mine if you show me yours," he invited. "But not here!"

"La, sir, what is a lady to make of that?"

"Whatever said lady cares to," he chuckled.

"Back at the hôtel, then? You're on a promise!"

"Pity we've already ordered, then."

We spent the afternoon being lovers again, and chatting in a companionable manner between bouts of activity. He had found some Pashas, and we decided that while we were in Paris we would smoke – everyone else did, like chimneys on fire, to be honest. The clubs were eye-watering towards the end of the final set and any perfume you might have put on at the start of the evening lost out to the smell of old ashtray. Our clothes and hair stank of Gauloises and cheap dark cigarettes. So we enjoyed the tobacco, and knew that in England things would, of necessity, have to be different. The cost alone was a deterrent.

Around eight o'clock we sallied forth to find food and music by straying back across the Pont au Double past Notre Dame, to the right bank and heading north. It was a good evening and people were out enjoying themselves.

"What did you make of Stefan and Elisabeth's idea of cleansing the site?" Jeremy asked.

I thought. "She'd mentioned it to me before, but I'm not sure how we'd do it. Something about clearing the long dark shadows of the people involved and their actions. What is this Stefan? What does he actually do?"

"This and that around the corridors of power as far as I can make out. But he is a fully trained ritual magician. Well, that's what he told me, and he taught me how to use the rings, so he knows something and is willing to pass it on. Do you really want to continue in esoteric work?"

"Do you?" I asked, hoping he'd say yes.

"It's interesting. I can see it becoming addictive," he mused. "And with you beside me, I think we could make a great team. But I rather fear there will be a lot of study involved."

"Ah, a book at bedtime... Let's do it! Remember when we were at Elisabeth's that first time?" When our minds had melded with hers and we had been quietly blown away from reality.

He smiled at the memory. We had staggered out, hanging on to each other and wandered round the Boltons until we were fit to drive. "Yes. But didn't it feel right?"

I nodded. "I don't think there is any question that we continue, do you? I got some black cotton today for robes, if you want one. I'll make them when we get back to London."

"And I thought you were buying stuff for our wedding."

"I was. But mostly for Maman, Angelique and Maddy. They've missed out on good fabrics these past years and they all wear them so well." I smiled up at him. "I have earmarked a bit for myself, of course. I couldn't have you marry me looking like a rag-bag."

"Certainly not – but I would! And you could never look like a rag-bag, trust me on that! You have too much style."

"Thank you, like attracts like. I do hope Laurence's suit will be OK."

"Oh, we're about the same height, so I won't have the trousers having arguments with my shoes, nor the cuffs with my wrists. The rest can take care of itself – I will either be tight-fitted or fashionably loose. It's the ladies who steal the show, anyway. Fancy a drink? And a bite to eat?"

Some time later we found ourselves in the Rue de Martyrs once more. It was dark by now, and there was a lovely local atmosphere far removed from the formality of the grand houses and boulevards. People were chatting and eating in cafés, calling to each other, greeting with kisses and handshakes, shops pulling down their shutters, music coming from upstairs windows, and generally normal life was going about its business.

As we passed Rue Navarin I sneaked a look back at the lovely renaissance building where we'd seen the Windsors exiting their limousine and entering the portal. Of course, we only had Sylvia's word that that was what it was, and I wondered about Felix taking clients there. But in business, of course, anything went, especially if you dealt in high-class merchandise. Which he did. Was Sylvia another bit of high-class merchandise, I wondered.

"What do you make of Felix?" I asked.

"Not sure now," Jeremy replied. "At face value, I'd say he comes across as perfectly nice. And successful. But I wonder what that chap in the check suit was saying to him. And also what he's doing with Sylvia."

"Having all his birthdays in a week?"

"No... And she is desperate to please him. Do you think she's a bit scared of him?"

"Didn't look like that to me last night. They were all over each other."

"Yes. But I think that's the only card she has to play with. Well and her youth, but she can't rely on that forever. Why do you ask about Felix?"

"Because since we spoke to Laurence, I can no longer take him at face value. Is Laurence's assessment valid?"

"He may be a gossipy old queen, but I think he's sharp enough to know what's what. It's the other chap I'm interested in. What's he up to? With Felix, I mean. Of course, it could simply be two fellow countrymen in a foreign land. But I think not, somehow."

We walked on arm in arm, each in our own thoughts. As we got further up the hill, there was a definite change. It was seamier. You could feel Pigalle coming down to meet us, the bohemian and local feeling of the quarter being taken over by the louche and the darker side of humanity. Street people were out now, men who swaggered and would almost certainly have carried a knife or two around their persons, women with too much make-up, especially around the eyes, and clothes that gave promise of easy access to what lay beneath.

"Feels like walking into an apache dance, doesn't it?" Jeremy said, holding me closer to him. He pronounced it properly – 'a pash', not 'a patchy'.

I smiled. "I'd love to do that, you know! I know it's horrible and supposed to be about a pimp beating up one of his women, but it looks such great fun to do. And the music. I love it, it's so blatant."

"Da da dada dada da, Dah! whack!" he chortled. "I'll dance with you, Alice. I promise I won't hurt too much or drop you on the floor."

"No dragging around by the hair, either, mine's too short." But it would be fun. "We could do it at our wedding! You wear a pimp's gear and I'll have a skirt split to my waist. That should set the ball rolling."

We were still getting over that idea when a fracas broke out in the street some way ahead of us. A young woman in a very tight red dress was being bundled by two men into a parked car. She was fighting back but no-one was helping.

We ran towards her, as she kicked out at her attackers. "Help! Help!"

Not 'Au secours!'.

She was English, and putting up a good show, blonde hair swishing as she hit out with her head.

Jeremy reached her first and pulled the first man off. I put my arm round the neck of the second man who was trying to push her into the car, and pulled backward sharply. He let go of her and grabbed my arm, to release his throat, but I already had my hand over his nose and mouth, and I just stepped backwards. I saw Jeremy land in a couple of good kicks at the first chap then drag the young woman away from the car to a sidewalk café where she could sit and recover herself.

She refused to sit.

She leaped up at him and began kissing him wildly.

That wasn't on.

The car was starting up, and I threw my man into the back seat, choking. Jeremy's man, clutching himself, crawled in beside him, I kicked the door closed as they were driving off, then turned angrily to sort out the female who was snogging my fiancé.

Already there was chaos behind me. From out of the sleazy bar came a large man, bellowing, running towards Jeremy and the blonde who were still entangled, mostly down to her clever use of arms, legs and face.

I was already dis-entwining this red-dressed hussy, when the angry man pulled her off and was about to thump both her and Jeremy.

"Felix!" I shouted. "Stop at once!"

Jeremy pulled himself back, free from her grasp. "It's not what you think, Felix, truly it isn't!"

Felix looked from him to me, and then, to Sylvia, who was dressed like a tart, but still dripping with jewels.

"So what is it?" he demanded. "I go to visit the gents and pay the bill and come out and find my fiancée, my fiancée, no less, entwined with a personal friend of hers. What is a man to think?"

"They saved me, Felix!" Sylvia cooed, linking his arm. "They came and protected me at my time of need. I had to say 'thank you', now, didn't I? It was only good manners."

He looked from one to the other of us. "And did you thank Mrs. Carson in the same way?"

"That won't be necessary," I told him. "But that is what happened, I assure you. Two men got out of a car and dragged Sylvia from her seat and were forcing her to go with them."

"They nearly strangled me with my necklace, Felix," Sylvia pouted. "And one of them was after my ring. I did fight, but Jeremy and A – Sally were wonderful. I think I need a brandy.

And I think these two do, too. It was very exciting, but now it's nasty. I think I'd better..."

She fled into the interior of the café. I followed to make sure she was alright. The loo, used by both sexes, was pretty disgusting, but was at least unoccupied. I waited while she threw up and rinsed her mouth out with the awful-tasting tap water, and splashed a bit over her face.

She looked up at me. "Thanks, Alice. For not being mad at me. I've always wanted to kiss Jeremy. You are lucky. And thank you for saving me. I don't know what might have happened..." she was still shaken.

"Nothing nice," I told her. "But what on earth were you thinking about, on your own dressed like a that?"

"You mean the short red dress? It's nice, isn't it? Felix bought it for me. He likes me in it."

"I've no doubt, but better at home. And the jewels? In daylight when you're with other people you know around, but at night in the red light district? You're asking for trouble, sitting out on the pavement like that, by yourself, surely you must know that?"

"I wasn't on my own. Felix was with me all the time. He'd only gone in for a wee and to pay the bill, Alice. Just a few minutes, that was all. It was just a bit of fun. Felix likes to live dangerously. That's what makes him fun." She twisted her hair back into a French pleat, and examined the abrasions where the necklace had scratched into her flesh, dabbing at them with a damp grubby handkerchief which probably did more harm than good.

"Come on, I'm fine now, and you were great, Alice. So was Jeremy. I owe you both one and Felix owes you several!" She pulled a tiny purse out of her cleavage and took a lipstick out. "I'll just fix my mask."

"Yes. Don't ever try your tricks on Jeremy again, Sylvia. I am not a forgiving woman."

She slipped the purse back into her bosom. "Absolutely. I wouldn't be if he were mine. No, I'll be a good girl from now on. After all I do have a very rich fiancé," she flashed a grin and her ring at me. "Do you want to borrow my lipstick? We should look our best for our menfolk."

I let her exit first, her lips matching the bright red of her dress, but with her hair pinned up she did look better.

I closed the toilet door behind me, and nearly stepped on the feet of a man on the telephone which was under a hood next to the loo. I felt a shudder down my back. I recognized the blue-gray check, and he was following Sylvia with his eyes.

I avoided his gaze, hastened after her and was blinded by the flashes of several cameras as we reached the pavement. I put my hands up to protect my eyes, and slithered sideways out of range. Sylvia was loving it, explaining in poor French that 'tout va bien, maintenant' and huddling into Felix's shoulder, while dragging Jeremy into view beside her.

Journalists were shouting questions at her, and as is usual in such cases, people gathered around to be part of the street theater. But no police.

I looked questioningly at Jeremy, who was inching away, allowing journalists to take his place beside Sylvia.

He shrugged. "They just turned up," he said while Felix was chattering to the gentlemen of the press in fluent but strangely accented French and Sylvia posed and pouted prettily for the cameras, and showed off the scratches on her neck. The café owner came out, now, to give his version of what had happened – it was, after all good publicity – and pointed to us, as the saviors of the young lady.

"Mr. Brouk's in there," I whispered.

"Indeed! There's a brandy and coffee for you, Alice, let's drink up and go?"

I downed them both in that order, a quick restorative, and together we slid away from the chaos into the night, trotting swiftly over the cobbles to the métro at Saint Georges, all thoughts of going to a club and dancing the night away forgotten.

Back at the hôtel we considered what had happened, and Jeremy used lighter fuel on his shirt to remove the stains of Sylvia's lipstick. We smoked Pashas and drank a very good Côtes du Rhône that we had picked up that morning.

"Mr. Brouk was there," he said. "And Felix left Sylvia on her own on the pavement looking like an expensive piece of totty while he paid the bill. Why wouldn't he call the waiter?"

"He went for a wee, Sylvia said. He couldn't have done that on the pavement," I reminded him.

"But he could have got the waiter to keep an eye on her.

Surely? Or Brouk?"

"If Brouk was was tailing her for him. Which we don't know."

"True, but if not, was he involved in the abduction attack? And on whose orders? Whatever the answers, he'd failed in his duty. That would hurt his reputation."

"Who do you think sent the press round?" I asked.

"Are you saying it was a publicity stunt, and we blundered in and messed it up?"

"No. As a publicity stunt we were good. But as for blundering in and stopping a possibly lucrative insurance scam, we could be construed as a nuisance, something to be got rid of. After all, they can't play the same stunt twice."

"Do you think Sylvia knew about it?"

"I don't know. But she did come out smiling, make up and hair ready for photographs. Of course I may be very wrong, but she did mention that Felix likes to live dangerously, and that's what makes him fun."

# 45

We were on the front page of Paris-Dimanche! It's a scandal-rag, but surely they would have had a bit more scandal than Sylvia Cavendish, lovely young fiancée of the great diamond merchant Felix van Buren, being unsuccessfully abducted. I managed to be deep in the background, my face hidden by my hand, but Jeremy was there as the hero of the hour, with Sylvia looking at him coyly and Felix pumping his hand with gratitude.

I read it over breakfast in the hôtel restaurant. The coffee was good, and so was the bread and black cherry jam; there was a lot of it, too, which surprised me as there was a bread shortage currently, something that the French found very difficult to deal with.

The maître d'hôtel brought over the paper, and asked if this was indeed Monsieur.

"Yes," said Jeremy, and poked his finger at me in the background "and Madame."

The maître d'hôtel puckered up. "Then would you kindly do me the honor of signing it – I should so like to show it to people. You saved a millionaire's fiancée. He must be very grateful to you both. A little present, eh? A diamond would be nice! I'm sure he could spare one. You did leave him your address here?"

I hadn't thought of that, but Jeremy chuckled with the man, "Oh, they know where we are, monsieur, je vous assure!" and took out his fountain pen and signed the newspaper photograph, and handed the pen to me. "Fame at last, eh, Mrs. Carson?"

We spent the morning in the Musée de Cluny, something I'd not done since I was a girl, and I found it even more of a delight than I had then. I'd not been to a museum with Jeremy and was a bit apprehensive at how he would take it. He'd only really been taken to the Walker Art Gallery on a school trip – which he had paid for himself from his paper round because any day out was better than a day in school – and had loved that, but here was something totally different, an amazing building built on the site of a Roman baths, and full of such wonderful things that he was dazzled, wandering around with a smile constantly lighting up his face, it was a revelation to him, and, I must admit, his appreciation was a revelation to me.

"I've never seen such stuff, Alice," he kept saying. "I had a vague idea it might have existed, but this ..."

"Today Cluny, tomorrow the Louvre!"

"Tomorrow Blois!" he corrected, "with our own precious artifact. Is it as beautiful as I imagine?"

"Probably more so," I told him. I'd forgotten he'd never seen it.

We finished at the Lady with the Unicorn tapestries, and just stared at them. I loved them as a girl – what teenager wouldn't? – but their beauty was now enhanced by my appreciation of how skilful were the weavers, the designer, and the story behind the legend of the unicorn. Other visitors came and went, but we stayed, trying to commit the wonderful works to a special place in our minds so that we could recall them in all their glory at will.

Finally we wandered back through the galleries to the entrance courtyard into bright warm sunshine.

"That was amazing, Alice. Thank you so much for showing me such a wonderful place." He was blinking rapidly. "My eyes hurt from looking."

"Art historian's eyeballs," I said. "It happens to the best of us. We were in there a long time – four hours to be exact - and I'm feeling a mite peckish."

Back at the hôtel there was a message for us from Laurence. Jeremy rang him, but he was out, probably drinking another restaurant dry.

The dining room was cool and welcoming. We ordered the pâté de foie, poulet aux champignons, and tarte au citron, then sat back with a bottle of Quincy, chilled to perfection to wait for the meal to arrive. It didn't disappoint, and we took it slowly, savoring every mouthful. About an hour later we were in the lounge sipping espresso and a very good cognac when a whirlwind in blue thundered in.

"Jeremy, A... Sally, how glad I am to find you in!" Sylvia greeted us loudly, rushing over and pulling up a fauteuil. "I've brought you these as a thank you!"

She plonked herself into the armchair and deposited on the

tiny table a bouquet of white lilies and red roses, and a box of very expensively wrapped chocolates.

We said our thanks. "Do you want a drink? You look terribly hot," I said.

"Love one. It's scorching out there."

She ordered Perrier citron, and the waiter took the flowers, "I will put them in your room, Madame, so you may enjoy them."

Sylvia slipped out of her little blue bolero and hung it over the back of the chair. "I didn't come this morning, I thought you'd need some time to yourselves, Sunday lie-in and all that..."

"Sally took me to a wonderful museum," Jeremy told her.

Sylvia's nose wrinkled. "Well, if you like that sort of thing, I suppose."

"So is Felix having a siesta after your morning activities?" he asked with grin.

"Unfortunately not!" She was cross.

I wondered what had happened after we left them last night.

"So where is he?" I asked.

"Gone to bloody Antwerp! We were having breakfast when the phone rang and everything started to go wrong."

Jeremy's cigarette case and lighter was out in a flash and she selected a Pasha. Still no holder, I noticed, and the lipstick stained the thin white paper like blood. As she inhaled her drink arrived, and a fresh ashtray.

"What happened?" I asked.

"Well, Felix got the call and told the person on the other end to come up. I wasn't best pleased, but what could I say. I went and got dressed, and when I came back into our lounge there was this chap with frizzy dark hair jabbering with Felix in some funny language, so I couldn't understand a damn thing and they were gabbling at each other for ages. At last Felix nodded and said in English, 'Yes, of course I'll come.' Then he turned to me and said he had to go to Antwerp. This man was the son of a very old friend, a diamond cutter, who was dying, and asking for him. There was a private plane waiting for them at Orly, as the old man only had a short time left. So he would go and see him, to say goodbye, and do a bit of business while he was there."

"What about you?" Jeremy asked. "Did they ask you to go?"

"No, of course not. It was business, anyway, hardly treats. I bet the plane would be one of those things that make you air-sick and it would be no fun sitting round a Jewish deathbed with a load of old people dressed in black. Felix knew how I felt. He told me to enjoy myself, he'd only be a day or two, and then told Bif and Bof to get ready to travel."

"Bif and Bof?"

"They're what I call his protection. They've got funny Afrikaans names. They live down the hall. If he goes anywhere with merchandise they are always with him. Heavies. Don't speak English, just keep the diamonds safe."

"And then they all just went?"

"Well, not exactly. It took a bit of time to get things sorted, packing bags and the diamonds and stuff, then he gave me a kiss and tucked a big sheaf of notes down my front and told me to have a good time. So here I am. Where shall we go? What shall we do?"

I sipped my coffee. I didn't want to go anywhere or do anything with Sylvia, except possibly avoid her.

"I don't know," Jeremy said. "I'd like a quiet afternoon, after that Museum and my lunch. And another cognac. Perhaps we could go out this evening. I'll try Laurence again" He signaled to the waiter.

"I'll get these," Sylvia told him. "What was the name of that drink I had with you the other day?"

While Jeremy went to the phone, Sylvia decided to tell me all about how her life would be in South Africa. I must admit to glazing over and nodding occasionally. I caught bits like 'and I shall have two servants, a maid and a boy, all to myself, and another just to keep my clothes looking wonderful, isn't that amazing, and I'll be in charge of all the other servants, only I'll let the housekeeper think she's doing it all, like before... and there's the polo, he's got horses. And dogs. He's promised me a hunting dog, and we'll go on safari. I'd love to shoot a lion or two... there'll be so much to do, and then there'll be parties, because there's nothing else to do if the servants do everything for you. And he says I'll be the most luscious creature in the room because the sunshine makes the women's skin very wrinkly very soon. I must take care to use lots of cream...'

At last the drinks came – yes, I needed the cognac! – closely followed by Jeremy. "Laurence will be over very shortly," he said. He looked at Sylvia. "I think you'll like him, he can be great fun."

Hell, I thought, two rattles! And the day had started so well.

As it happened Laurence was just what Sylvia needed. He flattered and admired her, and talked mischievously. He was obviously far more to her taste than we were. We watched him draw her out.

"How could your fiancé bear to be away from you for a moment, my dear?" he asked. "If I were he, and of course, if I weren't quite so bohemian in my tastes, I'd have taken you with me, just done the duty call, then rushed you off to a little love-nest somewhere. Who were these people? Did you catch their name? I have friends in Antwerp, perhaps I've met them?"

"Shouldn't think so," Sylvia said. "Jews. Diamond-cutters, something olowsky I think, and the chap who came was called Samuel."

"Sam Kowalowsky? Pushing fifty, dark frizzy hair with a bit of gray in it and a big nose, wears black?"

"That's right! You do know them! How amazing!"

Jeremy's eyes met mine: "racial stereotype" they said.

"Know the family well. Of course they 'disappeared' during the war, but they're back to stay now. Very orthodox. Felix does business with them from time to time, I imagine?"

"That's right. He supplies their diamonds. From his mine."

"And... er, what was Sam's father's name, now? It escapes me for the moment." Laurence's brow wrinkled. "Getting old already! A... something?"

"I think I heard Abraham mentioned," Sylvia said. "He's the one that's only got a few days to live at the most."

"Then Felix will stay for the funeral?"

"I don't know. I suppose he will want to. But that will mean he'll be away ages." Her face crumpled. "What if the old man hangs around. I'll be stuck here all by myself. It'll be horrible."

"I shouldn't think he'd be that long, if his son came to get Felix. I'd say it was on the cards that he'd go in the next forty-eight hours, and Jews like to bury their dead swiftly, so Felix will be back by what, Wednesday afternoon, at the latest. Probably before."

Sylvia's face dropped. "That's three days. What am I going to do for three days here by myself?"

Now we all looked at each other. We could all think of lots of things to do, places to visit.

She looked at Jeremy, pleading. "Oh, you must see how it is. I'll be bored to tears. I'll just spend my time with you two. And with Laurence, if he'll have me," she blew him a kiss. "You'd take pity on a lonely girl in Paris, wouldn't you?"

Jeremy said very gently, "Sylvia, we understand how you feel, but Sally and I are working. We can all go out tonight, but not out terribly late as we've got to get up for work tomorrow."

"But I could work with you. I'd be no trouble. I'd be quiet as a mouse," she looked up at him from under her eyelashes.

"No can do, Sylvia," he said firmly. "This is government work. We aren't here for a holiday. We have to meet some people out in the country somewhere. I can't even tell you where it is or who they are, and certainly couldn't take you along. I'm sorry."

"Well tomorrow evening. We can go out on the town."

"No, we already have an engagement that cannot be broken," I told her.

"Where? Perhaps I could come along?"

Laurence caught my eye and gave me an almost imperceptible shake of his head.

"I'm afraid it's by invitation only and they are not handed out lightly."

"Huh, that's not on," she muttered. "I'll be on my own all day and all evening. Laurence, can you help me, sweetie?"

"Not completely, because I, too, have to work, but I could introduce you to a friend of mine who is staying in Paris and at a loose end, too? Would that suit? He prays at the same church that I do, so you'll be perfectly safe. I'll give him a call, shall I?"

# 46

I was glad to be sitting on the train to Blois. It had pulled out of the Gare d'Austerlitz on time and trundled through the suburbs of south west Paris. They were small compared to the sprawl of London and we were soon in open country. Opposite me Jeremy was leaning against the dark green leather seat, in his shirtsleeves. He looked less than his usual pristine self, and I suppose I looked similar. We had caught the train with just a minute to spare, having run along the concourse of the station, and it was a sultry day, dark heavy clouds blocking the sun's rays but allowing its heat through.

I put my shoulder bag, with its precious brown-paper covered parcel on the rack above my head, then pushed the windows open to their fullest extent. Any air was better than no air.

A warm blast with more than a hint of sewage hit me full in the face. I closed them again.

Jeremy chuckled. "That was ripe!" He pulled a cigarette case from his trouser pocket. "This should kill it!"

I took my cigarette holder from the pocket of my shoulder bag, and inserted a Gauloise. "This would kill anything," I told him. It was a Fûmeur carriage and smelt of stale tobacco anyway, but the scent of sewage was tenacious. I let him light me, then opened the sliding door to the corridor, slamming it shut immediately: all the windows were open there and a noisome gale was romping down the train.

"Can't see Sylvia enjoying that," Jeremy said as I settled down next to him.

"Good job she's not here, then, eh?" I knew that David was taking her down the catacombs today, and to other creepy places. Still, it would keep her off our backs.

"Yes. Laurence told me he'd keep an eye on her – David, that is. I think he's doing a bit more than that."

"Like what? Seeking information?"

"Yes, and they'll get it. I don't think she realizes how much she knows about things, and she chats away all the time. She never shuts up. Makes you wonder what Felix sees in her."

"I'm sure he can find ways of keeping her mouth otherwise occupied," I commented, sourly.

"But not all the time! He may look pretty fit for his age, but he's no spring chicken." He blew out a cloud of smoke. "Happen he arranged the trip to Antwerp for a few days peace and quiet!"

"You think he won't come back?" I hazarded.

It just popped out. Hell, that would cause trouble!

"Ooh, Alice, you have such a nasty mind sometimes!"

"That's why we suit, darling. Don't say it hadn't occurred to you."

"Probably at the same moment it occurred to you, Alice. There, two nasty minds in harmony. How good is that?"

Pretty damn good, actually. We were alone in the carriage, so I let my head rest on his shoulder until we rattled into Orleans, where we bought bottles of water and pains au chocolat through the window from the refreshment trolley on the platform, and the carriage filled up with four more passengers, two well-dressed elderly couples, bearing beautifully wrapped parcels and a huge bunch of flowers, who were off to Tours for the seventieth birthday party of their brother/brother-in-law, who had no idea what had been planned. "He had a small party with his local friends, yesterday," Madame told me, "But this is the big one – in the Hôtel de Ville, friends and family from all over. His son's even come across from Canada!"

They chattered on happily until the train chugged into Blois, where we shook hands all round and wished them a wonderful day before we climbed down to the platform.

I looked around for Père Laval. I was expecting someone like the Rev Simmons, and there was no evidence of anyone like that. We wandered through the arch to the main entrance, and there, beside an early Citroen Traction Avant, stood a jolly-faced man in full soutane, mopping his bald head with a handkerchief, his biretta in his left hand.

He stowed his handkerchief when he saw us, replaced the biretta and came towards us beaming, his hands out in welcome.

"Mademoiselle Chamberlain? Monsieur Arkrit? I am Raymond Laval, welcome to Blois, please come with me."

He shook hands warmly, waving our passports aside, "You are

the only people off this train I do not already know, so I know who you are. Come, Madame de Lanteuil is waiting." He ushered us into the back seat of the car and drove off, passing the chocolate factory and out of town.

"Madame lives in retirement now – she was with her family in the south during the war, but she prefers it here, even without Monsieur. She would very much like to speak with you about that man of whom I wrote."

We turned from a small country road onto a track bordered by walnut trees, which led to a small château, the three-storied central block having a high pitched roof with fish-scale slates, attached to two lower mansard-roofed wings. Père Laval pulled up under the porte-cochère, and opened the car doors for us. "Please, come in. Thank you Amélie," he nodded to the maid who had opened the front door for us.

"Madame is in the library," she said. "I'll tell cook you're back."

We passed through a very grand, if rather faded entrance hall, to a room on the left, before the staircase. It was quite dark, cool, and smelled of old books, dusty drapes and pot-pourri. I noted several bowls of dried flower petals, mostly rose and honeysuckle, even before I focused on the tiny woman sitting by the window at a small table.

"Père Laval, you've returned. Bring these people into the light so that I may see them. Mademoiselle, Monsieur, please forgive me for not standing to greet you, rheumatism is an awful thing." She held out a minute knobbly hand to each of us, while Père Laval introduced us to Madame de Lanteuil. She was dressed in black, and wore her gray hair in plaits coiled on top of her head. Her eyes were intensely green and bright, her cheeks slightly rouged, and her lips wore red sweetheart lipstick. The smile when we took her hand gently, lit up her face like a beacon.

"How lovely to have young guests here again," she welcomed us. "Do take a seat, both of you. Père Laval, a little apéritif for us all, don't you think?" She turned to us. "Was your journey pleasant?"

Père Laval dispensed tiny glasses of clear brownish liquid. "Pousses d'épines," said Madame. "We make it every year. Santé!"

It was delicious, refreshing.

"Almonds?" Jeremy asked.

"Blackthorn," said Madame.

"Delicious!"

I put down my glass and opened my shoulder bag, handing the packet to Père Laval. "I am asked to give this to you, Père, and to make sure that only you open it. You will see it is sealed. This was done in London. It has been either with me or in the hôtel safe ever since."

Madame handed him a paper-knife from the tidy on her table. "Bring it over here, mon Père, I want to see this."

Slowly he cut into the wrapping paper, carefully unfolding it, until the Book of Hours was revealed.

Madame and M. le Curé both gasped. "It's ours, it's Lanteuil's treasure," she said. "It's the very one we showed that evil weasel of a man!"

"Yes, Madame. It is," Père Laval said, and delicately opened the clasp. "You permit me?"

"Of course," I said. "Please, go ahead."

Together they examined the book, remembering pages, their faces lighting up at the delicate painting and penmanship. Jeremy stood behind them and I watched his smile spread as the pages were turned.

I sipped my apéritif. I hadn't really expected anything else to happen, but it is always good when things go as you hope.

"Well, Mademoiselle, Monsieur, we can authenticate this as the Lanteuil Book of Hours. What else do you need from us?"

"A sworn, witnessed statement from each of you to that effect and to what happened to it during the war. I can type it if you wish."

"No, no, no, Mademoiselle, I have a person to do all my correspondence. She will do it after lunch. You know, of course, who took the Book. It wasn't the Nazis, although they took what they wanted. No, it was that evil weasel who insinuated himself into my husband's good offices. He was a clever man, an educated, cultured man, but he was not an honest man! I knew he was involved with the Germans before he last came here. I told Edouard not to trust him, but he wouldn't listen."

"His name, Madame?" Jeremy asked.

"John Anselm-Jones. I will get my secretary to let you know all the times he stayed here. I wasn't here when the Germans came. That was both lucky and sad for me, for I doubt I should have survived. I was with my daughter in the South – she had married very well and was expecting her first child and wanted me there. They wanted me to stay on, but it gets too hot down there in summer. I go in the winter to escape the cold."

Père Laval said, "I assure you that it was Monsieur Jones who took the book, and the Lady, too. And I can get other witnesses – although all of them will only have seen through darkened windows. You might like to visit our local blacksmith, he's as honest as any man, and he came to help me when the Germans had left me sprawled in the nave."

There was the sound of a gong from somewhere in the depths of the house.

"Lunch, my friends. I hope you will enjoy our humble hospitality," said Madame, and for the first time I realized that the pretty wooden bergère chair that she was sitting in was in fact a wheelchair. Père Laval stood behind her while she locked the book in the drawer of her table.

We processed into a dining room where the best china, glasses and flatware were laid out before us on a white damask cloth, where we were treated with the best 'humble' food and wine I have ever experienced. A goat cheese tart, with a cabbage and walnut salad, pike in beurre blanc and new potatoes, and a dish of local cherries just as they were, all washed down with the local Vouvray. We took a glass of home-made walnut liqueur with our coffee, and retired to the sitting room where we were introduced to Vivienne, her secretary/companion who had been out earlier.

Vivienne shook hands briskly and produced a file containing details of John Anselm-Jones's visits to Lanteuil. "May I bring the typewriter in here, Madame, there isn't enough room for us all to be comfortable in the office?"

Jeremy followed her out and lifted the heavy piece of equipment while Vivienne brought paper, carbons and flimsies, and a rubber.

We spent the afternoon doing and signing the statements of Père Laval and Madame de Lanteuil regarding the theft of the Book of Hours and the Lady.

"The Book of Hours belongs to the Church," I said. "I am empowered to give it back, but do you have a safe place for it?"

"It will stay in Madame's safe until I have such a place in the church," Père Laval told me.

"I am paying for such a display unit," Madame said. "Vivienne, you might ring M. Leblanc, he's promised me he will be available to make such a thing. It will be set into the church wall, Mademoiselle Chamberlain, and impregnable – only Père Laval and I will have the keys – it will need two to open and close – and mine will be locked away, only as a precaution against theft."

I looked at Jeremy and translated. "You happy with that?"

"Sounds good to me. I think Leggy would be fine with that. He's got what he wanted from it."

Père Laval coughed. "You wrote that you had the Lady of Lanteuil. Would you let us have Her back some time? She belongs here with us."

"At the present time She is part of an investigation, but I can assure you that She will return to you, hopefully sooner rather than later, although I cannot say when."

The priest nodded. "Whenever you can let me have Her, I shall be most grateful," he said. "We are delighted that you have been so good as to return the Book."

We left shortly after with the statements and a receipt for the Book of Hours in envelopes in my shoulder bag, with invitations to call again any time we were in the vicinity.

Père Laval drove us down the walnut avenue to the tiny village. He took us into the church and showed her where the Lady had stood, the broken 'safe' from which the Book of Hours had been liberated and the exact spot where he had been pushed down, unconscious, to the floor, then hustled us back into the Citroen. He dropped us at Blois station, shook our hands heartily and then drove off.

We spent the half hour before the train arrived in a local cutler's shop, where Jeremy bought a couple of spring-loaded knives, and I purchased a fine carving set. The day had been good.

## 47

We used the hôtel safe for the documents then went upstairs to prepare for the evening.

Despite my telling Jeremy it would be fun, I had some misgivings. Not about him, perish the thought, it would be good practice for him and he did look good in his penguin suit, but I was flying under false colors and I was concerned lest my cover be blown by, for example, an old school-friend who had done well for herself and was, with her husband, attending the function.

I knew what shrill voices some of the ladies had, and how a gushing 'Alice, darling, it's absolute ages since I saw you, where have you been, my dear?' would cut through any buzz of small-talk like a hot wire through butter.

We arrived at Laurence's in a taxi just after 7pm. He lived on the top floor of a grand house in the Marais. I hadn't known that such houses were being partitioned into apartments, but it had been tastefully done and made good financial sense. The concièrge let us in and gave us directions.

"This is worse than your place in Chelsea, for steps," Jeremy commented, as we left the opulent wide staircase behind and continued up the narrower one that led to what had been the servants quarters.

"Welcome to my eagle's nest," Laurence greeted us with open arms and open door. "And what have you been doing today? Come in, come in, do!"

He popped a bottle of Mercier and poured three flutes. "Cheers, my dears, to the good life, eh?"

We clinked glasses. The champagne was chilled, dry and very welcome.

"Now, Jeremy, let's get you looking the business. You, Sally, look wonderful. Far too young to be a widow – excuse me, not the embodiment of tact, and I've been hitting the Mercier since five – apologies if I've offended, but you seem to be coping with things very well. Oops, there I go again. Better stick to what I know. The suits..."

I smiled at him. "For this champagne I can forgive a lot; I've been widowed for longer than I was married, Laurence, and I actually find the state agrees with me."

"And black suits you so well, my dear. I love the hat!" He took Jeremy into another room – probably his bedroom, where I heard the two men chattering and clothes being shed and replaced. There was a peel of laughter, and I heard Laurence say, "I've got a longer pair. Just a moment."

Eventually the two of them returned to greet me with a flourish 'Ta-da!' and then a bending of the knees and 'Oh, yea-eah!', hands, in white gloves, waving back and forth in the air.

I laughed and clapped. "You'll do!"

They both stripped their gloves off and slipped off their jackets. They had the full works on, stiff shirts, ties, cream waistcoats and of course the heavy wool trousers. It was far too hot for all that. No wonder Laurence had been at the Mercier. I only had a lightweight dress over some thin undergarments, stockings, shoes and a hat – and of course my jewelry, none of it heavy, and I was hot.

Laurence refreshed our glasses and phoned for a taxi. "A propos of nothing," he said, "I telephoned Antwerp today. The Kowalowsky family are alive and well and old Abraham is not at death's door." He looked at us meaningfully. "And there is no report of Felix van Buren and his two henchmen entering Belgium."

"Oops!"


The Embassy was amazing!

It wasn't yet dark, but the way to the entrance, once we'd been admitted through the grand street gates, was marked by two rows of lights.

Laurence was less than impressed. "God, that brings back the war! I used to fly Westland Lysanders and have to land on paths like this. Bloody awful landings in bloody awful fields in the middle of bloody nowhere, on moonless nights as cloudy as this, always fearing you'd be shot down by Jerry or crash into some blasted tree because the runway was too short and the fog too dense. A wing and a prayer, eh? And you had just four minutes before you had to be airborne again!"

Then he brightened. "But see, I survive. I am alive and well and living in Paris. Which is more than Hitler is, God rot him!"

We were welcomed charmingly by the Ambassador, and his lady, the beautiful Diana. "Duff and Diana, to you two," he said, plonking a kiss on my lips, rather than the more usual handshake or double-bise.

"Work going well?" he asked Jeremy, pumping his hand.

"Completed, sir."

"Well enjoy tonight, my dears," said Lady Diana. "I'll come and chat later, but you know how these things are. Go and find some refreshment, it's so close, isn't it. I'm rather hoping for a storm to clear the air."

"Ambassador," Laurence said, clicking his heels and nodding.

"Oh, go and look after these two, Laurence. I know you're only here for the bubbly and the boys."

So we went in and handed our cards to the Master of Ceremonies who introduced us to the glittering world within the even more glittering rooms beyond. Behind us in the queue others were being greeted.

Laurence led us through the throng of fashionably dressed women and elegantly suited men and sequestered champagne. It was as good as the Mercier, but probably cost twice as much. I sipped it and looked around. It was extremely hot although the windows were all open and a small band played standards in muted tones at the far end. We mingled and chatted to various people to whom Laurence introduced us. We spoke English and French, which meant Jeremy spoke English and I spoke French, and Laurence kept us all supplied with drinks and canapés by flashing his eyes at the young waiters.

The Ambassador approached with a lovely young woman on his arm. "Je vous présente, Madame La Princesse, Mrs. Sally Carson and Mr. Jeremy Arkwright. Sally, Jeremy, meet my friend, the Princess Ghislaine de Polignac. She wants to enjoy herself. I'm sure you will all get on so well together."

We did the enchanté bit, and the Ambassador moved off, kissing her hand as he left, with a wink and a whispered "I'll be back!"

"Of course you will, darling, but be quick. I'm off to stay

with Rosita at the Château d'Horizon very shortly, which is where you'd be, too, if you had any sense!"

Then she turned to us, and smiled. "He's such a dear man, you know. All the women are crazy for him and, to be honest, he doesn't let them down. And his wife's an absolute darling. She knows he'll always return, once he's had his little fling. So civilized, don't you think? I mean marriage is not about love, it's about alliances and money, so once you've done your duty, and I have – four children is more than enough to keep the old Polignac line going, and I do have very good bones, which has improved the stock no end – I think a bit of pleasure is in order, don't you, Mrs. Carson? Or can I call you Sally? I can see you do. Mr. Arkwright, what exactly is it that you do? I came across your name recently somewhere. Delighted to meet you, Jeremy isn't it? I'm sure we'll be great friends."

She sparkled.

She was my age, born in the South of France, had huge bright eyes and thick blonde hair; she stood elegantly and wore her lovely clothes and jewels with grace. I admired while Jeremy gave her his best smile, and said, "I'm sure we will."

The sun had set now, the Ambassador and his lady were mingling in the brightly lit room, when suddenly a flash of lightning and an almost immediate rolling crash of thunder rent the air. The room gave a squawk of surprise, then, having ascertained all was well, heaved a collective sigh – the storm had broken! - everyone settled back to what they had been doing before, eating, drinking, gossiping.

The Master of Ceremonies rang his bell and introduced the late-comers. I felt the tension as he solemnly intoned "His Royal Highness, Edward, Duke of Windsor, and Her Highness, the Duchess of Windsor," followed by "Lord Oswald Mosley, and Lady Diana Mosley."

You could hear a pin drop.

Even the band stopped playing.

The Duke and Duchess had somehow got invitations which were not theirs to have.

He was a small man, small and slight, with a world-weary look on his face.

She, too, was small, upright, and incredibly thin, not an ounce of spare flesh, her face pinched, but they presented the epitome of the elegant society couple, exuding confidence and glamour.

Such was their charisma that people started forming a queue to greet them, a line of honour. Ghislaine swiftly tugged us into it, anxious to be part of it.

"Damned if I'm going to salute a bunch of Fascists," Jeremy muttered. "They've no right to be here or expect anyone to welcome them."

It seemed his attitude was only shared by me. With the Princesse de Polignac on Jeremy's left and Laurence on my right we were hustled into the impromptu line up. The Ambassador and his wife were nowhere to be seen at that moment, or things might have been very different.

Edward Windsor took it as his due, and greeted friends and 'subjects' down the line, having a word or two here, a smile there, with Wallis, wearing white from neck to toe, including long gloves, awash with diamonds, following him, supporting him with a smug smile that said she knew exactly what they were doing.

This was an invasion, cocking a snoot at Britain, the country that, they believed, had let them down so badly.

I didn't feel for them at all.

I felt angry that they should have been able to gain admittance.

Edward, Duke of Windsor approached.

Princesse Ghislaine dropped a deep curtsey and looked up into his eyes winsomely.

He smiled and raised her. "You look ravishing, Princesse, as always."

She gave a little quiver of delight. "Thank you, your Royal Highness," then cast her lovely eyes down to the floor.

"Ah, Mr. Arkwright. We meet again, I see. I thought you'd gone back to your little fiancée, but no, I find you here in Paris with a particularly ravishing lady at your side. What about poor Lord Wethersley's daughter? Not that I care. Wethersley's a waste of time, insufferable man. Do you know, he turned down a chance to paint our royal portraits? Twice! And I shouldn't be at all surprised if he's not behind the death of my poor friend John Anselm-Jones. No love lost there, I believe, and no smoke without fire... Still, you have a delightful companion tonight." He turned to me, "And what's your name, my dear?"

I was seething.

Suddenly everything made sense.

I'd met him before, too, not just when I came out as a debutante, but later, and I'd never liked him. This evening I wanted to throttle him.

I refused to meet his watery gaze but had to reply to his question.

"Mrs. Sally Carson," I spat the words out. "Sir!"

"'Your Grace', you should call me 'your grace' or 'your royal highness', but 'your grace' will do."

I said nothing, just stared straight ahead, avoiding this short, supercilious man who looked like Queen Victoria, my teeth clenched, jaw fixed, rigid in every muscle.

He eyed me up and down. "And you curtsey, too, there's a good girl."

I stood my ground, didn't move a muscle, looked over his shoulder at the band at the other side of the room.

"Well, well, well, what are we to make of you? Absolutely no manners but a pretty face... and somehow familiar. I've met you before, haven't I? Some time ago. Refresh my memory, eh? I'm sure we would have had fun together."

So he remembered me. Or thought he did. Dammit, I let him have it with both barrels, but I kept my voice dangerously low.

"I was sent by the British government and the French government, to implore you to come back and serve your country and your regiment, sir." I used 'sir' as an insult, and he knew it. "You abandoned your country and your friends, and stayed in Biarritz and then went to Spain in the company of Nazi sympathisers. And yet you expect me to bend a knee to you?"

He took a step backwards, but I wasn't finished.

"You've no right here. This is British Sovereign territory, and you have been exiled!"

Now Wallis leaped forward, snarling angrily.

"How dare you speak to his Royal Highness, the Duke like that, you insufferable young woman!" and raised her diamond-clad arms to slap my face.

I blocked the move, throwing her slightly off-balance, then brought up my other hand to clap at something. "Oh, the flies, they get everywhere these days. Excuse me, I need some fresh air."

I stepped out of the line and marched out to the terrace where the electrical storm was bringing in the rain. I didn't look behind me, but almost immediately there were people following. I heard Lady Diana's voice encouraging the band to resume their music and then tell her husband that gatecrashers would not be welcome and he should get rid of them.

"Major diplomatic incident, Mrs. Carson," said Laurence, at my elbow. "Well done!"

"I won't bend a knee to such people," I said. "Especially after what he said about..." I bit my tongue, "about Lord Wethersley."

"Oh, I thought you were making a political point, sorry!"

"You are right, I was."

Jeremy lit me a Pasha. I smoked it nude; Pashas didn't fit into my holder. "Lord Wethersley has more ethics in his big toe than those two have in their entire bodies," he said. "Come on, Sally, I'll take you back to the hôtel. I could do with a walk."

"Come back to my place, and pick up your clothes," Laurence said. "I'll just see if the Ambassador needs me."

"I suppose we must go and say goodbye, but I doubt we'll be in good odor!" I said, gloomily.

"Oh, I don't know, Alice," Jeremy chuckled. "Someone had to tell the buggers to get lost, and better you than me. I've got a career to build, after all!"

The rain that had started slowly was now hammering it down. I put my arm out beyond the terrace roof and let the drops cool me and began to laugh.

"I'll never tease you about your lack of subtlety again," I promised. Below me, along the drive with its two lines of lights two limousines were heading gatewards. One I had seen before outside a maison close. I smiled.

When we went back into the party everything had changed. The line had disintegrated, the band resumed their instruments and couples were dancing; the Windsors and the Mosleys were nowhere to be seen.

The Ambassador and his wife were toasting each other in champagne by the entrance as we approached.

"Well, I thought that went very well, dear," he was telling her.

"Of course they'll get over it, but we can't have them playing king and queen, can we?"

"Dear me, no, Duff." She turned to us. "Well, thank you, Mrs. Carson. You did us all a service. Now why did you take such a stance? Not that I don't applaud it. You gave us just the introduction we needed to act. Here, have some champagne."

"Er, no. I believe I've had enough for one night. Thank you for a … an interesting evening. I need to leave. I'll be going back to England tomorrow."

"Oh dear, so soon? And you, too, Jeremy?"

"Yes, Lady Diana."

The Ambassador shook his head. "Can't think what's happening with the world, everyone's deserting us, Ghislaine, you two, there'll be no-one around left to talk to. Well, safe journey both, and when you come back, do keep in touch."

He put down his glass and looked at his wife. "Come, my dear, let's go and join the dance."

# 48

My hallway was cool when I stepped through the door, and there was a pile of mail awaiting me. I left the suitcase beneath the telephone, and started sorting it. Messages first, one from Sam, which said simply "Ring me!" and another identical from Elisabeth, both with numbers attached. The rest were either from friends or bills and could wait. Jeremy closed the front door and put his case next to mine while I dialed Sam.

"Alice, listen. According to the Registrar who admitted Cissie, she was semi-conscious. When he asked if she could tell him who did it, she said, and I quote, 'no, my Dad would kill me.' Just breathed it, but Billy Laycock has a record of not being very nice. He asked her where she got the abortion, and she said 'London'. It's not very helpful. I wish I knew where the bastard took her. We could bring this to a close if we did."

I listened and thought. "Leave it with me, Sam. I'll get back to you. It may be a long shot, and I'm not promising anything. And thanks."

I relayed that to Jeremy. "How many abortionists do you know?" he asked.

"Personally, none. But I know a man who might know."

We locked up and took the taxi to Leggy's to report and hand over the papers.

Bobby greeted us, "Oh, milady, and you, Jeremy. Good afternoon. Come on in, the pair of you. I'll put the kettle on. Leggy's in his usual place."

Leggy was dozing slightly in his armchair, Nuts on his lap. He stirred when Bobby announced us and started to busy himself with his pipe. The room was almost back to its pre-Thelma state: the net curtains had lost their pristine whiteness and there was a feeling of orderly disorder about the place. "Come in, my dears, I'd not expected you back so soon."

I took the easy chair. Jeremy perched on the arm and opened his briefcase.

"Excellent!" Leggy said, taking the folders from Lanteuil and the originals of Sylvia's statement which we'd wrapped in a copy of Paris Dimanche. "Bloody Hell! What have you been up to?" He cast an eye down the newspaper. "Is that Sylvia Nesmith-Brown? She has changed! I suppose I ought to call her Sylvia Cavendish now, or is she already Mrs. Van Buren?"

"Sylvia Cavendish," I said, "But not for much longer, if she can help it."

"Well, good luck to her. She looks a lot happier than she was with young Guy," he chuckled. "And he looks a lot better without her, too, don't you think?"

He turned back to the paper. "So you saved her from being attacked? I hope Van Buren was suitably grateful."

"Not so you'd notice," Jeremy replied. "Oh, and Alice had a slight contretemps at the Embassy."

"I heard. Well done, my dear. I knew I could rely on you. But steer clear of the blighter from now on, eh?"

We went through our trip in detail – well, apart from certain bits which only concerned us – and Bobby brought in a pot of tea, and a plate of fruit scones and played mother.

"Do you still have John Anselm-Jones's telephone numbers?" I asked.

"Of course. Why?"

"Can I have a flick through?"

Bobby brought them over. "Anything in mind?"

"A hunch."

While the others ate scones and drank tea, I flipped through the cards, looking for anything to do with health or women. Nothing in the first coil, nor in the second, but I struck lucky on the third. "Anybody know what Panacea is?"

"The daughter of Aesclepius, Greek God of Healing, along with her sister,Hygeia," Jeremy said, surprising me. I hadn't got him down as a classicist. It must of shown on my face. "Got you, Alice Chamberlain!" he grinned. "I may be a rough diamond, but I've read a book or two."

"Panacea Advisory Bureau? No address, just a phone number," I told him.

Bobby chuckled. "I hope you won't be needing that, Milady. Amongst other things, it's a place where naughty girls go when they've got into trouble."

"Then can I use the phone? And no, Bobby, it's not for me."

The woman on the phone had the most calming voice in the world. She purred gently, "Panacea Advisory Bureau, here to help, whatever your problem. No problem is so large that it cannot be shared. Let me help you, my name is Dulcie, or Mrs. Dowsett, if you prefer. How can I be of assistance?"

I made myself tense and worried. "I'm in a bit of a pickle," I stammered. "I.. er... asked around and someone said you may be able to er..."

"Connubial emergency, is it?" she cooed. "I can see you within the next hour if that's possible for you, and give you an introduction for tomorrow. You do understand there will be a fee for the introduction, it's ten pounds. And you will have to negotiate with the doctor, too. Mrs. ...?"

"Carson, Sally Carson. Yes, yes. That would be wonderful... Can I have your address? I'll be over at once. And thank you so much Mrs. Dowsett, er Dulcie."

I scribbled down the address. "Bingo!"

It was on an upper story in a row of terraced houses to the north of Oxford Street. We entered and followed the cardboard signs to the door. Jeremy rang the bell. A whey-faced clerk opened the door. "Ah, Mrs. Carson? Do come in. Mrs. Dowsett is expecting you." She led us into an office, then knocked on the door. "Mrs. Dowsett, Mrs. Carson's arrived." Then she let me into the room, but kept Jeremy firmly outside.

"But I need to go in with Sally. I look after her."

"Perhaps you should have looked after her better so she wouldn't need our services, eh?" I heard the secretary say. "I'm sorry sir, it's house rules in this matter. We all have to abide by rules, sir, don't we, at some time or another, or things go awry."

She closed the door behind me.

Mrs. Dowsett of the calming voice stood up from her desk to greet me. "Oh, Mrs. Carson, I am so sorry to hear of your difficulty. Tell me about it, and, if you would be so good, how you heard about us. Whatever you say will be in total confidence and between these walls, I assure you."

I twisted my handkerchief between my hands. "I didn't mean

it... I mean, things just happen, don't they. And my husband had been at sea so long. I was lonely..." I looked at her pleading for her to understand.

"Of course you were, Mrs. Carson. A lovely young woman like you, and loneliness is so hard to bear," she purred.

"We were very careful. No, honestly, but accidents happen. At first I thought nothing of it, I was not that regular anyway, but then my breasts began to hurt, so I guessed what must have happened. And yesterday I got a letter from my husband saying he'll be back in England at the weekend and ... well, I don't have much time to prepare for him. He'll be wanting a lot of attention, you understand?"

"Oh, yes, I do, Mrs. Carson. Speed is of the essence. You want to be fit and ready for him, as any wife would." She let her hand hover over her telephone. "I'll check with our doctor to see how she's fixed. When was your last proper period?"

"The beginning of April, the sixth." I'd worked that out in advance.

"Then I'm sure we can sort your little problem satisfactorily, Mrs. Carson. For a fee."

I delved into my handbag and brought out two big white fivers which she received nodding, and stowed in a small cash-box that she took from a locked desk drawer. "No receipts, you understand, this is strictly between ourselves. You wouldn't want it on the books, now, would you?"

"I understand," I said meekly, and watched her dial – the number was on the London exchange, FRE 4708 – so very local to me, Earl's Court and South Kensington.

"Sister Margaret, how is Doctor fixed for tomorrow morning?" Mrs. Dowsett whispered, turning her face towards the window so I wouldn't catch the conversation.

I looked around. A comfortable spacious office, with good quality furniture, A view over the gardens, and, I noticed, access to a decent fire escape. Very wise.

Mrs. Dowsett turned to me, smiling. "Doctor will see you tomorrow morning. Her fee will be in the region of fifty pounds, due to the risk. Not to you, I hasten to add; she is fully trained and will expect you at 9.30. I know I can trust you not to pass on her address to anyone who could cause her a problem, as this would get you into trouble as much as her. If you are pleased with our services, do let any of your friends know. Word of mouth is so helpful, as you, yourself, will find out."

She scribbled the address on a notepad, ripped the page off and handed it to me. "It's been lovely to meet you, Mrs. Carson, despite the trying circumstances. I hope we may meet again in better ones, and that your difficulties will soon be over." She stood up and shook my hand, signifying that the interview was over.

I picked up Jeremy and we went down the steps swiftly.

"What happened?" he asked.

I told him. "And you?"

"They're not solely a front for illegal practices, but I'd guess that makes the most money. They will provide anyone to deal with any distressing circumstance – including private eyes, helpful household staff, and I should imagine people who are not averse to dirty deeds, a bit of duffing up, supplying things you might need that aren't available on the open market, that sort of thing."

"That mousey little woman told you all that?"

He pouted, "She was lonely in that dark little office all by herself, she wanted to talk, and I can be a very good listener."

"Damn right!"


As we got out of the taxi, George came bouncing over the uneven pavement to meet us.

"New skates, George? How wonderful!" I said, as he cannoned into me.

"Hello miss, hello mister, yeah, I got 'em for passing me eleven plus. Isn't that great! Mum saved up for them from what I gave her."

"Well done, George," said Jeremy, ruffling his hair. "Now you'll be a grammar school boy like me." He dipped into his pocket and brought out four half crowns. "There, spend it wisely." He handed over the big silver coins. "No, forget that. Have fun with it. You've earned it.!

George's face lit up. "You sure, Mister, cos it's a lot of money. I'd be perfectly happy with half that."

"So be doubly happy with that. And enjoy it. Want to come and get the red car with us?"

"Yeah. I wanted to tell you about that. I saw this bloke driving it down the Fulham Road, and I shouted at him at the traffic lights, but he didn't answer and drove off. So I followed him. I was on my skates, so it wasn't too hard. And I saw it outside this house in the Boltons, so I knocked and asked what the hell they were doing with your car."

"And what did they say?" I asked.

"That lady what came round with the short hair, she came down with this big fair-haired bloke, and said you'd let them have a lend of it. I guessed it was alright, cos I recognized her. Anyway, he gave me half a crown for being a good mate to you. He had a good laugh, though, cos I was puffed. It's a long way when you're doing top speed and you have to dodge old ladies with shopping baskets. They don't half know some rude words if you scare them!"

We walked, or in George's case, skated, round to the Boltons. Elisabeth gave me a sheaf of papers. "Some ideas for some work we're planning. Take a look and let me know what you think." Stefan handed back the keys, sadly, it seemed to me, while George took off his skates and got in the back, grinning like a Cheshire Cat. As Jeremy started the car, I slipped into the passenger seat.

"Fish and chips, George?" Jeremy asked.

"Cor, guv, I thought you'd never ask!"

# 49

When Jeremy turned up to collect me the following morning he looked decidedly louche. Unshaven, he wore black, in the style of the pimps we had seen in Pigalle, and moved with a swagger. "Da - da-da – da - da-da da Dah! Whack!" he greeted, grabbing me round the waist and sweeping me backwards. I squawked! He brought me upright with a mocking bow, then dropped a kiss on my cheek.

"Blimey, guv, you gonna knock me about a bit?" I asked. "I ain't done nuffink, honest!"

"Nobody knocks my girl about, love, you know that. I just thought it might give us an edge. I'm not sitting outside today. We go in together. And we work as a team, eh?"

He followed me up the stairs and took the coffee I offered gratefully as he inspected the work that had been done. "It's looking good, isn't it? Can't wait to move in."

"We could put the wedding forward," I suggested. "We only put it back because we thought you'd be out of the country for ages."

"We could indeed," he agreed, beaming through the stubble.

We were let into the flat in Barkston Gardens by a pretty woman in a blue uniform. "Mrs. Carson, is it?"

I nodded.

"So glad to meet you, Mrs. Carson. Do come in." She took us up in the lift to the second floor and ushered us into a waiting room. "I'll let the doctor know you've arrived," she said. "She will explain the procedure."

I looked at Jeremy, uncertainly, as we'd planned. He gave me an encouraging smile. "It'll all be over, soon, Sal, don't you worry."

"Of course it will," the uniformed woman said. "It's very simple, there's no need to be fearful. I'm Nurse Margaret, and I'll be with you all the way, to hold your hand and see that everything goes according to plan." She smiled at me. "It's not an easy decision to make, and you've been very brave. I'll just be a moment, then doctor will see you and we can get started."

Bloody Hell, I thought. It's all so matter-of-fact. But then, why not? It was only the illegality that made it all such a shady business.

"Doctor will see you now, Mrs. Carson. No, sir, I don't need to know your name, but you can't go in."

Jeremy towered over Nurse Margaret and said slowly, "I think you'll find I can. I stay with Mrs. Carson at all times. Understood?"

He lifted her bodily by her shoulders and removed her from his path, following me into the doctor's office, and took up his station, slouching beside the closed door.

"I take it my presence won't inconvenience you, Doctor. Anything you have to say before Mrs. Carson, you can say before me. Mrs. Carson has hired me to accompany her every inch of the way, and I earn my money. Her interests are the same as mine."

The doctor, a middle-aged woman whose short dark curls were flecked with silver, looked over her spectacles at him, displeased. She wore a white lab coat, and a stethoscope round her neck. "Then you may stay, but this is strictly sub rosa, none of what you hear and see here has happened. Just so you understand that, sir!"

She put the same insolent emphasis on the 'sir' as I used myself. I got the impression that she didn't like men very much, although they were the ones who kept her in work.

"I understand completely, doctor. By the way, where were you trained? And we'd like to see the surgery. We're very keen on the strictest hygiene. Don't want any problems afterwards." He pulled out one of the knives he bought in Blois, flicked it open and started cleaning his already-clean nails. I saw him twist his Abraxas ring, and did likewise. I needed to stay in contact even though he was out of my line of sight.

Her face darkened, the jaw set, her mouth a thin line. Then she turned to me. "Nurse will be preparing our surgery now. We pride ourselves on the strictest cleanliness."

"Thank you, doctor. And the training? I couldn't put myself into the hands of anyone who had no medical training."

She calmed a little. "Of course. Princess Mary's RAF Hospital, Halton, originally, but then I decided I didn't like what men did to women, so I took a course in Gynaecology and Obstetrics."

She drew a framed diploma from her desk and showed me. Dr. Hilda Scarsdale graduated from PMRAF Hospital, Halton in 1937. "The war brings out the worst in people, Mrs. Carson. I decided to help women such as yourself retain their equilibrium. If every child were a wanted child, the world would be a far better place."

I couldn't disagree.

"So how can I serve you, Mrs. Carson? Oh, there is a matter of the fee, of course. Fifty pounds, paid in advance. Mrs. Dowsett mentioned it?"

"Yes," I said, and opened my handbag. I felt Jeremy's warning: don't give it to her! Keep your hand on it.

"And for that you guarantee that all will go well? There will be no repercussions, no difficulties?"

She had reached out her hand to take the ten big white fivers. I held the notes down and stared her out.

"I am a professional," she spat.

"But accidents can happen. I don't want to be left in jeopardy."

"There is danger everywhere, Mrs. Carson. You could trip over the kerb and be run down by a bus!"

"True, but ... I need assurances."

"Mrs. Carson, you came to me, recommended by a friend, I understand, so you must know that my work is thorough!" She was needled. "Who was that friend, may I ask?"

I smiled. "I do hope you remember her. She came to you last year, around the end of October. Very young."

"A lot of them are," she said sadly.

"Cissie," I said. "I think she came with a much older man." I pulled out a picture of John Anselm-Jones. "Cissie Laycock." I said. "Tell me you remember her, please, Doctor. About five foot three, long dark hair, looked like a waif, big brown eyes. And about three months pregnant."

She looked at the picture of John Anselm-Jones. "I know him. Very smart gentleman, terribly generous. And very attentive to the child. Said he was her guardian, but I had my doubts, of course."

There was a knock on the door and Nurse Margaret came in. "It's all ready... Ohhh!"

Jeremy had slammed the door behind her, shot the bolt, and had Nurse Margaret in his grip, waving the knife before her.

"Enough of all this, Doctor. I shan't hurt Nurse Margaret at all if you tell us absolutely everything that happened between you and Cissie Laycock."

The nurse was squirming and screaming, terrified of the glinting blade. "Tell him, Hilda, for God's sake, tell him. He'll kill me"

I slipped behind the desk and caught the doctor's right arm up her back and held it there. "Cissie died of septicemia!" I hissed. "You understand what I'm saying? It's murder! Tell us what happened. How did you come to kill a child in difficulties?"

"Tell them, Hilda, tell them. Or I will. I don't want to die!" the nurse squealed.

"We've only their word for it, Margaret. Shut up." Even as I held her she was trying to wriggle free, to wriggle out of the situation.

"Tell us, Nurse Margaret," I said. "Cissie was my friend. What happened here?"

"Keep quiet, ouch!" shouted the doctor.

I slapped her face with my free hand. "Don't even think of stopping her!"

Jeremy led her to the chair I had vacated, kicked it some distance from the table and pushed the nurse in. "Have a seat, Nurse Margaret and tell us what you know. I'm letting you go, but I still have a knife, and so has Mrs. Carson, should she feel the need to use one."

The nurse rubbed her neck. "Please don't hurt me. I'll tell you everything. Just leave me alone."

The doctor continued to struggle.

Jeremy looked at me. "Mrs. Carson, do you want me to take over with Dr Scarsdale?"

He slipped round the other side of the desk and pulled the doctor's face towards him, staring straight into her eyes. "I know you think you're doing a service, but you really aren't helping very much. We want to find out all about Cissie's visit. If you and your nurse tell us everything you know, we'll leave you alone...

possibly."

She stared at him crossly, "You expect me to believe that? A vicious hoodlum like you! Coming in here and threatening defenseless women, why should I help you in any way?"

"I can think of several reasons, Doctor Hilda Scarsdale," I said. "Firstly, we would be very grateful, for your help. Which could be beneficial for your continued survival. You see, not only is Cissie dead, but her nice gentleman is also dead, and he was definitely murdered. We know that was nothing to do with you, but the deaths are linked, and there is a real murderer out there on the loose. That's who we are after. You may be able to spread some light."

"And you'd leave us alone?"

"We would show clemency," Jeremy said. "And of course, we could all be sitting far more comfortably if you complied. I really don't like threatening women. Unless I have to. What say we all sit down and you both tell us what happened?"

"Put the knife away!" the doctor said, still trying to deal. She knew that her future was going to be compromised.

"I think not. I find it concentrates the mind wonderfully. And we need your minds to be truly focused."

He nodded to me. I let her go. She was sweating profusely and starting to hyperventilate.

"The door is locked," I said. "So no-one's going anywhere. Take some time, ladies, to catch your breath, and then you can tell us all."

And they sang.

Cissie was brought by her Uncle Edgar at the end of October for a termination.

"She was terribly fearful," said Nurse Margaret. "I had such a hard job calming her, she was rigid. She wouldn't even put her feet in the stirrups. We had to give her something to relax her. I soothed her as much as I could, but the drug did most of the work."

"Did you ask her why she was so scared?"

"Of course," Nurse Margaret said.

"What did she say?"

"'My Dad will kill me!' Those were her actual words."

"You're sure?"

The nurse looked up at us sadly. "She was terrified of him."

"Did you ask her who had got her pregnant?" I asked.

"Yes," said the nurse. "I asked if the man who brought her was the father. And she cried, great big sobs. 'Not him. He's the best man in the world. He's taking me away from it all. He's getting me a position in London.'"

"So, who was the father?" Jeremy asked. "Did she tell you?"

"Yes." Nurse Margaret's eyes filled with tears. "It was her father. No wonder the poor little mite was terrified."

Dr Scarsdale said quietly, "From what I saw while I performed the operation, this had been going on for some time. There was a lot of scarring that you wouldn't have expected in one so young, believe me. She had been brutalised for a large part of her young life. If you can bring that man to justice you will be doing us all a favor!"

We were all silent. I knew we only had their word for it, and they would never testify, but it felt horribly right.

I said, "And the operation went alright?"

"We did our best. When she left us she was no longer pregnant and had had the best care we could give. We've never heard of any 'accidents' to our record before, which is why Panacea are happy to introduce us," the doctor said, wearily. "What happened after she left..."

"I think she was going home," Nurse Margaret said, softly. "She had a job to go to. I got the impression she would be moving up to London the following month. She would have got over the thing by then, built up a bit of strength, too." Tears rolled down her face. "No-one should be treated like that, poor little lamb!"

I stood up and to my surprised Dr Scarsdale pushed the pile of fivers towards me.

"No charge, Mrs. Carson. We're on the same side. I guess I should be looking for a new surgery."

"I think that would be very wise, Dr Scarsdale. Thank you for your help, and yours, too, Nurse Margaret."

Jeremy shot the bolt back and we made a swift descent to the street below. He slid a cigarette case into my hand, silently. We smoked fast and furiously as we made our way back to the tube, sickened by what we had heard.

# 50

"So how was France?" my sister demanded. "You dog, off for a dirty weekend with your paramour and getting paid for it!"

I chuckled. "It was wonderful! And it seems so long ago, already. I've brought you a present."

She cooed with delight over the fabric. "I'll get Angelique to make it up. I'd not trust my own skills on this beautiful stuff." She held it up to her face, and looked in the mirror. "Oh, Alice, it's so lovely, thank you so much," she said, hugging me and plonking a kiss on my cheek. "I hope you've got some for you, too."

I nodded. "But I need to make up a couple of things, could I use your facilities?"

"Of course, but, surely, with a decent piece of fabric... Wouldn't it be best to give it to Angelique?"

"No, this is strictly magic and needs to be made by me."

"Ooh, you're still into wizardry! How exciting. Let's have a cup of coffee and get started. You can tell me all while we're doing it. Nannie's taken the kids on a mass Nannie and charges outing; they won't be back for hours."

So we got stuck in, as we had as girls, pinning and cutting the paper patterns, tacking up the seams, setting in the sleeves, pockets and hood, of two black cotton robes. I played down the reasons for my trip, and my little contretemps at the Embassy, but told her all about Sylvia and Felix.

"Does Nigel know?"

"Shouldn't think so. She doesn't want him to know, either. In case he goes on the cadge."

"Do you think they'll marry?"

I shrugged. I'd no idea. And if what Laurence said was right, then Felix was missing, but I didn't mention that either. I kept it light, let her talk about Enid and Robin, her charity work, and various classes she went to until the robes were tacked up.

"Do the Aged P's know you're back?" she asked as we both

tucked into beans on toast with another cup of coffee.

"We're going down tonight."

"Good. Would you beg a favour from Angelique for me?"

Jeremy picked me up in the little red car from home shortly after five. He had shaved and was wearing a suit and a fresh shirt and tie as tomorrow he would be returning to London to work. I had decided to stay on for a day or two. I'd come back on the train if I needed to, but I'd packed the two robes as I would get a chance to fit them this evening, and hand-sew them tomorrow. Along with the robes were the presents.

Jeremy lifted the suitcase into the back of the car beside his overnight bag. "What have you got in here, Alice? I thought you were only going for a day or two."

"Sweeteners," I said, climbing into the passenger seat. "What have you been doing since I saw you last?" I dropped a kiss on his cheek as he slipped the little car into gear.

"Reporting. To Leggy, to Basil, and to various others. Oh, and I saw Stefan who gave me a letter for your Pa, and a ritual for us to read if Roger gives him the go-ahead."

"Blimey, that was quick. Have you read it?"

"Not yet. I'll do it tonight."

"Sam rang. He wants us to meet him at The Cricketers, Marsham, at about 9.30. I said yes, but if you don't fancy it, I'll ring and cancel."

"I'd actually quite like a quiet drink in a country pub among friends."

By half-past eight we had dispensed the presents: the fabrics and calissons for Angelique and Maman, pipe tobacco for Pa and Mr. Mac, chocolates for Mrs. Mac, several cans which included various pates and mousses, and anchovies in oil and 2 kilos of dark roasted coffee beans – all of which were embraced with delight. I took Jeremy up to the sewing room, and told him to put on his robe.

"I'll be wearing nothing underneath, won't I? Want me to strip off?"

"Yes, but no. Just the heavy stuff. And when you've done so, stand on that stool."

I fitted a piece of chalk into the clamp of the little wooden measuring pole and adjusted it to the height of his ankles when he was up on the stool.

"Now, do a full circle on the stool, and let the chalk brush against the fabric."

He chuckled. "That's pretty basic technology" he said, mincing round on the tiny surface.

"Don't knock it, it works. Alright, you can get down now. Are the sleeves too long for you?"

"Could do with a couple of inches off." He stepped off the stool. "Your turn?"

I stripped to my petticoat and slipped into the robe. Too loose, too long, but that was better than the other extreme. I stepped onto the stool. "Set it at the height of my ankle-bone." I, too, did the shuffle.

I pinned the robes up while the chalk marks were still visible and set them aside for completing the following day.

"You did all this this afternoon? Impressive."

"I had help," I told him as I slipped my skirt and blouse back on. "I'll just go and pick some flowers then we can go."

I waved him off to get the drinks in then passed through the lychgate.

Immediately the pinks and golds of the western sky were shut out by the trees and there was a loss of warmth in both temperature and color. Here, blues, dull greens and grays dominated, pale and misty against tall background of dark light-excluding yews, the church itself a bastion against the eastern sky. Bats were flying and in the distance an owl hooted.

I made my way to Cissie's grave with my little bouquet of white scented flowers, a climbing rose, sweet peas, carefully chosen for their lack of any extra color, and a tangle of jasmine.

Someone, probably Billy Laycock, had been hard at work. The grass between the graves and along the paths had been cut and spread to dry, prior to being raked up for hay. I guessed he'd be in the pub now, or back home. It was too late for working and I really didn't want to see him. Whether what we had been told this morning were true or not, I had seen his temper. But I did need to show Cissie that someone was on her side.

The little vase that I had filled last time was no longer there.

Now a glass jam jar filled with sadly drooping cow parsley and moon daisies that had been part of the greensward stood in its place.

She deserved better than this!

I refilled the jar with water from a standpipe by the church wall and cleared my mind.

Then I twisted my Abraxas ring, and felt myself drift.

I knelt beside the little grave and gently rearranged the wild flowers, adding my own garden varieties among them.

I called Cissie into my mind's vision. I had never seen her, but I sensed a figure appearing before me. Not exactly appearing, it was more a feeling, a shadow, but I could see her skinny body, her long brown hair that never quite stayed in place, and her big dark eyes.

In my mind I told her what we had found out today. Her young face crumpled and I heard words in my mind, felt the pain, the fear.

'It was so horrible,' she whispered. 'Nurse was kind to me. They thought it was Uncle Edgar. How could they? He never tried anything like that. He was helping me get away from Dad to a new life. But he said I had to go through this. It was wrong, he said, and he couldn't give me a good reference for a new job if I didn't do this thing. No-one would employ me like that, and Dad would kill me if I stayed. I didn't know it would be so horrible...'

I could feel her pain, her fear, and was shaking with sobs.

Her mind touched mine again.

'I didn't mean to cause so much trouble. It was all my fault for being a little temptress, Dad said. And he told me never to tell anyone, so I didn't... until Uncle Edgar asked me why I was crying. He was so kind to me. He never laid a hand on me, except to comfort me. Not like my Dad. When I got home, after that thing and told Dad I was handing in my notice and had a job in London, he went mad and beat me and kicked me, and ... he did horrible things to me. Horrible horrible things, and left me on the kitchen floor and went to the pub. He was so angry. It was all my fault. He told me I deserved to die.'

I didn't so much hear this as feel it. I experienced every kick and indignity. I was whimpering with pain, just as Cissie must have done on the dirty flagstones, when her voice shrilled through my head like a train whistle.

'Watch out! He's here. He'll kill you!'

And she was gone.

Behind me came a man, running, and as I turned, still groggy from the break between the two worlds, he landed a hefty punch on the side of my head.

I went down, smashing against the stone surround of the grave, and blacked out for a moment or two.

When I came to he was kicking me hard in the hips and ribs – I had fallen forwards – with angry blows of his hobnail boots.

I gathered what wits and what breath I could and screamed. It was a pathetic sound, and only made him angrier.

"Bitch!" he shouted, foam flicking from the corners of his mouth. "I'll have you, bitch!"

Now he was over me, clawing at my arms to drag me over onto my back.

I stayed curled in a tight ball and screamed again; it was louder this time, which encouraged me for a moment.

Now he renewed the kicking.

I didn't know how much more I could stand, but I didn't want Billy Laycock treating me the same way as he had poor Cissie.

Suddenly, my war-time training clicked in.

I span over and grabbed his foot and rolled sideways as fast as I could, as he launched another kick.

He was neither a big man nor used to falling.

He flew in an arc over me and landed hard on the stone grave beside me, knocking the breath out of him.

I hung onto his foot, yanking it as high as I could with both hands while I forced myself upright.

And then I kicked him where it hurt most.

For Cissie as well as for me. And screamed and screamed, clutching the filthy old boot tightly to my chest.

Now, suddenly there were people around me, coming to my aid.

Jeremy ran to me, and grabbed Billy's foot. "It's OK, Alice. I've got him! Sam, come and hold this for me, will you? Les, sort your uncle!" Then his arms were round me, holding me close while I shook and sobbed as all the hurts and pain returned now as the adrenalin slipped away.

I saw Billy, whimpering and whining, clutching himself, cursing me as an attacker, a madwoman, but they didn't listen. They had probably seen and heard enough to know what was happening.

Sam dug in his pocket and pulled out a hank of fairly strong string which he tied around Billy's hands and feet, hobbling him. Then he went to the phone box while Les spat venom at his uncle, slapping his face to emphasize his words..

I don't remember much of what happened after that, apart from throwing up and hurting like mad.

I know that I sat on Cissie's grave swaddled in Jeremy's jacket until Sergeant Bloxham and his duty constable turned up and I told them Billy Laycock attacked me. Jeremy took me to the local cottage hospital where I was examined, photographed and patched up.

"You should really stay in, but we're severely short-staffed, and there's a ward full of sick children – measles season," the duty doctor said, handing me a large bottle of aspirins. "Take a couple of these every three hours and don't drink any alcohol."

He looked at Jeremy. "If she looks poorly or doesn't respond when you speak to her tomorrow, we'll have her back in."

Jeremy drove me home. I wasn't good company, wincing over every bump in the road and having to stop to be sick again.

"Don't know how I'll explain this to your parents," he said, as he helped me out of the car.

"Just tell them I've been fighting again. They'll cope."

## 51

I woke with a start when Mrs. Mac put a coffee tray set for two on the table beside me and said "You have a visitor, Miss Alice. Shall I let him in?"

I sat up stiffly, moving my feet off the sofa. I felt like half a mile of road-up. "Yes, please, Mrs. Mac. Is it Sam Simmons?"

"No, Miss Alice, but he rang earlier. He hopes you are feeling better and will see you later."

I was just about understanding that when she showed in Les Broom, carrying a glorious bunch of lilac, three sorts, white, pale mauve and a deep purple double variety which brought their own special scents into the room.

"Milady? I hope you don't mind. I wanted to see how you are, and Mum said I had to call – she sends you these and says whenever she was poorly they always cheered her up. How're you feeling?"

"The flowers are wonderful, please thank her for me, Les." It was such a kind thought from a stranger. "I'll get them in water as soon as I can, the smell is lovely."

I pointed to a nearby chair. "Do sit down, Les, It's lovely to see you. You can tell me what happened. I was a bit out of it last night. Thank you for being there for me. It could have been so much worse, but we won't dwell on that. I feel like hell, but I'll mend."

He sat on the edge of the armchair, laying the flowers on a nearby table, and smiled. "I'm sure you'll mend quicker with that attitude," he said. "I was rather hoping you'd clear up a few things for me, too. Once they'd put Uncle Billy in a cell I went round to see Mum. She's got a good head screwed on her shoulders. We had a really long talk last night. You are pressing charges, aren't you?"

"Oh yes. You don't mind? I mean he is your family..."

"I'll not stand bail for him. Let it all come out. I'll look a damn fool, but he treated people so badly and took me for an idiot.

Throw the book at the bastard!"

I raised my eyebrows. This was a turnabout.

"So what makes you say that?" I asked.

He looked at me astonished. "He kicked you! He attacked you. No-one in our family attacks women, my dad taught us all that, before he died, and my granddad too."

He looked across at me. "I reckon he did the same to Cissie, only worse. A lot worse."

"Did he admit it?" I asked, eagerly.

"Not as such, but they're re-opening her case. Edgar Winthrop wouldn't have done that. He was too much of a gent. How come I didn't see that at the time?" He shook his head. "None so blind as them as can't see, eh? It might cause a lot of stink, but at least she will have had justice. He sickens me. When I think how he took us all in, how he mistreated her, his own daughter, too! How could he? She was just a little kid. She used to climb up in those lilac trees and sit there among the blossom pretending to be a fairy. That's how I'll always remember her, a little skinny big-eyed fairy child with all her life before her. I loved her. I couldn't have harmed her in any way. But he obviously could, the evil bastard. He deserves to swing!"

"So how did you find out? What did you find out?"

"I was the one who found Cissie, when I took Uncle Billy home from the pub. She was on the floor in a pool of blood. He told me she'd been out with her fancy boyfriend, that they were always rowing, but she loved him to bits. He turned up from time to time and took her out to flash places. He must have turned violent, for some reason. Well, I didn't know who the bloke was at that time: she wouldn't tell anyone his name or anything and Billy seemed so upset – and it shocked me rigid to see her little bloody broken body. I scooped her up into the back of the car and drove her to hospital at once, but I was pretty sure I'd be too late. Billy was snivelling about his little girl, he was a waste of time in getting help for her." He frowned, angrily. "And he'd done it all the time. He'd got her pregnant, and when she came back ... er not pregnant he brutalised her and left her for dead on the kitchen floor. That's not human behavior. It really isn't. Even animals don't behave like that! He really took me in. Well, he took everyone in round here. Poor little Cissie. I did my best, but

..."

"Why didn't you call the police?" I asked.

"Didn't think they'd get her to hospital soon enough. My car's fast and I drive fast. Here ... well, they aren't that swift, even in an emergency. Sergeant Bloxham uses his bike most of the time, takes a pride in it. We only got a car last night because Sam insisted, and Jeremy took you to the hospital while we went down the station." He reached into his pocket. "Do you mind if I smoke?"

"Not at all." I reached into my handbag for my holder. "I'll join you. Would you care for a coffee."

He nodded. "I would have taken you if Jeremy wasn't there," he told me as he lit us up. "He's made a right mess of your face, the bastard."

"I probably did that when I landed on the gravestone, to be honest," I said. "But he's a vicious kicker. I'll not be dancing for a while."

Slowly I poured two cups of coffee, stirred in sugar and milk for us both. I felt I needed the comfort of both today, not my usual black unsweetened.

I handed one cup across to him. "Les, I don't remember much of what happened after you three turned up. Did you hear my screams?"

He shook his head. "No, well not until we were in the churchyard. Sam asked where you were when Jeremy got to the pub. He said you'd gone to put some white flowers on the grave. I knew Uncle Billy was still up there. We legged it. First time in my life I left a pint unfinished!"

I smiled back at him, and reached out and touched his hand. "I really appreciate your quick reaction, and I owe you. Lots."

"Yeah, well..." he said, clearly embarrassed. "I'm glad to see you as perky as you are. You didn't look too good last night. I'll let you mend." He downed the coffee in one and replaced the cup and saucer on the tray. "I've got to get back to work shortly."

"Thank you so much for calling, Les. And for the flowers, they're beautiful. Tell your mother I am delighted with them, please."

He grinned, and nodded. "She'll like that. Oh, one thing more."

"Yes?"

"What are you doing on Midsummer Day? Or rather Midsummer Night?"

"We usually go down to Larry and May at the Wethersley Arms, there's dancing on the green."

His face dropped for a moment. "You wouldn't care to come across to Marsham at some time? We really know how to celebrate there. At the cricket club. Bring your friends, everybody welcome, and we've got a late license and a jazz band."

"Yes? But I feel bad about letting Wethersley down," I said. "Could I come along afterwards?"

"Of course, but don't leave it too late or you'll miss the good bit."

"And what's that?" I asked, intrigued.

"Fireworks. I've got hold of a load of fireworks. Everyone loves fireworks! We'll set them off at eleven."

His grin was infectious.

"All right," I said. "I'll buy you that pint then."


Maman and Angelique came in soon after – they'd been to a WI meeting that morning – and were impressed with my flowers.

"I know where they came from," Maman said. "So you've had Dottie Broom's son round."

"You know Les's Mum?"

"Of course. WI. And I know her garden too, very good jam-maker, Mrs. Mac will tell you."

"But she's from Marsham, not Wethersley."

Maman shrugged. "Just a bike ride away. We women aren't locked in our own villages any more, Alice. Anyway, she used to work here before she married her Les, the Farrier. She was Roger's nurserymaid when he was young, and she not that much older. Your grandparents set great store by her, even when she left to marry Les, and Roger says she was one of the kindest persons in the house when he was a child, full of fun, but full of good sense too. Both he and his brother adored her."

Bloody Hell! These villages were full of secrets and intertwining relationships.

"Anyway, dear, how are you feeling? Can I get you anything?"

"Just had another couple of aspirins, thanks. I need to finish this sewing..."

Angelique shook her head. "I can run that up for you on the machine. Just take a day off and tell us all about France."

"Thank you for the offer, but I'll do it by hand, if you don't mind. But bring your work and I'll certainly tell you all about France," I said, adding to myself, well, all you need to know!

So I sat with Maman and Angelique, me sewing, they knitting baby clothes – if they didn't find their way to Maddy, they'd reach the local hospital or children's homes. They were skilled knitters, having made beautiful complicated garments for all of us and themselves in the past, and always had some knitting on the go; baby clothes they enjoyed making whenever they could get the fine soft wool, as they were quickly finished, always looked charming and were always well-received.

Knowing their interest in fashion, I described the look there – slightly wide shoulders, but longer fuller skirts, and then described my visit to the Grandes Magasins, and they were happy to be sidetracked. They had been delighted by the fabrics and patterns I had brought them, and pretty soon they had brought the stuff down and were sorting out what to do with it all, and how to maximise the lovely cloth.

"You've got some for yourself, Alice?" Maman asked. "No, I don't mean that black stuff you're sewing, I mean proper material, fit for a bride or a young wife."

"Of course, but not here."

"Then bring it to me and tell me what you want made up," Angelique told me. "And tell your sister to do the same. I don't suppose you left her out."

"Angelique, you are a treasure!" I told her.

"Bien sûr, but not one to be buried. When you get married I want you all to be my advertisements, and then I will have local ladies willing to pay good money to look as smart as les dames de Wethersley."

At one o'clock lovely Mrs. Mac brought us pasties and salads on trays so that I wouldn't have to move too far or face the daily girls or Nigel.

Pa joined us.

He gave me a very gentle hug. "How's my best girl?" he

asked.

I smiled up at him. "The better for seeing you," I said.

"I had a word with your friend Elisabeth," he told me. "She'll be coming for the weekend, that's right, isn't it, Chérie?"

"Yes, it's all fixed up. We'll be having a full house but the Macs assure me we can cope, and it will be such fun. Midsummer on Sunday. Half a year gone already! Then we can go down to Wethersley for the dancing on Saturday night."

She turned to me. "Do you think you'll be up to it, Alice, dear?"

"I'll be up to having a drop of Larry's summer ale," I told her. "But I may not stay late."

"Of course you must do what you think fit," she said. "Do you know Elisabeth's friend? What's he like?"

"Tall, blond, Teutonic, rather gorgeous. Jeremy rates him highly. Quite different from Percy Meredith, although he is an occultist."

"You mean a white magician, not a black one, dear?"

I shook my head. "No. A gray magician, like we all are."

## 52

So, Elisabeth and Stefan would be here for the weekend, and I hadn't even read through what they intended us to do or got our robes finished.

I played the invalid card for the rest of the afternoon and went to my room, where I could study the ritual in peace and snooze a bit if I needed to. I could work on the robes this evening and tomorrow, but I needed to know what would be expected of me, and reading magical stuff always seemed to make me nod off. I'd noticed that with Elisabeth's father's magical diaries. Mind, I had had the same reaction from other books, particularly those I'd had to study for art history when I was being 'finished'. If I couldn't sleep, I only had to open the covers and after a few sentences I'd gone. Never got as far as the end of the first chapter, but the illustrations got me through the examination.

I brought a jug of water with me, closed the door and locked it, then opened the window as wide as it would go. It was a sultry day and I wanted as much air in as possible and no interruptions. Then I took off all my clothes, had a quick glance at my wounds, told them to heal fast and thoroughly, and lay on my bed, with the ritual in my hands, my head and shoulders propped on a couple of extra pillows and tried to empty my mind.

The scent of jasmine wafted in through the window, bringing back yesterday evening. I thought of Cissie, momentarily, and thanked her for the warning, then let her go, and remembered the smell attached to happier times, holidays at Grand-père's in the south of France when I was a child, where the plant grew rampantly and was one of Grand-mère's favorites. I brought these memories to the front of my mind, and let the perfume soothe me.

I poured a glass of water, took a sip or two, then opened the folder.

I had only ever worked in a magic circle once, and that was a full one, with the Merediths presiding and Elisabeth as High Priestess.

This was quite different, small and intimate. There would be four people within the sacred space: Stefan and Elisabeth in the East and West, Jeremy and I in South and North.

It was asking a great deal of us.

We had only been what she called upholders of power before, and that had blown us both away.

Elisabeth had written 'usual opening' – whatever that meant. I'd need to ask her about what we would be expected to do. I knew there were circles of protection and that the quarters needed to be called in, something we'd need to learn.

The Purpose of the Rite was threefold: to cleanse the clearing of all stain from actions committed herein, to contact those who had soiled it and pass them on on their spiritual journey to whatever awaited them, and to bring balance to the place and persons affected by the slaughter that had occurred therein. There was a note saying 'add anything else you think fit'.

I took some time to think about that. How did Billy Laycock fit in here? I knew Elisabeth was thinking of Archie Meredith and John Anselm-Jones when she wrote the second purpose, but Billy Laycock was part of it, as much as his nephews, Les and Joe, and Sylvia, of course. And then, Cissie, too. I scribbled their names down with question marks.

I read the invocations and the requests, the blessing of special water, special incense that would be taken to the clearing itself, the blessing of wine and bread that we would share together, and again take to the clearing. Stefan and Elisabeth would be doing all that, we would only be upholding, so no problems there, theoretically.

Any other business?

I'd think about that later. Perhaps that was where my list of people should fit in?

Then the closing. Again, we'd need to be taught how to do that properly.

But it sounded straightforward enough. And simple.

I liked simple.

I lay the folder on my bedside table and closed my eyes.

I awoke naturally some half hour later, feeling easier and more rested than I expected. It was always a delightful surprise when magic worked.

I spent the rest of the afternoon pottering; I took a gentle walk round the nearer parts of the estate, the flower garden, the kitchen garden, the poultry yard, just to get my body working. The day was heavy, and I couldn't move with any speed, but it was good just to be outside among the fresh air and living things. Even though the sky was mostly gray and cloudy, there was still a sense of growth and lots of color.

In the North I would be asked to mediate the powers of the Earth.

I put in some time preparing myself, feeling its strength and power, its constancy, stability, and its beauty, how it was part of me and I was part of it, let my mind wander back to France and the caves where we'd hidden weapons. Being inside a cave without a light, that was scary, but it was also safe, I remembered. It was like being in a nurturing womb. Of course, I did have a torch in my pocket, and a lantern and matches with me. I wouldn't have like to have been lost within the rock unprepared.

I wandered round the walled garden. The espaliered fruit trees were looking better than they had before, there were even some tiny fruit setting on the pears and apples. Nigel was absent and his cottage locked up. I wondered where he was. I hadn't seen him or Spider yesterday, either, but he had his own life to live. Not that he hadn't done a small miracle here. I picked some parsley and thyme for Mrs. Mac, and a big bunch of mint, enjoying the smells, and admired the neat rows of beetroot and carrots, both of which would need thinning soon. At last the weather was actually coming back to what it should be.

I closed the garden gate behind me, then started back to the house.

Sam's car stopped beside me shortly before I reached it. He opened the door with a flourish. "Alice, I didn't expect to see you up and about today. Hop in! Gosh, you're going to get a real shiner!"

"Thanks, Sam," I told him, as I took the passenger seat. "Make a girl feel good, why don't you?"

"Sorry, not exactly the soul of tact. I brought you a letter from the Rev. And some flowers."

He slammed the car into gear and we shot up the last fifty

yards at a rate of knots. "How are you?" he asked, as he braked suddenly and skidded to a halt.

"As well as can be expected," I muttered clenching my teeth. But he meant well.

We went in via the kitchen, where I knew there would be some tea.

I poured us each a cup and then found a vase. The flowers were from the Rev's garden, and delightful. "Thank you, Sam, and tell the Rev I thank him, too," I said.

We sat at the big table. We were alone, which was unusual.

"So what happened to you last night?" Sam asked. "Before we found you and after?"

I told him. He listened in silence, nodded.

"Did Jeremy tell you anything?" I asked.

"About yesterday morning? Yes. I checked out Dr Hilda Scarsdale. She doesn't appear to exist. No-one's heard of her at PMRAF Hospital Halton, and the College of Obstetricians and Gynecologists don't recognize her either."

"Shit!" I breathed. "Sorry, Sam. I was hoping she at least had some training."

"She might well have done, under another name. Or in another place. Or she may just be a chancer. A lab coat and a stethoscope are a good confidence-booster..."

Still, I knew that Jeremy had told both Leggy and Basil about our encounter, so there would certainly be some follow up on the Barkston Road 'clinic'.

I applied myself to the flowers, cutting the stems and placing them gently in the green glass vase. "I was doing this for Cissie," I said softly. But these were different flowers, glorious in their color, flowers for the living who enjoyed life, bright orange pot marigolds, yellow giant yarrow, deep blue lupins and delphiniums and huge ox-eye daisies. They looked wonderfully positive, this gift from the earth.

I took the letter that Sam held out to me, slit the envelope and read the greetings. Reverend Simmons had a lovely way with words. I smiled.

"Tell him I'm fine, and I thank him. At least things are moving in the right way now. You can't make an omelette without breaking a few eggs. At least I've got an excuse for staying at

Wethersley now, and doing very little. I'm rather enjoying it, but don't tell anyone, they'll think I've gone soft."

He chuckled. "Can't be on the barricades all the time, Alice. Look, I've got to go, but it's lovely to see you up and about. See you around, eh? No, don't get up, I'll see myself out."

I rinsed the teacups and saucers and put them to drain. Then I tucked my letter in my pocket and took the vase of flowers out into the living room where I found Maman, Angelique and Mrs. Mac, all knitting away furiously, listening to Wimbledon on the radio.

"More flowers, Alice. How lovely," Maman said, as I put them on the table before her.

"Where's Pa?"

"In his studio, with Mr. Mac and the cricket."

I went across to Pa's studio.

He was preparing a new large panel, while Mr. Mac sat in an easy chair quietly polishing the silverware. In the background a fruity voice kept up a constant slow-paced ball by ball commentary of what was happening at Old Trafford.

"Hello Alice, what brings you into masculine territory?" Pa asked, without moving from his stool.

"Need to have a word," I said.

"Do you want me to leave, sir?" Mr. Mac asked.

"Not that private, is it, Alice?"

I actually didn't know.

"Stay for a bit, Mr. Mac, you look so comfortable there," I said. "If Pa thinks it's private, he can ask you to go, but as far as I'm concerned it's not."

Mr. Mac looked up gratefully. He had got himself organized and to move would have been disruptive.

Pa turned on his stool and stepped down. "Then let's all have a break, eh? Are you smoking again, Alice?" He pulled out his pipe and tobacco pouch, and sat next to me on the settee. Mr. Mac tucked the polishing cloth away, and delved into his apron, bringing forth his own pipe and a box of Swan vestas.

"For the moment." I took my Gauloises and holder from my own pocket and fitted them together.

We went through the ritual of lighting up. "So, Alice, speak. You're among friends."

"Pa, I know who John Anselm-Jones was working for when he came to Wethersley."

"Ah!" said Pa, and sucked hard on his pipe.

"I won't say a word to Maman, or indeed to anyone else," I told him. "I met him in Paris, and ... well, he didn't know who I was, and he rather vilified you. He let it out that you had failed him, disrespected him."

"Did he indeed! Well, he always had a very high opinion of himself," Pa said with a smile.

"So I found myself telling him a few home-truths. He'd gate-crashed an Embassy Party."

"Good God, Alice, you could have started a diplomatic incident!"

"Oh the Ambassador and his Lady were behind me. They shooed him and his wife out!"

Pa's pipe dropped. "Alice, what are you saying? You ... you stood up to ...?"

"Yes, Pa. And I'm so proud of you, for not taking on his rotten commission. I bet he would have wanted it with the full royal regalia with his severely plain wife dolled up as Queen. He was terribly miffed. Well done you!"

I gave Pa a big hug, and plonked a kiss on his cheek. "You told the man who would be king, where to get off!"

"And so did you, by the sound of it. Alice, darling, you are a chip off the old block." He hugged me back. "I think this calls for a small celebration. Do you know what my daughter did, Mac? She told Edward the Abdicator off!"

"And Mrs. Simpson, sorry, Mrs. Windsor. She was going to slap me, she was so cross!"

Mr. Mac started to smile, and then to shake with laughter. "Oh, I never liked those two. Pair of spongers. I don't suppose they're actually working for a living?" He blew out a cloud of smoke. "No, I didn't think so."

Pa rooted in a desk drawer and pulled out a half bottle of Scotch and three small glasses. "Are you joining us, Alice?"

"Try to stop me." I figured the ban on alcohol could be lifted by now. "So must I keep silent?"

"I don't think it would be too wise to let the ladies know, Miss Alice. They may understand, but then again, " Mr. Mac said, taking the glass Pa offered. "A commission from an ex-king could be extremely lucrative."

"I don't think he flaunts the readies much, apart from on his missus," I said cynically. "It would be prestige only."

"That's what I thought," Pa said, handing me a glass. "And I don't need that. He's too fond of the Hun by half."

We raised glasses, and I sipped the golden liquid. A good single malt from the islands. I didn't ask how he came by it, but I was glad he was sharing it.

"Pa, where's Nigel?"

"Oh, he's off to London for a bit. Should be back by tomorrow night. It'll do him good to get back into the real world again. Not that he hasn't earned his keep here. He's a brilliant gardener, and it means I can concentrate on my painting again. Since those angels went on show last week, I've had several churches asking if I'd do them something similar – usually on a smaller scale, you understand. I'd never thought of myself as a religious painter, but actually, it's quite fun."

# 53

Jeremy rang me after supper and said he'd be down Friday (tomorrow) evening bringing Guy, and Stefan and Elisabeth would follow them. By then Maman had invited more people for Sunday, and she and Angelique and Mrs. Mac were sorting out sleeping and menu arrangements. I knew I'd be on cooking duty most of Friday, but this was short notice for calling in favors for extra foodstuffs.

"It'll all sort itself, Alice," Maman said, blithely. "Trust me, we'll do them proud. We always do. Besides, it will be nice to get the family all together. It will be little Robin's first visit to the family home, and I'm so looking forward to it."

"They're not staying for the weekend?" I asked, aghast.

"Of course not, dear, just the Sunday, for lunch and tea. It'll give Nannie a good rest, and we can enjoy the children."

"And Guy?"

"Oh, he'll come tomorrow night as usual, but he'll be bringing some food, I told him expressly to go and spend some points for us all. And then of course we'll have Leggy and Bobby down on Sunday, too. They'll bring something. They always do, and it's always good."

"Ah," I said, relieved.

Angelique looked over her glasses at me, "Nothing to worry about, everything's in hand," she whispered.

"I managed to get access to some pork belly," Mrs. Mac said. "Quite a large piece as it happens. We can get soup, cold meat and crackling to go with the drinks, plus all that lovely fat for frying and baking. It seems a shame not to share it. We'll cook it tomorrow, Alice, you and me."

So basically, I spent Friday morning in the kitchen garden, picking the first of the new vegetables while Pa dug up the new potatoes and thinned the carrots, lettuce, radish and beetroot for salads, and the rest in the kitchen with Mrs. Mac preparing and cooking food for the masses.

Maman and Angelique organized the rooms with the two daily girls, who were on overtime and happy to be so. My flowers had been spread about the house, and more had been picked, small scented posies in the guest bedrooms, along with clean glasses and flasks of freshly drawn water.

In the interests of propriety, Maman had placed Stefan in the blue room with Jeremy, and Elisabeth in Maddy's old room that adjoined mine. I could see that some rejigging might be necessary.

I sat outside after lunch, with a glass of water. We'd all done well, and were feeling pleased with ourselves. Mrs. Mac went in to check the pork which was simmering gently, but told me to finish my drink and have a break. I wasn't going to disobey.

Then, as Maman disappeared into the kitchen to check what we'd been doing there, Angelique whispered to me, "Regarding the sleeping arrangements, Alice, I've been told to say that they aren't inscribed in stone. They can be changed, should you or your friends feel the desire. It's just that Marie-Thérèse wants her guests to have the right to choose to sleep alone should they wish to. In the heat of summer, sometimes … I always felt a certain perfectly natural longing... "

I was stunned. "Blimey, Angelique, that's a turn-around! She or Pa used to escort Jeremy and me to our respective rooms not that long since! And wait for us to start getting undressed, I've no doubt."

Angelique chuckled a deep throaty meridional laugh. "I don't suppose that stopped you. It wouldn't have stopped her or Roger, either. Or me. You are a young woman, Alice, of course you have needs, and you are so blind, sometimes. She told me if she'd been in your shoes she'd have run away and got married weeks ago. Not that I'm advocating you do it, but … she understands, don't you see? Which is why she didn't kick up about you going to Paris..."

"As someone else," I reminded her. "No stain on the family name – and she did get some great fabric out of it. So did you."

"Yes, and a lot of work, too. Not that I mind." She put her arm through mine, pulling me closer, and whispered. "And she told me, if this Stefan is the piece of beefcake you described, well, Elisabeth isn't getting any younger. She ought to take advantage of the warm weather. After all, it is Midsummer, and St John's night on the way."

"What's St. John's night got to do with it?" I asked.

"June 24th – when all the boys and girls get together and alliances were made."

"I thought that was May Day," I said.

"It was. But now the girls have something extra, and that was good for the future of the community. So now, they have proved to be fertile, they get engaged, and dance all night under the moon and stars. Well, that's what happened when I was young. We had some good music, too, to dance to. I rather miss that. I loved the hurdy-gurdy."

She smiled wistfully, then patted my hand in her small one. "So, dear Alice, do what you think fit."

I kissed her small round cheek. "I shall be very discreet," I promised. "Although I don't think I'll be amazingly active with all this bruising."

"Oh Alice, I always found making love a brilliant painkiller. I'm sure Roger and Chérie will be diplomatically deaf to the creaking of floorboards and other extraneous noise – so long as it doesn't get too loud!"

"I will endeavor not to frighten the horses," I chuckled. "And instruct Elisabeth and Stefan to do likewise, should they choose to … well, you know... indulge themselves."

"Good girl! I knew I could rely on you. Now let's find out what needs to be done next."

By the time our visitors arrived around half past six, I had managed to finish both robes, and even press them. I was very proud of myself. I'd forgotten the cords, of course, but to be honest, I didn't like cords around robes; it broke the line.

Guy gave me a hug and I winced. "Who's been beating you up, Alice?" He frowned at Jeremy. "It wasn't you, was it?" and he meant it.

"Don't be an ass, Guy," I told him. "Now what's been happening at the bank?"

"After you left, you mean?" He sighed, shook his head. "God, that was ages ago. Lots of changes, believe me. Dugdale has been suspended. There's an enquiry going on, but it looks pretty clear he'll be out on his ear. Which is good news for me. I had a long talk with Mr. Jellicoe. He was most sympathetic, and the upshot is, I'm going to be promoted. Acting, only at the moment, but he has confidence in me, he says, and I'm not stupid enough to let him down by another lapse of judgment."

"I should hope not," I said. "It's the chance you wanted."

"Too right, Sis!"

He went in and hugged the rest of the family, telling them his good news, while Jeremy and I waited on the front porch for Stefan and Elisabeth to arrive. It was good to have him back.

They arrived in a hired Austin 8, shortly, and we took them in. Elisabeth was known to the family, but Stefan was new to them. He disarmed them all with his manners which were those of old Mittel Europ; it couldn't be easy being Teutonic in an Anglo-French house, but the Poles had been on our side, or we on theirs – before we sold them down the river.

We all ate informally in the kitchen. Nigel was still conspicuous by his absence, which surprised me, but it didn't seem to phase anyone else, not even Guy, who was commandeered by Maman and Angelique to help with the washing up.

Pa took Elisabeth, Stefan, Jeremy and me into the library. "Now," he said, producing a bottle of whisky, "What exactly do you need to do the work you proposed?"

"We need to see the site," Elisabeth said. "We've brought all that we need." She turned to Jeremy and me. "Have you read through the ritual."

We nodded.

"And we have robes, but no cords, I'm afraid."

"Don't need cords, necessarily," Stefan said. "They're handy if the robes are too long, that's all."

I said quietly, "I don't think I could walk down to the site and back. It's a long way when you've been beaten up. Sorry to be a softie."

"You're not a softie, Alice," Jeremy said. "We could go down there in your car, Stefan, and then decide what's to be done." He turned to Pa. "Have you a space where we could work undisturbed?"

"I have, indeed." He looked at Elisabeth and Stefan, "How big?"

"Nine foot square?" Elisabeth suggested.

The stile was a bit problematical, but I managed. I'd had aspirins with my supper but I was still stiffening up. I told them how I'd run along here and found Guy, then I led them to the clearing. In silence.

It felt strange, being in the woods with Elisabeth and Stefan. They were not their ordinary selves. As soon as we went off the path along Mr. Balfour's woods, a quiet had descended on them, a quietness so intense that you could almost touch it.

Once I was in the clearing I turned to speak, but Jeremy shook his head.

I closed my mouth and retreated to the far side where I leaned against an oak tree and watched.

They circled three times, looking, listening, smelling the air, tasting it, and touching with their inner senses, trying to get a sense of what had happened and what needed to be done to bring the place back into balance.

Because it did need to be brought back.

I could feel the ragged hurt, a strange ripping, scream that had taken hold here.

Normally there would have been rabbits on the greensward at this time of the evening, or at least the little currants that they left behind.

Nothing.

It was as if the place had been bombed, abandoned, despite all the lovers who had used it as a trysting place.

Now Stefan walked into the center of the clearing and pulled out a small pocket compass.

He looked at me. "Excellent, you found the North, Alice, without even trying."

Then he made a quarter turn and walked to the edge of the clearing and took up his station there. "Jeremy, opposite Alice, Elisabeth opposite me."

They were already there.

"Now, feel the energy of your quarter, and when you've got it, nod."

I wasn't expecting that. Practical work outside.

I closed my eyes for a moment, and felt the strength of the

oak tree supporting me, so that I became part of it. I melted into it, feeling my legs and feet delving downwards as they joined with the roots taking the power from Earth beneath us, my body the strong trunk, my arms and hands becoming at one with the branches and leaves, my head the crown of the tree, glorifying in the last warm rays of the sun. I felt totally at one with the earth and the tree, this particular patch of earth and this particular tree, but also with every part of the earth and every living thing within and upon it, and the energy coursed through me in a way it never had before.

I pulled my consciousness back and opened my eyes, and felt the others' eyes upon me.

I nodded to Stefan, and looked at the others. Jeremy appeared to be standing within a teardrop of flame. He looked so calm, so in control, so himself. Elisabeth was in a teardrop of water, and looked just as she had at Beltane, the complete High Priestess. Stefan wore a teardrop of pale yellow, and despite it being a still evening, he seemed to be surrounded by a mischievous, fluttering breeze.

"Good," he said. "Now, bring your energy into the center of the circle to join together as pure light. This is preparatory work."

I felt the oak tree solid and steadfast behind me and did my best, sending a sense of the Earth and all its beauty and strength in a green stream of light into the middle.

"Now, send all your good wishes into this clearing. When you have done so, stamp your foot. Then we will withdraw the energies." That was Elisabeth.

I closed my eyes and brought back the image of the clearing as I had known it as a child, and remembered it with love.

Then I stamped. I saw the others do likewise.

Stefan talked us through withdrawing the power, and I felt it slowly sink back through me and the tree, back into the earth itself.

"Make sure you are completely back," Elisabeth told us. "Stamp your feet, wiggle your fingers, and blink a few times. And when you are, join me in the center of the clearing."

I expected the pain would return when the power had left me, but I found I was walking lightly, as I did normally.

"That was amazing," I told her.

She nodded. "You look so much better. And you both did really well. It was a bit naughty of us, bringing you here to open up, but you handled it properly. If you can contact the elements outside, it's often easier to do it inside, but if you never work outside, how can you hope to contact the elements fully?"

"Have we done the work, then?" Jeremy asked. "I thought there was a lot more to it."

"Oh, there is," Stefan told him. "This was just for us to find out what was needed and to give you two a bit of training. Let's go back and see where we will do the actual ritual. If we do it tomorrow morning, we can bring some stuff down here in the evening."

"It's Midsummer," I said. "There'll be dancing down at Wethersley Arms – as a family we always go, so does everyone else - and we're invited to a celebration with fireworks at Marsham afterwards."

"All the better," Elisabeth said. "No-one will be wandering around here tomorrow night."

## 54

Saturday morning. I helped Mrs. Mac with the breakfasts and the washing up, then joined Elisabeth, Stefan and Jeremy cleaning one of the unused maids' rooms up on the top floor. They had already cleared it of what little furniture it contained, and were dusting and sweeping. I set to on the windows, cleaning the dusty glass inside and out with vinegar and old newspaper.

We rifled other rooms and eventually found what we needed, a small wooden table and four cream painted wooden chairs. These got dusted and washed too. Already the room was feeling more loved. It had some very old wallpaper based on autumnal leaves twigs and berries, which I found pleasing, now the cobwebs had gone.

"Why don't you two go and have a break?" Elisabeth suggested. "We'll set up." She checked her watch. "What time does lunch take place? We don't want to upset the rhythm of the house."

"One o'clock," I told her. "But it could be delayed a bit."

She shook her head. "No. That won't be necessary. If you're back here robed up by a quarter past eleven, that should be adequate, don't you think, Stefan?"

"An hour in circle, quarter of an hour to ground and change? Half an hour leeway, Yes. That should do it." He shooed us out of the door. "Go and do what you have to do, and we'll see you in half an hour."

"Do you want some coffee? It'll be downstairs shortly."

"We'll come down. Now, off with you, bitte."

"Everything all right?" Pa asked.

"Yes, Pa. Nigel returned yet?"

"No. And no word. I confess to being a little concerned. Not least because it will mean I have to do the gardening. I've got lazy since he's been here, and I must admit, I've enjoyed it."

He picked up a copy of 'The Times', opened on the foreign

news. "Did you see this?"

He pointed to a headline: MAJOR DIAMOND-DEALER MISSING; FEARS FOR HIS SAFETY.

We grabbed the paper and scanned it.

"Felix? Holy shit!" Jeremy breathed. "Sorry, didn't mean to offend."

"Look, his fiancée, a Miss Sylvia Cavendish raised the alarm when he didn't arrive back at their hôtel on Thursday."

"He never arrived," Jeremy read. "He's been missing since last Sunday morning!"

We knew he hadn't arrived at his destination last Monday.

Obviously Laurence had kept quiet about that.

"And his bodyguards and his diamonds vanished with him," Pa murmured, raising an eyebrow. "Do you two know anything about it? You were in Paris at the time."

"No, Roger," Jeremy said. "Although we did meet him there."

I shook my head.

It wasn't exactly lying: what we knew was there in print for all to read. We didn't know anything more than Sylvia and Laurence had told us, which wasn't much. Nor was it our news to spread or, for that matter, any of our business. Besides, there was no picture of 'the fiancée', so Pa couldn't be sure who she was, despite being shrewd enough to have made a guess. Still, he had the decency not to ask further questions.

"Oh well, I hope they find him safe and sound, but the longer he's missing... Come and have some coffee. You both look like you could use one!"

We joined Maman, Angelique and Guy who were chatting on the terrace.

"Where are Stefan and Elisabeth?" Maman demanded.

"Still setting up. They'll be down soon," I told her.

"Do you think it'll work, what you're going to do?" Guy asked.

"Don't know until we've tried," Jeremy said.

Maman looked fiercely at my brother. "If people are willing to help in a way they feel is appropriate, then we allow them to do so, Guy. And are suitably grateful, too. Manners cost nothing and open many doors."

"Yes, but... I mean, wouldn't you do better getting a priest over to exorcise the place, or whatever they do?"

"No, dear. Can you imagine if it got out? That we were exorcising the clearing? They'd think we'd all gone doolally. This way the locals need never know. You hear what I'm saying, Guy. Not a word. This is between us here at Wethersley only, and Stefan and Elisabeth, of course, but they understand the need for secrecy. Very nice people, by the way, Alice and Jeremy." She sipped her coffee daintily and set the cup and saucer back on the little table beside her. "I'm glad you've found some suitable friends. It's important to have people around you that you can trust."

I poured the last of the coffee between two cups, for Pa and Jeremy, then went into the kitchen where there was another pot and a plate of biscuits waiting.

On the way back with it I met Stefan and Elisabeth coming downstairs. "You've passed the test," I told them. "Maman approves of you both very much!"

Elisabeth smiled. "And we approve of her," she said, helping herself to a biscuit. "Isn't that nice!"

When we went back, suitably robed, to the room, Stefan said quietly, "Elisabeth is in there. Center yourselves. Leave all the mundane stuff that might be going around your brain out here, and when you are ready, I'll let you in."

No passwords, then.

I had been thinking about Sylvia and what she must be going through, but now, as I closed my eyes and turned the Abraxas ring once on my finger, those thoughts drifted away to be replaced with a core of peace.

Stefan opened the door and nodded. I looked at Jeremy, smiled, and let him pass me and walk through into the room, hailing the Light as he did so. A blast of incense hit me, then it was my turn.

I walked through the door, hand raised in greeting, into another time, another place. The room was set up four square, Elisabeth sitting in the West, serene and balanced in her dark blue robe, and Jeremy in the South.

I took my place in the North, and was followed by Stefan, who sealed the door, and came round to the East, facing the small center table, dressed as an altar, on which stood a gold candlestick with a tall white candle and a single deep red rose. Beside each of us were stools on which stood the symbols of the quarter.

I sat and gazed at the altar candle, and allowed what was about to happen unfold.

Stefan and Elisabeth went through the purifications. Salt and water, air and fire, then light, were blessed, taken round the room and shared with us all. Spiritually both we and the room were cleaned and ready. The room sparkled in its clouds of incense smoke,

Elisabeth regained her seat and Stefan opened the quarters. All Jeremy and I had to do was envisage two great doors open behind us and the power of Fire or Earth coming through into the temple. Easy, I thought, after last night, building the great gates behind me as he opened the East.

Wrong!

Stefan invoked and drew in the swirling of Air. The room was full of Light and the sound of wing-beats as he called in the archangel and holy living creature, the winged man of St Matthew. I cast a quick glance at Jeremy, then he was eclipsed by Stefan who was invoking the Southern Quarter. A roar of a lion, a winged lion, and more wing-beats and a blast of heat. In the West Elisabeth, eyes closed and lips slightly parted, sighed as the gate opened to Stefan's invocation, and I sensed a raincloud, a waterfall, a deep pool, a river, an estuary and the sea, with the path of the full moon upon it, being blown, so that the clouds formed and the whole cycle began again. And up in the clouds, the Eagle of St John hovered above the Archangel of the quarter.

Now Stefan was standing in front of me. I felt my roots go down, my body become a tree, my arms the branches, and then I went deeper, far into the earth where there was still fire and molten rock, and crystals were being born, up into limestone caves of stunning beauty, and then out through the tops of high mountains, and with me all the time were growing things – crystals, plants, animals and humankind, all within the enfolding arms of the archangel Uriel and protected by the Winged Ox, the symbol of St Luke, patron saint of painters. I let them through. Stefan bowed his head and returned to the East.

"Brothers and sisters, let us unite as we did last night."

The powers met on the central altar. It felt so right.

Elisabeth rose from her chair and joined Stefan at the altar.

"This temple is open for the purpose of setting things right," she said quietly, raising her palms to him.

"And to bring Midsummer joy to this area, freeing the people and the land to experience the harvest time as it is right for them," Stefan stated firmly.

I watched and listened as they described what had been done in the clearing in the woods, a place frequented normally by lovers and rabbits, both sacred to Venus, of the muddles, mix-ups, connivings and violence that had brought about the assassination of a man who, at this point, was actually in the throes of redeeming himself.

I found myself back in the clearing, watching it all again, unable to detach myself. But at last I understood what was going on. Whatever else he might have been or done during his life, and there was a lot of dodgy stuff, at the moment he was killed, he was trying for justice for his wondrous waif, Cissie. It was he who was attacking Billy Laycock, demanding the truth about her death and threatening to bring the full weight of the law down on him. John Anselm-Jones or Edgar Winthrop, whoever he might be, wasn't there to pay the man off, he was there for vengeance for a young girl who had been betrayed by her own father.

Archie Meredith was out for vengeance, too. I knew the man, had been threatened by him; he was a ruthless cold-blooded killer where self-interest was concerned. Had I known this – for I could see it so clearly now – I would have thought twice before entering his orbit and infiltrating his circle. I was glad he was dead.

Then there were the Brooms, Les and Joe, and Billy Laycock.

When they appeared I shuddered at Billy. The feeling he brought with him was awful: resentment and viciousness, lust and anger, all held in check by the very thinnest of fine threads. Well I'd seen, nay, felt, what happened when that thread snapped, but he had a persuasive tongue, and people felt sorry for him, a widower, bringing up a young girl. He could make people believe what he told them, how he and his only daughter had been betrayed by some nob.

Joe was a follower, also ruled by his emotions, and what he

saw as right; there was a touch of violence in there, too, for it's own sake. He enjoyed a brawl, just as Billy did, but wasn't a bully.

And then there was Les, who had set up the meeting, believing his uncle had a just cause for redress from the person he believed had ruined and killed his little cousin. There was a deep sadness in Les, but contained within it was a flame of pure golden light, the same flame that had inadvertently attracted me to him when we first crossed paths. I smiled.

In my inner ear I heard a whinney. Sylvia, mounted on her horse, had arrived.

She was there for the 'fun' of it. There was a very dark side to her, a side that enjoyed both inflicting cruelty and watching it being inflicted, but even here as I watched, I saw her flinch as the deed was done. But she pulled herself together and played her part well, impressing Archie Meredith.

I continued to watch as the scene played out on my inner eyes. It wasn't pleasant, but like a violent film, I knew it would stop.

Then I heard Elisabeth's voice. "Brothers and sisters, you have seen what happened. Let us now cleanse the place and the people so that they may continue their journeys and existence without these acts attached to them. May the clearing be healed, may the people therein get whatever they need in their journey so that things are brought into balance and no shadows remain."

We rose and joined around the altar, put a right hand on the shoulder of the officer in front of us and held our left hands out, then we circled, sweeping up the memories and turning them back upon themselves, as if rewinding a film. I felt what I had just seen and experienced being brushed like a whirlpool into the floor surrounding the small altar and when all was safely there, we each raised our hands in the air, caught any extraneous memories and passed them down into the altar too, to be reabsorbed into the earth.

And suddenly the temple was empty of it all, and there was nothing within but light and our four selves.

"Let us join together in thanks," Stefan said.

Elisabeth and I brought the cakes and chalice to the altar. Stefan brought a small envelope, which he placed there, and Elisabeth went back to her table and brought, to my surprise, a bottle of brown ale.

"It should be bread and wine, but we thought that the locality would feel more at home with cakes and ale," she said. "We'll share some here now and take the rest down to the clearing tonight."

She and Stefan blessed the ale and cakes, which she had made herself on Friday morning and we shared them, silently, with smiles.

"Anything else?"

"Cissie Laycock," said Jeremy. "We told you about her."

"Then just a prayer for healing and peace, freedom to continue her journey," suggested Stefan.

Some time later Jeremy and I sat in my bedroom in our normal clothes. We'd shared a glass of water and were smoking together on the window seat, the window wide open, too blasted to communicate in any way but by holding hands.

Jeremy looked out of the window. "There's Nigel and Spider," he said, waving.

As I turned and waved too, Nigel threw the much-chewed tennis ball for Spider, and waved back, a beaming smile on his face. In his other hand was a huge shopping bag, very full by the look of it.

Spider retrieved the ball, wagging his tail and laid it at Nigel's feet. The game was on. Nigel bent and then threw the ball onwards towards the house, and Spider raced after it. Nigel hefted the bag in his two arms and gave chase.

"Looks like he's come home," Jeremy mused, smiling.

I found myself very glad they were back.

# 55

I never found out why or where Nigel had gone, or what he was doing.

When we reached the living room, he had plonked the overflowing bag on the table and was apologizing profusely to everyone for not phoning and letting them down in the garden department when there were so many guests, although to be honest, the party had been arranged after he had left. But as he had brought a whole Gala pie, five pounds of fresh asparagus and four bottles of champagne, everyone forgave him.

Lunch was delayed while his presents were admired and stowed safely for tomorrow, which was handy as it gave Elisabeth and Stefan time to finish what they needed to do.

When we went back to shift the furniture back in the maid's room after lunch only a faint whiff of incense remained as witness to what had gone on.

"It's all downhill, now," Elisabeth said, as we came down the stairs. "We'll finish the job this evening in mufti." She looked at me. "How are your bruises, Alice?"

I frowned. I'd not noticed any twinges or stiffness for some time, and in fact, I'd not taken an aspirin since breakfast. I'd simply forgotten about them.

"Much better," I said, amazed.

She grinned. "It can work like that sometimes. But you'll probably feel very drained in the next day or two. Post-ritual fatigue. It's quite normal. Especially when you're not used to working with power."

Pa, Nigel and Guy disappeared into Pa's study, shortly afterwards, but Maman and Angelique said they were going down to Wethersley to help set up things for this evening, and would be taking the Citroen.

"Can we help?" I asked.

Maman looked at me strangely. "No, Alice, that would be

impolite to your guests. You might show them the gardens, and do a bit of weeding and dead-heading."

Angelique broke in, "I could do with a hand loading the car, gentlemen, if you would be so kind."

Jeremy and Stefan jumped to it, bringing out boxes and tins from the kitchen, and placing them carefully in the boot. There was enough to feed a small regiment stashed in under Angelique's eagle eye.

Maman climbed into the driver's seat and wound down the window. "Alice, tell Roger I'll bring the car back safely around seven and he should be ready to go then. You all should, that includes the Macs and Guy and Nigel. We have to support the village. I trust you'll sort out transport for everyone." With only two little false start hops, she was off, haring down the drive.

"What would anyone like to do?" I asked.

"Take up your mother's suggestion," said Elisabeth. "Or was it an order?"

It was a pleasant way to pass an afternoon, admiring Nature on Midsummer's Day in warm sunshine. There were clouds, but it wasn't humid like yesterday and the forecast was bright and warm for the next few days which was cheering.

By a quarter to seven we'd all had a light meal and were ready for what Pa called an evening of bucolic entertainment. Jeremy and I would go with Stefan and Elisabeth in their car, Maman would take Pa and the Macs, while Guy, Nigel and Spider were setting off on foot over the fields.

Stefan and Elisabeth packed the boot of the Austin 8, and followed Maman down the drive to the village green and the pub.

There was bunting all round the place, and the local brass band were playing songs that won the War. People were outside drinking, chatting, and in the garden of the pub there was a coconut shy and a stand of four painted swingboats both with queues of people awaiting the fun. It wasn't exactly a fairground, but it was very popular. It was delightful to see so many local families enjoying themselves.

We were greeted by people I'd known forever. I stopped to chat with some, and introduced Jeremy as my fiancé, which actually sounded good and made them happy. We shook hands, hugged, and generally mingled. I introduced Elisabeth and Stefan as friends from London. "Stefan?" said one of the farmers. "Is that a kraut name?"

"Possibly, but I was with the Polish Air Force. I'm Polish, sir."

"Then you're most welcome, and your lady here. Most welcome."

Elisabeth smiled and said nothing, but I knew what she was thinking: her mother was full German.

We went to the bar and ordered, but Larry refused payment. "Your brother and his friend have paid for this," he said. "And all night too, so if you fancy a short or a cocktail instead of a pint of ale, don't be shy!"

We took our drinks outside, and found Nigel and Guy at a table on the green, with Sam Simmons and a few of the locals whom they had paid out the week previous. There was good-hearted banter going on, and I was glad to hear it. If Guy was to take over Wethersley, he needed to be popular. We moved over to join them, that is Jeremy, Stefan, Elisabeth and I did. The Aged P's, Angelique and the Macs went out into the garden and found their own space and friends.

The band had stopped now, to applauding and catcalls. It was good-humored, light-hearted, and the guys blowing their instruments in their heavy serge uniforms were probably ready for a pint or three.

"What's happening?" Stefan asked. "I thought there would be dancing."

"There will," I assured him.

From the back of the pub came the sound of a drum, deep and insistent.

The crowd gradually quietened.

The drum continued, deep throbbing sounds against the silence. Joined by a metallic jingling, and the rich tones of an accordeon, and above it the shrill piping of a fife.

I grinned, despite myself.

This was barn dance music, and my feet were twitching already.

Gradually the sounds grew as the musicians came out and stood on the road, between the green and the pub. And then came a tall man dressed all in black, with a top hat stuck with pheasant tail feathers, his clothes a mass of tatters, his face blackened by soot. He held up both hands on high and bowed to everyone. "Do you want us to dance in the summer?" he shouted.

A ragged chorus of "Yes." and "Oh, alright, then," greeted him.

"I can't hear you!" He raised his voice. "I said, do you want us to dance in the summer?"

A slightly louder chorus.

"Still can't hear you. Do you want us to dance in the summer?"

Now there was a loud roar of assent, and a lone voice shouted, "Just get on with it, Fred, then we can start enjoying ourselves!"

Fred pointed to the drummer, who executed a loud roll, and from out of the pub poured a crowd of similarly dressed black-faced men, with bells buckled to their shins that jingled as they step-hopped out onto the tarmac road. Each one carried a thick wooden stick.

They lined up in pairs and the music started. Strong and rhythmic, and the men began to dance, their heavy boots crashing against the tarmac, forward and back, forward and back along the road, winding off and rejoining the line, forward and back then facing each other and crashing their staves together, hitting the ground hard, and waving at the sky, then crashing them again, opposite, diagonally, to the side and then on the floor once more, beating them in time to the drum, leaping at each other, crashing the staves in mid-air, and all the time, hopping and stepping, their tatters flying around them as the music got wilder and faster to a crescendo when they rapped the staves together in such a way as to form a knot that was held on high.

The music ceased, and the original tattered man called out, "The sun is at his strength. This is the longest day. Come and dance with us!"

The tattered men split from the road and into the crowd, dragging women out from the safety of their seats. The music started again, less wild.

"Strip the willow!" shouted the caller, and a long line of dancers sorted themselves out on the road. "Sets of four couples. Come on, people! It's time for a bit of fun."

I saw Maman grabbing Pa's hand. I grabbed Jeremy's, "Come

on, this is good!"

He stood up. "Stefan, Elisabeth, time to dance the summer in," he said, pulling them upright. "You'll get the hang of it! And if you don't, no-one will mind."

We joined Pa and Maman on the tarmac, and Guy took Angelique.

"I've never done anything like this," Stefan said.

"Then time you did," Elisabeth hissed. "This is real magic."

The caller got us all in our sets and nodded to the band. "For those who forgot what to do because they drank too much last year, I'll tell you what to do. Right, and... honor your partners!"

The accordeon gave a great chord, five seconds long; we bowed gravely to each other and then we were off, skipping forward skipping back, casting off singly, and then clapping and swinging as the top couple stripped the willow, swinging with each other and then the next person on their side down the set until they reached the end, and it all started again.

I looked down the road as as we danced: all ages there, people older and stiffer than Pa and Maman were standing up, as well as children of four or even less. Every face sported a smile, and although the caller was telling us what to do, there was frequent happy confusion, but as Jeremy said, no-one noticed. Mistakes were hurriedly rectified, and a good time was had by all. When the music finally ended, there were shouts for more.

We danced three dances on the road, joining in the old patterns, the women and girls in bright summer dresses, the men and boys in open-necked short-sleeved shirts and, mostly, gray flannel trousers and shorts. All ties, neck- or social were loosened and abandoned.

The accordeon, drummer and fife-player continued their music and the tattered dancers returned, this time with a young woman, who, at the end of the dance was lifted on high, up on their shoulders. We clapped and cheered. It was May's niece, wearing a gown the color of the ripening corn, a crown of red rambling roses on her long fair hair, the personification of summer, and she was reveling in the attention.

The band broke for a drink. The bar was full, but we got another round in. The sun was sinking in the sky now.

"We should be thinking of going soon," Elisabeth said. "Not

that I want to."

"Then wait for a few more dances. They'll be on the grass," I told her. "Circle dances."

"Oh yes!"

So when the band resumed we all took our places on the green for the Lady's Excuse me, Lucky Seven and the Circassian Circle.

Then the black-faced Morris team came back and led us in a circle of a different sort.

Hands were held, man to woman, woman to man, at least to start with, and the caller stood in the middle of the cricket pitch. The music started slowly and the string of dancers made a huge clockwise circle, moving at a stately pace. As more people tagged on to the end of the string the leader made a second circle, within the first, a spiral, and we joined in on the end, with more people linking on after us. Gradually the spiral got tighter and longer, the pace gradually quickening.

Now the caller raised his hands. "The first part of the year is over, the sun is at its height, as you pass me make a wish on this Midsummer's Night!"

We danced, spiraling ever tighter, then suddenly we were next to the caller and I had no wish ready. I thought swiftly "Give us all what we need!" then swiftly spun widdershins as the string of dancers turned to spiral outwards round and round until we were led from the green into the pub garden and the bar, breathless and laughing, hanging on to each other to stay upright.

"That was amazing," Elisabeth said.

"We know how to celebrate in deepest Buckinghamshire," I said. "I'll say goodnight to Maman and Pa."

Sam, Nigel and Guy were moving on too. They were going for the fireworks at Marsham in Sam's car. "We'll see you there, then," I told them.

# 56

As we'd suspected, the clearing was empty when we arrived, and the stars were just shy of coming out. We lit nightlights in each quarter and one in the center.

We united, and Stefan said quietly "Let this place be healed!" and poured the consecrated water on the earth.

"Let those who have defiled it be gone!" said Elisabeth, and held the center nightlight high. "Let the Light radiate here for ever!"

Jeremy sprinkled the consecrated beer and cakes around. "Let those who enter this clearing feel its love and blessings in whatever way they can."

I scattered the packet of seeds around, wild flowers that would grow well and were native to Southern Britain and said, "Let this place be blessed with new life and the joy that brings."

We shared the last of the beer and cakes, and hugged each other, then withdrew the golden lines and put out the candles.

Then I heard a cough; we all did.

And none of us had made it.

I shuddered.

We had been overlooked.

Oh Hell!

Bad News.

I didn't want this getting out, I really didn't. I think we all felt the same, too, from the looks on the faces.

Then a voice I knew came from behind 'my' oak tree. "I'm sorry, people. I didn't mean to scare you all. Ma told me you'd be working here. I had to come and see. You done good, all of you. Very good. She's pleased. And it'll go no further from me. I know what you're all thinking."

Mr. Fletcher emerged from the woods, silently, on poacher's feet. I made to introduce him but he shook his head. "No need for names, but I'd like to shake your hands before I go on my way. " He held out both hands to Stefan and Elisabeth. "That's powerful stuff you command. Use it well!"

He came to me and Jeremy, took our hands in his gnarled ones and nodded, then, as quietly as he had come, he withdrew to the oak tree and disappeared into the woods.

Above us the sky was indigo velvet splashed with diamonds. The clearing felt sparkling, renewed. The lovers could return. And more importantly any shades were gone. It was a perfect night in a perfect place.

At Marsham we could hear the noise before we even stopped. There was no room in the car park, it was full of charabancs, at least three of them, and people were milling around everywhere, spilling onto the cricket pitch on the green, up and down the road, all ages, all intent on having a good time. The pub next to the cricket club was sharing the business opportunities. More bunting, more laughter, people in bright summer clothes and the sounds of a Dixieland jazz band in full swing.

Stefan parked next to the churchyard.

"I would like to check out Cissie's grave," I said softly.

I wanted to visit the place to see that she was all right. I know that sounded crazy, but ... well, I also needed to know that I could visit a place where I had been attacked and deal with the memories of that. Fear can make you weak.

"I'll come with you," Jeremy said.

"We all will," Elisabeth and Stefan added immediately.

So we went into the dark churchyard, where the thick yews dampened the sound of jollity, and walked through the cut hay. I didn't know where Billy Laycock was, but it was evident that he'd not been back to work since he'd attacked me.

We made our way round to the north side of the church and found Cissie's grave.

I smiled.

A huge bouquet of mixed lilac stood there in a round metal pot.

I thought of Cissie, but she didn't come.

There was nothing there.

Elisabeth took my hand. "She's gone," she said. "She's continuing her journey."

Les caught up with us as we were paying admission to the cricket club. "Lovely to see you all," he greeted. "Come in and get a drink. My round."

"It's mine, Les," I said. "I owe you, remember?"

"Won't hear of it. Name your poison, folks, we're sure to have it." He hustled us through the clutch of people who were blocking the way to the beer tent, bouncing up and down to the music of New Orleans.

"Nice band, Les," said Jeremy.

"My old comrades," he grinned. "They'll do anything for a gig and a skinful of beer, but they are good musicians. We had fun out in Africa!"

There were people dancing – not the country dances we'd been doing, but actually holding each other and some even doing a sedate jive – if such a thing were possible.

I followed Les and Jeremy, Stefan and Elisabeth stringing along behind me, but my eyes were drawn to the dancers.

Well, well, well...

Tight up against the bar in the beer tent we got served and Les managed to find us some fold-up chairs that had been hidden for such emergencies. We took them and the drinks outside and found a space to park ourselves.

"Where did all these people come from?" Jeremy asked, amazed at the throng.

"Everywhere. We advertised it well. There are a bunch from the Polish Camp at Amersham, and a lot of off-duty nurses, they like to party, and just, well, everywhere."

It was a mixed bunch, by and large younger than we'd been in at Wethersley.

"Polish?" asked Stefan, with a grin. "But of course there are, we are readily visible when one looks." He took both Les's hands in his. "Thank you. For a short while I will go and speak to some of my compatriots."

He looked down at Elisabeth, "Forgive, for a moment. It is such a treat to speak my own language." And he was off, into the mêlée of dancing bodies, and clapping men on the shoulder, being hugged by women and generally enjoying himself.

"Well I never!" said Elisabeth. "He's found a friend or two." She smiled at Les. "Fancy a dance, big boy?"

"I never refuse a lady," he said, saluting smartly then bowing from the waist as he handed her up towards the music.

"Alice? Or would you rather sit here."

"I'd rather sit here with you, to be honest," I said. "It's been a bloody long day!"

"How're your bruises?"

"Starting up again. But nowhere near as stiff as I was." I reached into my pocket where I kept a strip of aspirin, and tore off two, washing them down with a mouthful of shandy. "Do you see what I see, over there? Close to the band?"

He peered across the moving carpet of bodies. "I can see Sam, he's there. I hadn't had him down for a dancer... Bloody Hell, Alice, your brother's got a stunner of a partner!"

"And he's getting pretty close!"

"So he is. He didn't dance like that with Sylvia. It was more than a hand's width apart!"

"It's a lot less than that now," I murmured. "That's how we dance, Jem. I wonder who she is."

"It feels wrong to go and barge in. Look, there's Nigel, and he's got a partner too."

"Blimey, Guv', things must be looking up for them all."

I looked across at the girl Guy was nuzzling. She was slightly shorter than him, her hair in a curly fringe, the sides were pulled up into a red ribbon at the crown, and then the left to cascade down past her shoulders in loose waves. She was wearing a white sleeveless dress with a red necklace and earrings, and seemed to be enjoying my brother's company as much as he was enjoying hers.

"Well," Jeremy said at last. "I may owe you an apology for besmirching your family name. That doesn't look like ..."

"No, it doesn't. Dammit, they're snogging! And Sylvia said he didn't even kiss properly! What the hell's happening?"

The band eventually stopped. People applauded like mad, and then stood for a moment, wondering what was next.

Les sprang onto the stage and took the loud-hailer. "Another big hand for the Desert Rats Dixieland Stompers!"

More cheering and stamping.

"Ladies and Gentlemen... and Players, we'll be moving out across to the far side of the green soon for the fireworks. I suggest you all get the tipple of your choice and come and join us. Quarter of an hour, then, OK? We'll see you over there at eleven o'clock, then you can come back and finish your evening. The bars close at midnight. Enjoy yourselves, but don't scare the horses. And if anyone's listening, mine's a pint of best."

I chuckled. We were joined in the queue by Stefan and his friends, Elisabeth, Sam and his partner, a slender woman with spectacles and a ready smile, and Nigel, with Spider on his shoulder, perfectly content in that position, and Guy and their new friends who looked as though they were related. We introduced each other briefly in between ordering and chatting, getting in a pint for Les, who was running up and down behind the bar, opening bottles and filling glasses from the cask.

"Ta, for that, Milady. Enjoying yourselves? Good." He took a quick swig, then ducked out under the bar. "Bring your drinks and follow me."


The fireworks were wonderful.

And there were lots of them. It must have cost a pretty penny, but oh, it was such a delight for all those who watched them that Midsummer's night, outside the Cricketers at Marsham.

I love fireworks, the smell, the whistles, pops and bangs, the bright flower-bursts that exploded against the night sky, dimming the stars momentarily, the arcs of golden sparks, the brilliant fountains of magnesium that left shadows on our eyes, and the pure delight in sharing these wonderful fiery gifts with others, who 'oohed' and 'aahed' alongside us. As the spectacle unfolded, we hugged each other, everyone part of a great joyous event, and when after an amazing finale with a barrage of coloured rockets and a waterfall of brilliant flowery white and gold explosions, terminating in a huge single bang, we cheered them. And hugged and kissed each other round the group.

"That was something," Guy breathed. "I'd forgotten how good they could be."

He looked across at the young woman on his arm. "I'd forgotten how good life could be." He smiled at her. "Another drink, Veronica?"

"No thanks," she peered at his watch. "Told my Mum we'd be back by midnight." She tapped her sister on the shoulder. "Time to go, Joycie."

"Walk you home?" offered Guy, his arm already round Veronica's shoulders.

"That'd be nice. Joycie, are you coming? I'm sure your new friend will walk you home too, and his little dog can protect us."

Stefan and Elisabeth were off to the bar with the Poles.

"We could walk home, if you like, Jem," I suggested. "It's only a few miles by road, even less across country and there's a good moon tonight."

"You want to do that? I'm game if you are."

So we said our goodbyes to Stefan and Elisabeth and their friends – I think they were relieved that we were making our own way back because there was much buying of drink and I had a feeling that the party would continue elsewhere long into the night – and set off back past the churchyard along the Wethersley Road.

A car hooted us as it passed then skidded to a halt.

"Want a lift? I'm passing your front gates."

So Sam took us home, far faster than he should have done, but I didn't care. We waved him and Wendy, a librarian in Amersham, goodbye and walked hand in hand up the drive under a sky full of stars. A memorable midsummer day, I thought, looking up at the Milky Way. I felt good.

Pa, Ma, Angelique and the Macs were flopped around chairs and settees in the lounge with bottles of white wine in ice buckets and dreamy smiles.

"Come, have a drink with us," Pa invited. "You'll have to help yourselves, we're all done for, all that activity..."

"Where are your friends? We didn't hear the car," Maman asked.

I poured two goblets of Quincy, handed one to Jeremy. "They met some old acquaintances – well, Stefan did. They should be back later."

I sank into an armchair, Jeremy perched on the arm and raised his glass. "Your very good health, everyone."

We all drank to that.

Pa looked over his glasses at us. "They're welcome to come in whatever time they like," he said. "They've earned a treat. You all have."

"What do you mean?" I asked.

Angelique said, "We all went down to the clearing on the way back from Larry's. It was wonderful. Like it used to be, full of life and peacefulness. Not like when you and I went down and had a peek, Alice."

"I don't know what you all did," Maman said, sipping her wine, "but it certainly has worked. And no, I don't need to know, either." She took a cigarette from the box on the table beside her and fitted it into her holder. "Were the fireworks good?"

"Excellent."

"I suppose Sam will give Guy and Nigel a lift home," Pa said.

We chuckled.

"Eh?"

"Sam gave us a lift. Guy and Nigel will have to walk," I told them.

"They may be some time," Jeremy added.

"You don't mean they're still drinking!" Maman said. "And I've got a lot for them to do tomorrow."

"No, they struck lucky with a pair of sisters."

That shook them.

"Well, good for them!" said Mr. Mac. "About time, too."

"Names?" asked Maman, Mrs. Mac and Angelique in unison.

I shrugged. "Veronica and Joycie, that's all I know."

Angelique smiled. "Baines Agricultural Merchants, far end of Marsham."

"Could be worse," said Pa. "Everybody here uses them."

"Pretty girls," said Mr. Mac.

"Unlucky," said his wife. "Veronica lost two fiancés in the war and Joycie lost one."

"Well, that's three, so they should be all right now," Maman said, swiftly. "I, for one, am glad to hear that they're behaving like young men should."

Aren't we all, I thought.

And I could see that on everyone's faces.

Maman dropped a kiss on Pa's cheek. "I'm glad you had a word with them both this afternoon, Roger. It seems to have borne fruit."

Pa smiled. "Oh, I had many words with them, Chérie, and

they with me, too. But let's keep this between ourselves. Let them tell us when they're ready. Or not, as the case may be."

# 57

Jeremy and I heaved the mattress back on my bed and remade it. Then he kissed me and slid silently round the door and closed it without a sound. It was half-past six, already light, but the rest of the house was still sleeping. We'd been very quiet, and hadn't rattled the bedsprings. Having done it, I preferred the mattress on the floor to on my saggy schoolgirl bed; all four of us had used our beds as trampolines at one time or another, even Guy, and every one of them bore the scars.

I filled the sink and had a strip-wash, listening to the tail end of the dawn chorus. I was drying off and applying talcum when I heard a scraping on my door.

I opened it. Jeremy with his suitcase.

"Can't stay in the Blue Room, Elisabeth and Stefan are in there curled up in one of the beds wearing very little but dreamy smiles. Fast asleep."

"Come in then."

I finished my toilette and lay back on the bed while he made his ablutions and changed into fresh clothes. "We ought to get married soon," I said. "It's not as though we don't play the part of a couple at every opportunity."

"I've no problem with that. I'll get a special license if you want. Although you ought to meet what's left of my family first, to know what you're letting yourself in for."

"I'd like that. It won't change my mind, though."

"I was hoping you'd say that. And the flat needs to be done. Where do you want to go for honeymoon?"

I'd not thought. "Anywhere. Anywhere as long as it's with you. Somewhere with better weather than here would be nice," I mused.

"Sounds nice. You choose, and I'll fit in." He came over, fresh-smelling and kissed me. "I'd follow you anywhere, everywhere, you know that. To the gates of Hell, if you asked."

I grinned. "I don't think that will be necessary. How about

you meet my family? Southern France. We could help with the grape harvest."

"Oh, I like it. A working honeymoon!"

"I don't want you to get bored, Jeremy," I chuckled. "Besides, I want to show you off to my cousins, especially that little bitch Marie-Josette who told me I was like a jar of bad pickles, on the shelf and going off."

"Then we go. And I'll be the perfect English gentleman – she needn't know my antecedents. It'll be fun."

"Oh, yes, that I can promise you that!"

We spent the morning preparing for the party later that day, well most of us did. Stefan and Elisabeth rose late, looking the worse for wear; by contrast, Guy and Nigel were bright, energetic and wreathed in smiles.

I worked in the kitchen with Mrs. Mac, Pa, Jeremy and Guy got the trestle tables and chairs out onto the lawn, Maman and Angelique decorated them, Mr. Mac sorted the crockery, cutlery and glassware, and Nigel and Spider rang back and forth from the kitchen garden fetching whatever Mrs. Mac required.

By noon the guests had arrived, Maddy and Basil, little Enid and baby Robin came first, and were greeted joyously, followed almost immediately by Leggy and Bobby, bearing bags and boxes. I hugged them all then excused myself to finish in the kitchen, but everything was in hand. We unwrapped their gifts. Maman was right, as usual. There was more than enough for everyone.

Enid followed me in. "Auntie Alice, is your bike here? We could have a little ride?" she asked. "Only Grand-mère and Tantange won't play with me, they're too busy with Bobbin."

So I took her small hand and we went to the garage where the bikes lived. I pulled the smallest, Maman's, out and set her on it, and pushed her past the house, down the drive a little way and was about to turn back when Nigel appeared with Spider, with a bunch of herbs and flowers in his hand.

"Is that your dog, Mister?" Enid piped. "Can I stroke him? What's his name?"

So I lifted her down, and she made friends with Spider and brought a big smile to Nigel's face.

"Would you take her back, Nigel?" I asked. "I need to help

Mrs. Mac."

"Of course. You could take her the herbs she wanted." He turned to Enid. "I'm Nigel, what's your name, little fairy?"

Enid chuckled, "I'm not a fairy, I'm a big girl! I like your dog."

"And he likes you. His name's Spider because he's little and very fast. Would you like to throw a ball for him?"

I turned the bike and rode it swiftly back.

"So," said Leggy, leaning back in his chair. "We've eaten well, we've drunk well, I suppose it's time we all caught up with each other's news. I'll start."

He lit his pipe and took a few puffs.

"When that body was found uncovered in the clearing, I was rather apprehensive of a happy outcome, I must admit."

He looked at Pa, fiercely, "And you really didn't help matters much, Roger. Of course we knew it couldn't be you who killed John Anselm-Jones, because we all know you, but your reticence as to what he was doing here... well, it really got up Chief Inspector Murray's nose. Happily, though, he's been recalled to his normal manor."

"I'm sure they'll welcome him back with open arms," said Pa, with a grin.

Leggy continued. "Nigel was the key to our getting you off the hook, Roger, as you probably know, and from then on things seemed to snowball. We discovered a lot that we suspected but didn't know for sure about Mr. John Anselm-Jones, and his alias, Mr. Edgar Winthrop. We have him now as a known Nazi agent, a close friend of Edward and Wallace Simpson, and a collector of illicit antiques which he sold on through the International Galleries."

He turned to me. "By the way, Alice, there's a job for you, matching up the items and researching them, if you want it. I can't think of anyone better to do it."

"Thank you," I said. "Can I think on it?"

"Certainly."

He took another puff of his pipe.

"Then we struck lucky, again, because we found that he had a strongbox at Bathurst's bank, and was very close to a certain

Mr. Ferdy Dugdale, who had … shall we say 'sequestered' the contents of the International Gallery lock, stock and barrel."

"Mr. Dugdale was my immediate boss, the one who introduced me to the Merediths, and Sylvia."

"Ah, my sister, Sylvia," Nigel breathed. "How does she fit in amongst all this, sir?"

"All in good time, Nigel," Leggy told him. "Mr. Ferdy Dugdale reckoned without his mother and his sister. They sold it all to us. It was a pure stroke of luck, to be honest, and it opened up a whole new can of worms. We found certain items that were stolen during the war and brought here with some vague provenance. We also found Mr. Anselm-Jones's contact list, and it would appear that he was blackmailing some quite important people."

"Was he blackmailing you, dear?" Maman asked Roger.

"Perish the thought, Chérie. He had nothing on me."

"Well why did he come here to see you?" she persisted.

"Let Leggy tell the story," he said, patting her hand. I wondered whether that would be enough to head her off.

Knowing Maman, I didn't think so.

"No matter about that. He was staying at Marsham with the Nesmith-Browns a week after he called on you. And then suddenly, he disappeared. He was due in various places round the world, but never reached them. There were questions, but nobody actually bothered looking too much, as he frequently vanished on buying sprees. The staff continued to be paid at his London flat and the International Galleries. Before he came to Buckinghamshire he was last heard of in Verona at a conference in mid October. He traveled privately, you see, and left no trails. He had several passports and would have used them interchangeably." He looked pointedly at Nigel. "Remind you of anyone?"

Nigel tried to look innocent, but Leggy just chuckled.

"It was while he was at Marsham, things started to go wrong for him. Now that may sound strange, because he was a slippery character and knew well enough how to look after himself. He was confident, ruthless, had friends in high places, but he also had a weakness..."

"The wondrous waif?" Nigel suggested.

"That's right," said Leggy. "So while he was enjoying your parents' hospitality, while intimating to them and their friends –

including the Merediths, which was not a sensible thing to do – that he needed to be paid for his continued silence concerning their Nazi sympathies, he was being enchanted by a young girl, Cissie Laycock."

"Dotty Broom's niece," Mrs. Mac whispered to Maman, who nodded wisely.

"Cissie worked at Marsham," Nigel said. "Her dad got her the job when she was barely twelve. Ma took her because she came cheap. And she was a good worker, Ma said."

"John Anselm-Jones felt sorry for her. I don't know how it happened or what happened, but he formed an attachment with the girl. She adored him. Whether it was sexual – most people thought it was, isn't that so, Nigel?"

Nigel nodded. "No smoke without fire in our house."

"I don't know. If it was, it was wrong. But Cissie was a very mistreated child with a lot of love to give, and extremely vulnerable. Everyone saw how Mr. Jones and Cissie lived in their own world, but no-one stopped it. It wasn't their business. So long as they don't frighten the horses, eh, it's all fine."

Leggy looked around at us all.

"Only it wasn't fine. She was a young girl and she shouldn't have become pregnant in the first place. Those who should have been protecting her failed in their duty. John Anselm-Jones tried to make things better for her. He promised her a new job in London but she had to have an abortion. She couldn't go to a new position single and pregnant, obviously. So he set it all up, and, although she was terrified, she went through with it."

"You've spoken with the abortionist?" Basil asked.

"My agents have," Leggy told him. "I'm prepared to take their word for it. And as far as the doctor was concerned, she went home safely.

"But the next thing we hear of her is being rushed to hospital by her uncle, Les Broom, after he took her father, Billy Laycock, home from the pub later that evening. She died of a severe kicking and a septic abortion. Billy blamed it on the 'flash boyfriend' that she'd been talking about round the village, but as no-one knew his name, it was all hushed up, especially the bit about the abortion."

"Billy was very cut up, told everyone she was a virgin, and refused to put anything other than white flowers on her grave,"

Jeremy said.

"There was a lot of sympathy for him locally," Mrs. Mac said. "People said he should find the boyfriend and sort him out, good and proper – well at least the daily girls were of that opinion," she added, piously.

Leggy chuckled. "Billy had other ideas, though. He knew who the boyfriend was, and he wanted recompense for his daughter's death."

"Surely he could have gone to law with that," Pa said.

"It would have meant a re-opening of Cissie's death," Maman said. "It would have meant all the things he was trying to keep hidden would come out, dear, don't you see? And it would have cost a fortune. He probably didn't have the money for that, so best to sort it out privately."

"Exactly so, Marie-Thérèse. So he and his family hatched a plan. They would arrange a meeting with the man."

"Why should he attend?" Angelique asked. "If he was responsible for the girl's death, he'd keep away, surely?"

"One would think that. But he chose to go. He was eager to go, by all accounts. He was angry."

"Who told you this?" Basil asked.

"Les Broom, local entrepreneur, Cissie's uncle."

"Les Broom? The cricketer? The one who stopped the rest of them beating me up?"

"The same. He set up the meeting. Unfortunately, he told Sylvia about it."

"My bloody sister. What has she got to do with it?"

"She told Archie Meredith."

"Bloody Hell!" Nigel breathed. "Sorry, everyone. So she and Archie gate-crashed the meeting, am I right?"

Leggy nodded. "And before the meeting could really get underway, Archie shot John Anselm-Jones in the back of the head, paid the Brooms off quite handsomely to bury the body and keep quiet."

"So she didn't lie to me," Nigel said softly. "She really did see an execution. I didn't believe her."

"It doesn't stop there, though. If it had, none of the last few week's events would have taken place."

"Quite," said Pa. "He'd still be kicking up the daisies, and

356

Billy and his friends would have got away with it."

"I'm afraid the rest might be down to me, sir," Jeremy told Pa. "When she came round asking for her engagement ring back, I told her to find her feet and make her own life how she wanted it. For that she'd need money. And she knew that John Anselm-Jones carried three hundred pounds on him at all times for emergencies."

"So she dug him up?" Maman asked, horrified.

"Desperate times, desperate measures," Leggy told her. "Since the Merediths were killed the money supply had been cut off, and it was going downhill before, isn't that right, Nigel."

Nigel nodded. "How do you know this?"

"By pure good luck; she bumped into Jeremy when he first went to Paris. And introduced him to her new fiancé."

"She's engaged? Already? Who to?" Nigel asked.

"Well, let's put it like this, she was. She is no longer."

"What's happened? I asked.

Basil took the story up. "She became engaged very swiftly to Felix Van Buren, a South African diamond merchant. You may have heard that he went missing last Sunday."

I nodded.

I hadn't realized Basil was working on this.

"According to Sylvia, he went off to see an old friend who was on his deathbed, taking his stock and two bodyguards with him. He never arrived, and the old friend, who we have contacted, is alive and well, never better, in fact, are the words he used. Late on Friday night a body was found next to a burnt out car in a remote part of France. We think it is Felix's body. There were no diamonds in evidence. Sylvia is milking sympathy from the press as vigorously as she can."

Basil gave a wry smile. "I heard this morning that one of Felix's sons came to identify and collect the body, and has paid her tab at the Crillon, and dropped her a hefty sum to get out of their life. I also understand that she will keep the jewels Felix gave her, but a little bird has told me that they are very fine quality fakes. I'm not sure that she is aware of that. She is on her way to the Riviera as I speak."

We took some time assimilating that.

Then Nigel said, "Oh, she'll fall on her feet, she always does.

Who really did kill little Cissie?"

"The knowing money's on Billy Laycock, but he's saying nothing at the moment," Leggy said. "Still, the evidence is building up, thanks to Alice. He is in custody. He can't beat up anyone else," he looked at me. "I wouldn't have put you through that, Alice."

"Ways and means," I said. "If it brings Cissie's killer to trial, I'm more than happy. And I did have three very swift and thorough rescuers," I looked at Jeremy, "One of whom has an announcement to make."

All eyes turned to him.

He smiled, like a boy, a bit awkwardly, "Yes," he said. "You know Alice and I are going to get married, well, we'd like to bring it forward to September. Hope nobody minds too much."

Maman looked at me, "Alice, you're not...?"

"No, of course not, Maman. Just impatient. And it seems silly to keep on two flats for another month when we can be together in one as soon as its finished."

"That's all right then," she said. "What date have you set? So I can start getting things organized. Oh, this is so exciting, and it will be far nicer than the end of October. You can't trust the weather then."

"The sixth, it's a Saturday. We hope you'll all be with us."

After the congratulations had calmed down, Nigel came out with a tray of flutes and his bottles of champagne. "I can't think of a better reason," he said, opening the first bottle like a professional. "I hope you are wonderfully happy together always." He poured us each a flute, and then with Mr. Mac helping, dispensed the rest.

The party continued for some time longer, and then Leggy and Bobby started to make a move.

Leggy looked at Guy, "Can we give you a lift back to London? Now you've got promotion, you'll need to be at the bank bright and early," he teased.

Guy shook his head. "Very kind of you, Leggy, but I'll have to refuse. Nigel and I have appointments later this evening."

"Blimey!" gasped Maddy. "I thought you were wearing the willow."

"Come on, sis, if Sylvia can get a new boyfriend, the least I can do is get a new girlfriend."

"And she is so much better than my sister!" Nigel chortled.

"But is she better for him than your sister?" Maddy asked.

"And is he good enough for her?" I asked.

Guy turned to me, "Oh, Alice. How can you ask such a question? You saw her last night. She's an absolute darling and I adore her, isn't that enough?"

"Well...," Pa said, "It's a good start!"

www.ingramcontent.com/pod-product-compliance
Lightning Source LLC
Chambersburg PA
CBHW050914250626
47155CB00001B/229